The Pepys Conspiracy

James Long

**SIMON &
SCHUSTER**

London · New York · Amsterdam/Antwerp · Sydney/Melbourne · Toronto · New Delhi

First published in Great Britain by Simon & Schuster UK Ltd, 2025

Copyright © James Long, 2025

The right of James Long to be identified as author of this work has been asserted
in accordance with the Copyright, Designs and Patents Act, 1988.

1 3 5 7 9 10 8 6 4 2

Simon & Schuster UK Ltd, 1st Floor
222 Gray's Inn Road, London WC1X 8HB

Simon & Schuster Australia, Sydney
Simon & Schuster India, New Delhi

www.simonandschuster.co.uk
www.simonandschuster.com.au
www.simonandschuster.co.in

The authorised representative in the EEA is Simon & Schuster Netherlands BV,
Herculesplein 96, 3584 AA Utrecht, Netherlands. info@simonandschuster.nl

Simon & Schuster strongly believes in freedom of expression and stands against
censorship in all its forms. For more information, visit BooksBelong.com.

A CIP catalogue record for this book is available from the British Library

Hardback ISBN: 978-1-4711-8295-2
eBook ISBN: 978-1-4711-4944-3
Audio ISBN: 978-1-3985-5067-4

This book is a work of fiction. Names, characters, places and incidents are either
a product of the author's imagination or are used fictitiously. Any resemblance
to actual people living or dead, events or locales is entirely coincidental.

Typeset in Bembo by M Rules
Printed and Bound in the UK using 100% Renewable Electricity at CPI Group (UK) Ltd

I dedicate this book to my son Ben who was my learned co-writer for *The Plot Against Pepys* — a dissection of what happened to Samuel Pepys in 1679. That book was published back in 2007 after three years of detailed research. Also to the memory of the late Dr. Richard Luckett, the Pepys Librarian at Magdalene College, Cambridge who opened up so many avenues into obscure archives for us. That work of non-fiction left me deeply puzzled over the base ingratitude shown to the man who helped save Pepys from execution for treason. The mystery niggled at me long afterwards until a possible explanation finally forced itself into my head. With no possible proof, I turned to fiction to explore it further and this is the result. Balthasar St Michel has been treated with amused derision by Pepys historians and he deserves far more respect. For that reason I also dedicate this book to Balty.

CHAPTER 1

September 5th, 1678

DEAL, KENT

Two men are toe to toe on a shingle beach and any moment now it will be fist to flesh. The older man is two hundred pounds of trouble, twitching with violence. His grin frames a dark cavern as his front teeth are long gone. White scars on both arms decorate ropes of muscle.

The younger man is known locally as Balty and his face betrays dawning knowledge that he has no chance. Small stones skitter from under his feet, cascading down the wave-carved slope, but he cannot escape with them. He stumbles and half the onlookers shout derisive laughter. They are strangers. The other half are Deal townsfolk who stare silently at the mismatch in front of them. These days, they see him as a local man even if his roots lie on the far side of the Channel facing them, over there where the papists live. By Deal's rough standards, Balty is a dandy – tall and skinny, a plush jacket over an embroidered shirt, bright leather boots – much too clean for this business.

His opponent is rigged out in sea-blasted canvas, frayed and fit for brutal purpose and accustomed to soaking up other people's blood.

The semicircle of spectators mirrors the curve of ships moored out there in the Downs, the busy anchorage inshore of the Goodwin Sands, a haven that turns lethal in the wrong sort of storm. The wind has dropped but the anchorage is still choppy despite the sandbank's shelter. The navy's Channel Fleet lurks here in the Downs when all is quiet, surrounded by trading ships awaiting a fair wind. This trouble began out there, on a mongrel boat – a Whitby collier hired by the navy to transport cannon from a wrecked frigate far up the coast. Its skipper is a wily man who added eight phantom seamen to his crew roster, swelling the bill to His Majesty on delivery of his accounts at Deal. He thought no one would notice.

Balty noticed. Balthasar St Michel, or 'that fucking Frenchy' as the collier's skipper called him, is paid to notice. He is proud to be the king's muster-master of the naval base at Deal, tasked with challenging the oceanic waves of fraud crew lists stuffed with ghosts likes these. Then there are the real ghosts, the gaps left by naval mayhem in the crew rosters of the men o'war. It is part of Balty's job to plug those with the sweepings of the press gangs.

Today, the fucking Frenchy has halved the collier skipper's bill and the skipper has sent his bosun to take it out of Balty's hide. The collier's crewmen have come ashore to watch, standing with sailors from other merchant ships to make up half the crowd. The other half are local folk, fishermen, ferrymen and sea-hawkers, gathered on the beach to see the action. None of them are here to observe fair play. There is little chance of that.

Two children work the crowd, bright-eyed with pale skin and glossy black hair. Their linen shirts are faded to the pale brown of smoked mackerel, worn over patched storm-cloud trousers. They have been obvious twins for most of their brief years since birth, but the girl now branches away from the boy with early clues of beauty. They are eleven and a half years old and they go from man to man collecting the bets. The girl notices everything about how the crowd splits and what each half wants. The boy inspects his notebook as much as he looks at the faces. These are Balty's children, Betty and Sam St Michel, and they take after him in quite different ways.

The day is getting warmer after the rain. The children have bled the townsfolk of their cash and now they come round to the colliers' crew.

'Would you like to make your bets, kind sirs?' Betty asks. 'Or perhaps you are uncertain of the outcome?'

Not one of them looks kind or uncertain. Coal dust has turned their faces into black maps of trouble. 'What's the odds, kid? Even money?' one asks. He is young, lanky, and a bandage round his head shows a dark bloodstain soaking through.

His crew-mates laugh. 'Evens? Chance would be a fine thing,' one says.

Sam looks at his notebook. 'Betting on your man to win?' he says, as though surprised.

They laugh louder. 'Course we are.'

He looks at the coins already in the bag, stares at the contestants and says, 'Please do inspect the two of them, sir. You can't expect even money on such a mismatch. The odds are one to two on your man.'

'What's that mean, kid?'

'Bet two crowns and you get three back.' He knows the tally of the bulge and clink of the coins already in his pockets.

Money for jam, the crewmen think, and they open their purses. The young sailor takes pity on them. 'How will you pay the bets, kids? You're not telling me anyone's putting money on that streak of piss?' He nods towards Balty.

Betty gives him a wide smile. 'The people of this town are very loyal, sir,' she says. 'They don't like to bet against a friend.'

'Him? He's a Frenchy and he's made out of nothing.'

'He's fast,' says Betty. 'Your man must punch slow with arms that thick.'

'You're joking, kid. Our bosun? Slow? Feints with the right, then uses his left like a double-charge cannonball. First and last thing you know about the fight, every time.' The rest of the crew nod and grin fierce grins – realigned by the past impacts from those same fists. Sam takes their money and enters it in his notebook. The colliers' crew demand he sits down in front of them where they can keep an eye on their money. They can't imagine losing any other way except by the bookmaker's flight. Now Betty holds up a red kerchief. It is time for the fight.

'Would you mind', calls Balty, sounding still more irritatingly French, 'if I remove my coat? There is no point in spoiling fine clothes before I have finished with you. The stitching could split.'

'Finished? With me? I'll split more than stitches. Quick now. Then down to it.' The bosun spits to one side and his crew cheers.

Balty tries to pull his jacket off but his wrists catch in the narrow cuffs and he wrestles with them behind his back. Betty goes to help, tugging the stiff cloth over his hands. Her mouth is close to his ear. 'Take care, papa,' she whispers, 'he fools with the right, then he throws a mighty left.' She folds the jacket over her arm.

'Thank you, my dear,' he says and steps towards the collier's mate, still keeping his hands behind his back, his chin unprotected – as if he has no sense of the cloud of violence leaking from the man a foot in front of him. His white shirt flashes back the sun.

'Dancing clothes,' says the mate. 'Not fighting clothes.' He looks past Balty. 'Hey girlie,' he shouts. 'This yer daddy? Send him home. You fight me. You look tougher.'

Betty smiles.

Balty raises his eyebrows, his hands still behind him. 'You are vairy right,' he says. 'She is tough indeed but she also has such grace. I will show you how she dances. Watch me closely. She can do this . . .' He attempts an absurd caper but his legs slide from under him on the sloping shingle. The mate jerks back off balance, starting a laugh which soars to a shriek as Balty's right foot crashes into his crotch. The Frenchman's hand whips to the side of the mate's descending head. It grips the lead cosh smuggled into his hands by Betty and the fight is over. The mate collapses backwards down the slope in a shingle cascade. He lies still and the last ripples of the wasted waves wash over him, a delta of blood spreading through the sea-foam from his split scalp.

Well practised in this, the Deal folk move to surround Sam and protect their winnings from the collier's crew. Outnumbered, the startled losers are forced back to their boat. The fishermen sling the unconscious mate in after them. Betty collects her father's share as Sam carefully distributes the rest according to the figures in his book.

Balty pulls his jacket back on, slides the cosh into its inner pocket and looks at his daughter, awaiting judgement. 'Well done papa,' she says, 'but . . .'

'But what?'

'It was so very quick. Your friends will not bother to come anymore if you cut it too short. They want to see more.'

'Child, you tell me I should not take risks. I'm tired and I am hungry and the man was a monster and you told me yourself that I should not let him get in the first blow. How much did we make?'

'Almost a guinea,' Sam says. He only lies when he has to. They made more than two guineas but, knowing their father's slippery pockets, the children always hide half the proceeds against the next inevitable rainy day. They turn westward to head home along the shingle towards King Henry's old stone castle.

That castle, seen only by God and seagulls as a carefully shaped Tudor rose, marks the end of the navy's so-called port, which is little more than a short stretch of beach with supply boats dragged up in a line. Balty thinks of the daily report he must write for his master in London. He will say he took necessary steps to correct the collier's muster roll. He will not mention skulls and blood, because the man who will read it would disapprove. That man is little Sam's godfather and allows Balty to call him 'brother'. Balty's working life as the Deal muster-master, the local ruler of this naval kingdom, depends wholly on his brother's goodwill.

The landlocked navy yard is in the middle of the small town and the muster-master's house is framed in blackened age-twisted oak. Its rooms smell of cabbage, tobacco and burnt tallow. The supply depot surrounding it is modern, the most ordered part of the town. Most of Deal is a random mess of broken boats and narrow streets, home to smugglers, drunks and whores.

Esther St Michel, Balty's entirely English wife, is wrestling with a wooden keg and worrying as she does so often now about a place far, far away where she has heard that people are sent to die. It is a harbour town on the North African shore of the Mediterranean and she can hardly bear to hear its name spoken. Balty's posting takes effect in only one month's time. Just him. Wives are not allowed, unless their husbands are of much higher rank than Balty. She is quite sure the posting is a hideous ticket to widowhood. This deadly place is named Tangier. Esther may give her husband a hard time, but irritation is a diversion from despair. Under that, she loves him with silent ferocity.

A balding dog watches the still-sealed keg. His sense of smell surpasses Esther's a thousand-fold and no keg keeps all its atoms trapped, however hard the wood. He already knows what's inside it. Corned beef would have been acceptable, but not this . . .

Young Sam also knows what's inside the keg, by experience and logical extrapolation. Young Betty knows through her understanding of human nature. Only Balty and Esther regard the keg as a promising mystery.

For most of his disappointed life, the threadbare dog has been known as Mumper after the Duke of York's famous pet. That has turned sour. It is more than two lifetimes since Harry kicked out the Church of Rome, but now religion once again splits England. King Charles has many sons, but none by his wife. His brother James, Duke of York is heir to the throne and James, almost unthinkably, is a Catholic and so presumably is his spaniel. Balty called their balding mongrel Mumper as a joke, but deliberate irony is now a slender defence when the anti-Catholic mobs calling for the duke's downfall can't spell irony.

Last month they doubled down on irony and changed the dog's name to Tapski, which is those street mobs' chosen name for their hero, Anthony Ashley-Cooper, Earl of Shaftesbury, who leads the campaign to rid the nation of the Catholic duke. The mobs know their favourite earl has a brass tap stitched into his side to drain pus from something foul within. The nickname makes Shaftesbury less of a perfect earl and more of an imperfect mate.

This Deal version of Mumper didn't answer to his old name let alone the new, but that seems unlikely to matter for long. He is also foul inside and looks set for an imminent encounter with Sam's scalpel. In any case, he is under the impression that his name is 'Dog'.

Sam is currently dissecting a rodent splayed out and pinned on a board. A large mouse? A small rat? Hard to tell when they are inside-out. Balty inspects his son's sketchbook and appreciates the precision of the full-page picture. The twins always surprise him, but 1678 is a man's world and this father dreams mainly of his son's future. He privately wishes Betty would take a little more interest in becoming charming and a little less interest in giving him improving advice.

Betty and Sam are close, but she has got used to doing without her brother for much of the past year. Sam has been in London, living the rich life in his godfather's grand household and busy Navy Office, and he has come back changed as if time moves faster up there. He has put on much more age than just that single year, but he has still not quite caught up with his twin sister. They are both clever but she has more wisdom.

Their mother thinks everything moves faster in London. Esther feels unfairly exiled to this dull coast. Towns are circular in her mind, so Deal is only half a town, the other half being salt water. Despite that, she would be happy to stay here if only Balty is allowed to stay here too.

The barrel surrenders, oysters spraying their saline presence as the lid clatters across the tiled floor. Balty sees her scowl. There is much of his dear, difficult, dead sister in Esther's face. The big difference is that Elizabeth knew she was pretty and Esther does not. Hard life has worn away her sense of worth. She picks up the lid and snorts. 'Tell the purser of that scow, the *Stavoreen,* we get far too many damned oysters,' she says. 'The labour of opening them kills any slight pleasure in the swallowing. Good wine would be more welcome next time he passes.'

Balty's brow creases. Acceptable fees easily become unacceptable bribes when they cross a line, but that line wriggles if you stare too hard. The *Stavoreen*'s crew list was much nearer reality than that damned collier, but he agrees that a barrel of oysters is not enough. Against that, a dozen of good Bordeaux wine could be too much and leave him vulnerable.

'You well know how this works. King Charles pays us for part of the service we provide. Those who receive that service quite rightly contribute the other part. Our king is not made of money,' he says.

'How do you tell what is right?' Betty asks.

'I just . . . I just . . . know?'

Sam raises a finger. 'Father, what does a keg of oysters cost?'

'A keg? Oysters? Four shillings? Five shillings? It depends I suppose. I've never had to buy one.'

'My godfather' says Sam, and Balty shudders, knowing that a higher authority is about to be introduced into this difficult debate, 'has tasted a wondrous Bordeaux wine they call Ho Brian. He says the King's cellar master paid *one guinea a bottle* for that wine, ten times the price of lesser wines from fields nearby. In that case I would estimate that more ordinary Bordeaux wine would cost perhaps as much as two shillings? So the proper price for your services might be no more than two or three bottles of the ordinary wine and anything more could be seen as greed?'

'Well, I . . .'

'But he did also say that there has been a very substantial wine harvest in that region for two years now, so it is entirely likely that prices will fall.' Sam studies his father for a moment. 'I suppose that doesn't really matter if, as you claim, you *just know.*'

'Sam,' says Betty sternly, 'you are focusing on detail. This is about gratitude and obligation, which cannot easily be measured, against bribery and greed on the other hand, which perhaps can. It appears to be a very uncertain business and we can be glad that, as young children, we do not face the hard choices our dear father has to make on our behalf.'

Balty walks out into the navy yard to avoid further questions. His children are getting uncomfortably close to the disquiet that so often plucks at his guts. The simple fact is that he trades favours because that is how the creaking system works. The royal wage bill is close to becoming insupportable. The smaller cogs in the king's machine are expected to make ends meet by a direct levy on those who need their services, but at Balty's modest level you get greedy at your own risk. When his 'brother' reached high office twenty years earlier, he hoisted Balty a little way up with him but laid down strict rules. Balty tries to observe them and has never grown rich. Somehow, his brother has become very rich indeed.

After twenty deep breaths, he goes back in. Betty and Sam are discussing some detail of mouse anatomy and Esther is frying fish. Tapski is stretched out, motionless. Balty has a brief hope that the dog might be dead, but it farts and immediately wags its tail. This might be a sign of pleasure, but Balty has come to think it is intended to widen the effect of the smell.

A double knock shakes the door. The daily messenger from the London office is bent-backed and twitching from his gallop on the third leg of the long relay. He thrusts a dusty leather satchel into Balty's hands and accepts its twin, clean and bulging with the Deal muster-master's reports. Balty watches him go, then ruffles through the contents until he comes to a thick envelope addressed in that distinctive hand. His brother has schooled his office team in copying that writing, counterfeiting the intricate spirals of his signature to save himself time, but this one is the real thing and Balty's stomach lurches. That indicates a personal message and of late those are usually disturbing.

'Esther?' he says and she abandons the fish to come to his side because she still has hopes. They had been promised something much better than Deal before Tangier was first mentioned. She still dares dream of busy Greenwich, with its easy access to the great city itself. When their brother first proffered Africa as a golden chance for enrichment her world fell apart, but they have written to him at length, urging a change of mind. Could this be a reprieve?

Balty gasps in air, breaks the seal, scans the words and stares at them in silence. Esther looks at the sheet. She tries to read the writing but the sheet is shaking in Balty's hand.

'Has he listened? Surely he has. He will not send us there.'

'Not *us*,' he says. 'Not you, not the children. Still only me and still Tangier.'

'Our brother cannot have read our letter properly. We must write again.' That word 'brother' comforts her as if seven letters can bind him more closely as protector, but her hope trickles away as she reads his face. 'How can he be so cruel?'

Balty often avoids hard questions but unexpected clarity takes over. 'Our brother has lined his nest with Tangier money. It pays for his luxuries. He likes to paint his own picture of a heaven on the African coast.'

He knows that Esther's increasing irritation with him is a disguise for fear, to distract from looming sorrow.

'We have to face it,' he says. 'He is deluded. I am to be sent to hell. No words of ours can change that.' He sees too late that both the twins are watching and listening.

'Can we help, papa?' says Betty quietly.

'No,' he says. 'Oh no . . . it will work out.'

Samuel has been staring intently at his father, his mouth working with no audible results. Now he speaks. 'It will certainly be all right as you say, father. It will be better than that. It will be the making of you and . . .' he frowns slightly, 'and the security of our family for many years to come.'

'What? What did you say?' Balty connects. 'Did your god-father teach you that?'

Samuel moves his head, the first half of a shake, veering into a nod, then completing the shake.

'He did, didn't he?'

'He has your interests at heart, papa. He showed me his drawings hanging on his office wall. Tangier is a wonder. There are lines of fine houses and tall foreign trees and strange birds swooping round them. Anyone should be glad to go there. He said so. Quite often.'

'Those are palm trees' — he has seen that drawing many times — 'and the birds are . . .' He closes his mouth to swallow the word 'vultures'. He knows the sand hills in the foreground are soaked in stinking blood. The gracious villas sloping to the sea are crowded dens ruined by drunken soldiers. Balty has talked to many sailors and they all say the same. Stay away from Tangier or say hello to Death.

Betty has her hand on Sam's shoulder and is squeezing it as she studies her father with worried eyes.

The dog gets up and stumbles towards Balty, wheezing. It sniffs his leg. Once a month it bites him and this might be the day — but instead it dribbles piss on his shoe and lies back down to shrink its tally of remaining breaths. Perhaps it senses he has had enough for one day. More likely it has forgotten what it got up intending to do.

CHAPTER 2

Later that evening, three miles up the coast towards Sandwich, fifteen men are enjoying an unexpected treat. Floating on a tide of free alcohol, they are proud to be the latest recruits to a gallant band ready to face the vicious menace threatening England. Until an hour earlier they hadn't known there was a vicious menace, but then the word passes from door to door in their tiny village that a stranger has come to the St Crispin Inn. There in the taproom they encounter a holy visitation. Major Martin is old, scarred and talking up a storm while endless mugs of porter and nips of smuggled brandy ensure his listeners hang on every one of his deliberately simple words.

England is in the grip of a virulent contagion spread by truth-twisters and the fever cells are multiplying in the sheltered minds of men such as these. The listeners have no clue that their new hero spends his master's money in a different inn every night to stoke the national fever. The major carefully explains that he works with Sir Frances Rolle, a Member of Parliament. In their eyes, that makes Sir Frances nearly as important as the king himself and certainly as truthful.

'I tell you,' says the major, 'I saw the villains in the jail.

Saw them myself as close as I am to you now. A dozen papists, dressed up to look just like you and me, and do you know what the searchers found hidden in their houses?' He stares at the nearest man, who nods his head three times, stops himself, shakes it once. 'Grenadoes,' says the major, 'they found grenadoes wrapped up ready and hidden in priests' robes.'

'What's they for?'

'Fireballs, ready to lob in through your windows and burn you in your beds like they did last time.' All the men in the taproom nod. They know the papists started the Great Fire of 1666. No question.

'Those murderers stood there in the dock, shrieking out that a thousand more stand ready to fill their boots,' says Major Martin. 'And will the king move against them when they do?'

'Course he will.'

Wrong answer. The major tries again.

'Really? Charlie-boy with his Portuguese queen, hissing in his ear? All smells and bells and Latin prayers. She don't hide her Catholic ways. Enough to muddle any decent man.'

Until this very evening, the lonely village has been beyond the hum of false news spreading from London, so they're not yet ready to hear 'royal' and 'treason' in the same sentence. They still remember Charles's gaily decked-out fleet of ships passing close by, bringing back their young king from his exile and ending the hard and heavy years. They remember the unearthing of the hidden maypoles and the thrilling return of the dancing, the sports, the music and all that had once spelt fun before the puritan clampdown. Wine and beer flowed freely again to wash away the Cromwell years.

'You're not saying the king is a bad man?' asks ploughman Harold. 'That ain't right.'

The major considers launching into Charles's shocking secret deal with King Louis. That works with a town audience, but he judges it's a step too far for these folk, so he backtracks to where Charles is the victim, not yet the villain. 'Well now, you spoke a truth there, matey.' He throws another coin on the counter and the jugs go round again. 'But that's the worst part.'

'Worst part?'

'When the Romanist assassins murder our very good King Charlie, they'll put his brother on the throne and we all know what Duke James is like, don't we?'

They don't know whether to nod.

'Our Duke of York is papist through and through, ain't he? You wouldn't think they were from the same womb, would you now?' Major Martin has been schooled in this game, because when you ask the questions just right, one after another, bang, bang, bang, and then you nail on those little confirmations after each one – that's when your crowd has to start agreeing and agreeing can be baked hard into believing.

'The duke doesn't hide it, does he? Right? You remember all the years he commanded our navy, our precious wooden walls to keep out King Louis's Catholic armies? Can't forget that, can you? God's truth, you men can see the Frenchy coast from here on a clear day. Packed with soldiers, ships all ready. Waiting for the word to set sail and slaughter us. And . . .' He turns slowly around with one finger raised and looks into their eyes, one after another. 'And if Duke James has his way, he would send our ships far away on some nonsense mission and those Frenchies would be over here already. That's what papist Jamie wants. Have you forgotten what happened last time we had a papist on the throne? Good men's flesh sizzled.'

His words carve out a deep slice of silence. They don't know much history and one hundred and twenty years is a long time, but four generations of parents have used that story as a threat to unruly children – the bonfires of the Terror, fuelled by the blazing fat of fourteen score good Protestants lashed to their stakes. They know about Bloody Mary's bonfires and no, they don't want those back, thank you.

This tavern is on the very edge of England. No political pamphlets reach it yet, but lurid words of printed threat and hatred are now on their way. The locals sense the ripples of the fear running just under England's skin. Rumours with the solidity of a vicious ghost are dripping down from the heights where powerful men prepare. They whisper that hidden Catholic assassins sharpen their stilettos, waiting for the signal to hand the country back to the pope. Duke James? He's in there with the assassins.

An elderly shepherd is stirred to prove he is up there with this craggy hero. 'We'll hunt them. That Frenchy in Deal, we can start with him.'

'Saint Michael?' says the tavern owner, who has seen a bit more of life. 'He's a Huguenot. That's French for Protestant. Louis bin killing 'em off. That's why there's thousands come over here. They hate Louis.'

The major frowns. 'That will be Monsieur Balthasar St Michel,' he says, deliberately pronouncing it the French way and savouring their frowns. 'He may *say* he's a Protestant but we know he's a Jesuit. They're taught to lie for their church so they get to heaven quicker. Am I right? I am, aren't I? And we know the Jesuits are plotting against us, don't we?'

'You've heard of him then?' says the tavern owner.

'Oh yes,' says the major, 'he matters.' He invests in more jugs of ale and by the time those jugs are dry they have come to loathe Balty as much as they fear the French.

The old shepherd Samson and his son Nazareth stagger away when the liquor runs dry, primed to see devils in the dark, their heads full of fire and daggers. Their eyes dart one way and another as the path twists, the moon edging clouds to spread silver on scattered water. Ghosts coalesce when fright is planted, as a stake in a stream builds a dam of floating foliage. Terror stops the son first. His father's eyes follow his shaking finger and their guts churn at the dim outlines of countless men filling the field in ranks to its far curve and beyond towards the sea. More clouds speed across the moon, giving only glimpses of the disciplined ranks facing them. English soldiers would not need to be silent and secret. These lurkers can only be King Louis's men, the midnight vanguard of the French king's move to put the pope back in charge of England's souls.

They duck below the hedge in mortal fear until the old man's knees force them to crawl away, then they hobble towards the town to find anyone who might know what to do. It takes time to rouse the defence force, so the Sandwich militia, three dozen ill-prepared men, arrive at the hedge two hours before dawn. They have moved as fast as they can because they are nearly as scared of the veteran soldier in charge of them as they are of invaders.

The moon has set and they creep along the hedgerow sensing only the outlines of the enemy ranks. Taking up positions on a whispered command, they know they are doomed. The three musketeers aim towards the field, though one of the three weapons rarely produces anything more than a flash in the pan. The other men hold pikes in shaking hands. The old soldier is behind them with a drawn sword so they can't run before the battle starts.

It is breathless deadlock until the sun bounces its first flash off the clouds from below the eastern horizon and glints on mounds of turnips lined in ranks across the field. The militia shout their relief. The turnips stay silent. They are English turnips to the core and not about to murder anyone except by choking.

Very much later, when the months of madness have dried to a dark stain on the fabric of history, historians will explain how the terror was fanned from old embers. They will struggle to capture the scale of the national hysteria. What made an entire country terrified by turnips in the dark? A gunpowder keg of a plot, that's what, planted by political interests at the same time as those turnips.

It takes three to make gunpowder. Saltpetre feeds rapid ignition, sulphur organizes the explosion, and charcoal provides the carbon to fuel it. In the England of 1678, sulphur and saltpetre are embodied in two ruthless politicians whose different aims chance to overlap. They need angry people for their charcoal and that fuel is everywhere you look in London thanks to the events of twelve years back, when Thomas Faryner forgot to quench the ovens where he baked ships' biscuits and set the whole city on fire. All that was left of fourteen thousand homes was the charcoal from half a million oak beams.

Until the fire, the ramshackle timber houses ever crept

upwards, jettied out at the top, often close enough to step across
a street from window to window. Sunlight struggled to reach
the ground where a foetid mesh of alleys linked the stinking
underworld. The old city's crowded complications imposed
rough and ready rules to keep life going, but the fire pried the
raucous citizens out of their ruts. A dozen years later, charcoal is
still heaped in piles between new-builds made from safer brick
and stone. The destabilized city has shed those old rules and it
is now ripe for violent realignment.

CHAPTER 3

October 18th, 1678

The tavern absurdly called *The Good Woman* stands on the edge of Deal beach where the narrow street, known as Goat's Jig Lane, heads up hill from the sea. The lane is home to rather less good women. The tavern is the closest drinking place to the navy yard and Balty often uses it when he needs to think – and today he has to think very hard, because this is the day he will demonstrate his new invention. He plans to invite the highest-ranking officers from the nearby ships to observe it. He is almost confident they will be impressed enough to spread the word and he is writing his 'brother' a letter describing the difference his invention will make to the safety of ships out there in the Downs, but only so long as he can remain in England to take the project further.

Esther has sent Betty and Sam to help him. She knows what can happen when Balty writes any important letter. His pen gets drunk on ink and dances to flowery excess. The children are sitting at the next table. Sam is reading a book. Betty is studying a pamphlet from a small pile on the chair by the door.

They are all the same – single rough-edged oblong sheets of lumpy paper, printed in harsh gothic letters, an unexpected new arrival. Mary washes mugs behind the serving bar. Her only other customers are two fishermen over there in the window that looks out towards all the masts. Betty frowns at the pamphlet. She doesn't want to ask her brother but she needs to know. 'Sam?'

'Yes?' He is concentrating hard and his voice sounds as if it has answered without telling him. They started the day with a minor dispute about the past history of the Stuart royal line and it clearly still rankles.

'Do you know what recusant means?'

He looks up, frowning. 'Oh, so now you need help from your older brother, do you?'

'Older by seven shrieks and a howl, as mama says. Are we still squabbling, twin?'

'You admit that I know things you don't?' Sam trades on his months up in London steered through chosen books from his godfather's library shelves. That hasn't stopped. More books sporadically arrive from passing naval vessels. Sam reads them first but does sometimes share them so they can discuss the hard parts.

'Brother, I wasn't invited to London. I wish I had been.'

'But you're a girl.' He manages to affront himself with these words and makes a face. 'Yes, I do know what recusant means.'

She looks down at the pamphlet again and her silence compels him to offer peace. 'A recusant is a person who disobeys the law by refusing to attend the services of the Church of England – usually because they are members of the Church of Rome.'

'Does that make them traitors and assassins?'

'I don't know,' he says. 'Why?'

'Because this ugly sheet says they are.'

He peers at it. 'Who wrote that?'

'Nobody brave enough to sign their name.' She points at the pile on the chair. 'Mary said they were left at the door.'

Major Martin's dawn delivery man had taken care not to be seen. 'This one is short,' she says. 'Shall I read it? "The English hero Titus Oates, recently escaped from the Jesuitical hatcheries of Spain, has given notice of the papist plot to destroy our king and murder true Englishmen in their beds. He has sworn it on oath to Justice Godfrey in London who can be relied upon to ensure that the guilty recusants planning this outrage will soon face justice."'

'Justice Godfrey? Sir Edmund Berry Godfrey? I have met him. He came to my godfather's house. Twice.' Sam exaggerates. He did see the famous lawyer being ushered across the hallway into his godfather's study but at twenty feet's distance and from behind. 'My godfather knows him very well. He says the man is a brave hero for all he did in London during the plague . . .'

A noise from his father stops him. Balty is staring out of the side window towards the narrow lane. The light makes shadow ridges from the wrinkles in his brow and his mouth is open. A fraction of his distress has got out. They both go to his table and see his half-finished appeal to the Navy Office. Betty hopes he will ask for her help quite soon, but Balty listens to Sam more easily than he does to her and the children don't agree on the subject of Tangier.

'Sister, it cannot be as you say,' Sam has insisted. 'My

godfather is in charge of the funding of Tangier port. He sends great sums out there in gold. He says it is an excellent opportunity for our papa to enrich himself and to enjoy a beautiful town with magnificent views over a warm sea.'

'Has he been there?'

'You know he has not.'

'Papa has spoken to seamen whose faces darken when they talk of plagues and snakes and scorpions and attacks from besieging armies and bad water and rotten food and many, many English graves.'

'Stop it. You are ungrateful. My godfather is thinking of us all.' He cannot bear to hear the contrary. They both love their father for his humour and bold spirit.

Balty looks up at them now and forces a smile. How simply he loves them. Every other relationship in his life is shadowed by some silent contract. Here in Deal, it all comes down to deals and gratitude is rationed.

Hooves clatter on the road outside and a horse whinnies. Seconds later, the inn's front door crashes open. A man stands dark against the sunlight, looking around at the surprised fisherman then squinting into the more distant gloom. 'St Michel?' he calls.

'Here,' calls Balty, jumping to his feet.

'Most urgent. Direct from Mr Pepys in London.'

'Wait,' says Balty. 'I may need to reply to . . .' but the door is already swinging shut and in another moment he hears hooves on the hard road picking up the pace into a gallop and fading away.

'Great God,' he says. 'Something's happened.' He takes his knife to the wax seal, shakes the message open and reads it rapidly, once then twice. 'What?' he exclaims. 'How am I supposed to . . . ? How has this . . . ?' He stops himself. 'Sam, you must run a message to the signal tower. I will write it quickly.'

'Say it to me,' Betty says. 'I will write it neatly for you.' She knows how her father's thoughts fly apart when ink meets paper, even when he is calm, and at this moment there is no trace of calm left in him.

'Yes, yes.' He sits down, frowning, and she takes his quill and a sheet of his paper.

'To the signallers. Hoist immediate signal to all ships, private and navy,' he says. 'No ship to depart until further notice. All navy captains to come ashore immediately for orders.'

'Come where? The navy yard?'

Balty thinks of the discomfort available there and shakes his head. 'No. Here will serve.' He calls to the woman at the bar. 'Mary, I need this room for the rest of the morning. Two hours maybe. The navy will pay.'

Mary looks around the nearly empty room and smiles. 'All yours,' she says and calls to the fishermen who are waiting for a different tide, or for the wind to change, or more likely for a refill of their mugs. 'You heard the man. The navy needs me. Off you go.'

Balty looks at Betty. 'Have you got it?'

'Yes.' She waves it in the air to dry the ink and hands it to Sam. The signal tower is not far along the beach and she keeps her question until he gets back. 'What has just happened, father?'

'An important man has been murdered in London and his killer is seeking to escape across the sea.'

'What man?'

'A man of the law. You won't have heard of him. Sir Edmund Berry Godfrey.'

Both children gasp. Betty hands the pamphlet to her father. 'We were talking about him,' she says. 'Sam saw him in London. Read this.'

A mystery is mushrooming. Sir Edmund wakes up in his London house a few days earlier as the first copies of this pamphlet are coming off the laborious iron press close by. He levers his old body off his horsehair mattress, dresses and goes out into a damp morning. He is seen walking in the fields north of Oxford Street, then misses a luncheon appointment and is not back home when evening comes. The alarming story that he is missing spreads rapidly across the city – which is odd, because Sir Edmund's daily perambulations normally escape comment. Days, weeks and months usually pass without Londoners giving his movements a thought.

Sir Edmund Berry Godfrey had achieved lasting fame during the Great Plague thirteen years before. As the lethal disease surged across the city, killing one person in every five, he worked day and night to organize the isolation of the sick and to arrest looters when fellow officials fled to safer places. However, Godfrey has recently been in contact with a brand-new plague of the mind, not of the body, and the pamphlet tells the truth. Godfrey has taken down the sworn testimony of the moon-faced ex-Jesuit Titus Oates, who has laid out all he claims to know of the papist plot to murder the king.

Five days after he goes missing, three men discover Godfrey's corpse in a Primrose Hill ditch, strangled then run through by his own sword. Wax has been spilt on his clothes. Clearly assassins holding ritual papist candles have taken revenge because he has helped Oates to expose the plot.

'Children,' says Balty, 'you can be proud. My brother, your uncle Mr Pepys, is taking swift action to find the killers.'

He reads out the message from London. After the terse instruction to freeze shipping movements and search the ships in the Downs, it says Balty should brief commanders that a suspect boarded a vessel at Gravesend in the Thames estuary. The ship may be waiting in the Downs for a fair wind and the fugitive may contrive to change ships. A reward of no less than £500 is offered for his capture.

Betty and Sam had once asked their father how Uncle Samuel came to be so important. Balty did not mention the detailed diaries Pepys had kept for a decade for the simple reason that he, along with everyone else, knew nothing at all of their secret existence. 'He is a very clever man,' Balty told them. 'Smart as a jackdaw and as organized as a queen bee.'

'But he's not an admiral, is he?' Sam had said.

'No ... but he was right-hand man to the king's brother James, the Lord High Admiral. Then Duke James got sent away for all his Catholic stuff and your godfather stepped into the breach as Secretary of the Navy. Been doing it ever since and to great effect.'

Now Balty puts aside his half-completed letter. The tavern's spyglass shows him the first longboats heading his way from the anchored men o'war and he knows he must delay the spectacle he had hoped to demonstrate to some of these same officers later in the day.

Betty looks at him closely and sees signs of disquiet. 'What's wrong, papa?'

'I may not enjoy this,' he says. 'Captains are proud men.'

'And?'

'And they don't all like receiving orders from such as me.'

'But those are your brother's orders, not yours.'

'This is a moment when some may resent the connection, my child. Now, both of you, go away until the captains leave. Can you first give Ezra a message. He may be in the yard.'

'No, father,' says Sam. 'He and his men are working up the hill at the launch house. He told me so.'

'Ah! Good for Ezra. Then warn him we may have to postpone our experiment until later in the day and to be ready for my word.'

When they leave he looks out to sea again. The longboats are making slow progress into a westerly wind and a big swell. He reckons he has at least fifteen minutes to wait for the first arrivals and his mind floats back to the great invention which might yet save him from Tangier. Balty believes he has inherited his father's inventive mind.

Alexandre le Marchant, le Seigneur de St Michel, recently dead, turned Protestant at the age of twenty-one and was thrown off the family estate in France, drenched by a bucket of holy water and prodded by the muzzle of Balty's irate grandfather's musket. For a month, Alexandre somehow found employment as court wood-carver to Princess Henrietta Maria when she crossed the Channel to marry England's first King Charles. It took the new queen that time to realize he was neither a good wood-carver nor a good Catholic. Marooned in England, he lived on his wits by inventing things. His device for stopping smoking chimneys brought in a modest income, but other ideas never made it beyond the drawings. Balty is giving one of those a second chance as one half of the great idea that might just save him from Tangier. It is his father's design for a trolley for launching heavy boats over rough beaches. The other half of the great idea is also borrowed, this time from something Balty once saw at the Goulet de Brest narrows in Brittany, the treacherous passage where a turning tide endangers ships leaving or entering the great French harbour. It was a rowing gig kept in its own special house at the top of a long ramp leading right down into the water, ready for launch at any state of those tides to rescue others in trouble or rush a commander out to his warship. Balty watched the gig race down the ramp on greased cow-hides and had been deeply impressed. Ezra is the giant Cornish bosun of a wrecked frigate's crew, left with Balty for the past month, waiting for a new ship. They became an instant nightmare at the hands of Deal's whores and innkeepers, so he has been keeping them busy turning his idea into reality.

The navy owns a tall, semi-derelict store up in the town. Ezra's men have built a steep ramp down from the top floor, aiming straight down the narrow length of Goat's Jig Lane towards the shingle beach. Balty assigns a redundant navy gig – a battered heavyweight, thirty feet long and planked with iron-hard elm. It has been hauled up Ezra's ramp and tethered by chains in the top floor of the old store. Needing a suitable trolley for its wild ride down the lane and across the shingle to the sea, Balty borrows his father's idea. Carriage wheels wouldn't cope for a second but Alexandre's invention uses willow. Balty dragoons basket-makers into weaving bulging willow rings for his trolley wheels. Ezra's team is waiting up there now to close the street and set the gig free at his command. The residents of the lane are in no position to complain. They depend on the averted eye of the naval authorities and mid-morning is their quietest time.

The first arrivals interrupt his thoughts and Mary provides them with drinks. As ever, in Balty's experience, the commanders divide into two groups – the inward starched sort, there by divine right of birth and wealth and the others, the outward facing, more dependable men who put their task first and their comfort second. He knows which ones he prefers. Today he is lucky. It splits one-third, two-thirds, and the majority listen attentively to him as he explains what Mr Pepys has told him.

'Gentlemen, you are required to look for a burly man . . .'

'Required?' interrupts a captain of the first sort who is also a marquis. '*You* require us?'

Balty holds his tongue in check. 'I simply relate the instructions from the Secretary of the Navy.'

'Ah yes, him. Secretary for the time being,' says the marquis, but others shake their heads and young Captain Elliot winks at Balty from the front row of chairs.

'To continue, he is said to have a cast to one eye. Thick eyebrows. Perhaps forty years of age with a military look and rough skin to his face, an out-of-doors complexion.'

'Does this man have a name?' asks Captain Elliot.

'It would seem he uses several names. He may have a campaign coat with him, trimmed with a brown fur collar, and two ornate pistols with silver curlicues on their grips. He is said to be highly resourceful and adept at escaping. He joined a ship called *Assistance,* aided by a captain sent to help him escape, but he may have transferred to another.'

'We had better get busy,' says Captain Avey from the back

row, currently senior commander of the Channel Fleet. 'As soon as the searches are complete, we will set a patrol in mid-Channel as the wind is set to change.'

'Chances are he's already past us and gone,' says the marquis, and Balty reluctantly finds he agrees.

They return to their ships and the twins come back. 'Ezra awaits your command, father,' says Sam.

'That may have to be another day. We will see.'

Balty goes back to his letter to London for half an hour by the chiming of a distant church bell as the inn starts to get busy. He wants the children with him for the trial run because they will enjoy the spectacle. Ideally, it would be witnessed by a pair of captains, or even an admiral should there be one handy. That would ensure they take note up in London. Should he test it out today or wait for a better moment? A smile spreads across his face in anticipation and then he turns at a sudden noise behind him and someone throws a mug of ale straight into his face.

For a moment, he can't see, let alone work out how to deal with such smelly, soaking aggression, but his children are across it. He blinks away the beer to see them busy at the back window, checking the yard beyond. 'This way, papa,' Sam says firmly. 'Right now.'

He looks back to see the bruised face of the collier's bosun who is waving a club at the head of a small crowd swarming through the tavern towards him, then he is pulled through the open window by his children. Shouts burst out behind him.

'Run to the boathouse,' he yells. He knows they are faster than him. 'Bring Ezra and his men, quickly now' – but they are already racing up Goat's Jig Lane.

Balty makes the big mistake of glancing back. A dozen men

have fanned out into the lane. His lead cosh will be no match for what's coming at him. His gaze fixes on them for a moment too long and he stumbles in the gutter, sharp pain stabbing his right ankle. Limping as fast as he can, he looks far up the lane towards the boathouse doors. Salvation? Only if the children bring the sailors in time. Are the sailors up there even on his side? Has he upset any of them? Yes of course he has, Ezra himself, but at least they got drunk together afterwards. He has to risk another quick glance behind and sees he is losing ground, but his pursuers are bunched up behind the collier's bosun, who is built for killing but not for speed.

For a moment, it might still be all right, but then it clearly won't be as he feels something in his damaged ankle give way. He finds a little more speed with a painful hopping motion, but they will soon be on him and there is no sign of help from the boathouse. Then something ahead changes. Both doors are opening at the top of the building. Shapes move high up there in the darkness around the tethered gig and he sees small figures which must be the twins. The bow of the gig emerges into daylight and as it starts to tilt downward on to the ramp a stentorian voice from up there bellows, 'Ouvrez une porte.'

The accent is horrible but Balty understands. The crowd chasing him do not. The door of the first house he tries is bolted. The second opens so easily that he sprawls into a dark hallway. The whore the sailors call Haystacks stands there with nothing better to do than wait for the next man. She grins and her two arms wrap around him in the pungent gloom.

Screeches erupt from the street outside, overlaid by a rising, creaking rumble. He battles to the open front door, towing her behind him as the noise increases to a roar, overlaid by yells of terror. He stops just in time as the great length of the heavy gig sweeps past, swaying on its trolley, its wooden sides scraping against the houses, spraying splinters and shavings as he lurches back. Craning out to peer after it, he sees the boat careering on down, deflected off the cottage walls from one side of the narrow lane to the other. The shouts turn to thuds and screams and the runaway boat bounces to a halt at the edge of the shingle, leaving prostrate bodies strewn across the cobbles behind it.

Ezra and his sailors are hot on its heels and puzzled drinkers are coming out of the tavern, baffled by the carnage. Balty limps slowly down to join them.

'That did it, sir,' gasps the giant. 'What a show! They're the business, your two. Little Sam – he comes yelling at us to open the doors and he knocks out the shackle to let the gig go. Your pretty Betty, she sees you in trouble and starts shouting those Frenchie words at you.'

'But that wasn't her.'

'Oh no, no, sir. Her lungs being too much on the small side, she hands over the shouting to me. Me speaking French? Oover oon port. What about that? It was so you would get out the way and they wouldn't – not speaking French. Eh?'

'Yes, I think I understand, Ezra.'

They inspect the result. The colliers' bosun will never pick another fight, nor will three of his shipmates, but others are stirring and clutching at their injuries. Two of the prostrate men are not from the collier's crew. They wear shepherds' smocks.

'We'll fix this, sir,' says Ezra. 'You sit yourself down.'

The sailors separate the living and the dead and drag them all down the beach to a longboat. Balty sits on a bollard, resting his ankle, and watches them pull out towards the ships anchored in the Downs. A small hand tucks into his and Betty is standing there with Sam next to her.

'Your trolley works quite well, papa,' Sam says, 'though I believe its directional guidance is not ideal. The friction of its encounters with the walls slowed it too much for it to cross the beach. Guiding timbers nailed to the house frontages and painted with tallow might make for a better result.' He paused. 'But one might also suppose that it lost necessary momentum when it collided with all these men.'

'Samuel,' says Balty slowly. 'Samuel and Betty. I know you have saved me just now, so it might seem ungrateful to point out that in saving me you appear to have done away with quite a number of those who were after me. There is a commandment specifically against that, I recall.'

Betty and Samuel look at each other. 'You forget yourself, pater,' says Sam. 'We are after all only eleven and a half years old, therefore any reasonable person would conclude that we could not possibly have foreseen the consequences when I chanced to trip over the release lever on the cordage restraining the chock at the top of the ramp. No mere child could be held responsible for so unfortunate an action, nor his sister.' He shades his eyes and stares out towards the Goodwins. 'Besides, I think Ezra is a man to be relied on and I did promise them all a drink at your expense when they return.'

'I did not agree to that,' says Betty and cuffs her brother gently.

Sam looks smug. 'Now, come pater and order yourself a glass of malmsey wine and I will take a sip of it to see if I have developed the taste for it yet.'

He does, indeed he takes five sips, carefully spaced out, and then opens his notebook. He appears to Balty to be noting down the changes he observes in himself as a result and takes his own pulse every now and then, counting silently, though his lips move with the numbers. Betty refuses malmsey and stares out to sea in silence, following the progress of the longboat and moving her lips in what may be a prayer but is more probably a decision.

Ezra's sailors come back after two more glasses of malmsey have passed and Balty makes sure they are rewarded with the best barrel of the hopped beer that the tavern owner has aged for three whole weeks.

'They're all safely back on board, sir,' Ezra reports.

'All? Even the dead ones?'

'Oh I don't think you'll find there were any dead ones, sir. The collier skipper seems to think you'll sign his final muster list without arguing just this once. There might be some real ghosts on it this time.'

'I shall sign it,' says Balty. 'Did I see two shepherds?'

'They'll be heading to pastures new. On our way to the collier we rowed by the old *Portland*, in sore need of more hands after the press left her short. Next mooring for her is the far-off Bermoothes. I gather there'll be some sheep towards Sandwich needing a new owner should we need supplies.' Ezra hands him a pamphlet. 'It was lying in the road with the bodies,' he says. 'I would read it to you if I had the trick.'

This one was headed 'Good Protestants to Arms Whilst There is Still Breath in Your Body.' It tells of poison-smeared stilettos, of ten thousand trained foreigners ready to cut out the livers of sleeping Englishmen, awaiting only the instruction from the devil in Rome and his tame king in France to go into action. It tells honest Englishmen how to recognize assassins by their accent, clothing or unusual names. It details the precise techniques they will use to slice through the neck and slit the stomach.

Betty frowns. 'Papa, people know you are French by the way you speak,' she says. 'But sometimes you sound more French and sometimes less.'

'Do I?'

Betty weighs her words. 'You choose to put yourself in danger, papa. This cannot be a wise approach. Even our family name shows us to be French.'

'Of course it does.'

'But your friend André Le Prieur is now Andrew Pryor and nobody calls him a fucking Frenchie.'

'Betty . . .'

'I am simply reporting what the man said before he threw his beer at you, papa.'

'But child, your grandfather was Alexandre Marchant, le Seigneur of our great estate of St Michel. You think we should forget his pride in that title?'

'If we had, your ankle would be unharmed and those men would still be breathing. Should you perhaps consider tempering that pride with caution in these dangerous times? I would enjoy becoming Betty Merchant if it stopped men trying to kill you.'

His face betrays the depth of his discomfort, so she waves the pamphlet in the air to change the subject. 'Tell me, papa,' she says, 'have all these Catholic assassins actually killed anybody yet?'

CHAPTER 4

London – ten weeks earlier

These pamphlets may not yet have gone far beyond London, but they are spreading through the capital at extraordinary speed. That is all because of a social network created by a recent arrival in England – not a lethal foreign assassin, but the kernel of a small fruit. The great Mr Pepys has shown his favoured godson the evidence of this during Sam's stay in London and Sam so enjoys Pepys's style of passing on his knowledge that he strives to copy it from then on.

'I understand the fruit to be cultivated in the mountains of the Yemen,' Mr Pepys tells him. 'It is known in those parts as kavhé and its hard seeds are shipped through the port of Mokha to the Turkish Ottoman Empire and thence to Venice, then on north, east and west to many lands where their flavour, rich and bitter, joins with their remarkable effect on the physical and mental sensations of those who imbibe them to inspire a very dedicated following. On arrival here in England, they first came to Oxford and then rapidly spawned kavhé houses throughout this, our city of London, though the English tongue has transmuted kahvé to this word coffee and they will insist on describing the seeds as beans, which must surely be held to be entirely incorrect.'

Many of these coffee houses are no more than coffee shacks, built to hold a crowded dozen standing, but some develop higher aspirations. One such has appeared where Chancery Lane meets Fleet Street, a substantial place built by a flame-haired Bristol man with a business head on ambitious shoulders. Sniffing the air, he scents a ready market in these buzzing zealots and realigns his coffee house to suit angry people of a radical persuasion. This catches on very fast and coffee becomes the fuel for both sides of the new political divide, but mostly for those on the side of extreme change.

As an open Tory royalist, Mr Pepys would never be welcome in this one, but had he taken his godson to see it just a few weeks before Godfrey's murder, they might have witnessed a remarkable event. On that day, the place is packed, cheap tables rocking as new arrivals push through the crowd. The prices scrawled in chalk on a hanging blackboard have been partly rubbed off on the shoulders of those shoving past. It doesn't really matter. The price and quality of the coffee aren't critical. The strong scent of trouble in the air is driving the customers towards the comfort of like-minded folk. The coffee buzz fans their fears as they concoct still more trouble. Three men have jumped the queue that day to snatch a table, but no one argues because two of them have a tough ex-military look. The third is a large man, mostly silent, who keeps a scarf wrapped round the lower half of his face. He reeks of wealth and power.

The first of the tough guys is well known. He is John Wildman, a Roundhead officer in the civil war and a trouble-maker all his long life. Don't be fooled by the half-closed eyes. Wildman only feels alive when he is plotting something. The second tough guy is less likely to be recognized. He has a rough complexion, thick eyebrows and a slight cast to one eye so you can't be sure if he's looking at you or at his assassin coming up behind you. You can't be sure of much else about him either. His life story is very fluid. He is here to be assessed.

'Colonel Scott,' says Wildman, 'you have a chequered reputation.'

'Chequered?' The voice sounds amused and annoyed in equal parts.

'You are truly a colonel?' The hunching of Wildman's shoulders says his fist is only just behind his words.

'*Major* Wildman,' says the newcomer. 'I know your rank so do not question mine, sir, which was earned in hard combat in the Americas. Do you know Barbados?'

'A little.'

Scott seamlessly changes tack. 'And do you also know the island of St Kitts?' It is nearly three hundred miles from Barbados to St Kitts by way of Martinique and Montserrat but he guesses Wildman may not know that.

'No, I do not.'

'It was there I reached my rank fighting the French and Dutch. I went on to advise King Charles's forces in the taking of New Amsterdam.'

Wildman snorts, 'Renamed for the glory of James, Duke of York. Did York show you any gratitude for that?'

'Such a thing would not occur to him.'

'No surprise,' says Wildman mildly and the brief

confrontation is over – a crude first snarl between scarred dogs, put aside for another time.

The third man lifts the scarf from his mouth to take one sip of coffee. 'Ugh,' he says and pushes the mug away.

Wildman glances at him, sees the ghost of a nod and goes one step further. 'The duke is not like his brother the king, is he? What do you make of him?'

'The duke?' Scott recognizes the key question. How bold should he be? He knows Wildman's reputation but is only half-way sure about the man behind the scarf. 'The king's brother is a harsh man stiffened by the starch of bad beliefs,' he says. 'That should concern all of us.'

Wildman grins. 'He is a danger, permitted to parade his Roman beliefs by his brother's softness.' The silent man's forehead contracts in a brief frown and Wildman quickly moderates his words. 'May God preserve King Charles, but if not, then James, Duke of York becomes king and the country we love becomes an adjunct of Rome and a vassal state to King Louis's France with no true Englishman allowed to follow his beliefs. In short, a bloody disaster.'

The third man displays no further sign of disapproval. Wildman checks the crowd around them. Has he spoken too loudly? The nearest of them are busy offering loud opinions to each other and thinking up their own next lines instead of listening to replies. He lowers his voice anyway. 'Tell me, John Scott. How far would you go to correct that?'

'With the right company, I would do whatever is needed. The project would call for precision, subtlety and daring.'

The third man nods. Wildman says, 'But you are sometimes described as a rogue.'

Most men would bristle, but Scott recognizes a fellow in the other man. 'Indeed, I am.' He sees Wildman smile and he turns his head to address the paymaster. 'Sir, please know that I am a very useful rogue.'

The third man breaks his silence. His voice is luxurious, port-soaked and in no hurry to reach the end of the sentence. 'Wildman. Tell him how this will work. I need to take a piss.'

They watch as he forces his way to the back wall. The men standing by it split apart as he fiddles with his clothing and lets fly an arc of urine against the plaster, splashing down on the floor. They chorus disapproval as the steaming river trickles round their shoes. This is too much even by their loose standards. The man responsible calmly buttons himself up and turns round to face the protesters.

'Something bothering you?' His voice is very sure of itself.

The red-haired owner speaks into the sudden silence. 'You, sir,' he says. 'You're what's bothering me. That's not the pissing wall. The clue is the colour. The pissing wall is over there and it's yellow for a good reason. You've splashed my customers.'

The man snorts through his scarf. 'I piss where I choose,' he says. 'And my piss tastes no worse than your coffee.' No one contradicts him. That confident patrician tone carries the day and has the ring of truth on both counts.

The owner retreats to the back room where he roasts nettles, acorns and mangel-wurzel leaves to dark brown bitterness to bulk out the expensive beans. He is sure the customers won't desert him as they pore over the latest partisan pamphlets and find them to be God's only truth. With new strength in numbers, they can't wait to take to the streets to wield the power dribbled down to them by powerful men with a secret agenda.

These fervid clusters are ripe for cultivation and this very coffee house has become the main recruiting place for a new club, shaping to be the most lethal powder keg in the whole of explosive London.

The man who has spawned the Green Ribbon Club serves as sulphur in the new political mixture. One night earlier in that same week, he was huddled at home in a dim parlour deep in the Dorset countryside, two days' journey southwest of the capital, dissecting England over a single candle with his small circle of confidants. Sulphur has a fine mind and the divine right of kings sticks in his throat. In the middle of nowhere, he and his circle concoct a way to melt all that seems solid. With not a second to spare on fools, he makes sure they test their best ideas in red-hot argument to undermine the walls of power.

Do not misunderstand. He is not seeking revenge for poor birth and poverty. This cramped parlour is somewhere near the back of his house, which has one hundred windows and four hundred acres of parkland. Sulphur's name is Anthony Ashley-Cooper, Earl of Shaftesbury and he looks to change the course of the nation's history.

An orphan by the age of nine, he becomes a baronet before he can spell the word. His father's hard trustees put him through a puritan education before he turns to study law, preferring the logic of fixed rules to unchallengeable royal power endowed by a mysterious deity. No king, he thinks, should be exempt from law. His supporters know him as a fervent Protestant but at heart he is still the 5-year-old, questioned by one of his train of temporary nurses when she finds him staring at the empty sky.

'What are you doing?' she asks.

'Looking for God,' he says, 'but if he's up there, he's keeping very quiet.'

Pain sharpens its teeth around his stomach in his late forties and early one evening he retires to bed, unable to concentrate on the discussion downstairs. He has no desire for pity. That would unstitch relationships constructed entirely around intellectual merit. He has kept this distress from his wife, inventing reasons to sleep apart. When the knock comes on his door, he is curled up to contain the pain.

'Not now,' he calls, fearing his voice wavers. 'It will wait for morning.' Everyone in that vast house obeys his commands, but not this time. The door opens and his secretary walks in.

'John, go away,' says the earl. 'I have colic.'

'Colic? For three months? To hell with that. Where precisely is this pain?'

Seeking relief from a liver infection two years earlier, the earl came upon this man studying how the body works and how the mind works too. Recognizing brilliance, he has hired John Locke to join him as secretary, physician and philosopher, using their journeys between institutional politics in London and unfettered thought in Dorset to explore the range of Locke's brain.

Shaftesbury does not answer, because answering releases his illness into the realm of the undeniable, but Locke, a gaunt man who looks older than his thirty-five years, pulls back the bed cover and lays a cool hand on the earl's side.

Shaftesbury cannot avoid a gasp and the secretary nods. 'Your liver again. A cyst. We need a surgeon. I know the right man.'

'It is not for you to decide I must be cut.'

Locke shakes his head. 'Nobody should harm another.

Unnecessary death is surely harm. It is therefore my moral duty to save you. Can you find a valid counter argument? No?'

They travel to the appointment with the knife in the softest-sprung carriage available. Locke insists a tube is left in place to drain the cyst – the product of a tapeworm's egg. The tube saves Shaftesbury's life but the ever-dripping infection twists him inwards. His pure faith in the law curdles to a sulphur-ous willingness to use any means. The earl's circle of thinkers continues to discuss moral philosophy in the elegant rooms at the front of his house, but a much tighter inner circle now meets late at night in that dim parlour, warping the movement towards violent action.

Shaftesbury is joined by ambitious Parliament men and greedy merchants in the growing Green Ribbon Club, but he remains a little outside the ranks of England's longer-established aristocrats. There is one particular nobleman who might offer an entrance key to that group. They have met in public many times though exchanging only few words, but never in private. One night in this August of 1678, Sulphur travels through the charcoal streets from north to south to meet saltpetre, the man with the power, just possibly, to curate this explosion. Fastidious folk prefer the twisting routes through rebuilt dis-tricts, but Shaftesbury orders his coachman to take the direct way south past the rising building site which is to become the new St Paul's. There, he raps on the window and the coachman pulls up.

Half the columns of the old cathedral still stand. In 1666, lead had poured off the roof in a flood of fire as scorched stones burst. Today, they have been blasting the eastern stonework and Shaftesbury watches the men up there who will carry on until they cannot see, swinging picks to tumble loosened stone. Thirty of them have been killed so far. He keeps count. Shaftesbury stores such facts in case someone who gets in his way proves vulnerable to blame.

Passers-by cannot clearly see the beginnings of the new cathedral. Wren hides his secrets behind tall hoardings, but a wagon-load of fresh Portland stone, just off the boat, shines as clean as sunlight against the tar-black of the remains behind it. Shaftesbury enjoys the symbolism. The old wreck was always a luridly painted Catholic place, finally whitewashed at Henry's command, but that ancient paint had begun to loom faintly through to disturb those who prayed with their eyes open. This new cathedral will be pure and Protestant from the very start unless the Duke of York becomes . . . He chokes off that thought. It must not happen. The postillion jumps down to intercept a man hurrying across the road towards them. Shaftesbury nods and the door is opened. The newcomer sits down opposite the earl, out of breath, and takes off his hat to reveal his red head of hair.

'You have news?' says the earl.

'Wildman came in yesterday,' says the man in his Bristol burr. 'Him and another. Wildman treated the other man with care. That's rare for the major.'

'The other man? Short, tall? Fat, thin?'

'Tall, well-fed, wearing fine cloth. Mighty certain of himself but mostly silent. Clearly the boss.'

'Could you hear?'

'I had men either side, taking care not to be seen listening. Wildman was questioning a third man like they might give him a job. Army of some sort from over there in the Caribs, Colonel

Scott. They wanted to know what he was ready to do. My men missed some of it cos folks around were shouting.'

'They heard nothing useful?'

'The man spoke louder at the end. Described himself as a rogue . . . no, a "very useful" rogue – then they stopped talking because Wildman's boss went and pissed on my customers.'

'This boss. Describe his face.'

'He had a scarf wrapped round his mug.'

'A slight lisp?'

'You know him?'

'Perhaps. Now, pay attention. Plans for the next parade of the Green Ribbon Club. Bigger crowds. More clever stuff. Who is making the pope?'

'Four men from the theatre. Twice life size.'

'Twice? Three times. No, four times. Make it burn slower somehow . . . and there must be screaming.'

'Actors?'

'No, no. Screaming that somehow comes from the pope himself.' Shaftesbury snaps his fingers as a solution wanders past on the roadside. 'Cats. Sew cats inside him. A dozen cats. Two dozen. They'll scream when they start to roast. Now go.'

The carriage heads towards the river by way of the rubble that had been St Matthew's church. A hoofed and shrunken leg projects from the heap – a coachman's nag buried at dead of night? Easier than dragging it to the knacker's yard. Watling Street allows a wider horizon and only one spire cuts the sky here. Other churches have sprung back up, but putting a roof over worshippers' heads comes first. Fancy touches will have to wait. They rattle round curves and dogs-legs, Bread Street, Basing Lane and St Thomas Apostles, all witnesses to lost opportunity.

Parliament drew up geometric and grandiose plans for the rebuild of the city, great avenues in grids or in radiating spokes from circuses at their hubs. No chance. Angry Londoners raced to hammer wooden marker posts into rubble which was still hot. They reclaimed the outlines of their burnt houses, preserving old street tangles, but still the fire tore citizens loose. Primed for something new, they need people to blame.

Near the river, the carriage turns into a grand driveway. Shaftesbury steels himself to explore the possibility of secret co-operation. He is certain this is the lisping man who pisses on people and superficially, the two of them seem to be on the same side, but he knows he may get pissed on himself. Liveried servants run to open the carriage door, but the earl pushes out his crutches and the servants stare at them, undecided. This man has a harsh reputation. Shaftesbury mutters as he levers himself out. They see that eagle's beak nose and keep a safe distance as they shadow him up the steps.

Countless candles light the grand hallway and the long gallery, burning up the sovereigns, each flame multiplied by opposing ranks of mirrors. His host stands waiting in the plush salon at the far end. The powdered face and fine wig complete the famous figure, matched in the full-length portrait on the wall behind him. 'Shaftesbury,' he says.

The man on crutches stops and surveys him. 'Buckingham.'

The duke's face freezes. 'Shaftesbury, you will find "Your Grace" is still the correct form.'

'Then afford me my own correct address,' says Shaftesbury.

'Of course . . . my Lord . . .' says the Duke of Buckingham, but his sarcastic tone, practised in poetry, drama and public oratory, strips away any dignity.

Port is poured and servants waved from the room. Two mouths and four ears are the maximum for what may follow, but still they circle. The duke rambles about theatre. Shaftesbury has no time for the plays his host writes. He thinks the dialogue is not nearly as funny as Buckingham thinks it is. This conversation is a monologue.

Pouring a second glass, Buckingham turns to business.

'Let us be open. We have much in common, but I am very sure that we also have objectives that clash.'

'Would you list them?'

'My Lord, you have other things to do to fill the time before Doomsday comes. Let us start with my greatest friend the king.' He nods towards a portrait of Charles.

Shaftesbury turns to look, noting it is a foot smaller than Buckingham's own portrait and hangs in a gloomier corner.

'We go back to childhood,' says Buckingham. 'I was sent to the Tower on his behalf.'

Everybody knows that. Shaftesbury's irritation rises in his throat. 'Because you took to fisticuffs with Dorchester in the House of Lords?'

'No, sir, no. Not that time.'

'When he had you imprisoned for treason and for casting his horoscope?'

'Don't play with me, sir. I mean my imprisonment towards the end of Cromwell's disaster when I was enabling the return of my king to his rightful throne. We were as close as brothers.'

'Were?' Shaftesbury has the sharpness of a prosecutor.

'We were then and we are now. I fought for him. Warfare is, of course, a little too hot for one with your unfortunate disabilities?'

'Let us leave that. There is a greater game before us. We both know your great friend the king lacks legitimate, Protestant offspring and therefore . . .'

'He should have asked me to do the job. His queen and I would have . . .' Buckingham stops mid-sentence. Bawdy stories please his supporters, but this is going too far.

The earl stares at Buckingham and sees a man who hides his sharp mind behind the disguise of a witty rake. He is charming in his apologies when it serves him and Charles always forgives him in the end whatever the depth of his crimes. Can they work together?

'As I began to say, the crown may pass to his brother and Duke James will bring back papism. Our nation needs us to . . . to find a different way.'

'Us?' says Buckingham. 'What is this "us" exactly? I support the king. You are a radical in disguise. Given your way, you would leave no space for kings, not even for ceremony to maintain the loyalty of the downtrodden. I would take on a bet that you would not share your two grand houses with the common people if your dream came true.'

Shaftesbury stares and finally he shrugs.

'I am no revolutionary,' says Buckingham slowly. 'I want to preserve my king's life against those who wish him dead. I will join you to protect him but only if that is the purpose of the action. Do you hear?'

'You will help prevent his brother from taking the throne?'

'I will act to protect my king's life.'

Shaftesbury knows the duke has played away his money and lives on an income rationed by strict trustees. That's why he has sold his great London estate and Shaftesbury knows how that sale reveals the extent of the duke's ego. Buckingham has imposed a condition. The roads the developers build across his old gardens must follow an exact sequence – George Street, Villiers Street, Duke Street and Buckingham Street. A short link between the last two is to be named 'Of Alley.'

He tries a different tack. 'Patriots must wake Charles to the full danger his brother represents. I would like your advice.'

Buckingham nods. 'The Jesuits are especially devious. You must match their tactics.'

Shaftesbury inches closer. 'The Duke of York is beyond our range. Men close to him could be our target.' There is one man they both hate. Shaftesbury wants Buckingham to name him first.

'The way to the master may be through the servant,' says Buckingham. 'The duke is no longer High Admiral, but his pompous lackey still controls it for him. Mark that, Shaftesbury.' He already thinks this is his own idea.

'Who do you mean, your Grace?'

That pleases Buckingham enough to dull his suspicions. 'We have both crossed swords with him, have we not?'

'But who . . . oh, do you mean Mr Pepys? Ah . . . yes perhaps.'

'He is too full of himself and not to be trusted. It would be a service to the nation.'

'But how . . . ?'

'A clear Catholic atrocity to wake up the people. What shape might that take?'

'I . . . don't know.' Shaftesbury wants this to come entirely from Buckingham.

'The death of a good man by the thrust of Catholic daggers,' says the duke. 'It has been forecast for long enough.'

'But will they do such a thing?'

'A dagger will do it.' Buckingham smiles. 'The hole in the air from the man who wields it may be labelled Catholic.'

'I would not know where to find such a man.'

Buckingham stares. 'This is your scheme, not mine. To save my king, I may agree to stand in the shadows of it, but you must stand in the light.'

Shaftesbury considers, then he nods. 'We need a rogue – better still, a *very useful* rogue.'

That startles the duke and the earl takes care to maintain the blankest of innocent looks.

'You might choose to consult Major Wildman,' Buckingham says. 'He possibly knows such men.'

As Shaftesbury struggles up to his feet, he cannot resist a final question. 'You believe we have a duty to do what truth requires, do you not?'

Buckingham laughs with savage derision, broken halfway through by a belch. 'Do not pretend to be so pure, my leaking lord,' he answers. 'The people love strange things to light their drab lives, They will unwrap your truth if you wrap it up in bright paper and when they have sucked out all the sweetness, they will have no doubts. Their anger will put your truth firmly on the throne and all you have to do is say it loud enough and well enough and do not stop saying it.'

'There is also the man Oates,' Shaftesbury says as they wait for his coach to be brought round. 'He is offering further information about plots.'

'The Jesuit?'

'The *reformed* Jesuit, I have met him briefly. You might wish to do the same.'

'Certainly not. I hear he is a hideous creature with a face like a full moon. His mouth lives in the centre of it, his voice assaults the ears like a seaman's whistle, and the contents of his trousers are a danger to any young man passing.'

Shaftesbury nods. 'I will speak to your people.'

'That is entirely up to you, but do nothing to harm the king.'

Shaftesbury ponders during his ride home. He smiles to himself as they pass St Paul's again. The options coalesce behind his hard eyes and the great plot takes a big step forward.

CHAPTER 5

When young Sam went to Derby House to stay with Uncle Samuel, he found there was a third Samuel living under that roof, which doubled as the Pepys residence as well as Admiralty headquarters. Pepys's loyal clerk Sam Atkins is ten years older than Samuel St Michel, but they get on like brothers from the day they meet. Sam Atkins is about to find out that the flames of the Sir Edmund Berry Godfrey murder will singe him.

Two weeks before the killing of Godfrey, Titus Oates is working hard to spread his dramatic story. The king's Privy Council calls the Jesuit informer in to question him about this plot of his – cleverly uncovered, he explains, while studying at Valladolid. He confirms Charles is to be killed and his brother James crowned in his place. Valladolid is a good place for such a plot, as it contains a royal palace packed with the Spanish king's courtiers alongside the Catholic secret service, those devilish Jesuits.

In front of the Privy Council, Oates faces his first public test. His first inquisitor is Danby, an earl who likes to be seen as King Charles's leading protector against the dangerous Catholics, while secretly negotiating private deals with the Catholic

French king. 'Oates, you claim you spied on a meeting of the plotters,' he asks in a low rumble. 'Who was there?'

'The King of Spain's bastard son,' says Oates. 'Don John of Austria.'

Gasps come from the Council table. Don John is a powerful name, the sort of enemy you really don't want.

A tall man uncoils himself from a chair in a dark corner of the chamber and his high-pitched voice cuts through the clamour. 'Oates! Tell me more of Don John? I can only imagine the fella.'

Oates thinks fast. 'He is, what shall I say, sir? He is dark-haired, tall, a lean and muscled man with a commanding presence.'

'Interesting description. Would you describe me perhaps in the same way?'

Oates squints at him. 'You appear less obviously command-ing, sir.'

Uncomfortable murmurs rise from all around the table.

'I must try harder,' says his questioner mildly. 'To clear up any doubt, I am Charles, your king. You are an idiot and you should now consider yourself under arrest for mischievous untruth.'

Oates's narrow mouth forms a small 'o' within the larger circle of his face. His words burst out wrapped in panic. 'Your Majesty? Oh lord, I did not mean that. I abase myself to you. Please sire, I do tell the truth.'

'Nonsense. I know Don John very well. At twenty he was dark-haired and muscled but now he is fifty. His hair is grey and his muscles hide under folds of fat. He is not tall but he has not shrunk. He was always short.' He turns to the law officers in the room. 'Take him to the dark, damp place he deserves.'

It should end there, but political power is shifting at dizzying speed. Wise old Henry Coventry, the king's spymaster and clear-sighted fixer, is a key support for Charles, but acute pain is ageing him rapidly. His office in Whitehall Palace has its own bedchamber for when he is too unwell to go home. Late that evening, he calls 'Enter' to a gentle knock, then starts to struggle to his feet as the king walks in.

'Stop that, Henry,' Charles says. 'Lie back. Gout is a blade that pierces the flesh all the way to the soul. We will not stand on ceremony. Indeed we will not stand at all.' He slumps into a chair. 'Oates walks free,' he says. 'This is a pretty fix.'

'He named one of the plotters. I was waiting for more details before informing you.'

'Who did he name?'

'Edward Coleman.'

'Oh no.' Coleman is a blatant Romanist, recently secretary to Duke James but serving the Duke's Catholic Duchess.

'They take aim at your brother,' says Coventry. 'It's good you had him move to a safe distance. They search Coleman's rooms as we speak. They will find something though it may have arrived with them.'

'What now, Henry? Has my brother drained my credit?'

'My dear king. Many of your subjects are too young to remember when pleasure was banned. They have enjoyed almost two decades of dancing and feasting. The Puritan times are back in the past with Noah's flood. Their gratitude to you is fragile.'

'Will they cut off *my* head? I could disband the Privy Council. Shall I have Shaftesbury arrested?'

'It is too early to challenge the lies. It will make us sound more guilty.'

A fresh knock at the door. 'Stay,' calls Coventry. 'Who is there?'

'A message from your office, sir.'

'Push it under the door.'

Charles fetches it for Coventry who turns up the lamp, checks the heavy seal for signs of tampering and cuts it open.

He sighs. 'Coleman is as good as dead. They found a box hidden in his fireplace filled with Jesuit correspondence. Oates is given his own militia to hunt down plotters. By tomorrow he will be a hero. Untouchable.'

'Men will die.'

'My job is to make sure you are not one of them. Please, my friend, let us take the cautious route for now.'

Coventry's information is correct. The Privy Council hands Titus Oates money, power and his very own force of musketeers. Whitehall Palace is surrounded by artillery and Parliament's cellars are searched in case of a new Guido Fawkes.

Godfrey's funeral on the last day of October is a huge public event, taking so long to organize that the coffin stinks as it is carried through roaring crowds accompanied by a thousand gentlemen in black. Oates's accusations send a group of Catholic lords straight to the Tower.

Empowered by national panic, Shaftesbury sets up a 'Secret Committee to Investigate the Plot' with an inner core of his conspirators, cloaked by an outer circle of useful idiots. They listen to the denunciations of dubious adventurers drawn to the bright light of huge rewards. Justice is not involved.

A three-letter word is coined.

The Green Ribbon Club bulges with new members, taking

to the streets to spray out vitriol. All this rouses what Seneca called the *mobile vulgus,* the common crowd, but that's a mouthful and it soon gives up two thirds of its letters. Now, the mob is on the street, thrilled by its new sense of self importance.

Shaftesbury becomes the mob's popular leader. On the evening of Godfrey's funeral, he calls the hard core within the Secret Committee to a darkened house beside the royal park.

'This new name on the list,' says the old intriguer Major Wildman, Shaftesbury's expert in brutality, 'Atkins? Who's he?'

'He was seen to lead a papist ritual around Godfrey's corpse,' says Shaftesbury, 'His arrest is a step towards a higher member of the conspiracy.'

The Marquis of Winchester stops fanning himself. 'Where was this ritual?'

'In Somerset House, the home of our Catholic queen.'

'This is madness.' Winchester's voice squeaks. 'We cannot move so high.'

Wildman laughs. 'The queen's home is not the same as the queen herself and it is bloody well chosen. A mad warren of rooms. She might have known but she might not. Let the mob decide.'

Winchester still struggles. 'And who exactly is this Atkins?'

Shaftesbury cuts in. 'Samuel Atkins is clerk to the Admiralty Secretary Mr Pepys, who is the surrogate for Duke James.'

Winchester shakes his head. 'Then we should arrest the duke's lapdog, not his lapdog's clerk. Why not seize the grocer who once sold the clerk a bushel of flour?'

'Because Pepys has a perfect defence.'

'In my wide experience of the law, Shaftesbury, no defence is ever perfect. A good lawyer can always challenge an alibi.'

'One hundred of my guineas say you are wrong.' Shaftesbury offers a hand to seal the bet.

The marquis reaches for it, thinks twice and frowns at him. 'Explain yourself.'

'His witness is a man entirely above suspicion.'

'There is no such person.'

Shaftesbury proffers his hand again. Winchester again ignores it. 'His witness,' says Shaftesbury slowly, 'is His Royal Majesty, King Charles. Mr Pepys was watching the racing at Newmarket as the King's personal guest throughout the crucial days in question. Atkins remained in London, supposedly prohibited from leaving the house but observed by no one. We will produce witness testimony that he sneaked away.'

'Is your witness practised?'

'I will rehearse him to perfection.'

'That still hangs the servant, not the master.'

'The servant is human and young. Once he understands the degree of pain he faces, he will blame his master for the deed. Have no doubt.'

None of them understand friendship and loyalty between master and servant. Shaftesbury's circle of thinkers are valued assets – but they must perform well to keep their place. Wildman follows jungle laws. The rest are men who call their successive butlers by some unchanging generic name. The committee members know nothing of straightforward respect from a young man who truly admires his master's quick-witted determination. Pepys is now famous for running the cash-starved navy with unflagging efficiency. It is largely because of him that the nation has a strong navy to take on whichever of the Dutch and the French is the current enemy. As a Member of

Parliament, Pepys defends his king against Shaftesbury's Whigs in the ferment of the House of Commons. He may not abide by quite the same moral rules that he sets for those who serve him, but Sam expects that.

The following day, Shaftesbury forces Henry Coventry to deliver Sam Atkins to the full committee. Tom Smith, the king's messenger sent to do it, takes his task lightly. He drops in to the Rhenish wine house in Channel Row, orders a bottle of their cheapest and sends their boy round the corner asking Sam to join him. Sam is annoyed by the summons.

'Master Atkins,' Tom calls as he enters the crowded room. 'Over here.'

'What do you need, Master Smith? The Channel Fleet papers are not yet ready.'

'Let me explain. Unbuckle your sword first, there is little space. Pass it over here and I will tuck it away. Pour yourself a glass. I regret I have something unexpected for you here.' He passes a document across.

'What is this?'

'I am told it is an arrest warrant.'

'For my master?' Sam has been fearing such a move.

'No. Of course not.'

'Oh . . . good.'

'No, it is for you yourself. Don't take it personally. Likely it's all a mistake.'

Two men take Sam from Tom Smith, bind his wrists and squash him into a cab which sways through gathering gloom to a large house in Lincoln's Inn Fields. He is prodded into a room before seven gowned men in a predatory line. Ordered to sit down on a stool, he recognizes Shaftesbury at their centre.

'Atkins, how long have you known your master is a Catholic?'

'He is not.'

'How did he persuade you to take part in murder?'

'What murder?'

'Just tell us. You were seen by witnesses.'

It goes on and on, glissading away from facts whenever Sam thinks he is about to understand the accusations. After an hour that feels like four, Shaftesbury takes on an expression almost like a smile.

'Atkins, I understand you have been forced into this matter through no choice of your own. You may be saved if you answer with complete honesty. Tell us the truth or you will be forced to by most painful means then tried for treason and executed – all to protect a traitor who seeks the downfall of our king.'

Indignation boils out of Sam's mouth. 'You have been misled. Neither my master nor I are traitors.'

Shaftesbury summons three men. 'Take him to Newgate. Atkins, it will be your final home.'

In Westminster, Pepys is already annoyed by his clerk's absence. His butler opens the Derby House door to tendrils of cold mist and a cloaked man with upturned collar. 'I am commanded to pass this to Mr Pepys,' he says, showing a vellum envelope.

'Wait here. I will take it to him.'

'I am ordered to hand it directly to Mr Pepys. Tell him I come from Secretary Coventry and the matter is urgent.'

Pepys is in the study with the wide windows looking out across the Thames. He hurries down, breaks the seal and scans the message. 'Secretary Coventry says you can speak for him,' he says to the cloaked visitor, 'and I must forget your visit as soon as you leave. What is this news?'

The cloaked man looks towards the butler. Pepys waves dismissal and leads him into the morning room.

'Well?'

'Hard news, sir. Your boy Atkins is taken.'

'Taken? Who has taken him?'

'Shaftesbury's council.'

'Why?'

'For his part in the murder of Godfrey.'

'What? Young Sam?' He looks down at the note, sees Coventry's private symbol and his face hardens. 'I see. They aim this at me.'

'Secretary Coventry is forbidden from speaking to you. You should be aware there is a new secret group within the Privy Council. This is their doing.'

Pepys clenches one fist, turns to stare out of the window, then swings his gaze back to the messenger. 'Hurry to tell your master they're not having Sam Atkins. I will make sure of that.'

Cold, wet, hungry and bruised, Sam resists his interrogators but he knows he is in bad trouble. He comes from a family that only just avoids the word poor and his bed in Pepys's house, the upper bunk shelf of a narrow cupboard with Pepys's boatman on the shelf below, feels like luxury compared to the old days. That's already a faint memory. He is in the worst of Newgate's cells, dripping, surrounded by brutes, reeking with jail fever and prisoners' shit. Loaded down with chains, he is slapped and punched every hour of every day.

Now he forces himself to do what his master does when things get rough. He thinks. Over Christmas in his freezing cell, he is entirely cut off from outside contact except when hauled back before the committee to face another string of alien assertions. He canes his memory for anything useful, but that is hard when nobody will give him any details of the charges against him.

Men accused by Titus Oates have begun to die and that is the only news encouraged to spread through Newgate. Edward Coleman is hanged, drawn and quartered for aiding foreign devils. At the end of his third month in jail, Sam, thin and with a jail pallor hidden only by jail dirt, is told the barest details of his supposed offence: direct control of the notorious Godfrey killing. Crucially, he is told the exact date the witnesses swear they saw him standing over the corpse in the queen's house. He has no plausible way of escape.

However, now he knows that date, and Sam delves deep. As his hearing with the King's Bench judges approaches, it dawns on him that the date is one of the very few for which he does actually have an alibi. The question is how can he prove it?

Above all else, Sam Atkins loves the feeling of a girl's arms around him, but that is a very rare event because his master sets monastic, deeply hypocritical rules for his staff. Sam is only allowed out of Derby House for short periods on approved business, so he usually has to fall back on imagination to enjoy a girl's embrace – except when his master's absence lets him break the rules. His master was indeed absent on that particular date, but the realization gives Sam a deeply embarrassing problem. Even if he could contact his master, he really might prefer to die than to own up to what he was doing on that night when the king's Newmarket invitation to Pepys created a very rare opportunity.

As Sam heads towards the court, three men convicted of Godfrey's murder are jeered all the way to their appointed execution place close to the spot where the corpse was found. Robert Green, Henry Berry and Lawrence Hill are working men, ill equipped to defend themselves against heavily loaded dice. Their guards taunt them in the cart as they duck to dodge the horse crap and dead cats hurled by crowds lining their route. They burst into laughter as they tell Green, Berry and Hill that their place of execution has been renamed Greenberry Hill in their honour. The three corpses-in-waiting don't find it funny.

The charge against Sam is that he did command, counsel and abet Green, Berry and Hill in committing the murder. He has no idea what witnesses will be ranked against him, but he knows now that he would babble his entire alibi to Mr Pepys if he only could.

CHAPTER 6

February 11th, 1679

Guards rush Sam into the vast gloom of Westminster Hall close to the Parliament chambers. The arched Norman stonework of the ancient entrance is obscured by the chaos of drinks stalls and food booths propped against it. A weaving drunk throws the dregs of his sour ale at them and splashes the guard to Sam's right, who cuffs him hard. Inside, they force a way through shoppers, gawkers and cutpurses towards the courts at the far end, passing the rough shop counters lining both sides of the hall. He stares at second-hand books, spectacles, felt hats and all the other startling flotsam of a bright, free, busy world he has almost forgotten. Dragged by the guards' grip on both his arms, Sam's feet skid on damp rushes strewn across the floor to soak up the piss of the animals wandering there. A dog runs barking behind them. Cats twist through all the legs. Two bemused sheep block their way, shepherded by a man holding an upside-down cluster of shrieking chickens, tied by their feet. It is a brain-jamming change from the monotonous dripping echoes of his cell — a breath of real life on the path to real death. His destiny looms at the far end and he cannot bend it away.

The court of the King's Bench stands under a wide royal crest behind it. Judges sit in a row along the high oak bench itself, looking down across a green baize table where a score of clerks work on parchment rolls. The crowd is already there, waiting for the fun. Early birds cram the high viewing platform to the left of the court. Two lesser courts stand next to it with no divisions for privacy. Witnesses, judges, plaintiffs, defendants and lawyers all need strong lungs to work here.

The crowds buzz, catcall and ignore the ushers' calls for decorum. A guard shouts into Sam's ear. 'All right chum? Ready to cough up? Clear your conscience to meet your maker. Better that way, eh?'

They push past two men without taking note of them. One is tall, tough, tanned, with a slight cast to one eye. The other is a youth with parchment cheeks above clerical black. They are agents of the men who have contrived this trial, sent to report back later.

Sam twists his head from side to side as he devours every detail around him. He expects to be put in the prisoner's dock, but instead he is made to stand in the crowd of lawyers, witnesses and hangers-on. Could this be deliberate, he wonders? Is there an assassin with a dagger close by in case the court sets him free? Sam pushes the thought away to keep his nerve with his mind running at double speed. He can identify no friendly faces in the huge crowd.

'He's done for,' says the tall man watching. 'Dead already and that bastard he works for is going down with him.'

'The earl is quite sure of the outcome,' says the clerical youth, who is uncomfortable in the other's presence – too much of the killer shows in his face. That would be better hidden.

A scatter of gaunt men stand ready at the front of the crowd, displaying a piece of straw tucked in their cap band or held between their teeth to advertise their availability. These 'men of straw' are opportunists, available for hire as instant witnesses. The judges accept that such men are useful for open-and-shut cases when the facts are so obvious that all they need is convenient testimony to validate their decision. The massive hammer beams of the roof high above rest on angels carved in stone and Sam knows the old joke: 'Angels work wonders in Westminster Hall.' It's a joke, because angel is the common name for the gold coin bearing the head of St Michael – and much testimony has been changed by the passage of angels. That seems a lot less funny to him now.

His jailers have told Sam with glee that this can only go one way or the mob will want to know why. They say Green, Berry and Hill strangled Godfrey with a sixpenny linen handkerchief before running him through with his sword. They tell him the prosecutors know that Sam organized it all and remind him that his face was seen grinning through the black mass candle smoke above the corpse.

A vast and choleric man presides over the hearing with a face crimsoned by decades of wine and beefsteak. His very name echoes the crunching of neck vertebrae in the shock of the noose. He is Lord Chief Justice Scroggs and he needs little convincing that the papists planned it all.

As the case opens, he shouts at Sam. 'Prisoner Atkins, look at me. Of what religion are you?' Scroggs has been merciless in his sentencing of accused Catholic plotters.

'Protestant, sir. Through and through.'

'Your Honour,' interrupts a grey man with the eyes of a hound watching a limping rabbit. Sir William Jones, the Attorney-General, leads the prosecution. 'We will produce evidence against that lie.' He whispers urgently to an assistant who pushes away through the crowd.

The first witness speaks against Sam, and he recognizes a drunkard ship's captain who owes him money. The man tells a tale of Sam seeking to hire an assassin to kill Godfrey on his master's behalf. Scroggs shifts in his chair, frowning.

'Our next witness will attest to the attendance of the accused at Catholic rituals,' says Jones. The witness is pushed forward – a teenager in the filthy uniform of the blaggards, the unofficial wolf-pack who loiter near the Whitehall barracks, selling themselves one way or another. The boy is an apprentice man of straw, but the other justices mutter. This is a shade too blatant for them. Sam knows they will get over their concerns because the Catholic infection requires cauterization. This dirty little chancer may be their single attempt at proof that Sam Atkins is on the other side.

Sam's brain delivers a blaze of inspiration from nowhere. 'Boy,' he calls, 'over here. Do you know me at all?'

The boy turns his head, startled, and sees only a strange man standing in the throng. 'No, sir,' he replies, 'I do not.'

Chaos in the court. The boy rushes away. The prosecution makes excuses. Scroggs turns to Sam and booms, 'You are too bold, sir, altogether too bold,' but there is a searching quality to his look and something like a malevolent twinkle at the end of it. The crowd is nowhere near changing sides but it is certainly enjoying the unexpected drama.

It is a start, but Sam has no idea who else he may be up against. Attorney-General Jones questions the next witness.

'William Bedloe, you were present in Somerset House on the night in question, the night following the murder of Sir Edmund Berry Godfrey?'

'I was.'

'At what hour?'

'Between nine and ten.'

'And did you see the accused at that gathering?'

Bedloe has seen what just happened to the last witness and his small store of courage abruptly fails him.

He is silent for a count of ten and the crowd rumbles. 'There was very little light, sir,' he says in the end. 'It is hard for me to swear that this is he. It was probably him, no, I should say possibly him – either that or perhaps someone very like him.' Scroggs snorts. Bedloe sees disaster looming and decides to step out of its path. 'No, now I consider it carefully and seeing Atkins in this better light, I believe the man I saw had a more manly face – and . . . and a beard perhaps?'

Scroggs dismisses him with contempt and turns to Sam to call witnesses for his defence.

Sam is bewildered. He hasn't considered this. How can he call even a single witness? He has been given no opportunity to assemble a case – hasn't even known the details of the accusations against him until the last minute. More than that, he is undermined by another factor. Like the rest of England, *he believes in the plot*. Someone murdered Godfrey and the authorities are quite right to pursue it. They've just made a mistake, that is all. Sam believes he and these prosecutors should really be on the same side. He looks up, unsure what to say, and then movement catches his eye. A man is waving both arms wildly at him from the far edge of the crowd. He blinks, stares and recognizes the waving man with a flood of utter shock.

Salvation and perdition in equal measure are trying to attract his attention combined in one person. This is his key witness, but how in heaven is he here? His spirits soar, then they sink. Only his master could have arranged this miracle and that means Mr Pepys must know everything and will never wish to employ Sam ever again once this witness gives his testimony.

One way, Sam loses his job. The other way, he loses his head. 'I call Captain Richard Vittles as my witness,' he says and hears his voice shake.

The captain pushes forward and the crowd jostles to see him. You could not mistake Vittles for anything other than a bluff sea dog with a direct manner. 'Captain Vittles,' says Sam, marshalling his thoughts as the muttering subsides. 'Were you with me on the night under examination?'

'Oh yes,' says Vittles with a grin that makes Sam squirm. 'It was Friday the 11th day of October and you and I drank a great deal of fresh wine from soon after four of the clock throughout the evening until we got, shall I say, a little unseasonable.'

Attorney-General Jones is extremely displeased. He is hungry for another neck and far too close to the men behind this twisted case. 'Captain, how can you be so certain it was that same night?'

Scroggs turns and bellows at him as if Jones were the accused, not the prosecutor. 'This man, sir, is a mariner. Mariners are most exact and very punctual in their comings and their goings. Mariners are particular, sir. They keep precise accounts of every day and they keep logs listing details of all their passages.'

Sam is fairly sure that this particular mariner would have gone out of his way not to list precise details of the passages they encountered on this particular night, but he begins to hope, just a little.

'So you drank too much and that was that?' interjects Jones. 'If you were replete with drink, sir, then you cannot know for certain what the prisoner did afterwards.'

Vittles throws back his great head and roars out laughter at the far-off beams above. The crowd catches the laughter and they fix their eyes on him, eager to hear what is to come.

'I am very used to drink and we were not alone, you might say,' says the captain. 'There were two fine young lady witnesses with us and they held back on the drink.'

'Their names, sir?' barks Jones.

'They are the Williams sisters,' Vittles is emboldened by cheers from the crowd. 'Sarah and Anne. Buxom girls and very well presented.'

Jones is at a loss for words. Scroggs, now grinning broadly, piles in.

'These buxom girls, what course did the night take with them?'

'Early in the evening, it seemed a wise idea to take them to a quieter place, my lordship – so we boarded to my boat.'

Jones sees a chance to regain control. 'Your boat? A boat of your own? Is it the kind of boat perhaps that regularly provides hospitality to young ladies of a certain sort?' He leers. This witness will not keep his authority for much longer if he has his way.

Vittles's expression changes abruptly. He does affronted dignity as well as he does man-of-the-world knowingness.

'No, sir, indeed it is not my boat and I have to say I would never agree, and nor should you, to such a demeaning description of the owner of the boat, sir.'

Jones sneers. 'You protect him because he is the owner of a floating brothel?'

'No, sir, I do not.'

'Come on Captain. Why then?'

'I protect him, sir, because he is Charles, King of England, the second of that name. I was at that time the captain of his royal yacht *Katherine*. That is the boat to which we repaired.' His voice rises to a shout. 'Do you persist in describing him as the owner of a floating brothel, sir?'

Pandemonium in the great hall. All other cases in the adjoining courts come to a halt and crowds of lawyers, witnesses, prisoners and judges clamber out of their various boxes to swell the crowd.

Jones fans himself with a piece of parchment. 'Enough of this witness,' he says. 'I have done with him.'

'Speak for yourself,' says Scroggs. 'I am nowhere near done. Captain Vittles, exactly what did happen next?'

'May I ask that you use your own imagination to answer that question, your honour,' says Vittles, 'as there may be those here of a sensitive conformation. The fact most necessary to this case is that at half past the hour of ten by the very fine royal chronometer on board, it became clear that some of our party were too deep in wine to function correctly. As we were lying at Greenwich with the outgoing tide running with full strength, we loaded the two ladies and this man Atkins here into the royal four-oared wherry commanded by the royal bosun Tribbett and I had them rowed up to London Bridge. The tide there sluicing through the arches with full force, my royal bosun put them ashore close by Billingsgate, as he will testify, and loaded them somewhat like sacks into a cab accompanied for their later sustenance by a royal Holland cheese and half a royal dozen of good royal wine.'

Jones is forced to clutch at straws. 'These sailors of yours, they are Catholics I presume?'

'No, sir. English Church to a man, like myself, and here to testify if you require.'

'That may be, Captain Vittles, but you can have no idea what Atkins did after that.'

'In the first place, sir, that was after eleven of the clock so it shows that Atkins was not where you say he was and yes, as it happens I know exactly what happened to them after that and there are other witnesses today who will testify to it. Mrs Bulstrode, the landlady of the house where the sisters live, is here in court and she will say, should you choose to expose her finer sensibilities to this crowd, that Atkins recovered his faculties sufficient to spend the rest of that night with young Sarah, as poor Mrs Bulstrode discovered to her shock and dismay in the morning. I am happy to tell your worship that Anne, the other sister, was not so discovered with them.'

The pandemonium reaches new heights. 'Thank you, captain,' says Scroggs, He stares at the crowd, holding up his hand. A wolf's grin is on his face and utter silence falls on the room. He turns to Sam. 'Mr Atkins, you are free to go. The both of you deserve to share another bottle of wine, I think, in whatever company you may choose.'

Sam, colour back in his cheeks after weeks away from the light, endures the back-slapping and ribald remarks as he makes his way through the hall. His anxiety remains, but it has rapidly switched to thoughts of his master and what must now follow. Should he run away? Must he now go back to the Admiralty Office to face vast displeasure? There seems no real choice.

The rain has stopped and he sees a familiar figure outlined against the sun at the doorway. Will Hewer is a fair-haired, open-faced man with a ready smile, a fine brain and a quality of politeness rare in families as rich as his. Hewer has spent years as the protégé of Samuel Pepys and is now Pepys's friend and closest colleague.

'Sam, thank the Lord. I have a coach waiting. Let us go quickly to somewhere less dangerous.'

Less dangerous? 'But I must first go to Newgate to pay my jail bill, Mr Hewer.'

'No need. We will sort that out later. There is more pressing business.'

They travel the very short distance to Derby House in silence. They could have walked it in three minutes, but Sam suspects his master does not want passers-by to see him arriving there. He follows Hewer up the stairs to the great bookcase-lined room that looks out over the Thames. A bewigged and mildly corpulent man is gazing across the river, his back turned to the arrivals. His master, Mr Pepys.

He turns. 'Atkins,' he says. 'I am greatly pleased to see you.'

Sam is astonished at the smile on his master's face. 'Sir, I am ashamed of the circumstances which have . . .'

'Circumstances which have saved your neck, young man. If you had followed my instructions and stayed at home, you would also be following those others to execution because it is very hard to prove that you were *not* in a place. Much better to prove where you were and that others were with you, whatever you were all doing or perhaps failing to do through drink.' Unbelievably, he is still smiling.

Sam blinks and sees his master in a new light. 'But . . . how did you know what I did?'

'Captain Vittles came to me and told me the whole story. He is well known to me and I have had cause to use the yacht *Katherine* on many occasions. After that it was a case of following your path through that day. You left a vivid trail.' He turns to a document spread out on the desk. 'Here, let me show you.'

Sam sees it is laid out in four sections, starting with the harmless words 'To prove Sam Atkins' education and profession of the Protestant religion' with six witness testimonials listed. The second section is 'To prove he lay at lodgings on Friday night the 11th of October and went out on Saturday morning till 12 o'clock' and he sees that the testimonials are by Mrs Bulstrode and her maids, though whether her maids and the Williams sisters might be the same people is now lost in the mists of time and fresh Rhenish wine.

'I am in your everlasting debt, sir, though I expect you will now require me to leave your service.'

Pepys looks hard at him and walks round him to close the door. 'Atkins, none of us are perfect, though you may be more imperfect than many. You will learn.' He pauses and adds, 'Or at least learn not to be caught.'

Sam looks at the carpet and shuffles his feet.

Pepys puts both hands on the young man's shoulders. 'Look at me Sam,' he says gently. 'I know what Newgate is like. I know they threatened you with all sorts of terrors. I know they tempted you with survival if you did what they demanded, but above all I know that you never gave way. You do know that it was me they are after, not you?' Sam nods. 'So,' Pepys goes on, 'temptation comes in many guises and the two sisters are much more forgivable than the Earl of Shaftesbury.'

'Why is he out to get you, sir?'

'For his greater goal, but also because I once defied him in a public matter and he does not forget such slights.'

'Are you safe now?'

'Far from it. He thought we would both try to save our necks, you and me. You would be forced to accuse me and then I would accuse the Duke of York to save myself. Lord Chief Justice Scroggs may have the power to terrify but, at heart, he believes justice matters. He says it should never be used to please the people but should flow like a mighty stream even in a corrupted age.'

'And what now for you?'

'With friends like you, I need not fear.'

Pepys is wrong. He discovers just how wrong three months later.

CHAPTER 7

May 21st, 1679

Balty rears bolt upright in bed so that Esther mutters and shrinks from the swirl of cold air. Spring is slow coming this year and they still sleep downstairs to glean some heat from the banked-up kitchen range. It is not yet dawn and most of that warmth has drained away. Fists pound again at the front door. He wonders how Esther slept through it, unaware she has spent the first half of the night wide awake with her worries. He takes the short sword from the hook by the door, holds it behind his back with one hand and slides the bolt with the other, stepping back as the door swings open. All he sees is the glint of moonlight on a pale rectangle thrust towards him by the shape of a tall man. A horse snorts at the gate.

'Who . . . ?' he starts as the rectangle falls to the mat, but the silent man is already away and seconds later, he is back on his horse, hooves striking sparks from the cobbles. This second abrupt and unexpected messenger leaves him feeling a little sick. Over a brace of tallow candles, with the stove doors open and tongues of fire licking at a fresh cone of sticks, Balty studies the familiar florid signature. Another terse command from London.

'On receipt, make utmost haste for Gravesend. Announce your presence at the searchers' office. I will meet you there.'

Cold hands gently squeeze his neck, thumbs working to ease the muscles by his shoulder blades. Esther blinks at the paper.

'Our brother?'

'Yes.'

'And this came *now*? On a Sunday?'

They both consider that fact. A message brought all the way from London, charging non-stop through the night hours on a single horse? That demands a strong horse and a stout-hearted rider. Regular messages from the Navy Office always come in daylight stages via Chatham and that system isn't set up to work at night.

'It must matter,' says Balty. 'He would never waste the navy's money on something that . . .' A terrible thought stops him. Is this a trick? Has their brother divined that he would do anything to avoid the Tangier posting? Make utmost haste for Gravesend? Gravesend, where the Thames widens towards the sea, is the embarkation point for men bound far overseas and its name is an accurate prediction for many of them. Will he be forced onto a ship as soon as he gets there? Esther divines his thoughts.

'He would not do that,' she says gently. 'It must be something else.' She looks at the dark windows and shudders. 'How will you travel?' Not *will you travel?* – they both know this instruction has to be obeyed.

Balty has a choice of sorts. As muster-master, he could requisition the navy's fast yawl moored at Sandwich with its small cabin down below. It is kept ready for officers needing sleep on an urgent journey, but where is the wind? Opening the back door, he steps out into the garden and shivers in the sharp air. The trees show dark against dawn's first fingers. They bend the breeze and he cannot be quite sure of the direction, so he sniffs instead, hoping for a whiff of cow shit, though chicken shit would be second best. Instead he gets unmistakable ammonia from the tannery north of town, newly rebuilt after it was razed by unknown townsfolk infuriated by its stink. A second whiff of salt sea comes mingled with a hint of the tanners' old urine. That adds up to a north-easterly, and no chance of a rapid sea passage. Cows lie to the south. Chickens to the west. How much easier it would be if he could smell a blend of those two.

The shed beyond the vegetable plot shakes with the vast snores that have punctuated their nights since Ezra moved in. The giant Cornish seaman melted into the stews when a ship came for his crew, then reappeared like an unshaven angel the next time Balty found himself outnumbered in a tight spot. It seemed sensible to find him a job in the depot and now Ezra has completely adopted the St Michel family. There is much comfort in his huge presence. Balty is growing a little tired of always having to fight and having Ezra next to him tends to save him the trouble.

He bangs on the door until the snoring stops and is replaced by an interrogative grunt. 'Ezra,' he says, 'I need a horse saddled now if you please. It is urgent.' Another grunt possibly indicates reluctant consent.

Back in the kitchen, he rubs his hands to restore some warmth. Esther's worried face asks silent questions. 'Not by sea,' he says. 'Not against a nor'easter.' He imagines a sickening crawl all the way to the far end of France on a cross-swell heaving the boat from side to side before there would be any hope of weathering the Margate pig's snout on the next slow beat towards the Thames. It could take a week. A carriage? A guinea a day to hire and two whole lurching days through the ruts.

'Horse,' he says. 'No choice. Ezra will saddle Rhaebus.'

Rhaebus used to be known simply as the navy horse, but Sam reads about the brave steed of the Etruscan king Mezentius and gives him a new name. Since his elevation, his former title has passed to a much less impressive beast. This brute is an ill-meant bribe from the captain of a horse transport who sailed away before the true nature of his gift became clear. The new navy horse has a deep hatred of people coupled with a deep hatred of other animals and, on a bad day, a deep hatred of all inanimate objects. Balty has that man marked down on the revenge list next time he anchors in the Downs.

There is also Moll, the small mare with the sweet nature, beloved of Esther and the children, but Rhaebus is the obvious choice, although every journey is a contest between what Balty thinks might be best for himself and what Rhaebus knows to be best for Balty.

Ezra appears, gets his instructions and leaves. Balty notes he is wearing good seagoing gear last seen on a troublesome and equally large ship's mate the previous day when Ezra took him away for a quiet chat.

'I will get your bag ready, and some food.' Esther is clearly worried. 'We need to change the powder in your pistols,' she adds. 'The weather has been damp.'

'The highwaymen will be asleep.'

'Don't put your faith in that. Change it.'

A sleepy voice says, 'What highwaymen, papa?'

'Back to bed with you,' says Balty, turning to hug his son. 'There will be no highwaymen.'

'I will dress myself,' says Sam. 'I am coming with you. The men of this house must stick together.'

'Back to bed, I said. I will be perfectly safe.'

'Safer still if I ride behind you facing backwards. I will watch for ambush and keep my pistol ready.'

'*Your* pistol? What pistol?'

Sam looks away. His sleepy voice has spoken before his brain could stop it. 'Nothing much. A very small pistol that Ezra gave me. He took it from a drunken sailor. He said to keep it hidden just in case.'

'Back to bed with you. Now. We will discuss your pistol when I return.'

Sam goes. Balty and Esther get busy with their arrangements. When they are done, Esther hugs Balty for a long minute just as she once used to do and he goes out to where Ezra waits with the saddled horse. Out on the road, Rhaebus immediately tries to show who is boss by shaking his head and threatening to bite him. Balty is ready for it and anyway the horse doesn't mean it. It is his way of showing who is in charge. At the outskirts of Deal, Rhaebus begins to take an interest in his surroundings. He breaks his stride and flares his nostrils when they turn off the Sandwich road into the lane through Staple towards Canterbury. Balty urges him on, but Raebus opts for a more measured pace. This is a clever horse and he knows the choice of route indicates a long journey ahead.

The sun clears the horizon. On higher ground now, the wind chills Balty's right cheek and all down that side to the top of his thick leather boot. He slaps at himself and rubs his right arm with his left. It is a relief to reach the brief windbreaks offered by each clump of woodland, although both he and Rhaebus are on the alert for anyone who might be hiding among the trees. Many desperate people find a precarious living along that road. The clump at the top of the Sheepwash rise worries the horse and he keeps looking behind him for the next furlong. After a long time, a Canterbury inn with a small livery stable provides hay for Rhaebus, coffee and last night's beef warmed over the embers for Balty. They both eat fast.

Leaving the cathedral city behind, Rhaebus suddenly seems to regret their departure. They have gone another mile on Watling Street's straight and ancient roadway when he turns his head back to the road behind and snickers. Balty has a brief fear that they are being followed, but the road behind looks as empty as the road in front. It provides good going on a firm surface with only occasional approaching horsemen to send Rhaebus to the left verge and Balty's right hand to his pistol butt. In late afternoon, they reach Sittingbourne with Rochester still at least two more hours ahead. Gravesend is another two cold hours beyond that. Balty invests in an hour's break at the Red Lion Inn, where the owners are unreasonably proud that nobody has refreshed the dining-room whitewash since old King Harry stayed there a century ago. He has Rhaebus rubbed down by the stable boy and given a tub of oats. Inside, more coffee warms him and his thirst is slaked by a quart of black ale. Watching the window as it grows dark again outside, he is briefly jolted by a white face pressed against it peering in. Back in the saddle, horse and rider hasten on under scudding clouds.

The wind goes on rising, still from the bitter quarter of the compass, penetrating Balty's layers of wool and canvas. The inside of his thighs start to chafe and the small of his back sends a complaint as his tiring horse fails to spot a pothole. He can sense the horse's growing discontent.

'Imagine the sun burning you,' he says to the horse to cheer it up, to cheer them both up if the truth were known, as Balty likes to talk and the twilight is too silent. He could imagine anything behind them on that road, or lying in wait ahead. 'Pretend you are too hot, Rhaebus, then you will take pleasure from this chilly air.'

The horse snorts, unimpressed. Balty tries out a horse voice inside his head, a deep voice that would use few words and speak simple, strong truths. What would it say about burning sun?

The single word 'Tangier' bursts through his head in the horse voice he has conjured up and plunges him into immediate despair. Was Esther too quick to dismiss this? Is this where his journey really ends, in the sort of trap he himself has staged many times when a navy ship is short of crew? A rendezvous in Gravesend with a gang of sailors who will beat him with a knotted rope's end – maybe some of the very same sailors he has hijacked in the past in back alleys behind taverns?

'Why would he do that?' he asks.

'He can do what he wants,' the horse says.

'But I am his brother.'

'Brother to his wife, not to him – and his wife is dead these past seven years.'

'He has been our friend.'

'He has kept you fed and housed. You gave him no choice. That eats at friendship.'

'Be quiet. You have said enough.'

'I have said nothing. I'm a horse.'

They plod onward, Balty's concentration drifting back into stupor tied to the rhythm of the horse's hooves. Afterwards, he could barely recall passing through Rochester. Only once does that rhythm falter as Rhaebus whips his head to look behind, making a harrumpf deep in his throat, but Balty can no longer bring himself to care.

Darker straight edges up against the sky finally rouse him – a man-made structure so tall that it can only be a church tower. His spirits lift because he immediately knows where they must be – the village of Milton and its church of St Peter and St Paul rearing up to the right. That means Gravesend and warmth are only a short mile ahead, but the dark church spooks Rhaebus, who is suddenly very uneasy indeed, giving little snickers and turning his head this way and that.

'Don't be daft,' says Balty, but he is wrong and Rhaebus is right. Another horse answers from the graveyard behind the church wall and as Balty twists to look back, hooves clatter on the stones. Two riders burst from the church gate in the light of the slim moon, an ambush just as he thought they were safe from the highway predators.

Rhaebus lurches into a heroic canter for the first time on this long, long journey. Balty's spirits lift. They can make it to the safety of the nearby town. No they can't. Three more horsemen block the road ahead.

Balty puts his hand on the butt of his pistol, then takes it off again. He can make one shot count, but it would take him most of a minute to reload and his powder flask is in the saddlebag with the other pistol.

He pulls Rhaebus up, searching around him in the dark
for any prospect of escape, but with two behind and three in
front, there is none. The rider in the middle of the three opens
the shutter of a dark lantern and holds it high. Balty blinks but
cannot make out the face behind the sudden glare. It's all a bit
pointless, he thinks. He has a paltry sum of money and the
pack of Esther's food. They will want his pistols and they will
want his horse, but he knows Rhaebus won't stand for that. He
braces himself.

'Stay calm,' says the man behind the lantern. 'We mean no
harm. We are here to escort you to your true destination.'

Oh Lord Almighty, thinks Balty. That's a ditch if they are
highwaymen or a Tangier ship if they are not.

'Who are you?'

'That does not matter, Mr St Michel.'

He knows my name and he is well-spoken, thinks Balty,
astonished. That must mean Tangier.

They surround him and jog onwards.

'Are you taking me to meet my brother?'

'Wait,' is all the leader of the group will say.

They go in silence, not to the port office where the searchers
work but to the courtyard of a large townhouse two streets
away from it. A groom takes Rhaebus and the men escort
Balty inside to a dimly lit reception room where a man is
waiting, half-hidden in a winged chair turned away towards
the fireplace.

'Brother?' Balty asks, unsure.

'No, not he,' says the man, and Balty knows him immediately by those three syllables, by the bulk of him and by the
turn of his head. The man in the chair has sent him into danger

before. This is not Pepys. This is a man who is more powerful still. This is Henry Coventry, the king's loyal fixer and spymaster. He has one foot propped up on a stool.

'You are surprised? Sit down,' says Coventry. 'Food is coming. It will make up for your cold ride.'

'My brother summoned me, sir.'

'No. I summoned you in his name and with a fine copy of his signature for which I hope he will forgive me. I think he will because, believe me, he does need help from both of us.'

'Why is he not here himself?'

'Ah. You have not heard yet. The news will reach Deal today.'

'What news?'

'Mr Pepys has been arrested by Parliament at the bar of the House of Commons and he is now in the custody of the Commons' Sergeant at Arms. Brave Pepys is on his way to being locked in the Tower. He will be bound speedily to the gallows if his enemies succeed and I fear that looks all too likely.'

It is the most unexpected forecast Balty can ever remember hearing.

'Why?' he says. He neglects the 'sir' but Coventry could not care less.

'He stands accused of high treason as a secret Catholic plotter against the king.'

'My brother? He is no Catholic.'

'You know that and I know that. Nor is he treasonous.'

'But . . . what is the supposed nature of this treason?'

'Oh, a small matter of selling the secrets of our ships, our ports and their armament to Louis of France to support a

French invasion intended to reimpose the Catholic faith on this Protestant island of ours.'

'My brother? You have come here to tell me some sort of joke, sir?'

'St Michel, listen carefully to me. I have come here because I believe you and I can save him, working closely together, but we must not be seen to meet. This is a desperate and secret business and I can only help Mr Pepys effectively if none know I am doing so. Is that understood? Yes?'

'Yes, sir.'

'Pepys has been under mounting attack from the king's enemies for many months and now that they control Parliament, they have made their final move against him. I suffer from the gout and my journey here should indicate the size of the stakes in this game. Believe me, it takes a great deal to persuade me to leave London these days. His neck is under immediate threat. My only question is will you help me try to save it?'

'I will. So . . . what must I do?'

Coventry waves Balty to a seat by his chair. A servant brings a steaming mug of grog and a plate of sliced lamb. Coventry watches as Balty wolfs it down.

'The last time you worked for me, you did very well,' says Coventry. 'I believe I can trust you. Am I right?'

Balty stops chewing and thinks back to that unexpected mission which started when Coventry sent him to King Louis's court to arrange the delivery of two yachts, a gift from Charles. It soon got much more complicated when Coventry added military espionage to his list of tasks.

'You are right, sir,' he says.

'You met King Louis himself?'

'Only in the sense that a man may meet a mail coach that sweeps past him at full gallop,' said Balty. 'I visited Versailles to inspect the lake where the yachts were to float, but the palace was yet half-built and the lake was a malarial marsh. King Louis passed by with a mask to his mouth and nodded in my direction. He and the court still dwelt at the Palace of St Germain, a distance from Versailles.'

'As they yet do,' said Coventry. 'He is delaying his move until Versailles achieves complete perfection. Strange that he does not like his fine capital city. I would happily live in Paris given the choice, but he dislikes Parisians.'

'They say the city is too full of people for him,' said Balty, 'and those people are too ordinary for his taste.' That wins a bark of laughter from Coventry.

'You performed extra duties for me,' Coventry says.

'I did.'

'Investigation around the ports, to see if Louis was preparing an invasion fleet. Your reports were of great assistance.' Coventry pondered. 'First I want you to understand why I chose to travel here, at great cost to my comfort. You will now sit very silently behind the screen over there, do you see? I will summon a witness to describe events that took place here last October. Do you recognize the significance of the date Sunday, October 13th?'

'No, sir.'

'A murder?'

'Ah, yes. The day of the death of Sir Edmund Berry Godfrey?'

'No, but it was the day his body was discovered on Primrose Hill. You are about to hear of events in Gravesend very soon

after. Go behind the screen and make sure you keep your
silence.'

Balty sits on a stool out of sight and hears Coventry ring a
handbell. The door opens and footsteps tell Balty that one man
has been brought in by another. The first man leaves.

'Sit there,' says Coventry.

'Yes, my lord.' The man's voice has a powerful Kentish accent.

'I am not a lord. I am nobody in particular and in any case
you are not here meeting me and I am not here meeting you.
Is that quite clear?'

'Yes, sir.' The voice says it is not at all clear.

'Not even a "sir" from now on. Regard me as empty air and
never refer to this again on pain of losing your employment
immediately.'

'Yes, sir . . . er, yes.'

'Tell me your name.'

'My name is Henry Gals.' Balty imagines him as burly, in
his forties. Possibly once a soldier.

'Your job?'

'I am an officer of the Port Authority for Gravesend.'

'Monitoring those coming in and out by sea?'

'That is one part of my job.'

'You were doubly vigilant on October 14th last year?'

'I was. We had received an urgent message from the Navy
Office – from Mr Pepys himself. He said we were to watch for
the escaping murderer of Sir Edmund Berry Godfrey trying to
flee the country.'

'Mr Pepys was warning all the ports?'

'I believe he was, sir . . . oh there I go again. Mr Pepys has
a special concern for the Kentish ports being as how he serves

as a Justice of the Peace in the county of Kent, and Gravesend would be the obvious port for a fugitive from London.'

'Do you remember it clearly?'

'Oh yes. It was plumb in the middle of our yearly fair. Tradesmen by the hundred, people by the thousand flocking in to the fair-fields up towards the windmill. Not just that, but we had an eclipse of the moon, a rare sight.'

'And then a stranger arrived?'

'They sent for me from the Horns Tavern, up the road. The landlord told me a stranger armed with pistols had ridden into town on a lathered horse. The landlord asked him for his name and do you know what name he gave? He said his name was Godfrey.'

'A strange name to give you on that day of all days, but hardly the one you would pick if you really were Godfrey's fleeing assassin.'

'Unless you were taken aback by the question, sir . . . I mean, by the question. Then might you blurt out what was on your mind? That was my thought. Any road, the two of us, me and my comrade Mr Skarr, went straight to the Horns to see for ourselves. I should explain it is one of the finer inns, not usually frequented by the worst sort.'

'And?'

'And we got into conversation with the man.'

'What sort of a man was he?'

'A big man, bushy eyebrows, one eye pointing a little away from the other. The sort of man you might think twice about going up against. I've served in the army. He looked like he had lived through a war or two in a campaign tent.'

'You spoke with him?'

'We drank with him to get the measure of him. We got him in his cups and we rumbled him for a liar.'

'How so?'

'Oh, for a start, he boasted of some mission to Jerusalem. Said he landed at Alexandria near Aleppo when we folk who have travelled know that's Alexandretta. Alexandria is nowhere near. So we asked him, all innocent and ignorant like, about the inns between Aleppo and Jerusalem and he started on such a list you would not credit. Names plucked out of thin air. Mad names, English names like the Saracen's Head and the King's Arms. Not at all the sort of thing they would call the inns in that country if there were any.'

'How do you know that?'

'I've been there with a sword in my hand and I can tell you there are no inns on that road. None at all.'

'Did you arrest him?'

'To my shame, we did not. We knew he was pressing the master of the *Assistance* for passage on his vessel but we told the port searchers not to let the boat sail. Sad to say, but money changed hands. The *Assistance* was cleared to leave and he slipped aways. I sent my report to Mr Pepys at the gallop as soon as I had that news and he alerted the navy in hot pursuit. We are still looking for the searcher who allowed this.'

'There was something about a coat?'

'Yes there was. This man who said he was Godfrey claimed to have been two weeks on the road running around the countryside on his master's business. I could see that weren't true. He arrived with no coat at all and his clothes were clean and dry. Then we heard he purchased a campaign coat up at the fair-field so our mayor searched out the stall-holder who sold it to him.'

'And?'

'The man who sold him the coat was a Londoner and by the greatest good fortune, he recognized this Godfrey – even knew where he lived. This coat-seller worked at a Cannon Street tavern when not attending the fairs. The man Godfrey lived right opposite, lodging with a haberdasher. I put all that in my report.'

'Thank you. You may go. You will keep your silence regardless of who asks.'

When Gals has left, Coventry calls Balty from behind the screen.

'I wanted you to hear that account in this place where it happened.'

'Did something come of it?'

'Everything came of it. I believe that all of this, every single bit, starts with what your brother Pepys did next.'

'Yes?'

'You know what he is like. Imagine it. This likely murderer has slipped through his fingers. Mr Pepys's navy has failed England. He moves heaven and earth. He sends his orders to all the ports to intercept the *Assistance*. He takes Judge Jeffreys with him to search Godfrey's lodgings. He questions the haberdasher. He finds out who Godfrey really is.'

Balty stares and Coventry winces, stretching both hands towards his swaddled, swollen foot.

'The man at the heart of this,' he says eventually in a thin and painful voice, 'is one Colonel John Scott. You need to know this, but remember we must keep our cards hidden close. Colonel Scott has spent his recent years in Europe doing many hidden things. This time, he switches ships twice and gets across to France despite our efforts. Mr Pepys pressed for a warrant for his immediate arrest if he came back here. As a result, Scott was obliged to stay in France for many months and that is why he hates Pepys and it is why on his return he has moved against your brother.'

'But how did he come back without being taken?'

'Ah! More harsh news is crawling towards Deal. The Whig Party has swept to power at Westminster.'

'I know that.'

'But you will not yet know that yesterday the Whigs passed their bill to bar the Duke of York from ever becoming king and they set the scene by launching their attack on Mr Pepys in the House. Scott led that attack.'

'He smuggled himself back to do so?'

'He was summoned back from France by leading Whigs. On landing, he was at once seized on my warrant, but his friends freed him and brought him to London to wreak his mischief.'

'The king did nothing?'

Coventry sighed. 'The king's enemies control his Privy Council and are bent on limiting his power. Scott stood at the bar of the House of Commons yesterday and denounced your brother as a traitor. He intends to destroy Mr Pepys.'

'But . . . how can I help?'

'We need to understand exactly who controls Scott. The possibilities include that old bastard Wildman and . . .' Coventry hesitates, '. . . a certain man of noble rank. A man of such status that the king cannot proceed against him until he is entirely sure of his facts.'

Balty has heard the stories. He wonders whether he dare name the Earl of Shaftesbury, but before he makes up his mind, rapid footsteps approach and a fist raps on the door.

'Enter,' calls Coventry.

Balty recognizes the leader of the horsemen.

'Captain Clifton,' says Coventry. 'I said we were not to be interrupted.'

'Sir, my apologies but I must. We have taken two people attempting to spy on your meeting. It is not clear how much they have already heard.'

CHAPTER 8

Clifton's words bring Coventry to his feet with a gasp of pain. 'Eavesdroppers? How can that be?'

'All I know so far is that they followed Mr St Michel, a brute of a man and a small boy. The man was attempting to insert the boy through a window. They refuse to explain but we will sweat it out of them.'

'No you will not,' says Balty.

Coventry's gaze swivels to him. 'Why so? Do you know them?'

Balty remembers Rhaebus's behaviour at points on the journey. 'I do, though I am astonished. The brute works for me. He is a loyal brute. The other ... the other would seem to be my son.'

And so it is. Captain Clifton ushers them in, then stands guard at the door. Ezra looks exhausted and sheepish. Sam is dishevelled and dirty but displays his usual calm and certain self.

'Of course we came after you, papa. It was folly in the extreme to go off through the night by yourself.'

'I was safe enough, as you can see. I arrived here untouched.

You could have got yourself into terrible trouble doing such a thing.'

Sam looks at him as if deeply disappointed and adopts a tone of patient reproof. 'You arrived untouched only because we were behind you, pater. Ezra grabbed the two ruffians following you up the Sheepwash hill. They won't trouble you again. We flanked you out of Canterbury in the fields to your right and I shot the villain with his musket waiting in ambush. Did you not hear it?'

'A fine shot, sir,' says Ezra.

'It was not,' says Sam. 'I aimed at his hat but I hit him in the foot. I thought I had missed him entirely because it took some time for him to fall over. The barrel of my pistol is much too short.'

Balty is having trouble taking this in. 'You were riding?'

'Of course we were,' says Sam, betraying a little exasperation. 'We could find no friendly eagles to carry us. We rode the navy horse.'

Balty's astonishment rises further. 'The navy horse?' He turns to Ezra. 'You persuaded the navy horse to take you all the way here carrying both of you?'

Ezra frowns as if the question makes no sense and Sam answers for him. 'The horse kicked Ezra when he went to mount it. He knocked it down with one punch then he sat on its head while it woke up.'

'And then . . . what? It agreed to go wherever he wanted?'

'With horses, it is all a matter of respect I think.'

Coventry seems to have forgotten his gout. Captain Clifton is gazing up at the ceiling.

'Clifton,' says Coventry, 'will you take these two to the

kitchen and feed them anything they want. After that, we will discuss arrangements for their return journey.'

'Thank you,' says Sam. 'A very small glass of Malmsey wine would balance the dispiriting nature of the journey without proving too deleterious to my powers of reasoning, I think.'

Left to themselves, Coventry stares at Balty as if framing a question, then smiles and shakes his head. 'I have taken certain covert actions to help Mr Pepys so far as I can. He will be able to communicate through my office without our enemies knowing and I will be able to alert him to the machinations of those who would destroy him.' He sighs and drums his fingers on the arm of his chair, then reaches a decision. 'St Michel,' he says, 'the clearest way to save your brother Pepys is to tear to pieces the testimony of the villain who calls himself Colonel John Scott. You do understand that they need only one more witness to swear your brother is a traitor and then he is done for.'

'I fully understand,' says Balty. The law holds it to be unthinkable that a person who swears on the bible would risk eternity in hell by lying. One unnatural man might do such a thing, but two sworn testimonies against the accused allow no possible defence in a treason trial. It is even worse when the accused is a Catholic because they may swear the truth of anything they choose. Everybody knows that Catholics have a special dispensation from the pope to lie with impunity if it is done to secure their Catholic ends.

Coventry is clearly weighing the risks of revealing more, staring at the wall beyond Balty, but he nods once, decisively, and continues. 'There is a capable man in our Paris office who has the power to help, because it is in France that we may uncover the truth about Scott. I have sent a message, but that man may not agree to my request and it is more than possible that I will need to call on you.'

'Why me?' says Balty.

'You have shown me in the past that you have the right qualities. You are a clever fellow when it comes to uncovering information and we share, I hope, a strong interest in keeping your brother alive.'

'But my brother is bent on sending me to Tangier,' says Balty. 'That is not calculated to keep me alive.'

'If you take on this task, you cannot also be in Tangier. You need have no such future worries while I am in charge.' The gleam in Coventry's eye shows he has been leading the whole conversation towards this moment. 'There is something else. It is not one person whose life you need to save. It is three. Our friend Sir Anthony Deane shares Pepys's imprisonment, though in different corners of the Tower to prevent them conniving . . .'

Balty's breath goes out of him. That only makes two and Coventry circles a finger into the air which moves slowly to point at him. 'And if I told you that Pepys and Deane also face charges of piracy? Then perhaps you will understand who that third person might be?'

Balty is suddenly extremely weary. A minute ago, he hadn't seen this coming – that feels like a bygone age now. 'You mean . . . it is me.'

'So you will do this for me, for Pepys, for Deane and for yourself?'

'Do I have a choice?'

'Think of your wife. Think of your son.'

'And what about his daughter?' says a small voice from behind a curtain.

'Oh dear God above,' says Coventry as Betty steps out into the dim light. He raises his voice, 'If there are any other St Michels in here, could you show yourselves now please? I've had enough surprises tonight.'

'Sir, there is no reason to shout at the Lord in that way.'

Balty is horrified. 'Betty, you are speaking to King Charles's Secretary of State, the noble . . .'

Coventry holds up one hand. 'Stop there. Little girl, you are quite right, but I speak to my God with a great deal of personal affection and after all this time, I feel he allows me a certain measure of informality as he expects us to meet in person quite soon. Were there really three of you on that poor horse?'

'No, sir, certainly not. Ezra and Sam didn't know I was following them.'

'You mean you came here by yourself?'

'Oh no, sir. I had my horse Emma. She was most supportive.'

'I'm sure she was, Betty.' Coventry rings the bell again and Captain Clifton appears at the door.

'Clifton,' says Coventry mildly, 'it seems one more member of the St Michel espionage circle has managed to evade your security entirely. Let me introduce you to Betty and I would like you to bring the other two back in here with enough food for us all. There is a further story to uncover.'

Ezra and Sam stare at Betty in complete astonishment. 'You foolish girl,' says Sam. 'That was a most dangerous thing to do. If we had not dealt with the villains lurking along the way before you reached them, you would be dead by now.'

'Oh Sam, Sam . . . Really? I caught up with you before you ever reached the Sheepwash hill. That was just as well for both of you as I was able to lead them a merry dance.'

'Them? The two men Ezra dealt with?'

'No, no. The other three. The bigger men you never saw. I thought five might be too much even for Ezra, so Emma and I lured them away. They were struggling out of a ditch when we left them. After that I mostly rode ahead of you because I know the navy horse moves more rapidly when he can smell Emma ahead.'

'That horse has a soft spot for the filly,' says Ezra.

Sam frowns 'An odd expression,' he says. 'It would be more accurate, according to my understanding of the natural sciences, to say that the navy horse displayed a strong desire to embark upon the reproductive act with Emma while Emma, having no such matching desire, made sure to keep her distance ahead of him to prevent that outcome. So, sister, that does explain how we were able to make quite good speed, though, papa, you would keep stopping.'

Betty looks at him, pursing her lips and the three adults avoid each other's eyes.

'But then of course I also dealt with the felon with the musket,' Sam points out and Betty says nothing.

'I did,' says Sam firmly. 'I shot him and I saw him fall over.'

'As soon as you fired?'

'No. It took a moment because there was an echo of my shot as if . . . he . . . Oh, no. You shot him, didn't you?'

'In the foot, yes. It was a very lucky shot,' says Betty.

'What did you shoot him with?' Balty demands.

'The other pistol,' says Ezra. 'The one I gave *her*.'

'But of course, Sam's shot distracted him first,' says Betty. 'He was whirling around. It made him an easy target.'

'Extraordinary,' says Coventry. 'I have no words. Eat. You

will need all your strength because you must now return to Deal. St Michel, come close.'

Balty stoops over the old man. 'You will take on this task for me?' Coventry whispers.

'Do I have any choice?'

'Yes of course. Your other choice is a reasonably certain and fairly rapid death for Pepys, for Deane and probably for you yourself afterwards.'

'But you said I might not be needed?'

'Probably not immediately but very soon, as I foresee problem with those I trust in Paris. You must return to Deal now, but be ready to go as soon as I call.'

'Please, sir, we need to rest here for a few hours first. It is a long ride home.'

'You can rest for longer than that on board.'

'On board?'

'On board the very fast and fine frigate *Moonstone* which I have ordered to transport you and your three estimable bodyguards back to your home in the most comfortable style. Captain Clifton commands that frigate when he is not imitating footpads on my behalf and he will take you there. He enjoys my full confidence and he will pass on to you all the information that I have managed to accumulate to date. When the time comes, he will transport you across the sea to France. Now, I shall return to the London I never left in a comfortable barge and you will abandon any false memories of our conversation. They were but drunken dreams. Yes?'

'Yes, sir.'

He rings the bell and Captain Clifton enters so quickly that he must have been waiting outside the door. Balty sees him through fresh eyes, not as the mere army captain he had assumed but as a navy man instead, and the whole of that efficient ambush crew must be seamen too, though they ride well for sailors.

'Sir, we have arranged transport for the horses. A cavalry troop is on their way to Dover tomorrow. They will deliver them to Deal.'

An hour after dawn the next day, Balty comes on deck to see Sheerness and the beginnings of Sheppey island on the starboard bow as the *Moonstone* knifes through the waves, shrugging off the swell on a fast and sure track. Clifton welcomes him to the quarterdeck. Balty looks him up and down in the daylight and takes him for not yet thirty, young to have command of a frigate and showing a lithe intelligence that marks him for even greater things.

'Your children have beaten you to it,' says Clifton.

Balty inspects the gun-deck ahead of them. 'They are up and about?'

'Up certainly.' Clifton points to the top of the main mast. 'They are very far up.'

Balty tilts his head right back and far aloft, under the high curve of the topgallant sails, he sees a distant figure which looks more like Ezra than Sam. Then his eyes adjust for the height and he sees it is indeed Ezra and the two much smaller figures next to him can only be Betty and Sam. Although Balty has spent large parts of his life at sea, he has never been entirely at home aloft and it turns his stomach to see them so high up, their existence threatened as every heave of the frigate on the beam seas sends the tops of the masts sweeping through an immense arc of sky.

'Get them down,' he says as calmly as he can. 'Do please get them down. That could be their death.'

Clifton smiles. 'I have been watching them for the past hour. Your man Ezra is a fine seaman and he has already schooled them well. They have been scampering around the rigging like natural top-masters. See now?'

One tiny figure is coming down, not the obvious way, not hand over hand down the ratlines with the heart-stopping, backward-bending jink through empty space at the crow's nest overhang. This one, who must be Sam, comes straight down the quickest way, as near to falling as you can get, rocketing all the way to the deck with his arms wrapped around the main-stay, his life depending on a single, slanting piece of rope. He sees a widening grin as the figure reaches the deck and he also sees it is not Sam, it is Betty. Sam is coming down after her. The pair race straight to the ratlines, climbing fast to do it all over again.

'Could you perhaps spare me your man Ezra?' Clifton asks. 'I need a good bosun and he is very much my sort of seaman.'

'Ask him. He is not really mine to command. So long as you don't ask for Sam as well. He is too young to be a midshipman.'

'Too young? I think he may be too old, don't you? He appears to me to be passing thirty in most respects. No, I think there might be other paths for him.'

'What does that mean?'

'Later. We have limited time and a lot of ground to cover.'

The captain's cabin is spacious, its gallery windows spanning the width of the stern, the climbing sun splashing their arrow-straight wake with arcing sprays of silver.

The steward brings the best coffee Balty has ever tasted.

Clifton opens a small black book. 'Now,' he says. 'I know you have experience of the administration of ships, but perhaps not so much of their design?'

'Some.'

'Sir Anthony Deane is accused alongside Mr Pepys. Do you know why that matters?'

'Of course. He is our finest ship designer.'

'By far. The *Moonstone* and her similar sister *Sapphire* are perfect products of his craft – a sharp bow to cut through the water and the slender grace of a greyhound for remarkable speed. However, that comes at a price when the broadsides start. You haven't been in action I think?'

'I have,' says Balty slightly stung. 'I was muster-master of the *Henry* flagship when Harman was Rear Admiral of the White in '66.'

'Good Lord above. You were at the St James's Day battle?' Clifton's expression alters. He looks at Balty as a man looks at his equal. 'And I was foolish enough to question your experience. The White Squadron had the worst of it, did it not? Tell me more, please.'

'I was below helping the surgeon prepare when the fireships struck.' Suddenly with the *Moonstone's* deck rolling under him, he is back on the *Henry*. 'The heat was hellish. The fireships were burning from bottom to top and the flames came straight up at us. The rigging was already on fire and our sails were catching it.'

Balty feels the axe thrust into his hands by the first mate who sags to his knees, blood spurting from his scalp. Then he is running to the nearest Dutch grappling iron, hacking at the rope as burning canvas falls around him, forcing him to beat fire from his hair. A sailor lies in two halves on the deck in front of him, guts sliding out from the gap. After the pictures comes the noise, the screams of seared men leaping into the water between a fireship and the *Henry*'s hull, one of them thudding into an out-thrust cannon barrel and plunging on down, limp as a rag doll, to splash and vanish.

'Harman was the best of commanders,' he says. 'He was alongside us with an axe in his hands until a topmast spar came down and snapped his leg. We went to carry him below but he wasn't having it. The surgeon's loblolly boy came up to splint it and he went on yelling his orders.'

'He stayed up top?'

'Oh yes. We were ordered back to Harwich and he refused to hand over command. We set up a bed on deck, fed him rum through the night. He watched over all the repairs. By mid-morning, we had sail up again. On our way back out, we met all that was left of the White Squadron retreating into the river. leaving the *Prince Royal* burning on the Galloper Sand. Harman was beside himself.'

Balty forces the pictures back to their prison beyond the past and turns to look around the cabin, surprised to see the polished woodwork and perfect paint. 'We had it better next time,' he says, half to himself. 'We shattered a score of ships that time, chased them back to hide behind their islands, so . . . yes, Captain Clifton. I know what lower gun decks are like when broadsides hit them. Sharp oak splinters flying and smoke to blind you. The top deck is easier. The wind blows away the smoke.'

Clifton's tone is full of respect and his voice is more gentle. He knows when theory is a safer place than memory. 'Sir Anthony's greyhounds will win us battles but not if we overbalance them with too much top weight. So Prince Rupert's new guns may complete Deane's magic. The place those two secrets meet is at the heart of all this and that yet may hang both Pepys and Deane, who should rather be seen as heroes.'

Prince Rupert? The inventive nephew of the first King Charles led the king's cavalry in the civil war before he turned magician. Now he creates clever, practical wonders out of glass and metal – but guns? He follows Clifton out on deck. The cannon are lashed down. Clifton pats the nearest. 'Look closely. These are Prince Rupert's new wonders. What do you see?'

The cold iron has a browner sheen. Balty reaches forward to feel the muzzle and he is startled. The cast metal is much thinner than he expects. 'This barrel must be lighter by far. Why does it not burst?'

'Rupert calls this his turned and nealed gun. Turned on a spinning lathe to grind away the bumps and bulges. Nealed, because he fires the finished castings to red heat, then cools them in a very precise way. The saved weight and the new strength are supposed to give our greyhounds powerful teeth and not overbalance the ship in the midst of battle.' He pats the barrel. 'I have yet to try them in action but do you see now? These are the secrets King Louis desires to have, the same secrets our friends are accused of selling and that may kill them.'

'But . . . the making of the guns sounds quite simple?'

'Until you try to do it. The purification of the molten metals. The exact heat of the nealing. The skill of the lathe work. All need perfect precision. Get it wrong and barrels explode, arms are severed, skulls break. Get it right and your ships blow the enemy to splinters.' He bangs a fist on the barrel. '*These* guns in *these* ships may rule the seas unless the traitors win.'

Seamen nearby, attending to a gun carriage wheel, are muffling their profanities because of the captain and his guest. Clifton takes Balty to the quarterdeck where his first mate, standing at the steersman's elbow, salutes. Clifton crosses to the weather rail, the captain's private side. 'Pepys and Deane stand accused of selling the secret of the guns and detailed maps of our harbours and defences. Coventry must catch the men responsible and prove whether the French now have Rupert's secret. You are caught up in all this.'

'Am I accused of this as well?'

Clifton shakes his head but Balty's relief lasts only two heartbeats. 'For you,' says Clifton, 'the danger is the matter of the *Hunter* ship. Piracy. A capital crime.'

Here it comes, thinks Balty, its fingers clawing for my neck. 'What do you know about it, Captain?' He finds that Clifton's opinion matters to him.

'I looked into the matter for Secretary Coventry to determine the truth. I am seconded to him by the king when he needs help or sometimes just a fast ship and a loyal crew.'

Balty struggles with what he is allowed to say. 'It was not as it seemed.'

'From the very start, it stank in every way. I see that.'

Balty sees his children slide to the deck yet again and race up the mast, cheered on by watching seamen. They plunge even faster, but now his heart plunges too. 'But how do you see it?'

Clifton glances up at the masthead pennant, then at the coast and back at their wake. He walks across to make a quiet comment to the first mate. The mate nods and the steersman turns the wheel two spokes to starboard. Balty can feel the ship pick up a fraction more speed as the curve in the sails hardens.

Clifton takes his time walking back, thinking something through.

'A cabal of rich investors buy a ship and fit it out as a privateer to fight our enemies. They are out to seize valuable merchantmen, not dangerous warships. A common enough affair. Yes?'

'Yes.'

'But the *Hunter* attacks a ship which is not an enemy at all. Don't argue. Not yet. St Michel, you and Sir Anthony Deane are listed among the *Hunter*'s owners. You note I said *rich* investors and with no disrespect you are not rich. You fight hard to provide for your family, which I admire, but . . .' He shrugs and smiles. 'Eight shareholders funded this venture but you could not have run to an eight hundredth share, let alone an eighth.'

'I can't speak of that.'

'I salute your loyalty. I know you never were a part-owner of the *Hunter*, but you had to pretend you were. The ship's owners included Mr Pepys and your name was borrowed because Pepys, as Secretary of the Navy, could not openly be seen to have a private venture.'

'It is an old matter.'

'But it has not yet been put right and that is still high in the mind of our embassy staff in Paris. You will need to sort it out when you get there.'

Balty bridles. 'I may yet choose not to go.'

Clifton glances up at the sails again and seems satisfied. 'But you will, won't you? Secretary Coventry needs you and if you are in Paris, you cannot also be in Tangier.'

Balty finds he dislikes this polite coercion. 'I have become quite reconciled with the idea of Tangier,' he says as lightly as he can. 'A short posting there will be a good for me. I will make money and it seems a most interesting city.'

'I have changed my mind about you, St Michel,' says Clifton. 'You came on board as a landsman of uncertain quality and you will leave as a seaman with a practised approach to danger. Now listen to me. I have experienced Tangier and you have not. That place makes sense only in the mind. The maps show it commands the Mediterranean at its narrow entrance but the map is flat and made of cloth while that coast is mountainous and made of sand and venom.'

'I will take care.'

'Open your ears, man. I have been very close to death in that same cabin below, brought down by fevers. Beyond the disease and the things that bite stand the armies of the Moors who were here long before us. They hate us with good reason as *we* are the trespassers, an alien intrusion, celebrating a different god. They know the land much better than we do, so they are held at bay only by bribes and powerful guns. I have buried ten of my men there. I have heard the screams of soldiers captured from our outpost forts by invisible men who took them in the darkness and staked them out in the African sun to have their eyes devoured by ants. I have seen . . .'

'Enough. My brother Pepys is convinced I will find it a paradise.'

'A rapid route to paradise if your soul is spotless.' Balty turns away and Clifton looks at him with some degree of sympathy. 'You may yet see Tangier if you fail in Paris.'

'But . . . at what exactly?'

'At uncovering the precise intentions of Colonel John Scott, the man who entertained Parliament with his list of what Pepys sold to King Louis and how Deane delivered it.'

'And the answer lies in France?'

'Lies is the right word. Coventry says the treason is real but the perpetrators' names are not. The crimes Scott places at Pepys's door are his own. He spent many months in France demanding cash for his information. We need proof of that. He planned to come back in glory when his masters won political control but Pepys chased him out of England and blocked his return. Scott hates him for that. He works closely with those who would destroy the Duke of York and hang Pepys.'

'You want to preserve Duke James?'

'Your task is to preserve Pepys and uncover the hidden history of Colonel Scott to learn who steers him. That is rich and dangerous territory.' Clifton takes a small book from his pocket. 'Listed here is much of what we know. Repair to my cabin and read it carefully, then I will answer questions.'

'And then?'

'I will leave you at Deal to prepare, then I may carry you to France and brief you further on the way. Just think, a frigate detached from duty entirely for your convenience.'

'How long will I be there?'

'At least a week. At most a year. That depends on you.'

'How will I explain my visit?'

'As a Frenchman why would anyone ask? The *Hunter* business may be a good excuse if you need one. There are loose ends there which need splicing.'

'Who will pay for this?'

'A wealthy Huguenot merchant, Mr James Houblon has volunteered his help.'

Balty knows Houblon as a good friend to Pepys. 'But . . . will I be by myself?'

Captain Clifton looks up the mast to where the children are far out towards the end of the topgallant yard, stepping sideways like seasoned seamen. 'I have an idea about that,' he says, 'but your wife may not approve.'

CHAPTER 9

Esther is delighted to see them safe but very unhappy over what is to follow. 'You will go to Paris to do something you know nothing about, and you want to take little Samuel with you? Are you off your head?'

'It will be good for his French.'

'Frenchmen say his French is perfect. Sam and Betty are both taken for natives. Have you forgotten?'

'They were younger then. It is time Sam had proper experience of Paris. After all, half of him is French.'

'Only a quarter, thank the Lord. You forget your English mother! What are you up to? You come back here after a mad escapade, luring the children after you . . .'

'You could have stopped them.'

'I could not. When Sam's determined, he won't listen. At least he was with Ezra. I didn't even know Betty had gone until I found her note. I was terrified. Then you come back in a great ship without our horses, telling me our brother may lose his head and now you have to take Sam to France?'

'It may never happen, but Captain Clifton will deliver us

there himself if it does. He will be at my command to fetch us back here afterwards.'

Esther's eyes had widened at the sight of Clifton and he had taken care to charm. 'The captain himself? I will consult Sam. I expect he will have a strong opinion.'

Somehow Sam's opinion rapidly persuades her, helped by a note from London that Pepys's wealthier younger colleague, William Hewer, would welcome Esther and Betty to stay at his London house while Balty and Sam are away. Hewer's grand townhouse is right on the river by Westminster and his rural manor near the quiet village of Clapham is close by when a day or two of peace beckons. Hewer promises she will be looked after by proper servants – a butler, her own maid and one of the best cooks in the city. She starts to hope Balty's trip will be longer.

There is just time to prepare. It takes three weeks for the word to come from London. Balty hires two retired officers to do his work and the *Moonstone* appears in the Downs. Ready to depart, Balty corners Sam in the garden. Esther and Betty are out of earshot. 'What exactly did you say to mama to change her mind about you coming with me?'

'Only that I would look after you, papa.'

'She wouldn't have liked that. It makes it sound dangerous.'

Sam turns pink. 'It wasn't that sort of looking after.'

'What sort was it?'

'I told her I had heard Paris was home to friendly ladies and I would rescue you from being misled by them.'

Balty shakes his head as if that could fling Sam's words back out of his ears. 'You thought that up by yourself?'

'Captain Clifton told me stories of fine men who have been lured into difficult positions by bad women. He said he was quite sure you would be resolute, even without someone there to help you.'

'He was right, so why ...?'

'Betty and I were less certain. You do like to think the best of such ladies, papa.'

'And ... you told mama that?'

'I chose my words carefully, but she speedily decided it would be good for my education if I were to come too.'

'Sam, perhaps it would be better if you did not involve yourself in this sort of adult matter. You have no idea what this is all about.'

Sam sighs. 'Pater, Betty and I have talked this through. We know you are going to Paris to save my godfather from a rogue by uncovering his activities in France. Those activities may include the ladies of what Captain Clifton carefully described as the Paris demi-monde so as not to offend our young ears but Betty says they practise the same trade as the whores of Goat's Jig Lane, though she adds that they are almost certainly more slender and more appealing in every way. Now, it is quite clear to both of us that you have an eye for a certain style of lady, as I expect I will too some day, though I cannot quite imagine that yet. It seems a lot of trouble to go to and all for what exactly?'

When the departure day dawns, Balty and Sam are ferried aboard the *Moonstone* in the frigate's longboat. A cutter from the Deal depot brings Esther and Betty out to see them off. Clifton greets them on deck and insists they take his cabin for the voyage. As the crew spreads the canvas and the frigate gathers way, Balty goes to the rail to wave farewell to his wife and daughter in the boat they are leaving behind. He sees Esther waving both arms. 'Where's Betty?' he says to Sam. 'I can't see her.'

His son giggles. 'She's standing behind you.'

'What?' He whirls round. 'But your mother . . .'

'. . . thought it a good idea for my education and your further support that I should come too,' says Betty, 'and as Captain Clifton himself puts it, whatever it is exactly that you have to do, you may attract even less suspicion with two children under your care than with just one.' She beckons him to bend down to her and whispers in his ear, 'Besides that, I shoot straighter.'

It is a rapid passage across the Channel with the *Moonstone* revelling in an unseasonal north-westerly. 'A little abaft the beam,' Clifton says. 'Do you feel the boat loving it?'

At dawn next day, the *Moonstone* swings to her anchor off Honfleur in the Crique de Rouen. Balty is deep in discussion with Betty, Sam and Clifton in his cabin. Balty has given up trying to play the protective father. Sam is taking notes and when Clifton gently questions this in case their true purpose might be discovered, Sam shows him a page covered in the secret method of speedy writing taught to him by his godfather.

'There are powerful forces at work here in France as well as England.' Clifton pauses. 'Secretary Coventry says you must understand what he calls the triangle of religious diplomacy. Do you know what that means?'

Balty has heard that phrase many times before. 'It's a complicated way of saying the obvious. The English, the Dutch and the French are three sides of the triangle, so the points where they meet are the possible alliances of any two of them against the other?'

'Exactly so.' Clifton turns to the children. 'We've fought the Dutch thrice in three decades for trade advantage while France cheered us on. King Louis likes it when Protestant

England is battling the Protestant Dutch. He would be much less happy if those Protestant nations united against Catholic France. Louis dreams of turning England papist again. Think about that. Now, we have much to do. Your transport is due here in an hour.'

Clifton spends that time going through the short list what they know of Colonel John Scott's misdeeds in France and the much longer list of what else they suspect. 'Two Paris merchants await your arrival,' he says, 'friends of Mr Houblon. They have found you rooms and will supply you with funds. You will supply full accounts in return.'

'Certainly,' says Balty, who has no intention of doing anything of the sort.

'We will,' says Betty, who has every intention of so doing.

'There is also a man of ours in Paris, a valued agent of Secretary Coventry, half-French with many looks and identities. He will only make himself known to you if it is necessary and safe.'

Balty frowns. 'How will we know him?'

'By the first words he will say to you: "I do not like your hat." He will go by the name Captain René Augier for this purpose. Remember that and take care you do not expose him. He has done us a great deal of service, to his constant peril.'

He glances out of the stern windows. 'Your transport upriver is coming now. It is a hundred miles to Paris in a straight line but the Seine's loops make it much further. However, you will arrive unnoticed, whereas every passenger on the Messagerie coach from Calais is carefully observed.'

'But we might be seen leaving the *Moonstone*.'

'This barge always brings us fresh water barrels. You will be offloaded in the empties. We pay the man well.'

'A barge?' said Balty, looking back through the gallery windows. 'We will travel in a goods barge?'

'Were you expecting a royal galley? They know their business, these bargees. They have sails for a fair wind and draught-horse teams waiting when the river swings round the wrong way. You will be in Paris in three days.'

'And when we get there?'

'Your first visit must be to the ambassador, Mr Henry Savile, and his assistant, both well known to Mr Pepys. They may tell you about Monsieur Barillon, Louis's ambassador in London, who pays bribes to Whig politicians to unsettle the equilibrium of our country.'

Sam is shocked. 'Englishmen take foreign money to do that?'

'Gold has no smell but a seductive voice.'

Betty holds up a hand. 'How do we report what we discover?'

'A good question. Your letters will go to a secure address. A trusted team will monitor them and get them to Mr Pepys, who has been moved to the King's Bench prison in Southwark. His replies will go via Coventry to your Paris rooms. It takes a week to send post from Paris to London and another week for it to come back, longer if the winds and the weather are opposed.' He smiles. 'You will not be surprised to hear Pepys is leading his own defence and gathering information from everywhere. Expect him to write to you every day with fresh questions. He expects rapid replies.'

Balty knows that means a flood of instructions telling him exactly what he should and should not do. 'He can do that safely?'

'Arrangements are being made, but . . .' Clifton looks at the three of them in turn. 'It is likely that some of your letters will be intercepted, opened, read and then re-sealed.'

'Who will do that?' says Sam.

'Agents of the plotters. Agents of King Louis wondering why you have come. Agents of other nations who know your connection to a high-ranking man held as an enemy of England. Anybody else who sees a profit to be made. Take your pick.'

Balty frowns again. 'But our focus will be on Scott, nothing to cause wider concern.'

Clifton shrugs and Betty stares at him. 'That's not so, is it Captain? I see it in your face.'

He returns her stare, then gives a single nod. 'Please understand that Secretary Coventry is using up his remaining strength in the service of his king and country. He . . . he needs a further service from you. You should learn what you can about Louis's military preparations. We fear he may decide to intervene directly in England's affairs.'

'Oh, not that again,' says Balty. 'Great heavens, I did that for him last time. It got me into all sorts of trouble. What if I say no?'

Clifton points out of the stern gallery windows at the approaching barge. 'Almost nothing. I will put you into that boat just as we intended and it will take you to Paris with your baggage.'

'Good,' says Balty. 'Let's get going.'

'*Almost* nothing?' says Betty.

Clifton looks down at the table as he speaks. 'Forgive me. I have to follow my orders. Once you are in the barge, I must send a message to the office of national security over there. Do you see the building with yellow windows?'

Balty's question comes in a whisper. 'What will you say?'

'That you are a man of doubtful character set on actions likely to harm France.'

Balty glares but Betty laughs. 'That is a big *almost*, Captain,' she says. 'Papa, shall we do as he asks?'

'Let us get on with this,' says Sam. 'Captain, you say our letters may be read by others. How do we stop them?'

'As you write, leave a little space between the lines and use this liquid as ink to enter your private information in that space.' He pushes a bottle across to Balty. 'It requires treatment to become visible. Your letters will be carefully copied. The copies will be sent on to Mr Pepys and Secretary Coventry will keep yours to study what else you have to say.'

Sam frowns. 'He will copy every letter? That will take time.'

'His staff can copy eight pages every hour,' says Clifton, 'with every sort of blank paper to choose from. Mr Pepys knows all about that but even he will be unable to detect the difference.'

Sam uncorks the liquid. 'Lemons,' he says. 'Diffused into a volatile spirit? Yes, not visible until you apply heat sufficiently to read it. I was going to suggest the same as I have done it myself in my godfather's office. Good, but there will be others who know this trick.'

'You will number your letters so we will know if any have been intercepted. Once the secret writing is heated, it does not disappear again and they would have to destroy it. That would leave a gap in the sequence. There is a further precaution.' With sealing wax and a hair plucked from his head he shows them how to seal a section of hair discreetly into the wax, a giveaway sign of interference.

'And . . . if we are found out,' says Balty. 'What then?'

'An emergency place of safety. The same one as you used on your previous mission. Do you remember where to go?'

'Le Tréport on the coast. The track by the old oak? The fisherman's house and the signal.'

'Still our secret. A ship, this one unless I am required elsewhere, will look in every two weeks after dark. One more thing. You two, Sam and Betty, are your father's best protection. No father would willingly take his children into danger. You must be ordinary children and nothing more. Try to ask the sort of questions a child would ask but observe everything for when you can talk privately together.'

Betty nods. Sam frowns. 'I will have to think how best to do that,' he says.

'Finally, be on constant alert for anyone watching you. If you are observed, we need to know. So, one week after your arrival, Sam, you must write a letter to your godfather. Address it to him as if he is still Secretary to the Admiralty in his offices. It will make it seem that you know nothing of what has happened. Coventry will intercept it. I hear you can write in other languages?'

'Latin, French and a little Italian.'

'Then use both Latin and French in the letter. If you are quite certain you are not being watched, start with the Latin. If you detect watchers, start in French. Presume it will be read by unfriendly eyes. Keep it simple, perhaps some short expressions of delight that you are in Paris.'

Three days later they arrive in Paris where everything immediately gets much harder.

CHAPTER 10

John Brisbane has just hurled a small plaster bust of King Charles across his room in the Paris embassy, scattering gilded splinters from the frame of the king's portrait and denting the canvas. It is no great loss, a degraded copy of a copy which could be any moustachioed man with a black wig. Brisbane is the hard-working assistant to Fat Harry Savile, as even Savile's friends call him, and this is not how he normally behaves.

Technically, Savile is not a real ambassador but merely the Envoy Extraordinary to the court of King Louis, a lesser title intended to reduce the embarrassment if he behaves badly, as he has so often done in the past. Fat Harry appears to be a fair-haired and jovial buffoon but he cultivates that reputation to blind people to his darker purposes. Those purposes may occasionally be for the benefit of his king, but they are more often designed to further his own ends – his endless need for money coupled with his endless need to couple.

Fat Harry, despite his unkempt appearance and substantial girth, sees himself as irresistible. So many women have heard about his reputation that some come to believe it. Those he considers truly worthy of his attentions are usually far up the ranks of the nobility and that is why King Charles keeps Savile in Paris, not London. Charles is at home with debauchery but he values discretion and Fat Harry is unfamiliar with the word.

Anne Hyde is noted for her beauty and for something that came over her in late April of 1659. It is unclear whether that was lust, ambition or both, but she changed the course of English history in late November when she was seven months pregnant. She did that by marrying the man responsible. He was the king's brother, James, Duke of York, and she quickly converted him to her own staunch Catholic faith. James went on to beget eight more children with Anne.

Inexplicably Harry Savile saw Duchess Anne as a suitable target for his advances. She found him briefly amusing while fully dressed but had no wish to see the rest of him. When she had to repel him, screaming, he was frogmarched to a cross-Channel packet and exile. Returning and staying at Althorp House, he tried his luck with the newly widowed wife of the Earl of Northumberland. She too screamed for help to find him standing by her bed, naked from the waist down. Challenged to a duel, he chose escape and the steward of the cross-Channel packet was soon plying him with consoling brandy once again.

Fat Harry pays little attention to his job in Paris. John Brisbane is the man who makes it all work, but the letter he has just read has horrified him, which is why he has just bust the king's portrait with the king's bust.

The letter comes from his imprisoned friend Samuel Pepys. They first met at a wedding where Pepys led Brisbane into the bride's chamber to kiss her rather too enthusiastically and was forcibly shown the door. The pair then staggered off to a high-stakes gambling den run by a royal porter in the depths of Whitehall Palace and that set the pattern for their friendship.

That shared history is now threatened. Pepys's letter tells a more sober Brisbane that brother Balty is on his way to knock on his door as a vital first step in the Scott investigation. Pepys does not know that Brisbane is convinced Balty is the worst sort of criminal pirate and wants nothing whatsoever to do with him, but now Balty is in Paris. After the slow barge journey, he is pleased to be met on the quay by Antoine Pelletier, one of Houblon's merchant friends – a man he already knows. Pelletier is a stocky, smiling man of forty who helped host that sad visit a decade earlier which resulted in the death of Balty's sister and Pepys's wife, Elizabeth.

'I have chosen a place for you close to the church with which you share your name, Monsieur St Michel. You will know it is close to our great cathedral and it has many fine places to get food and drink all around it. The proprietor will meet your every need.'

He ushers them into a fiacre and drops them off at the selected lodgings in the Rue de la Huchette, just inside the great scar where the city walls have very recently been demolished. Balty is even more pleased to meet their landlady. Madame Florentine greets them at the door, wearing a blue silk dress which caresses her figure and salutes her eyes. 'Sir,' she says, smiling, 'the gentleman from England. I am delighted. Your apartment is ready and I am entirely at your service. Do follow me and my houseman will bring your baggage. These are your sweet little servants?'

'Madame,' says Sam, 'while I may be only one quarter of your age, as I judge you to be perhaps exceeding forty, I may not accurately be described as sweet. I am Samuel St Michel, no servant but rather the attentive son of my father here.'

'And I am his daughter and pine for my beautiful, youthful mother who sighs at home in England, always in our thoughts and waiting anxiously for our speedy return so that she and my father here may continue their ecstatic marriage.'

Betty's smile dissolves Madame Florentine's own. She shows them their rooms. The bed chamber has dark tapestries, tall shuttered windows and five beds of different sizes. The day room has desks, tables, bookcases and an equally varied collection of chairs. Balty thanks her and she leaves as soon as she can. Balty looks at his children as a mouse looks at a pair of cats, but Sam smiles back as if nothing important has just happened, finishes off a note he is writing and begins to sort out his books. Betty is unpacking clothes.

'Sam,' says Balty. 'What are you doing?'

'Merely writing a description of the features of the fiacre that carried us here.'

'It's just a hackney cab.'

'Did you not look properly? It is ingenious, made to give the passengers a good view, with its small front wheels able to negotiate sharp street corners easily and I think . . .'

'Sam, there are more important things to consider. Children, you must be careful what you say in this city.'

'I am always careful, papa,' says Betty. 'Why in particular?'

'Protestants are not popular here. Louis would like them gone but the city would not function without them. They are allowed one church, outside the walls, and they are pelted with rotten vegetables when they leave. Foreign Protestants are even less welcome. We must be invisible.'

'My French is good enough, is it not? And Sam's certainly is.'

'Your clothes are wrong. We will get you new ones. For now you must stay here. I go to announce myself at the embassy. It will be a short and simple matter.'

Balty is right about the short part. He is ushered into John Brisbane's office by the ancient and very deaf doorman, who announces him as Mr Samuel Shell.

Brisbane reaches out a hand in surprise. 'Mr . . . Shell? Forgive me, I was not expecting your visit. How can I help you?'

'Do excuse me Mr Brisbane. I am St Michel not Samuel Shell. In full, Balthasar St Michel,' says Balty, doffing his hat and bowing. Brisbane stands rooted to the spot with his eyes widening, then reaches for a walking cane propped against his desk.

'You . . .' he says.

'You are expecting me, I hope. My esteemed brother has . . .'

'You . . . you come in to my office as if . . .' Balty begins to understand this is not going to plan. He had imagined Brisbane saying some gratifying words about his regard for Mr Pepys, then enquiring after Balty's well-being and the comfort of his journey, moving on to discuss arrangements to introduce him to a network of useful Paris contacts. That way, Balty thinks, they could be back home in a week or two with a job well done, but when he holds out a hand, Brisbane lashes at it with his cane. Balty snatches his hand out of the way.

'You are a scoundrel, a villain, a greedy misbegotten mountebank, not even truly a man at all but some vile chimera from the depths of hell,' declares Brisbane with the volume rising from word to word. 'What are you? What do you think you are doing here?'

'Mr Brisbane,' Balty says heavily as it all sinks in. 'I think, sir, that there may be a misunderstanding. In your earlier enquiries, you have mistaken me for someone else.'

'I know precisely who are you are.' Brisbane's voice approaches a screech. 'You are the criminal who purchased the *Hunter* ship with a royal warrant to seize the ships of our enemies and instead you seized an ENGLISH SHIP. You are a pirate, sir, and if you do not leave this room at once YOU WILL HAVE TO FIGHT ME.'

Balty returns to their rooms. Sam is concentrating on his notebook. Betty looks up at him, concerned. 'Did you see them, papa?'

'Yes.'

'Did it go well?'

'Not entirely.'

'Why so?'

'Mr Brisbane hit me several times around the head with a stick then announced to the entire embassy that he had finished with Paris and was determined to arrange his return to England at the earliest possible moment.'

'And . . . Mr Savile?'

'Mr Savile heard his screams and, though he did at least relieve Mr Brisbane of the stick, he too left the building rapidly, though in his case by way of the back cellar. He told me that if a Monsieur Carpentier was to stop me as I left, I was on no account to say that I had seen any sign of Mr Savile and, if I found the opportunity, to point out forcefully that Mr Savile barely knew Madame Carpentier.'

'When you said "not entirely" I took you to mean that there were some parts of your visit that did go better than others. What were they?'

Balty thinks. 'I did not meet Monsieur Carpentier,' he said.

'But what exactly were these terrible things that Mr Brisbane accused you of doing?' Sam asks.

'He said I am a pirate.'

'That would concern the ship called the *Hunter?*'

'What on this earth do you know about that?'

'Oh papa, you and mama have often discussed it.'

'Only when you were asleep.'

Sam shakes his head sadly. 'Loud sounds, though interrupted by strong well-fitting flooring, have no difficulty in finding their way through our house as good floorboards are among the many things it lacks. My godfather told me that his learned friend Mr Newton says sounds are like powerful waves hitting a wooden jetty and spraying through its gaps.'

'Papa,' adds Betty, putting her arms around him. 'We followed the matter of the *Hunter* quite closely from our beds when it was upsetting mama so greatly every evening.'

'It was all a mistake.'

'Which part of it was a mistake, papa?' Betty asks innocently.

'My brother Pepys and Sir Anthony would not have pilfered naval stores to equip the ship. Yes, the *Hunter* seized what appeared to be a London ship according to the registry, but it was crewed by the Dutch and carrying Dutch cargo. It was entirely the fault of the *Hunter*'s captain, who was a drunken rascal.'

'Make up your mind, pater,' says Sam. 'You cannot have it both ways.'

Balty twitches. He has come to recognize that there is trouble ahead when his son switches from 'papa' to 'pater'.

'Both ways?'

'You cannot say it was completely justified by circumstances then say it was the captain's fault. The two claims sit unhappily with each other.'

'You can,' says Betty, 'because the captain was driven by drink and mischief and neither knew nor cared about the true identity of the ship.'

'Sister, you . . .'

'Sam, another time. Papa, you came to France to deal with it at the time, did you not?'

'I did. Her captain took the prize into a French port. I had to persuade the French authorities that she had been rightfully captured.'

'How?'

Balty thinks of the bag of gold Pepys had given him to change the mind of those avaricious authorities. 'By the powerful force of my arguments,' he says.

'Yes, papa,' Sam says and one of his eyebrows seems to be very slightly raised.

Balty looks at him doubtfully. 'It leaves me in a very difficult position,' he says. 'The embassy is not likely to help us now. We will need a plan.'

A knock comes at the door. The deaf doorman from the embassy thrusts a package into Balty's hands. 'Came for you just after you left, sir,' he says. 'Followed you here. Couldn't catch you up. Not as quick as I used to be. Lost you where you turned the corner. Looked all around but you had disappeared.'

'A thousand thanks.'

'What was that, sir?'

'I said a thousand thanks.'

'There's no need for that sort of talk, sir, if you don't mind me saying so. I did my bit and I shouldn't be spoken to like that.'

'I didn't . . . I mean . . . oh look, here's something for your trouble.' Balty finds a coin in his pocket, presses it into the old soldier's hand and spots the gold glint of a Louis d'or too late. He has handed the man a month's pay. He tries to think of a plausible way to get it back, but Betty is now speaking to the man slowly and loudly.

'Then how did you discover which house we were in?' A puzzled frown is the only response. She repeats it louder still and the doorman's eyes light up.

'The feller told me.'

'What fellow?'

'The feller staring at the house.'

'Show me,' Betty leads the soldier to the window.

'Can't see him now,' says the old man. 'Funny sort of bugger, excusing my French. Kept asking me questions but he would mumble so.'

When he's gone, they open the fat packet. Inside is another one, sealed with four stamped discs of wax. It is marked 'Please pass to Mister Balthasar St Michel on arrival at the Embassy.' It contains all the statements made by Pepys's accusers to the House of Commons and they pore over the documents in horrified disbelief as they read a vivid portrait of an arch-traitor.

The lesser accusations start with the employment by Pepys of a tame Catholic priest, living in his household and masquerading as a musician, but the main thrust of the accusations depends on a single stark event, witnessed by a particular man at a particular time at a particular place. That man is Colonel John Scott. The date is four years earlier – an evening in late

August of 1675, and the place is here in the very centre of Paris.

Sam reads that part out loud. The place is a fine house on the narrow curve of the Rue Cléry. It has black and white marble floors and an inner courtyard with orange and myrtle trees, the home of Georges Pellissary, Treasurer of the French navy and, because they are both Protestants, Pellissary shares a great secret with Colonel Scott. He shows Scott papers just brought to France by Sir Anthony Deane, the evil Englishman now dining elsewhere in the house as they speak. Standing at the bar of the Commons, Scott describes those papers to the massed members of Parliament staring at him. Fourteen sheets of close handwriting detail the English navy's readiness for battle and the armament of its ships, focusing on the poor morale of unpaid crews and the ways they might be subverted. Five large maps detail the approaches to England's major naval bases.

Sam looks up. 'Oh, this is not good.' He reads on and the words carry them into that packed Commons chamber, stuffed full of enthralled Whigs and horrified Royalists, including Samuel Pepys himself. Colonel Scott declares that the documents include a personal letter from Pepys to the French leaders commending Deane as a trusted friend who can explain all. Scott says he recognizes Mr Pepys's florid signature so he knows the documents are real.

Pellissary returns to his dinner party. Scott is dining alone in a room with a high window open into the garden when he hears English voices. The traitor Deane is right under his window, explaining to someone unseen that Pepys would not have accepted King Louis's forty thousand pounds 'had it not been that he agreed with the greater end'.

'Sam, remind me,' says Balty. 'You noted down all that Captain Clifton told us.'

Sam studies his notebook. 'Sir Anthony Deane delivered the two yachts to Versailles in August four years back,' he says. 'Oh dear me, papa, it seems you made the arrangements.'

'That part is true,' says Balty. 'Deane came here with your godfather's great friend Mr Hewer. It was hard. The yachts were more like flat-bottomed barges because Versailles' lake is shallow. They pulled them miles overland with huge teams of horses.'

Sam looks back to his notes. 'Captain Clifton agrees that they were entertained by the French navy treasurer *at his home* in Paris. What is that last document? You haven't broken the seal.'

The letter from Pepys is headed 'My jail cell' in stark letters. It commends Balty to his worthy friend Mr Brisbane at the Paris embassy. It tells him to only take actions approved by Brisbane and not to draw attention to himself.

'A little too late. The only action I could take to earn Mr Brisbane's approval would be to run myself through with my own sword,' says Balty. 'What in heaven do we do now?'

Sam is still looking back through his notes. 'Have you met any Benedictine monks in this city?' he asks.

'No. Why?'

'Captain Clifton said Scott somehow defrauded them in Paris. I think you may have been looking out of the window at the time, papa.'

'No, I wasn't. I don't know any monks.'

'We could visit the house where this conversation is said to have happened,' suggests Betty, 'perhaps to see if it fits the description?'

An excursion sounds slightly better than doing nothing. It might be stretched to three paragraphs in the letter his brother will expect Balty to write today. Twenty-five minutes takes them across the narrow Pont St Michel which supports two rows of tall houses, testing the strength of the bridge's high wooden arches and blocking any view of the Seine running beneath them. They pass the clattering shops of the tinsmiths and finally reach the narrow Rue Cléry, lined by the tall, hewn-stone houses of the rich, their lower windows protected by iron grilles. A man and a woman come out of a door to their right and the man turns to lock it behind him.

'Excuse me, sir,' says Balty. 'I am looking for Monsieur Georges Pellissary. I believe he lives somewhere nearby?'

The couple are of middle age with tanned skin and the man replies in a pronounced Gascon accent. 'I am afraid he is nowhere nearby.'

'You are sure?'

'I regret to say I am quite sure because the dear man went to his maker perhaps two years ago.'

'Oh.' Balty searches for a plausible reason to ask where his house had been and Betty beats him to it.

'Sir, I so want to find his home. They say it has fine myrtle trees in its courtyard and I long to see them. Myrtle trees are a great passion of mine.'

The woman smiles at her. 'An unusual passion. His widow still lives there. It is further down on the left side, just before the Rue des Poissoniers, the house with the light blue door. I do hope she lets you inspect her trees.' She looks Betty up and down. 'You are wearing strange clothes. I have not seen the like of them before.'

'They were made far away, madame,' says Balty.

'Papa is going to get me new ones,' Betty babbles. 'He knows I like the Parisian style better, don't you, papa?'

The house with the light blue door has a blank frontage with a row of shuttered windows at street level hiding any courtyard beyond. Loitering would make them conspicuous, so they turn and walk slowly back.

'Let's go a different way,' says Betty. 'The long bridge with no houses on it. I want to look at the river.'

CHAPTER 11

The great Pont Neuf vaults the Seine in two leaps, touching down on the pointed end of the Île de la Cité on its way across. A gusting wind carries the smell of manure from the west and the bustling crowd clutch hats and wigs to their heads. A procession of lawyers approaches, their gowns held high by pageboys, half-running on shorter legs. More boys follow, pushing hand carts laden with the lawyers' bundled papers. A train of black-robed monks ahead of them swerves to avoid the legal phalanx and Balty, Betty and Sam catch up with them, following in their vacuum as the monks divide more respectful people in the oncoming crowds.

'Papa, might these be Benedictines?' says Sam.

'They might very well be,' says Balty, who is hazy on the dress differences of the various orders and even uncertain of the distinction between monks and friars. 'The St Germain-des-Prés abbey is up ahead and that belongs to the Benedictines. They're a sort of Jesuit.'

'Shall we follow them? We could ask if they know of Colonel Scott?'

'Sam, don't be absurd. You want me to ask men we have

never met before, religious men who have little association
with the world and who may or may not even be Benedictines,
whether they have heard of an Englishman called Colonel
Scott, a man who we only suppose they might have had some
difficult contact with because ... Oh, do excuse me, sir.' He
has switched into French for these last four words as the monk
in the hind row of the column has stopped dead in his tracks
and swung round, causing them to collide. The monk is tall
and very well-padded, so Balty rebounds without moving him
an inch.

'Colonel *John* Scott?' says the monk in strongly accented
Yorkshire English. 'Of course we knew him and I bloody well
hope you're going to tell me the bastard's dead.'

Later, sitting in the otherwise empty abbey refectory, drinking an infusion that both children find challenging, the monk
apologizes. 'I'm devout enough in French most days,' he says.
'That's the freshly whitewashed Brother Ash. It's only when I
speak English again that the profanity comes tied to it. Can't
help it. English is who I was, a proper sinner. I'm a little bit
closer to a saint in French.'

He grins and Betty smiles back at him. 'How long have you
spoken French?'

'Four years solid, little miss. Bits and pieces back in my other
life.'

'What was that?'

'I were a seaman in King Charles's navy. Sailmaker, gunner
and a good foretop man with a musket. Didn't do me much
good. Never elevated, except up the mast.' He bellows with
laughter then stops himself, puts a hand over his mouth and
winks.

Betty nods sagely as if that was what she suspected.

'I could see the way the wind was blowing,' says Brother Ash. 'Me, wrong-side-of-the-sheets but proud to be fathered by a Catholic Scrope from Bolton Castle even if his bible looked the other way while he was doing the fathering. We're only human, at least I used to be. My side of the family line dribbled itself away and it is too late for me to revive it, being as how I'm what I am now and not supposed to do any reviving.'

'You left the navy?' says Balty.

The monk spreads his arms and looks down at his robes. 'You're a very observant fellow,' he says. 'I jumped ship in '74 when France looked a safer place for the likes of me, but I'm no sort of Jesuit as I heard you say back there. Oh no. Those Jesuits go off and do their complicated interferences, directed by the pope himself, they say. Us, we help out where we can with the folk around us.'

'And you really did know this man we seek?'

'The swaggering colonel? Oh I knew John Scott all right. He made your mistake, thought we were entirely of the Jesuitical persuasion. That's why he came knocking on our door hoping to brew up a good conspiracy with fanatics. Course, he don't speak proper French. Pretended he did, but the abbot needed me to turn his gabble into sense. Now, before I say more, you be straight with me. Exactly what is your interest in the man?'

Keep the mission entirely hidden, thinks Balty. Draw no attention to yourself. His brain races in a circle but Sam steps in. 'My dear godfather has been wrongly accused by this man and we want to help him live. My sister and I asked our father to assist us.'

'Bless you, young man,' says Brother Ash. 'I hear the truth

in your voice and I will tell you what I know and in case I get a bit too divine at the expense of honest loathing, I will continue to speak in my native tongue so as to be the sailor not the monk. Please ignore any unintended profanity. It is merely punctuation.'

'Thank you.'

'I were still what they call a candidate, not even a novice, when Scott popped up here. Thought they might turf me out on the street any moment, so it was my chance to impress the abbot. I took the colonel to one side for a chat but I could soon smell him.'

'How so?'

'His voice and his eyes. Two different men. He reeked of duplicity, said he had a scheme to help the true religion but I smelled his god was gold. I had to tell it all to the abbot in French and I wanted to warn him but I couldn't be sure this colonel didn't speak the lingo a bit better than he were making out. He were listening hard to every word. You know how some folk like to keep an advantage up their sleeve. Sometimes it's sharp steel, other times it's knowledge.'

Sam waits with his notebook open. 'Would you tell us exactly what happened?' he says quietly.

'It ain't my place to say anything bad about our abbot but . . . he is impressed by more worldly men. A bit of envy you might think. Anyway, through me, Scott told the abbot there were a powerful plan afoot to turn England back into a proper Catholic nation and he was here to help make that happen, assisting King Louis, being a good Catholic himself. I knew that was bollocks, excuse my English. He weren't no Catholic. He didn't have a clue.'

'Where did gold come into it?' Betty said.

'He said all he needed was the ready money to complete his great work. When he delivered his map to the minister, the navy would sweep into English harbours just like the Dutch did in '67 and that would be the end of Protestant blasphemy.'

'The navy minister?' Balty asks.

'That's the man. The Marquis de Whotsit. The crazy one.'

'Crazy?'

'Too much religion gives you a fit of the vapours like too much Jamaica rum. The marquis spends his life on his knees lamenting the sins of the world. Mebbe not the best way to manage your ships. Can I top up your mugs? Good stuff, this tisane. It's usually a bit watery for my taste but you can chew on this one. I like the lumps. No? Suit yourselves. Anyways, Colonel Scott tells my abbot he's making better charts so the French navy can free the English from their servitude. He says he's been doing it all himself but now he needs skilled men to finish it and if the abbot would lend the money he will pay back double – well not exactly, he had some fancy phrase about straddling the financial gap. I turn that into "lend the money" when I say it to the abbot and the colonel gives me a hard look, making me think again that he might know a bit more French than he let on.'

'The abbot believed him?'

'Led by the nose. Also by the fancy map Scott brought along. Biggest I ever saw. Three yards long, on two shiny rollers with a blue silk fringe. The south coast of England, and Portsmouth dead centre with every last detail. The castles, the gun batteries and the regular anchorages of the great ships with their names and the numbers of their cannon. It showed the clever ways into those anchorages and the dangers along the way. That made a grand sight but I knew it for a load of old shite, begging your pardon.'

'How?'

'I were a sailor, weren't I? Seen a lifetime's maps and charts. I knew it for a fancy copy of what they call the Dutchman's map except drawn out thrice the size, which is an easy trick if you use a grid.'

'Just a copy? Nothing more?'

'Ha! The Dutchman's map is for hanging on a wall, not for fighting battles. Scott's was worse. He inked in fortresses, copied castles he had seen maybe? There was a neat little sketch of Windsor, stuck on a barren lump of land at Hayling where there is nothing in real life but crows and cow shit. The cannon batteries just west of there? Not a single sign of them, only a tiny sketch of trees and a church. I could go on . . . but you follow my drift.'

Betty frowns. 'So . . . perhaps Scott was working for England to mislead them after all?'

'Naah. I heard the stories. He done the same thing between the Hollanders and the French. Got a lot of men killed. He told the abbot he had a dozen other maps nearly ready but the king wouldn't look at 'em if they wasn't perfect so he needed money.'

'The abbot believed the king would put decoration before information?'

'Well, he wasn't wrong there. Have you seen the piss-pots they're making for Versailles? They're so fancy you would rather burst.'

Sam holds up his hand. 'Do you remember what these other maps depicted?'

'London river from Gravesend all the way to the Galloper. The Island of Wight. The Medway from the Rochester bridge past Chatham and he must have seen that with his own eyes because he had the defences sketched in and only half wrong. One more. What was it now?'

'Was it Plymouth perhaps?' said Balty with sudden excitement, 'A map of the Sound and the harbour with the island and all the new defences?'

'Bless my soul. It was indeed, sir. How did you guess that?'

'These are the self-same maps that Colonel Scott claims were sent by . . .'

'Pater!' Sam and Betty say it together.

'By . . . ?' says Brother Ash. 'By who . . . ? By what?'

'By messenger,' says Betty firmly. 'Now please tell us the abbot didn't give this colonel his money.'

'Oh but he did. A heap of gold. I got him to ask Scott for a guarantee and that came the next day, signed by Jean-Baptiste Colbert no less.'

Balty turns to the children. 'The king's chief minister. The second most powerful man in all of France.'

'Papa,' says Sam, 'to be precise, he is King Louis's chief *counsellor* and whether he comes second or third in the French hierarchy is open to question, according to my godfather who . . .'

'Sam!' says Betty. 'We don't want to bore our new friend.' She smiles at the monk. 'What happened next, sir? Did the poor abbot get his money back?'

'The abbot went to Colbert who said the signature on the guarantee was as like to his own as a cowshed is to Notre-Dame Cathedral.'

'The money was lost?'

'It was.'

'Did the abbot pursue Scott?'

'The abbot stopped me taking the physical actions I proposed as prohibited by most of the ten commandments, but he had to blame someone, so he made me serve three extra months as a candidate before he would make me a novice.'

Balty considers. 'Would you swear to this story before a public notary if asked?'

'No, sir. I plan to stay here and the abbot keeps a close eye on me.'

'You like your life here?' says Betty. 'It suits you?'

'It's easier than a frigate. I get fresh food and a mattress.' He turns and points upwards. 'There's sunlight through stained glass and clever fingers on the keys of a fine organ. I've been in too many places where people are at each others' throats. Tribes, forgetting that we're all the same when it comes to food, drink and a place to sleep, but it's the people at the top who split the people at the bottom. We're saved much of that, tucked away. Sod them. How's your Latin, girl?'

'Sam's is better.'

Brother Ash looks at Sam. '*Ubi deus, ibi pax*? You know what that means?'

Sam doesn't have to think. 'St Francis. Where there is God, there is peace.'

The monk looks around the refectory to make sure no one is tucked away in the shadows. 'That's what we're told. Those Franciscans are good enough folk – out there doing their best for the sick and the starving. Bit simple though. Add in one more religion and what do you get? *Ubi dei, ibi* whatever . . .

Where there are Gods, there is war. Us Catholics and you Protestants, same god more or less, and we fight each other to the death. Peace? Sod that. Up against power, profit and politics, peace don't stand a chance.'

Back in their rooms, Balty says, 'I wish we could persuade him to testify.'

'Papa,' says Sam, 'even if we could, my godfather's accusers will say it is another sure sign of the Catholic conspiracy.'

Balty frowns. 'So we really have no choice. We must find Protestant witnesses in this Catholic city?'

CHAPTER 12

A Protestant comes to see them one hour later. Antoine Pelletier, who met them from the barge on arrival, introduces François Trenchepain, a Catholic, the other half of Houblon's team of friendly local merchants. Trenchepain is a lot less friendly than Pelletier.

Balty struggles with his letter to Pepys. He is trying to hint at a clever plan to inspect the interior of the Rue Cléry house. He has described the meeting with Brother Ash as another ingenious strategy, covering himself against Pepys's certain dismissal of Catholic testimony by making that point himself. He leaves wide gaps as instructed and stares at them, wondering what secret naval information might possibly be found to fill them. Should he invent overheard conversations about mass movements of invasion barges? He suspects he will be found out, not to mention letting England down. To his surprise, he discovers a passionate desire to do this properly and prove he can be trusted with a desperate mission. Why would anyone send such a man to his death in Tangier? Betty appears deep in thought and Sam has spent the entire hour staring out of the window. They make Balty nervous and he is glad to be interrupted.

Pelletier begins with polite enquiries as to their state of health and the suitability of their rooms. Trenchepain puts a heavy cloth bag on the table. 'Fifty livres, sir,' he says, 'and sign this receipt. I am anticipating accounts which demonstrate when and why you require more. I have prepared a sheet to show you the correct form.'

Balty tries to slip it under his own stack of paper but Betty intercepts it.

'How else may we help you today?' Pelletier says.

'Clothing for these two comes first,' Balty says. 'My clothes come from Paris and attract no attention. Theirs were made by the widow of a tavern keeper in Kent and they might as well be dressed as scarlet harlequins. People stare.'

'My tailor is in the Rue Dauphin,' Pelletier suggests. 'His clothes are cut well from fine fabric.'

'And very costly,' says Trenchepain quickly. 'There is a clothes market, La Fripperie, in the stone gallery near Les Halles. That way, you will have your clothes immediately.'

'Old clothes?' Pelletier is indignant. 'He does not want cast-offs.'

'They are mended with such skill that you would not notice.'

'Gentlemen, we can wait three days for the tailor. We will make sure we are not noticed,' says Balty.

'Pater,' says Sam, turning from the window, 'we need those clothes now. We have already *been* noticed.'

'How do you know?'

'Because I watched the arrival of these gentlemen and I saw a man follow them here. He waited at the corner until they came inside and now he lurks in the wine shop doorway.'

That brings them all to their feet, but Sam stops them

heading for the window with a raised hand. 'Don't let him see we are on to him. Better he does not know that I know. We must buy older clothes and I have a plan.'

Minutes later, Trenchepain and Sam turn left outside the house, walking slowly and looking straight ahead. The other three leave the house seconds later and turn right. Trenchepain hails a fiacre and they pick up the others two streets away. Looking back, Sam is reassured they have not been followed. At the far side of the Pont Neuf, a carriage sits across their path with a shattered wheel and two men are fighting. They take a narrow side street and pedestrians press back against the walls to get out of their way, excepting an athletic lad in blue and white uniform. He races towards them, hurdling over the small front wheels and jinking around the back wheels without breaking stride. He wears a sailor's hat and has a leather shoulder bag slung round his neck.

'What on earth is he doing?' asks Betty.

'The boy? A messenger for the Navy Ministry,' says Pelletier. 'They stop for no one. The boys get paid for their speed.'

'Where is he going?'

'To the old navy offices, I expect. Despatch riders take important papers to Versailles at full gallop.'

'So where is he coming from?' asks Sam.

'Offices here and there across town. They have opened a new one in the Louvre fortress. I see the boys running past my house.'

Children's clothes stalls are at the far end of the Fripperie market. The merchants are sharp of eye and tongue – at least as interested in buying Betty and Sam's clothes as in selling replacements. Betty finds a fancy outfit which fits her well and is perhaps only a year behind the fashion. Trenchepain unearths something suitable for Sam. Splits in the breeches had been repaired with tiny stitching. Then Betty picks up a well-worn sailor suit and holds it against Sam.

Trenchepain shakes his head. 'That is silly clothing for some spoilt child.'

'Good,' says Betty politely. 'We need to buy it.'

Trenchepain looks to Balty for fatherly approval. Balty shrugs. 'Just as she says.'

The twins walk along the other stalls, finding a leather shoulder bag and a fancy hat with coloured ribbons. Trenchepain takes Balty on one side. 'Those are needless purchases,' he says. 'You should resist childish whims.'

'Nothing my children do is childish.'

'Then what is their purpose?'

'They will tell me when they are ready.'

The twins are talking to Pelletier when they catch up. Pelletier is smiling. 'I have agreed to show you some of the sights if you don't mind a longer walk back.'

Balty shrugs. 'It is a fine afternoon.'

They zigzag through the streets. Pelletier and the twins are talking intently in front and Balty is left with Trenchepain, whose prickly reserve melts just a little at the mention of Pepys's great ally, Mr Houblon. 'A fine man,' he says, 'a merchant known across this country and far beyond for his utter trustworthiness.'

'He is,' says Balty, 'and the rest of his family are the same.'

'You know them all?'

'Indeed. Bankers and merchants. Huguenots, like you and me.'

Trenchepain actually smiles for a fraction of a moment.

They say their goodbyes before they get back to the house and approach it from the opposite end of the street to the wine shop where the watcher may still lurk.

On the way up, Betty knocks on the landlady's door and borrows a needle, thread and a pair of scissors. In the room, she explains their intention as Sam starts to cut the ribbons from the fancy hat.

'The messengers wait for instructions at a bench outside the old Navy Ministry. They are boys between 12 and 15 years old and they run messages between a dozen other offices in the city. They have much more work recently and the Versailles offices are not yet ready for all the navy staff.'

Balty thinks. 'More work? Why?'

Sam looks up. 'Because Mr Coventry and Captain Clifton are right, papa. There is something in the wind.'

'How do you know all this?'

'We questioned Monsieur Pelletier on the way back while you were talking to Monsieur Trenchepain. We asked to see the boys who wear the uniform. He humoured our childish enthusiasm.'

'What is all this about?'

The twins sigh in unison. 'You tell him, Sam,' says Betty.

'Papa, do you know what you will write in the first invisible message?'

'No . . . not yet. Something will come.'

'Only if we make it come. Did you notice the messengers waiting when we went past the old Navy Ministry?'

'Navy Ministry?'

'Monsieur Pelletier says the messengers prefer it. They have their favourite places. They don't like the new office in the Louvre fortress because there is no shelter from the wind and rain and they are not allowed to sit on the ground. It was most interesting.'

'You mean . . .'

'. . . that I can wait at the Louvre fortress and bring packets I am given back here for our inspection before taking them to their destination.'

'Oh, that does sound dangerous.'

'I can run fast.'

'You will get lost.'

'Papa, did you not notice that Monsieur Pelletier showed me the way as we came back?'

'You told him your plan?'

Betty looks up from her inspection of the sailor uniform. 'Certainly not. He is a patriot in his own way so we should not involve him too deeply, but we do have a plan. We will tell you tomorrow when we're ready.'

Next morning, they walk to David Chaliou's chocolate shop, for something to break their fast, eating Dutch buns with hot chocolate as they sit looking out at the crossroads. The road surface is covered in a mess of litter and remains of food, picked at by pigeons.

'I guess yesterday was a wheel day,' says Balty and regrets his words immediately.

Betty looks at him. 'What's that?'

Balty picks up another bun. 'These are good. Do you like them?'

Sam nudges Betty and she doesn't ask again. He read some books in his godfather's library that he was not meant to read.

He knows what it means to be broken on the wheel but wishes he did not. As they walk out of the shop, he sees the platform at one corner of the crossroads, not yet washed clean, and feels the hot ghosts of violence all around him, dragging him too quickly into the sort of adulthood that hurts. He will search for a softer explanation when his sister asks again, as she will.

Back at the Rue de la Huchette, Sam sews blue ribbons on to the sailor jacket while Betty alters the white trousers. 'That is the best I can do,' she says in the end. 'It is close to what we saw yesterday.' She knows she has told her father a small lie for his peace of mind. The ribbons match but the shape of the jacket is entirely wrong and they have no hat. Sam insists he can run fast enough if he is caught out.

'Time to try it out,' he says. 'Will you go out to buy something, papa?'

'Why? What do we need?'

'Anything that takes you two or three streets away that way,' he points, 'so that you get followed and we go the other way.'

From the window, they can see no obvious watcher, but when Balty appears in the street, a man walking past turns around and walks after him, keeping his distance. 'I'm going now,' says Sam. 'I'm coming too,' says Betty. They head across the Seine, Betty hanging back behind her brother.

The old Louvre fortress stands in its own grounds, part of it repaired, the rest more ruined than not. A boy is fidgeting near the door – a street urchin like so many others in the city in frayed and faded clothes. He stares at Sam.

'Who are you?' he demands. 'You're no messenger, chum, that's clear enough.'

Sam looks away towards where Betty is inspecting a far wall.

'I'll tell on you,' says the urchin. 'You're not going to mess me around. Sod off somewhere else.'

'Why would I do that?'

'Because I got here first and they give me the jobs when there's no proper messenger, don't they? I gets it there quick enough and they pay me for it when I hand it over. Not what a proper messenger gets but it helps me stay fed. So chum, I don't know what your game might be but it ain't honest. You better tell me quick or I will set up such a hullabaloo.'

'Why do you think I'm not a messenger?'

'You can't be that dumb.' The boy walks round him but now he's showing unexpected signs of smiling. 'Come off it. That bag. Where's the tag?'

'Tag?'

'Clipped on here,' he prods the corner of the bag. 'Case it gets lost – tells people where to take it. Your tunic – just plain wrong. No hat, obviously. But then the big one, you haven't got no number. Should be on your sleeve. Everyone knows that. Can't miss it. Yes? They note it down every time they hand over a message and all over again when it's delivered. Not me obviously, but they know me. You're a puzzle. You don't fool me and you won't fool them – not for long. So, before I hand you in, what's your game exactly?'

Betty assesses the problem and runs up to join them. 'Hello,' she says.

Sam says, 'Hello, my sister. That's a surprise. Meet my new friend. He's worried that they haven't given me a hat yet.'

'Well, you've only just got started and they ran short. They did tell you to go back when you had time.' She turns to the urchin. 'You look hungry.'

'Course I am.'

She pulls out coins. 'Go and get some food,' she says. 'We'll be gone by the time you come back.'

The boy takes them and smiles a gap-toothed smile. 'Beats running for the money,' he says. 'Don't know what you're up to, but good luck with it. Watch out, these guys are bastards. I'm Hubert, what's your names?'

'Sam.'

'Strange name, strange boy. You?'

'Elisabeth,' she says it the French way. Hubert walks off clutching the coins and looking back at them every few steps. Betty goes back to the gate and Sam settles in to wait.

The door opens a long time later as he is kicking pebbles aimlessly along the driveway with his back to it.

'You!' The summoner wears a long black cloak and holds out a packet wrapped in canvas. His fingers are inky. 'To the Versailles post. Where's your hat?'

'Blew off my head in the wind, sir,' says Sam. 'Snatched up by a dirty little boy. Couldn't catch him, sir.'

'Don't you come back here without one.'

Sam takes the package and races away. He hears a shout behind him. 'Oy, what's your number?' but he ignores it and sprints even faster.

In the cover of a half-built house three streets away, he takes his own jacket out of the bag and tucks the packet and the tunic away in its place. Betty catches up with him and they keep a keen eye out as they get near their lodgings, walking further along the street as a man approaches, then doubling back when the coast seems clear.

They shrug off Balty's anxious questions. 'It was simple enough,' Sam says. 'Shall we see if it was worth it?'

Betty picks undone the knots in the twine binding. The packet contains a long list of stores, marked as payment received. There is a summary of defective cannon returned to the armoury from four frigates. One document lights up Balty's eyes – an order for the commander at Brest to transfer thirty-five horse transport barges to Saint-Valery, in the Bay of the Somme, to arrive within three weeks of the date of the order. Le Crotoy is the alternative destination should the wind favour it.

'I know it,' he says. 'Between Dieppe and Boulogne. St Valery looks out across the entrance to the river. Le Crotoy is on the other side of the bay, facing south. Why there?'

'It has served them before,' Sam's voice conveys a hint of impatience. 'Papa, do you not know your history? A fleet once gathered there before a great victory.'

'Really? When?'

'Six centuries ago. William of Normandy assembled his fleet there to invade England.'

'Sam, you have had the benefit of an education. I only had my father.' The mercurial Alexandre St Michel's understanding of the world was an uncertain mixture of fact and fable, leavened by wild grabs at the emerging world of science.

His daughter smiles. 'Just think, papa. Already you have words to fill the gaps between the lines.'

Sam crosses to the window, looks down and is surprised to see a ragged boy staring up at him. 'Papa', he says. 'There is a boy down there. We need to bring him up here to talk. He is not very clean.'

Going quietly down the creaking stairs to avoid attracting Madame Florentine, he opens the door and gestures Hubert inside. He puts a finger to his lips and they tiptoe back up. Hubert flinches when he sees Balty. They seat him on a hard chair to preserve the upholstery of the others.

'Papa, we met Hubert at the Louvre fortress, but how did you follow us here?' he asks, looking at the boy. 'We did not see you.'

'Of course not. I know the tricks.'

Balty gives him a hard look. 'Tricks?'

'It is not an easy life, sir. My mother expired. My father vanished one night, pouf, just like that. Dragged down to hell. Left his crucifix behind. Just me since then.'

'So . . . why do you follow people?'

Hubert inspects the surface of the table. 'There is a man who shelters the wild boys. I sleep there. He sometimes gives us food but . . . he makes us find out things.'

'What sort of things?'

'Where the rich folk live and how they lock their doors.'

'I don't look rich,' says Sam.

'No, just strange. I followed you for my own reasons, not for Monsieur Bollard.'

Betty speaks gently. 'What reasons?'

'Only to know more so I could stop wondering. Like I said. The clothes – halfway right, halfway wrong. The money you gave me to go away, for which I thank you.' He turns his gaze back to Balty. 'I told them. I carry the packets when there's no proper messenger there. They toss me a coin or two.'

'That's how you survive?'

'I have a place where I hide the money. I want to be a proper messenger but you have to pay for that. If I save enough I will sleep somewhere else. I would like that.'

'Pay who?' Sam says, 'The navy?'

'No, no. You buy the job from another messenger when he gets too old or too sick or from his family if he gets too dead, then you take his number and his clothes. I will earn much more by running the packets with a uniform. I know a boy who will have to stop soon, Gerard from the Faubourg St Jacques. He has the coughing sickness but he wants more money than I have.'

'Can we trust you?' says Balty.

Hubert frowns. 'No, of course not. You don't know me.'

Betty smiles. 'But if we did?'

'Even then I would say trust me to do what? Trust me to kill my cat if you asked me? No.'

'You have a cat?'

'The cat has me. She shares my mattress when I sleep, day or night.'

'My father means can we trust you if we give you the money to become a messenger.'

'Why would you do that?'

'To help you?'

'If you say that, I know *I* can't trust *you*. People always wants something back. All else is lies.'

Balty can no longer keep silent. 'Hubert, you are a creature of the streets and you do whatever you need to stay alive, yes?'

'Otherwise I would be dead.'

'If we give you money, you might disappear?'

Hubert considers. 'You could take my cat as hostage,' he says. 'But she would scratch your eyes out.' He stares at each of them in turn and they each try to hold that steady gaze. 'This is the wrong way round. Tell me what you want. I might choose not to do it.'

With those words, they find themselves facing a real person, not just another rascal from a stinking street tribe but a boy whose eyes are bright with stripped-down honesty.

Betty answers. 'You might think what we ask goes against the good of France, though that is not our purpose.'

'France?' Hubert shrugs. 'I am a citizen of the streets, not of France. King Louis is moving far away because he does not care to see the likes of me. I care exactly as much for him as he cares for me, so . . . what is this about?'

Betty speaks simply. 'We need to save the life of one of our family and to be quick about it. This will help us do that.' She sees Hubert's puzzlement. 'Yes, it does sound strange but . . . that is all the truth I can tell you.'

Hubert stares into her eyes and eventually nods. 'I see you believe what you say.'

Sam thinks. 'Do they check the exact times you pick up packets and the times you deliver them?'

'No, course not. We all run like the devil's after us. That way we do more and we get paid more. Simple.'

'Then . . . you could run past here, show us the papers, then run on to deliver them?'

Hubert's brow furrows. 'Here? That would look crazy. This isn't on the way between any of the offices. No messenger runs a step further than they have to.' He closes his eyes tight and they wait, then he reopens them and smiles. 'Messengers don't come over the Pont Neuf and along the quay,' he said. 'but I *could* cross by Pont St Michel, then nip round the back and come past here as if I was heading for the old queen's hospital. That would work.'

'How will we know to be here for you?'

'The Louvre messages go out around midday and then again before the Vespers bell.'

'We can make sure one of us is always here.'

'They're not all easy to open. Some have wax seals.'

'I know how to deal with those,' says Balty.

'But you can't just keep coming to the door,' Sam says, 'People will notice.'

'Oh ha ha. They will not. I know all these streets from a burglarizing point of view. There's an alley behind this place that gets me into the yard and you have a back door. I will run past the front so you see me and go round that way. You will come very quietly down and let me in the first time. Then I'll rig a little tricky thing to open the door from outside when I need to.'

'Will that work?'

'Yes. I'm very used to making sure no one is watching.'

Balty nods. 'All right. Let us visit your sick friend and turn you into a true messenger.'

On the way, Hubert runs the packet of documents to the old ministry building. Balty looks after him. 'He thinks. He has a plan.'

'That is why he is still alive,' says Betty. 'He is a very direct boy. Nice,' She sounds unhappy. 'Maybe they all are, all the street kids.'

Hubert comes back jingling coins in his hand. He already seems part of the team.

Trenchepain delivered fresh funds and some go to securing the messenger post. Gerard's uniform fits Hubert well enough. He likes his number, 156, and gives Sam a spare cap that comes with it. Balty wonders how he will list all this in Trenchepain's accounts and that gets harder when they realize Hubert also needs somewhere new to sleep as he can't go back to Bollard. A vague tale from Balty about a friend's son needing lodgings, helped by a little restrained flirting, reveals that Madame Florentine has an old farm bothy where the cows' track crosses the Rue du Bac. She takes two months' rent in advance.

Balty struggles to write between the lines of their letters. He can't stop to think halfway through a sentence as he can't see where to start again or remember exactly what he has written. The twins get him to write it on a different sheet with ordinary ink so Sam can transcribe it in the lemon juice mixture, then Betty burns the original just in case. They add carefully worded lines asking Coventry for extra funds, then Sam takes up the normal pen and writes his own letter to his godfather as instructed by Clifton. He thinks about the man who appeared to have been watching the house, so decides his words must start in French then switch to Latin.

He begins: '*Monseigneur mon très cher oncle, Si je suis coupable comme je n'en doute point d'avoir tant vielly sans me donner l'honneur de vous écrire, je vous supplie de me pardonner . . .*' and carries on in that vein before switching to Latin, '*Quando veni ex Anglia in Galliam transivi per multas urbes quas miratus sum et commoratus sum lutetium in urbe pulcherrima . . .*' He signs it off with a flourish after throwing in a reference to his new dancing skills to show any illicit readers that he is a typical 10-year-old.

CHAPTER 13

Hubert comes twice a day, avoiding ears and eyes, slipping through gaps that aren't there. They give him food and drink and work fast, freeing wax seals with a hot blade, reading the documents, then heating the blade again to fix the seal back in place. Hubert gains weight and strength but all they harvest from his efforts is victualling bills, repair lists and crewing rosters.

Balty has seen such papers every day for years, so he adds his interpretation of frigates being moved from Brest to Dieppe and underlines commands to speed the launch of a new ship to show he is doing his best.

They enquire about that large blue-fringed map described by Brother Ash, hoping to prove that Scott was hawking the very maps around Paris that he accuses Pepys of selling. They visit the taille-douce shops displaying copper-plate prints and see no sign of anything in vast and glorious colour. They question the master engravers, Israel, Chaveau, Sylvestre, but none respond to mention of an English colonel. These are gloomy men, any humour eaten away by acid engraving fumes. Only plump Monsieur Morin nods. He has seen such a map.

'I forget the exact details, monsieur.'

'We believe this was a scaled-up copy of another map,' says Balty.

'Ah, to do that, a man needs good tools – compasses, set-squares, scale grids. You might ask the instrument makers. I don't suppose you speak English? The best of them is an Englishman but it is an ugly tongue.'

'I speak a few words.'

'His name is hard to spell and harder to say. I will write it down.'

Balty reads it out, 'Michael Butterfield.'

'You say it just as he does.'

The window of Butterfield's shop in the Faubourg St Germain displays a gleaming brass instrument on black velvet, a complex device with precision quadrants and intricate dials. Sam studies it. Inside, an old man bends over a workbench where minute components laid out in a row are lit by reflected sunlight.

'*Attendez*,' he commands and then in English, 'don't even breathe.' He tweezers the pivot of one tiny lever into the hole in another, puts them down and pushes a pair of lenses up his forehead. '*Qu'est ce que vous voulez?*'

'May we breathe now?' says Balty.

'Ah, now that's a relief,' says Butterfield. 'More new arrivals? Running from the London mobs?'

'We're not running anywhere. We're looking for some maps. They say you're the man to talk to.'

'Maps? If you think that is a map in my window then you need stronger lenses like mine.'

Sam walks to the window and stares at the the instrument on

display. 'Don't touch that please, young man,' says Butterfield, but he says it gently.

'I see you do fine work here, sir,' says Balty. 'Did you sell instruments to an Englishman to scale up a map?'

Butterfield's face closes. 'I have not made any such sale this year.'

'This was four years ago and I speak of Colonel Scott.'

'Scott never bought anything from me, or rather he never paid for what he took. Sir, you are treading into soft ground. I make instruments for the king's court and I have no wish to lose his favour.'

'I am nothing to do with King Louis,' said Balty.

'I don't much care. Your question is fraught with danger. Please leave my shop.'

Betty tries a smile. 'Can you direct us to someone else who might help, sir? A friend is in great trouble. My father will keep us walking the streets until we find the answer and my feet are tired.'

'You're young. Walking won't hurt you.'

'Sir, sir, sir,' says Sam in a squeakier voice than usual, turning away from the window display. 'I like all the wiggly things in your shop and the ones that have slidey pieces and number circles on them. We need you to help our friend. Please?'

'Young man, this is far beyond your understanding.'

'Can we have a game, sir? Can we?'

'What game?'

'Um . . . If I can explain all about that lovely, shiny, curvy thing in your window, will you help us?'

Butterfield's voice is kind. 'My boy, I applaud the fact that you want to help your father, but . . .'

'Oh please, please. I have guessed what it is and what it does. Pleeeease. May I try?'

An indulgent smile touches Butterfield's mouth for a moment. 'My son was a bit like you,' he says. 'Tell me what it is and what it does, but mind, you have to get it just right. "Lovely, shiny, curvy thing" will not suffice. You must tell me exactly what it is to win the bet, but ... I fear you will find that very hard.'

'Hurrah, and when I win you will answer our questions?'

'Questions? If you get it right. One question only.'

'Three please, sir, like stories of magic lamps.'

Butterfield smiles again. 'Ah, those stories. Three questions, yes.' He turns to Balty, 'I hope your lad does not set too much store on this.'

'Thank you, sir.' Sam's voice drops to its normal pitch. 'I would say, to use the French term, this lovely, shiny, curvy thing is a *graphomètre à pinnules*. It is for astral navigation principally for mariners, but I see yours has features to assist in solar navigation also. This one, I believe, must be a new development with a transverse scale and a clever shadow measurement facility. The addition of a monopod foot may be intended for stability onboard in inclement weather. A fine instrument, clearly superior to that produced by Johannes of Hamburg, especially, I would say, in the design of the swinging arm on the quadrant, though that might perhaps benefit from a larger pivot.'

It is some time before Butterfield is able to utter a coherent word.

Sam asks his questions.

Did Butterfield ever see a blue-fringed map drawn by

Colonel Scott. Yes, he did but, Butterfield being a Catholic, his testimony will bear no weight.

Does Butterfield have any knowledge of treasonous behaviour by Scott aimed at England? Yes, in particular the colonel's activities with a group of men brought over to make cannon. He sold one of that group some other instruments.

Can Butterfield direct them to others still in Paris who have more knowledge of this? A long, reluctant pause, then . . . yes, he will write directions to the house of an Englishman who stayed behind and may have something to tell.

On the way out of the shop, a pigeon shits all over Balty's jacket from quite a height. 'That's a lucky sign,' says Balty.

'That is unpleasing to the eye and disturbing to the nose,' says Sam.

'Let's go back to the rooms and get you changed,' says Betty.

Sam stops Balty at the corner of Rue de la Huchette, peers round it and then pulls his head sharply back. 'He's there again.'

'Is he? Well, I've had enough of this,' says Balty. 'You two go around and come up from the other end. He'll be watching you. I'll jump him from this side.'

Sam nods. 'He is in the doorway by the horse trough.'

The twins saunter up the road from the far end, looking up at the window and then waving as if they can see their father. The watching man's gaze is fixed on them. Balty walks quietly down the street then charges the last few feet, seizing him around the waist and tripping him so that he falls flat. The man yells and struggles to turn his head and that is when Balty realizes he has just made his relationship with the Paris embassy even worse — because the man is John Brisbane.

Upstairs, they wipe blood from his cheek and bring out

Balty's brandy. 'Mr Brisbane, I am very sorry. Have you been watching us before?'

'No, of course not.'

'We have been under surveillance. I thought you were that man.'

'Surveillance?'

Sam answers. 'He is not there now, sir, but I have seen him on several occasions. He wears a wide-brimmed hat and a dull coat. When he moves he limps slightly on his right foot. How is your head?'

'Better for the brandy. All right, St Michel, I am in my final days here and I find I was wrong. Mr Pepys did tell me you were coming, through Secretary Coventry. I wrote back that I would not see you but I learnt today that Coventry chose not to pass that on. I had assumed your visit was in flagrant breach of my wishes. I now know it was not.'

'I understand.'

'Yes ... but perhaps not fully. I still thought you came to change my mind about the business of *Hunter*. I do still hold you to be part of the *Hunter* affair, but I recognize it may not have gone exactly as I thought.' He stares at Balty, considering. 'This man outside, do you know why he is watching you?'

'Because ... King Louis does not trust his own people let alone foreigners?'

'Visitors arrive in this city by the hundred every day. Did you draw attention to yourselves?'

'We were smuggled ashore in barrels,' says Betty. 'It was entirely secret.'

'There is another possibility.' Brisbane considers his words carefully. 'Those powerful men playing dangerous games in London may have their own agents here.'

'Why were *you* watching?' Balty asks.

'I have letters for you and I was being careful.'

'Your porter brought them before.'

'He is choosing to be particularly deaf today. Have you made progress?'

Balty sees Sam holding up his notebook. 'My children will summarize it.'

'Oh, I do not think they . . .'

Sam interrupts. 'We have talked to an English Benedictine monk. He told us of a large map of the English coast, used by Scott to solicit a loan from his abbot.' Betty takes over with a fast analysis of their abortive journey to find the house with the myrtle trees in the Rue Cléry and hands back to her brother to cover the exchange with the instrument maker. They leave out their deal with Hubert.

Brisbane passes rapidly from irritation to focused attention. 'I see you have a formidable team,' he says at the end. 'You need to be aware that the man Titus Oates is cutting swathes through Catholic plotters. Five more Jesuits went to the gallows last week. Mr Pepys and Sir Anthony have used the rules of *habeas corpus* to force their release from the Tower.'

'That is most extraordinarily good news.' Balty beams. 'We can go home then . . .'

'No, no, no. They were immediately arrested again on the evidence from Scott, Moone, well known to you as former captain of the *Hunter*, and John James, former butler to Mr Pepys.'

'What? Moone is a drunkard. John James is a rascal, dismissed by my brother after . . .' He glances at the twins. 'Well, let me just say it concerned the housekeeper and took place on a Sunday, to make it worse.'

'Nevertheless, their word sent Pepys and Deane straight to the King's Bench prison at Southwark.'

'The Marshalsea? Better than the Tower surely?'

'It is riddled with jail fever. The case may still proceed to a treason trial at a day's notice. All they need is one more witness. You must move quickly.'

Balty nods. 'Where do we start?'

'This marquis who controls the French navy?' Sam says, checking his notes. 'He may be a Catholic but he is a nobleman.'

'Even worse.' Brisbane pulls a face. 'The Marquis de Seignelay. He is surrounded by preening flunkies fawning and flattering him. This very morning I travelled to the Palace of St Germain to say my official farewell to the court of King Louis. The marquis's coach halted close to me and I nerved myself to speak to him.'

'Did you ask if he ever had dealings with Mr Pepys?'

'Yes.'

'The actual words if you please. I must write them down.'

'I said something like "I would not touch on this business if I imagined it would cause you the least pain, sir, but . . . but an Englishman of repute, Samuel Pepys, the Secretary of the Navy, has been accused of criminal correspondence with you concerning our ships and our ports." Then I bowed deeply.'

'Did he answer you?'

'Unfortunately he did. He considered and then he said, "Mr Pepys most certainly did communicate to me the strength of the English fleet in ships and men and he told me their disposition around the ports and inlets of the coast." And then he walked away into his waiting gaggle of painted courtiers.'

Sam closes his notebook. He wants no record of this.

'How can that be? My brother is lost,' says Balty.

'Perhaps,' says Brisbane. 'The navy treasurer's house in the Rue Cléry may yet count for something. Madame Pellissary is absent at the moment. I have spoken with his private secretary, Landry, who still serves the widow. He will let you view the house.'

'The house with the myrtles and the orange trees,' says Betty. 'Colonel Scott gave a very exact description of parts of it only visible from within. If he lied then his story fails.'

'And Landry is a Protestant,' says Brisbane, 'able to swear statements, so is the widow.'

'Let us go at once,' says Balty. 'Mr Brisbane, will you accompany us?'

The four of them make their way back to the Rue Cléry. Monsieur Landry is a bright-eyed old man with a bent back.

Brisbane introduces them. 'Monsieur St Michel is brother to Mr Pepys, who stands accused in England. He also knows Sir Anthony Deane, the co-accused.'

Landry gives a staccato burst of nods, 'I remember the Englishman Deane very well. He and his colleague were here on an evening four years ago. Most polite gentlemen.'

'Sir,' says Betty. 'We hear the house has a fine courtyard with trees. I should very much like to see it.'

They hope Landry will look mystified, but he smiles and leads them through the inner door to a grand room. Balty looks at the black and white marble tiles and sighs, then Landry takes them into a courtyard beyond, where trees grow in large tubs.

Some bear small green fruit on their way to becoming oranges. Others display a profusion of pink flowers.

'Those are myrtles?' says Betty.

'My mistress is renowned for her cultivation of the myrtle with colours of a brilliance rarely seen in this city.'

The interior is exactly as Scott has described it and the windows on the north side of the courtyard are high enough that men could easily talk below them without realizing they are overheard by someone inside.

Balty tries to squeeze some comfort out of Landry. 'Did Sir Anthony Deane come to this house more than once?'

'No, sir, I remember he came on that one occasion only, accompanied by the other English gentleman.'

'Mr Hewer.'

'I believe that was his name.'

'Was any other Englishman here that evening?'

'I cannot answer for sure, sir. Madame had hired the great chef Roussillon to prepare the dinner at his own kitchens, so men kept arriving with dishes throughout the afternoon. Monsieur Pellissary was frequently called away to attend to this or that. I cannot say exactly who was here after such a length length of time.'

'Were documents and maps delivered that day?'

'No, I do not recall that – but my late employer had a room with many maps. It remains as it was then.'

'We seek maps signed by Colonel Scott. May we see it?'

'Papa,' says Sam, 'they cannot be here. Colonel Scott specifically claimed that the maps were passed on to a navy commander by the name of La Piogerie for his assessment of the information they contained.'

Betty sees the slightest of flickers on the secretary's face. 'Monsieur Landry, do you know an officer of that name?'

'No, my dear. I have heard the name La Piogerie ... but as a place, not a person, and only a very small place at that. I passed my childhood in Nantes and La Piogerie lies a little south of the city.'

'You were busy with the affairs of the navy for how many years?'

'More than thirty in the service of the Treasurer.'

'If there was an officer with that name, you would know it?'

'I am generally regarded as having an excellent memory.' He pauses, frowns and holds up a finger. 'There was indeed a man in the Channel Fleet, a captain of marines, Louis Heröuard, and he came from the estate that owned that village and its farms. He would perhaps have styled himself Sieur de la Piogerie. Could he be the man you mean?'

'Is he an expert on strategy and navigation?' Balty asks.

'Not at all, sir. An officer commanding marines is a leader of land warfare, not an expert on the sea. Navigation does not enter into it.' He screws his eyes shut for several seconds. 'I have him now,' he says. 'Heröuard's ship was the *Emerillon*, of twenty-four guns, used to put marines ashore for land attacks. He met his fate somewhere in the Indies, Tobago perhaps? His ship was wrecked on a reef.'

'He is dead?'

'Indeed, these past three years or so.'

Back in the street, Brisbane ponders. 'So we have two people central to this affair who you cannot examine in person, Monsieur Pellissary and this Sieur de la Piogerie, because they are unfortunately and quite recently no longer breathing. That is a very sad state of affairs.'

'No, Mr Brisbane,' says Betty. 'Colonel Scott may have named them for the sole reason that dead men cannot testify.'

'Young woman,' says Brisbane, 'my departure leaves a vacancy in our embassy here should you be interested, but I suspect the job is beneath you.'

CHAPTER 14

July 9th, 1679

Shaftesbury is worried and wondering how best to burn a pope. John Locke has told him that the ears and nose have more power to sway the mind than the eyes. Certain judges are demanding more proof and the tide of executions is starting to ebb. The mob must howl louder to reach those judges' ears but the outer circles of the crowd won't hear twenty cats over the crackling of the bonfire. There must be forty cats sealed inside the effigy next time, but he is not sure whether forty shrieks carry twice as far as twenty or whether they just sound twice as loud to those close by. He will ask Locke.

The eyes still matter. He needs a man to play the ghost of Godfrey, made up in stark white, but will the back of the crowd see that death face? Tall stilts. The ghost roaring lines from Dean Lloyd's funeral sermon? He flips through his copy of that best-seller and finds the few good bits mired in pages of theological boredom. 'Ensnared and butchered by wicked men – his mangled macerated body thrown out to birds and beasts.' That works but the dean only gets round to blaming the pope twelve pages from the end. An actor who can remember lines *and* be expert on stilts? Perhaps a clown to perform the least funny role of his career.

There is a knock. 'Enter,' he calls and a cloud of nothingness comes in. Any witness would struggle to remember his height or his girth or his clothes. This man takes care to merge into his surroundings. As fashion changes, he is always in the middle ground. Does he smile, does he frown? Shaftesbury can never remember and that is why he employs him. The earl usually calls him Harrington, but sometimes he is Benson and at others Wilson. When in France, he goes by French names, but Shaftesbury prefers not to know them so he can deny any future charge of conspiracy. Harrington, Benson, Wilson is a distant cousin and the most lethal member of his squad. 'Yes?' he says.

His cousin delivers his reports in a flat monotone. There are no hesitations or ill-chosen words. 'St Michel is active in Paris,' Harrington says. 'He was refused audience by the secretary at the embassy who holds him guilty of piracy in the *Hunter* affair. He has rooms near Notre-Dame. His children are with him, which limits his activities. I judge that to be for the purpose of their education. Their presence makes constant surveillance simpler but I do not at present recommend increased resources for that purpose. Our prison informants confirm Pepys is not allowed to send letters. St Michel has however received visits from embassy personnel. He assaulted one such, so we may assume their purpose was not friendly and reflects continuing disagreement over the *Hunter* affair.'

He falls silent, awaiting dismissal, but this time Shaftesbury does have questions. 'Tell me of Colonel Scott. Our project depends on him but I am associated with him only by necessity.'

Harrington is silent for some time, but Shaftesbury knows he is sorting out what needs to be said. Eventually he nods and addresses a spot on the wall behind the earl.

'Scott was sent to the Americas in his youth after offences here. He was later accused of fraud and of murder in Long Island and Massachusetts. He fought in the Caribs where he claims the rank of colonel but was credibly accused of cowardice. In England he has untruthfully portrayed himself as a high-ranking official in the Americas. On military service in the Netherlands he was accused of numerous crimes and sold information, true and false, to any nation's spymasters who would pay for it. In France, with little money and many debts, he found his way into a cannon-making project designed by an Englishman called Manning to . . .'

Shaftesbury holds up his hand to stop him and a flicker of surprise crosses Harrington's face – rapidly suppressed.

'I am concerned only in your assessment of Colonel John Scott as he is now. You have met on several occasions, I believe.'

Harrington thinks. 'He is a man driven by a desire to be important in the affairs of his betters, even to affairs of state. He displays grandiosity extending into fantasy. He becomes capable of intemperate violence though he is not otherwise brave. He nurses resentment for those who he feels have done him harm and is obsessed by his exclusion from England after the murder of Godfrey.'

'Surely a normal procedure for a valid suspect?'

'Sir, you will remember that Scott was arrested when he returned to England at the end of April, rowed ashore from a French vessel. He gave his name as John Johnson, which roused immediate suspicion.' He sees Shaftesbury raise an eyebrow and begins to explain, 'because that is the very name . . .'

'. . . that Guido Fawkes adopted during the gunpowder treason of 1605. Scott has a strange way with false names. What did he say when you went to free him?'

'After the Whig election victory it was clear that he expected a hero's welcome on his return at your invitation. He was infuriated by his arrest on the old warrant drawn up by Pepys and Coventry but gratified that I was able to free him with the order you provided.'

'Does Scott know our connection?'

'I was Cavendish, a maker of gloves. I have made sure he sees Rolle, Wentworth and Peyton as those in direct charge of him.'

'You rode to London together. Did he speak much?'

'Without ceasing. He swore repeated curses against those who chased him out of England. His wish for vengeance knew no bounds. As directed, he is preparing his accusations against Pepys, but the height of his emotions gives me concern that they may be poorly constructed. He requires more control and those to whom he answers directly are not of such a rigorous frame of mind as you.'

'The exact dangers?'

'I am often obliged to bend the truth. He has no notion of its breaking point. He is both a coward and a violent bully who can plot killings by others in a cold state of deliberation but can only himself kill in frenzied anger and then only when he feels no risk to his own life.'

'He was brought to me as a very useful rogue.'

'A rogue, yes. Useful perhaps, but precision would be preferable.'

Shaftesbury turns to the window and ponders on this dangerous alliance. 'Just how sure are you that there is no communication between Pepys and his brother in Paris?'

'I am assured that no letters leave his cell.'

'Keep a very close eye on Paris. If there is blood, it must be carefully spilt. You are going to Westminster Hall now?'

'I am.'

'Hasten back afterwards. I wish to know everything.'

In Paris it is July 19th by the new style. In old-style London it is July 9th, a warm, wet Wednesday in Westminster on the final day before the courts close for the rest of the summer. The Hall is packed with the crowds expecting entertainment. John Hayes, Pepys's clever lawyer, has procured this hearing, seeking to get his clients out on bail before jail fever kills them. Pulling strings has got them some privileges in their Marshalsea incarceration – but even the better cells are not proof against the fever, which carries off many more inmates than those who die by execution.

Samuel Pepys has a powerful desire to see his accuser again. A forensic listener and examiner, he is set to dismantle every word from this dangerous colonel. That first encounter at the bar of the Commons, in what now seems another age to Pepys, had seen him ambushed, overwhelmed, allowing him only indignant denials. This time he is ready, informed by answers through Coventry's secret channels from the countries where Scott has left his marks – uncovering fraud, espionage and acts of infamy in many countries. He knows France is at the heart of the story now – his fastest route to confounding the colonel. The court assembles, Scroggs, Dolben and the rest of the bench in the centre, the prosecutor, Attorney-General Sir William Jones to one side. Pepys and Deane stand in the dock and Pepys is quivering.

Three men watch from the back, half-hidden under the awning of a second-hand book stall. Harrington is one, his horse held by a hired man outside, ready for him as soon as the decision is reached. Two others stand beside him, hats tipped down over their brows and linen kerchiefs over their lower faces, feigning protection against the crowd's exhalations. The disguise has a measure of vanity. Even in this place, close to the Commons chamber, only another MP would recognize them. Sir Francis Rolle, Member of Parliament for Bridgwater, is not often seen in Westminster. Ruisshe Wentworth, the MP from faraway Liverpool, keeps himself out of the public eye because his main activities are nefarious. They watch as Colonel Scott takes his place before the court.

'He is sober,' murmurs Rolle.

Wentworth nods. 'We made sure.'

'You have prepared him thoroughly?' asks Harrington.

'I have,' says Wentworth.

'Watch Pepys,' says Rolle. 'See? Eyes darting everywhere.'

'Don't concern yourself.' Wentworth shrugs. 'Scroggs still believes. They won't get bail, not against the colonel's word.'

'But no second witness yet?'

'We still work on that.'

Attorney-General Jones leads the way. 'The prosecution urges that no bail be granted, your honours.'

'On what grounds?' booms Scroggs.

'On the grounds that the accused have threatened, attempted to bribe or otherwise subvert witnesses. We will have further evidence within a week and will move to trial on the main charges at the start of the next term.'

'You have proof of such subversion?'

Jones reads out sworn affidavits telling startling stories, then turns to Colonel Scott, who widens his earlier accusations, making great play of the maps and papers he says he was shown in Paris.

'They were signed clearly by Pepys,' he says, 'a fancy curling signature which seemed very fond of itself. It quite startled me as I had never seen such a signature before. I did not know his handwriting then but I saw letters from him in the months afterwards.'

He goes on to stress the role of Monsieur Pellissary and Captain la Piogerie, reeling off dates with panache to detail La Piogerie's actions in the Caribbean and demonstrate the man's key expertise in French naval strategy.

'Not bad,' says Rolle.

Wentworth shrugs. 'Scroggs didn't look impressed. Not enough meat in it yet. It hangs on this next part. I think Hill has the required detail.'

The affidavit sworn by George Hill, a London iron-founder, claims that two years earlier, he recognized a notorious Jesuit, one Conyers, infamous for his skill with a stiletto in the darkness. He saw Conyers offer heavy bribes from Pepys to Colonel Scott to forget his coming accusations. Westminster Hall echoes to the crowd's cries of outrage.

Pepys interrupts to say he has never met Conyers but Scott says that Conyers is not the only one. Twenty others have offered similar bribes. Pepys stares at him. 'Name them,' he says.

Scott stares back. 'I do not have to do that.'

'Yes you do,' booms Scroggs.

Scott frowns. 'There was a clerk of the accused. I met him in a coffee house.'

'His name, sir.'

'Lewis? Or Harris, or perhaps Morris?'

'No such person. Name others,' says Pepys.

'I cannot remember.'

'What, not *any* of them?'

Scott can only shake his head.

'Not so smart after all,' mutters Wentworth.

Pepys switches his gaze to Attorney-General Jones who is holding the iron-founder's affidavit. He waves his hand at Scroggs. 'Your honour, may I see that document?'

'That is not allowed,' says the Attorney-General.

'It is if I say so,' booms Scroggs, 'and I do say so. Pass it to the prisoner.'

Everyone watches Pepys leaf rapidly through the affidavit and the whole crowd seems to holds its breath. He closes it then turns back to that very last page, holding it close. They all know the man has poor eyesight.

'May I ask my prosecutor a question, your honour?' says Pepys.

'You may.'

'Can you tell me the date this affidavit was sworn?'

'Not exactly, sir, but I would guess it would be perhaps half a year or so ago, as the investigation widened.'

Pepys passes it back to Jones. 'The date is written at the end. Will you tell the court what date that is, please.'

Jones stares at it and silence stretches out until the prosecutor has to say something. 'It bears today's date,' he says in a low voice.

Scroggs roars. 'What? What? Do you toy with us, Mister Jones. Today? What is this? Was it got up this morning to fill a hole?'

Jones turns to Scott. 'Colonel, please explain to the court how it was that you could not share this information before today.'

Scott is silent for a long moment, frowning and looking up at the distant roof. 'Sir,' he says in the end, 'I had sworn to keep this secret while those who received the maps from Mr Pepys still lived. Only when I discovered that Messieurs Pellissary and Piogerie were both dead was I released from my oath and was then able to use this witness's testimony.'

Scroggs's brows knitted. 'Are you confused in your mind, Colonel?' he asks. 'I can make no sense of what you say. Why should two men in France have been concerned about the observations of a London iron smelter they did not know and which appear to have no direct connection to them whatsoever?'

The crowd is utterly silent as it tries to get to grips with this unexpected complexity.

Scott flushes. 'It could not be done before, sir. The Duke of York was not yet exiled, he was still in power and he is my greatest enemy because I have stood against him. Pepys is his lackey, his favourite and his confidant. I could have expected no justice then.'

'Colonel Scott,' says Scroggs in a slow and dangerous voice. 'The Duke was gone away a long time before you swore your first accusations and that was many weeks ago. Why could you not say it then? Stand down, sir, before I lose my composure.' Others on the bench are muttering to each other.

Pepys is deep in thought, staring at Scott. He holds up his hand.

'Prisoner Pepys,' says Scroggs. 'You have more to say?'

'I have a question, your honour, which may help clear the confusion.'

'Then ask it.'

'Colonel Scott, you kept your claims about my supposed actions a close secret for a very long time before you accused me in the House of Commons?'

'I did, though it was hard to hold myself back,' Scott sneers at his questioner.

'No one else previously knew you were in that house in Paris where you say you overheard Sir Anthony Deane incriminate me? Not me nor anyone else? This is all before you accused me publicly.'

'That is certainly so.' Scott looks around the crowd with a smile as if inviting them to ridicule his questioner.

'So how in heaven's name could I have known that I needed to offer you bribes to silence you when, as you yourself confirm, your so-called knowledge of this was utterly unknown to me?'

'What?'

'By your own account, I did not know you were there in Paris on that day. Your so-called overhearing of my friend Deane's so-called information would be entirely unknown to me.'

'So?'

'So why would I have sent this Conyers and a score of unre-membered men to buy your silence on the matter at a time when you say you had kept it all a complete secret from me and the world?'

Scott's eyes widen as he understands the size of the hole he has fallen into and a hubbub spreads as the crowd members catch on at various speeds.

Pepys's eyes are fixed on Scott, drinking in his reaction. Jones leaps to his feet. 'Prisoner Pepys,' he shouts, 'keep your tricky rhetoric for your trial. You will not save yourself by twisting words. It is your neck that will twist. Colonel Scott, remind the court of your charges and do not be diverted by these false facts.'

Scott looks down and reads from his own affidavit, faltering at first but regaining some confidence as Pepys listens in silence. Harrington, Rolle and Wentworth see what Scott is not seeing – the intense focus on Pepys's face as if he is waiting for something else. That something arrives when Scott reaches the part where he sees Pepys's signature on the documents in Pellissary's Paris house.

Without waiting for permission, Pepys interrupts. 'What, sir? How so?' and the judges swing their gaze back to Scott without chiding his questioner for this new breach of protocol.

'Why do you ask how so?'

'I am asking how you recognized my signature.'

'That is simple. I had been shown many documents you had signed in the past.'

Scroggs beats Pepys to it. 'Colonel Scott, you told us in this court, this very morning, not minutes ago that his signature surprised you in Paris because you had never seen so fancy a signature before. You then said you only confirmed it to be his when you saw other such signatures *after* that event.'

Scott snaps back, 'The court is mistaken. I never said any such thing.'

Wentworth groans. 'Idiot,' he says, 'you do not ever tell a judge he is mistaken.'

'How dare you, sir,' says Judge Dolben.

Scroggs points a shaking finger at Scott. 'You, Colonel Scott, you very plainly said it,' he roars. 'Do you accuse me of dishonesty or outright idiocy?'

The crowd is unsettled now, torn between delight at seeing any witness humiliated and their strong desire to see papist blood.

Pepys raises his hand again and Scroggs immediately gestures for him to speak. 'Colonel Scott,' Pepys says, 'please confirm who it was that showed you these orders I am supposed to have had signed?'

'It was Captain La Piogerie as I said. That should surely be obvious.'

'And when was this exactly?'

Scott thinks for a space of a dozen breaths. 'December in the year 1674 at the port of Brest.'

'You are sure?'

'I am.'

'Completely sure? There can be no mistake?'

'Just so.'

A puzzled look comes over Pepys's face. 'And yet you testified this very morning that this supposed naval expert Le Sieur de La Piogerie also called Louis Heröuard was based at Rochefort looking after his ship when you saw my signature at Mr Pellissary's house. You also said that you did not meet him in person until he came to Paris *the following January*, so he could not conceivably have shown you those orders supposedly signed by me *before* you saw this document.'

Scott's face suffuses as a hiss of whispering spreads through the crowd, then he turns without another word and forces his way through them out of the hall, passing the three men at the back without giving them a glance. Attorney-General Jones scoops up his papers, red in the face. 'The matter was passed to me by Parliament,' he says to Scroggs. 'In opposing bail I was but performing the task they set me.'

The crowd far prefers simple, reliable belligerence from Jones. A rising murmur grows in the hall and Jones responds. 'The detail of this treason may still be obscure, but treason it certainly is and all will be made undeniably clear at the trial.' He points at Pepys. 'This man will hang,' he says, 'and his body, tarred with pitch, will dangle with the other traitors.'

The crowd murmurs. That's the sort of thing they like to hear and they recover a little of their nerve, then they fall silent to watch what the Lord Chief Justice is doing. Scroggs is a massive man with a thick neck. He turns awkwardly round on the bench, forcing Dolben aside as he leans back to stare up at the vast royal crest on the wall behind him. The crowd has not seen him do this before. Scroggs extends his arm and jabs a finger at the crest. 'This is our complete and only authority,' he booms, 'the authority of our king.' He cannot lose his faith in the great plot. He has already sent men to their deaths because of it and must not think he has murdered them, but against that, he has heard things in the last few minutes that twist his gut. He turns back to stare at all these faces with their eyes fixed on him. Is this Shaftesbury's mob or just the usual fickle crowd of thrill-seekers? He tests the water with a loud aside to Dolben. 'They seek to impose their stories on us and fox us with their faulted claims. They shall not blind us to the truth.'

The response is something like a great sigh, broken by only a few jeers, soon cut off. Scroggs listens to his gut and turns to the prisoners. 'You are Englishmen,' he says, 'and God forbid you should not have the rights of Englishmen. I grant you bail.'

A partisan corner of the crowd at the top of the wooden tower howls at him. He slams his mace on the table top and multiplies the bail sums in his head by ten to keep a foot in both camps. 'Four of your friends must put up five thousand pounds apiece for each of you. You yourselves must each put up twice that.'

The howls are replaced by startled laughter. These are unimaginable sums. Surely so much money cannot possibly be raised? Is the judge toying with these two traitors after all? The three men watching know otherwise. 'Houblon will put that up by himself. With the East India trade and his port wine profits, he keeps as much under his bed,' says Harrington. 'They will be out within the day.'

'Tell your earl it gives us time,' says Wentworth. 'They are only bailed, that is all. We have the rest of the summer to find the second witness.'

Rolle frowns. 'Pepys has his spies working across the Channel.'

'He does,' says Wentworth, 'but we must plan to stop their mouths.' He turns round to Harrington but sees only a hole in the air. Harrington has vanished.

CHAPTER 15

Many people enjoy Samuel Pepys's lively company and admire him but Will Hewer is his only really close friend. That looks extremely unlikely when Will arrives in Samuel's life as a teenage manservant nearly twenty years earlier. For the first months Will is no more than a polite boy serving the blurred mixture of office and home that make up the Pepys residence. His uncle got him in there to be trained for higher things because he was set to inherit a great estate, but to Pepys he is just another face.

That suddenly changes four months in when Will finds himself trapped in a corner of a room, the forced witness of an appalling domestic scene. Pepys married Elizabeth when she was fifteen. Still only nineteen and ever passionate, she catches him fondling a new maid and is doing her best to inflict significant injury on him. Cut off from the door with no escape route past the screaming woman and the recoiling man, Will tries to blend into the plant stand next to him as if carved from the same stone. Quite by accident his eyes meet his master's and the boy blinks. Except he doesn't. One of his eyes is watering from powder hanging in the air, erupting from the jar Elizabeth has just hurled at her husband's head. Only that eye closes. His master's face changes, staring at the boy with an expression of incredulity.

Will freezes as a terrible realization blocks out all other thoughts – oh my good lord, he thinks I *winked* at him. He will send me away. He blinks three times rapidly, then something entirely unexpected happens. His master, himself covered in the powder and with a nail scratch down one cheek, opens his mouth and begins to laugh louder and louder, unable to stop, waving a finger, speechless, and after an endless minute Elizabeth cannot help joining in, though with no clear idea why.

Pepys soon learns that Will is a kind and clever man in the making who matures into a valuable colleague. His inherited wealth dwarfs his master's own riches but he chooses to go on working with Pepys. Hewer's new, grand home in York Buildings is only ten minutes' walk along the river from the Admiralty office. Now, ahead of the bail hearing, praying for success, he pours persuasion and cash into liberating everything important from their old office. The best builders in London work hard and fast to make a suite of rooms as much like Pepys's old rooms as it is possible to be. Before bringing Pepys back from prison to York Buildings, Will tells his butler, cook and the matron of the house that Pepys is to have exactly the same status in the household as he does himself. He makes space for Pepys's own maid, coachman and secretary, then addresses a trickier problem. Mary Skinner is just seventeen when Pepys chooses her to be his housekeeper nine years earlier, soon after Elizabeth's death from cholera. Her role changes rapidly. In the old Admiralty apartments, what they chose to do may have been shrouded by darkness, but now he must somehow address this more openly and he is not looking forward to it. Mary is known for her strong views and sharp tongue. She comes to tell them how the rooms should be arranged. At a signal from Will, the head builder finds a reason to leave the room, leaving the two of them to talk to each other. He sees a determined woman who looks ready to spring into some unspecified action.

'I must make sure we are as comfortable as possible here,' she says.

We. He was hoping not to hear that word. 'Of course we must be ready for danger,' he says. 'I will share that danger willingly with Mr Pepys and . . .'

'What do you mean? What danger? It is surely all over once he is released.'

'Sadly not so. The first danger is the work of the committee, driven along by dangerous and determined men. Their leader Shaftesbury despises Mr Pepys. They still seek to have him hanged.' It is brutal but he has to shake her.

She is not yet shaken. 'The second?'

'Colonel Scott is driven by malice beyond understanding. He is given to acts of extreme violence.'

Her eyes widen and she even steps backwards as if the words hanging in the air between them could harm her. 'You feel it would be dangerous for a woman to be a guest in your house?'

'I do, except . . . '

She nods her head. She already knew. 'You have made an exception for Esther St Michel?'

'A special circumstance. It is my duty to look after her in the absence of Balthasar.'

'And why exactly is he absent?' She spits the words out.

'He is undertaking a task overseas on behalf of the king.'

'Do tell me this. Have you ever noticed Esther's resemblance to the dear, departed Elizabeth? I have often heard it remarked on, though of course the years have masked much of that. How old must she be now?'

'Oh, um . . .' He doesn't want to go down that road. Elisabeth was still only twenty-nine when the fever took her. Esther? Probably looking thirty in the eye? Why is slightly scary Mary, as he privately thinks of her, so disturbed by Esther's presence in the house? Does she think Pepys will take Esther to bed? Of course she does and, knowing his master of old, Will realizes she may have a point.

'I don't know,' he says. 'You will certainly want to keep up with your master. Let me work out a way to keep you safe while this household is closely watched by those who would do him harm.'

That does it. Her face falls and she moves to look out of the window. 'Where are they?' she asks in a lower, quieter voice.

'Where they cannot easily be seen. Leave it to me Madam Skinner. I will make safe arrangements. No harm must come to you. Meanwhile, I will ensure Mr Pepys is well looked after. Are you currently staying in a safe place?'

'My brother's house. I will go back there now.' She switches her glance to the window again.

'I will call for my carriage.'

CHAPTER 16

In Paris, Balty and the twins are tracking down the Englishman who might know more. Butterfield's instructions are written in engineer's script, as if he had engraved them in brass. He describes an entrance on the Rue de Tournon and names Mr Charles Foster. The street is at the grander end of the Faubourg St Germain. on the way to the Chartreux convent. It has been colonized by foreigners, noble mansions divided, the glorious armorial carvings reduced to chipped stone with just a ghost of gilding left. Fashion is all and cleared sites wait for new builders.

They walk under the crest of a forgotten prince into a court-yard where a man sweeps leaves. When Balty asks for Foster, he pulls a face and nods to a stairway.

A haze of sour smoke hangs in the air as they climb to the second floor where faded blue doors flank a landing. A notice pinned to one says 'GO AWAY'. Someone plucks a stringed instrument in the room beyond with no evidence of any skill. Sam considers. 'He does not know we are coming therefore he has not written his notice with us in mind, so we may announce ourselves.'

'Also,' says Betty, 'it might stop that noise.'

Balty knocks and the noise is replaced by an English shout, 'Go fuck yourself.'

Sam calls out in his highest voice, 'Mr Foster! I wish to speak with you.'

Footsteps approach the door, interrupted by a splintering crash. The door swings open. A young man with dishevelled hair looks at Balty, straight over Sam's head. He wears a greasy oriental robe. His eyes slip down to Sam and he frowns.

'I took you for a woman,' he says, 'but you are not.'

'I know that, but my sister here is. I am resigned to seaman's language but she is not, so please watch your words.'

The sour smell is stronger with the door open. A table lies on its side in the middle of the room with broken glass around it and a pool of liquid spreading across the boards. Foster kicks the glass aside and picks a long-stemmed pipe out of the wreckage.

'Pomet sent you? Tell him I will pay his bill next week. My funds from England are delayed by the weather.'

'The weather in the Channel is fair,' Sam says, 'as we know from the rapid arrival of mails posted to us.'

'Also,' Betty adds quickly, 'we have some limited funds available which may address your bill if you help us. Who is Pomet?'

'Pierre Pomet? He has not sent you? He sells ... he sells wondrous remedies of all sorts.' Foster rummages in a drawer and produces a desiccated lump of something infinitely old and blackened. He holds it out and flakes fall from it.

'This is Egyptian mummy dug up by Pomet himself.'

Sam stares at it. 'Mr Foster, you owe money to this Pomet for *that*?'

Foster waves his arms, loses his balance and staggers two steps backwards. 'He stocks the very best mummy, not stuffed with dirt and beetles like the rest.' He leers at Betty and she takes a step back as he waves it towards her nose. 'Carpentier's shit from the rubbish tips stinks of pitch when you light it. This comes from new-found tombs far up the Nile river.' He holds out the piece of dead ancient Egyptian. 'It protects against certain diseases.'

Sam steps forward and runs his fingers over the lump. 'It could be a shoulder,' he says. 'Which diseases? I have a growing interest in such matters.'

'Diseases you are too young to know about.'

'You mean the pox. Do you smoke it? Is that the smell in the air?'

'No, no. That is . . . that is something else entirely.'

'How much do you owe to this Pomet?' says Balty.

'A trifle, but he is an impatient man. Two Louis d'or.'

'No trifle, but I may have two such coins in my purse,' says Balty.

Foster sweeps clothing from a couch, some of it clearly female. He kicks more chairs into a line and they sit. 'Why do you come here?'

'Butterfield the instrument maker sent us. You know a man we seek.'

'This is about guns?'

Balty stares at him. 'Maps first.'

Foster hisses, clenching his fists. 'You are after Scott? The price just doubled.'

The far door crashes open and a young woman reels in wearing a red silk mask, black hair hanging down below her shoulders. She is entirely naked below the mask and seems unaware of the strangers. 'You,' she says to Foster, 'whatsyourname. I want madak. Now.'

'You smoked it all. Leave us.'

She flounces off and both men look at the twins. Betty looks as calm as ever. Sam shrugs and goes on writing in his notebook. 'How is "madak" spelt and what exactly is it?' he asks.

'It is tobacco mixed with a substance brought from very far away,' says Foster. 'Pomet sells it. One d and a k.'

'And that substance is ⸫ . . . ?'

'A floral extraction boiled with hemp. Pomet gets it from traders in China. He says it washes through the channels of the brain, calms the movement of the animal spirits and restores pleasure to a troubled life.'

Balty nods at the far door, behind which the woman is now howling and throwing heavy objects. 'Your friend's animal spirits appear to be moving quite rapidly.'

'I have no more madak to give her. She has taken my share as well as her own. It is wearing off.'

Balty pulls out four gold coins and puts them on the table. He puts a fifth near the pile. It is a quarter of what they have left from Trenchepain's money. 'This will buy more if you tell us what we need to know.'

'I might not choose to answer you at all.'

'Then my brother and I will ask the questions,' says Betty, 'so that you have less to fear.'

Sam goes first. 'Mr Butterfield says you knew about Scott's maps. What did you think of the one with the coloured silk fringe?'

'The huge one? Fit for the king, he said, and set to make his fortune.'

'What colour was the fringe?' says Betty innocently.

Balty frowns. 'We know what colour it was. It . . .'

'Pater!'

Foster is oblivious. 'Blue. He went to Louis's palace with empty pockets and came back weighed down with gold. He's a wily fellow.'

'You know him well?'

'Well enough to have charted the entire story of his life.' Foster twitches and begins to scratch the back of his right hand, harder and harder.

Balty stares. 'You wrote it down?'

'I wrote the book, all his tales of adventure and daring.' His eyes are getting wider, staring. 'You question me, you think I lie?'

'Be calm. I believe you.'

'Believe? What am I? What is he? True, false? A hero, a villain, a beast? I don't know. Do you? DO YOU?' They see beads of blood on his scratched hand.

'I should like to read your book,' Sam says.

'Oh, so you say.' Foster's voice grows harsh. 'I would not trust you near it. God's teeth, I hate little shits like you. Keep your mouth closed, boy.' He knocks his chair over, crosses to a chest and pulls drawers open, one after another.

Balty looks at the twins meaningfully. 'Enough, children. You have had your fun. As an adult, may I read your account, sir? I will give you another coin.'

'It is hidden. Where? Somewhere.' He pulls open the last drawer. 'There is not enough gold in all of Paris to persuade me, Captain.' Foster's face is white and beads of sweat appear on his forehead. 'They are watching us. Up there.' He points to the top of the high cupboard. 'They are in the chimney.'

'I am not a captain. Calm yourself.'

'Why did you say you were?'

'I did not.'

'Don't fool with me. I will not put up with this. I come from a fine family, you know.' Foster strides towards Balty and with no warning, punches him hard in the stomach. Balty doubles up with a gasp, straightens again and swings Foster round, forcing his arm up behind his back and pushing his face into the wall.

'I have only one more question,' says Betty.

Balty eases the pressure. 'Answer it. Then you can run to your man Pomet with my gold,' he says.

'No more answers,' Foster yells, then screams as Balty increases the pressure. He tries to kick backwards.

'Your choice, Mr Foster. We can stand here for ever or you answer now and have your gold.'

'For God's sake ask it. I will answer or I will not. There are great lords who will not let me. My mouth is stitched shut. This hurts. Let me go.'

Balty releases the pressure and Foster screams.

'Quiet,' says Balty, 'I'm not hurting you now.'

'Every part of me hurts. Have mercy, man. I must have madak. Bastard. You have had your money's worth. My head. Leave me alone. I am done. Ask the cannon crew. They know more.' He starts to sob and his muddled words lurch into the gaps between the sobs. 'Ask the King of England. Join the watch. Make her leave me. Take these devils with you.' Balty lets go entirely and steps back as Foster flails at things only he can see.

'The money is on the table. Take it to your damned shop,' says Balty. 'Children, let's find cleaner air.'

Back in the street, Sam says, 'Is that opium they mix with

the tobacco? It seems to be a poor friend to the senses. What did he mean by telling us to join the watch?'

'He was raving,' says Balty. 'Let us restore ourselves.'

A wine shop at the end of the street has chairs set outside. Balty goes in. The twins sit down. 'Sam,' says Betty, 'the cannon crew?'

Sam nods. 'Yes. My thoughts too.'

'I am not sure our father noticed it.'

'We will tell him.'

'Yes, but lead him to it gently. He will be more committed when it becomes his own idea.'

Balty returns with a glass of burgundy for himself and two of muscat. Sam sips his slowly. Betty leaves hers. 'Papa,' she says. 'Have you marked the Paris fashion in boys' clothing?'

'All these boys parading around dressed up as officers in the dragoons and the grenadiers. It's colourful but perhaps a little strange.'

Sam is leafing through the notes he made as Clifton briefed Balty. 'Papa, there are some things that Captain Clifton told us on the *Moonstone* that I need to understand better, such as these new cannon.'

'Prince Rupert's special guns? You two were capering around the rigging when we discussed that.' He explains the advantages of turned and nealed guns.

'I see how they may beat old iron guns, but brass makes good cannon too,' says Sam. 'But brass is, let me see, perhaps three times the cost of iron?'

Balty's brow furrows. 'Is that so?'

'My godfather told me that. And a brass cannon would weigh much more than this new gun.'

'Would it indeed?'

'But I recall he told me even old iron guns will send a ball a quarter of a mile further than a brass gun because brass will not tolerate the same charge of powder while Prince Rupert's guns will outdistance the iron by a full half mile.'

'How so?'

'Isn't that clear? The barrel is truer and the ball fits better so it flies further and straighter. Also, if Prince Rupert's guns fail, they merely crack. Iron guns burst to pieces and kill the cannon crew.'

He gives a special emphasis to those last two words, but it passes Balty by. 'Sam, if you know all that, why did you ask me?'

'Papa, I may have easily misunderstood as I was only ten when my godfather told me this. You have so much more knowledge. It must be difficult to make these new guns or everyone would be doing it. The precise method of manufacture must be a secret?'

'It is a secret kept at Windsor where Rupert does his work. Clifton said it is all in the mix of the metal and the exact way it is heated and cooled.'

Betty steps in. 'Would the French have paid Scott well for those secrets?'

'I am sure they would.'

'Without proof? They must be very trusting.'

'Well no, they trust no one. They would require proof.'

'And did Scott know how to make the cannon?'

'I doubt that.'

'So . . . you mean he would have needed men who did? You don't mind my asking you these questions, do you papa?'

Balty smacks his fist into his open hand. 'I have it,' he says. 'Scott put together a team who *did* know Rupert's secret.'

'Where could they have learnt it?'

'Prince Rupert's Windsor foundry.'

'Oh,' says Sam. 'A *crew* of men who understood the method?'

'Yes Sam, that's what I've just been saying. You must listen better.'

'So ... the men, the *crew* you might say, wrote down those secrets and the French paid them?'

Balty smiles indulgently. 'No, King Louis's men do not trust anybody, least of all foreigners. I think they would have got Prince Rupert's men over here to show them how to make the cannon and then prove they worked. Ah ...'

It dawns on Balty. 'Do you not remember? Foster talked of a *cannon crew*. That was what he called them. That is what we must do. We must track down the traitors who came to sell our secrets.'

Betty smiles. 'Oh, well done papa. Yes, I see now.'

Balty is staring at the people passing by. 'Oh dear me. We may have to try our luck with Mr Foster a second time, but only if he has his madak again and has not smoked too much of it.'

At that moment Foster is heading for the door with the coins clutched in his hand, heading for Pomet's shop, when the door crashes open.

'You!' he says. 'Beelzebub. Your skin is green.'

'Foster. You are not alone?' The woman is now wailing loudly in the next door room.

'Take her away and I will be. Why do you whirl so?'

The man steps towards him and an iron hand closes around Foster's neck. 'Listen to me. There are new arrivals in the city who may try to talk to you. Do not speak to them. I will know if you do.'

The hand thrusts, releases, and Foster stumbles backwards over the end of the couch, falling onto the table and fighting to get air back into this lungs.

'Do you swim?' demands his visitor.

'Swim?' He shakes his head.

'Then keep your mouth shut. Otherwise the Seine will rush in and drown you.'

The man leaves and within seconds Foster's drug-starved visions erase any memory of him.

CHAPTER 17

The twins strive to remain patient as Balty insists on doing it his way, but days pass with little progress. Pepys uses his new liberty to write countless letters of instruction which arrive in bundles, taking an hour to read and three hours to answer. Hubert brings packets full of dull details about the French navy, barely worth the lemon juice. Pelletier comes smiling, offering help. Trenchepain comes frowning, to hand over reluctant cash and complain. Balty seeks an appointment with Madame Pellissary on her return to the house with the myrtle trees. Mostly he takes them on visits to metal-workers' yards, asking vague questions about cannon crews and cannon casting that get them nowhere.

On the seventh fruitless day, Balty runs out of ideas. 'All right,' he says, 'your turn. What do we do now?'

They explain. His face shows he is clearly not impressed. 'That won't work. You say we should stop some random boy in the street and find out what we need to know? That is just plain daft.'

Sam comes closer to being cross than Balty as ever seen before. '*Not random*, papa. Not at all. We have a detailed plan.'

'Trenchepain will be angry.'

'Monsieur Trenchepain is always angry. It is his immutable nature.'

'What will this cost?'

So they go in search of those same military children's clothes which have become all the rage on the Paris streets. Sam rejects them one after another. On the second day, he finds the right ones and puts them on once he has corrected the proud tailor who tells him the new uniforms are a brilliant French idea to stop soldiers shooting their comrades when gunpowder smoke makes their eyes weep. 'But what about the Romans?' Sam asks and gets no reply. He suggests they sit on the benches of the Île de France tavern which are set out along the street on the corner of the Rue de la Huchette. There, they settle down to study the passers-by, keeping an eye on the house in case Hubert passes.

Children stroll by, with mothers, maids and governesses. Some of the boys parade the latest rage, pricy tailored uniforms copied from King Louis's Royal Army. That mighty army has standardized weapons and particular clothing for each regiment – another brand new word. These uniforms have become quite the thing for the rich kids of Paris and that is why all the boys inspect Sam's new outfit as they pass. He is dressed in green with yellow trouser stripes and epaulettes and he studies the passing boys until finally a fair woman approaches holding the hand of a tall lad in that same green and yellow. Sam springs up. The boy stops, stares and doffs his hat with a flourish to reveal a light yellow wig. Balty bows to the boy's mother, who inclines her head and returns his smile.

'Your sword is not right,' says the boy in a shrill voice. 'The pommel should be cased in darker leather. Your stripes are too narrow.'

'I know that,' says Sam. 'It is the best artillery uniform I could find. Yours is better.'

'My father was killed at St Denis,' says the boy. 'This is copied *exactly* from his second uniform, sent back to us afterwards, because his best one must have been a mess.' There is more excitement than grief in his voice, but his mother issues a theatrical gasp and fans herself.

'Madame,' says Balty. 'I am so sorry. Do sit down. Will you take a glass of ratafia? It is very effective for sorrow.' He waves his hand for a waiter.

'My name is Lucien,' says the boy. 'My mother is Marie.'

Betty realizes they need to sound more French, 'This is my brother Jacques, the son of Balthasar. I am Elisabette,' she says loudly, hoping that Balty will hear, but his attention is fixed on Lucien's mother.

'Where do you live?' Lucien asks.

'Close by,' says Sam. 'I am sorry for the loss of your father.'

'Oh, I didn't really know him. He was off fighting the Dutch for as far back as I can remember. My mother knew him quite well though.'

'He died last year?'

'They had already signed the peace treaty,' says Lucien with mild indignation. 'It was a ceremonial salute and the cannon burst. His coffin was very light. I could pick up one end by myself.'

'What sort of cannon was it?' says Sam.

Five minutes later they are deep in a discussion of the relative merits of artillery weapons, with Sam making a strong case for the return of the demi-culverin and Betty asking Balty pointless questions to remind Lucien's mother of the presence of his children.

When Lucien is convinced they are the best of friends, Sam casually dangles the bait. 'I have heard of new types. They say a crew of English gun makers came to make them for King Louis.'

Lucien laughs and bounces up and down with excitement. 'Yes, yes,' he says. 'We heard they were testing in the fields beyond the Bastille out by St Antoine. Mama took me to watch. I saw it all. A disaster! Quite wonderful.'

'What happened?'

Lucien can hardly get the words out. Tears of joy are trickling down his cheeks.

'They had two fine-looking cannon and one mortar. When they fired the first cannon there was the silliest little plop you ever heard. Pouf! The ball fell out of the end and did not even bounce. Oh, you never heard language like it. I don't know English and mama covered my ears because they were yelling fuck, fuck, fuck, fuck, fuck.'

'Lucien!' said his mother sharply. 'Stop that!'

'And then?'

'They poured in so much powder. Half a tub! There was a crowd right around them but mama kept me back. Do you know what happened when they set the match?'

'Nothing good.'

'Oh no, no. Something very good. It burst apart! The whole cannon flew to pieces in a cloud of smoke. Screams and yells and people falling down. I saw a man with no head and a head with no man. It was so funny.'

'What happened?'

'They chased those English idiots out of Paris. I've got a piece of the cannon back at our house. It was still hot when I picked it up. I couldn't find a bit with blood on it. I looked and looked.'

'So the Englishmen have all gone now?'

'Oh yes. Well, nearly all. The big, bald man who set the match was really bad, bleeding all over. They carted him off to the nuns' hospital.'

'He lived?'

'He must have done, I suppose, because we saw him on the stairs last week when mama went to the Englishman who mends clocks. He came out of the Englishman's room.'

'A clock mender?' says Betty. 'We need someone to mend a clock. Who is he?'

'Don't know his name. He's a little man who looks like a rat.'

'Where is his house?'

'Mama,' calls Lucien. 'Where does the clock man live?'

Sam and Betty see that Balty is stroking mama's hand in a comforting manner. They know this encounter needs to end.

'Why do you ask?'

'Because these people have a clock that needs mending.'

'No we haven't,' says Balty.

'Yes we have,' says Betty. 'I'm very sorry to tell you it was broken this morning by that naughty boy called Sam or some strange foreign name like that. He said to me, "Please don't tell your father", but now I see that I must.'

'What are you ...?' says Balty. 'Ah, I see. Thank you for telling me.'

'I don't know if he mends clocks,' says mama. She is a little flushed and leaves her hand stretched out, even though Balty has stopped stroking it. 'The man is a watchmaker.'

'We can ask him, madame,' says Sam. 'If he does not fix clocks, which are not so different to watches except in the size of their cog wheels, then no doubt he will know someone who does. Where do we look for him?'

'The Rue des Fossées. It is not very far. You will see an inn on the corner. There is a sign. Monsieur Joyne. His apartment is up the stairs.'

Halfway there, they are overtaken by bearded monks running at full speed in two ranks, ten each side of a very long ladder and all of them carrying a bucket in their outboard hand. Around the next corner, the way ahead is blocked by a crowd, thick smoke drifting over them and the smell of burning spreading below it. The running monks don't slow down. They start to shriek in ululating harmony and the crowds part for them.

'Who are they, papa?' Betty asks.

'They are the Capuchins,' says Balty, 'come here from Italy many years ago. They fight fires. That is what they do.'

'Capuchin *monks*? Why?'

'They weren't doing well as monks. A bit too Latin for Parisians. They found a gap they could fill and they've been doing it ever since.'

They wriggle through the crowd and around the next corner to see smoke belching from an upstairs window. The monks fill their buckets from a trough and tip them over their leader, soaking his thick brown habit. He has an axe tucked into the rope around his waist and a hood pulled over his head. They tuck his long beard inside his sodden robe and prop their ladder up against the wall. He swarms up and climbs inside, then his arm reappears reaching for the first bucket in the chain. Two dozen buckets later, he sticks his head out, gasping in fresh air.

'It is out,' he announces to the crowd and gets a mutter of discontent. They were hoping for flaming catastrophe. 'A drunken pig, asleep in his bed, his pipe dropped into a pile of paper. Three chairs burnt and the room spoiled.'

'Dead is he?' calls a turbaned man, an Armenian coffee seller with a tray of small mugs and a tin pot. 'We must commemorate him with kahvé. It is our custom for the passage out of this world.'

'He is not dead.'

'Then we celebrate his salvation with kahvé. That is our custom for miracles.'

'He soaked his bed in piss,' calls the monk. 'That saved him.' He finds he is talking to the back of the disappearing coffee seller, so he turns back to the dwindling crowd. 'I cannot wake him. Shall we leave him sleeping? He will get a big surprise.'

The crowd laughs but the rest of them slip away when the fireman starts to intone a singsong prayer.

'Protestants,' says Balty. 'See Betty? See Sam? They're not hanging around for Roman prayers. We are not alone in this part of town.'

The Rue des Fossées shows what King Louis is doing to the city. For the last three centuries, the great ditch behind the houses has run round outside high city walls, punctuated by steepled gatehouses. Those were still there when Balty guided Samuel and Elizabeth Pepys around the city but, just as Elizabeth fell, so did the walls. Louis decided Paris was now too strong to need them and too big to be constrained, so the massive stones have been levered out to reuse in his grand developments.

Nine years later, it is still a messy work in progress, shouldered aside for the moment for other more grandiose schemes. The filled ditch lines the edge of the street and a short row of mismatched houses blocks part of the ragged view.

Lucien points to the larger building at the end of the row. 'He's in there.'

They wave goodbye and cross the street. Betty looks at the sign on the inn's wall. It translates as 'The Head of the English King.'

'Sam,' she says, 'you noted down Mr Foster's words? Please read out what he said towards the end.'

Sam studies his symbols. 'He said, "Ask the King of England. Join the watch."'

Betty nods and looks at Balty, 'Do you understand, papa?'

'Yes.' Balty experiences a surge of pride that he is ahead of them. 'He was trying to say "Ask at the King of England. Join the watchmaker." Do you see?'

'Look at the sign,' says Betty, pointing to the open door. It says 'John Joyne. Fine Watchmaker' in English.

An old woman sits on a chair by the stairs, knitting something shapeless and already very dirty.

'Monsieur Joyne?' Balty asks. She nods upwards and spits. The stairs bend under their weight. The first floor landing has two doors, one bearing a painted picture of a clock.

The man who opens the door has a canvas headband pushed up on his forehead. A large lens is attached to it. His thin face shows mistrust and he puts his hand to a serviceable dagger in his belt.

'Oui?' he says.

'Your name is Joyne?'

'As it says so down there.'

'Mine is St Michel. Do you always greet your customers with a knife?'

'Yes. You've come to buy a watch?'

'We have been sent to talk to you.'

'By . . .'

Foster's name would only increase the tension crackling from this man. Balty says, 'By Mr Butterfield.' He waves a hand at his children. 'I am indulging my son. He has a passion for artillery. Mr Butterfield said you know something of the subject.'

'Crap,' says Joyne, glancing at Sam. 'Boys like guns they can hold and point, not cannon. Have you come from the Rue Cléry? That whole affair is best forgotten.'

Balty is startled. The Rue Cléry? The house with the myrtle trees? Why would he come up with that?

'You know who I mean,' says Joyne. 'I see it in your eyes.'

Balty does.

Joyne nods. 'I mean Paul le Goux.'

Balty doesn't. The name means nothing. Joyne sees that and his own eyes narrow. 'No? This is not about Nevers?'

'The Rue Nevers?'

'The *city* of Nevers.'

'I know nothing of that city.'

'For God's sake. I am too busy for this.' His workbench is covered in clocks and bits of clocks. A display case shows a dozen watches hanging by their chains. 'Spit it out. Why are you here?'

Sam answers. 'To help my godfather.'

'Who is this godfather?'

'Mr Samuel Pepys. Have you heard of him?'

'Spare me. The grand Mr Pepys of the Admiralty who is either the saviour of our navy or England's greatest traitor depending on your party? News does reach us here, you know. That means you are really here to ask about Colonel Scott.'

'You know him then.'

'He was my lodger, here in these very rooms. That was his front door opposite mine.'

'Scott *lived* here? Is he a friend?'

Joyne stares at him. 'Your name is St Michel?'

'Yes. My late sister was wife to Mr Pepys.'

'This is a desperate business. How do I know that is true? Who in Paris can vouch for you?'

'Mr Savile at our embassy?'

'Savile would not spare the time of day for the likes of me.'

'There was a Doctor FitzGerald who used to live close to here. Does he still?'

'We all know the doctor. How does he know you?'

Ten years vanish to plunge Balty into a swamp of memory.

Paris, in the autumn of 1669 is hot – not merely Marseille hot, not even Algiers hot, but close to Sahara hot. Balty has orchestrated the trip to France, a treat to help his sister and her husband mend broken fences. Pepys likes it. They eat well, visit the great and good of Paris and over seven weeks they tour Louis's royal workshops which are working flat out to make all the fabrics, furniture and ornaments needed for the growing stone emptiness of the new Versailles palace.

Pepys, for the only time in his life, lets Elizabeth buy anything she desires and she starts to talk to him in whole sentences again for the first time since she found his hand up the girl Deb Willet's skirts.

Dr FitzGerald takes them to the Jardin du Roy to see the medicinal plants. He offers a visit to the dissecting room where surgeons-to-be practise on corpses found floating in the Seine. They politely decline.

Balty has been greatly disturbed by the seismic damage to his sister's marriage. Two weeks in, Samuel and Elizabeth are just slightly closer, though her tone remains haughty and her husband is more anxious to please than Balty can ever remember. His beautiful sister has always been wilful as her so-youthful marriage, against her mother's advice, had showed.

On the parched final afternoon before their departure from Paris, he turns to see Elizabeth taking a deep draught from the earthenware jug intended for the window boxes. That jug contains water straight from the river. Next to it is the glass jug with drinking water from the Maison des Eaux, brought safely to the city by the Arcueil aqueduct. By evening she is unwell and they take her to Dr FitzGerald. He smells of alcohol which may not be wholly medicinal and dismisses the fever as a passing effect of the heat and no reason for them to postpone their journey.

They had planned a roundabout route home to see Flanders and the lumbering carriage wends its way via Senlis and Guise. By the time they reach Brussels Elizabeth is very sick and other passengers will no longer share a carriage with her. Balty remembers the search for private transportation and the Brussels doctors shaking their heads at her fever. They wet her mouth with spring water and mop her brow, but that last leg of the journey, across the sea and up the Thames, is the stuff of nightmares.

Only days after they get back to Seething Lane, Elizabeth leaves this brief life in the soaked convulsions of typhoid fever.

When that Navy Office burns to the ground four years,

taking their living quarters with it, Pepys mourns the loss of so many things of beauty, saving only some precious books and those private diaries of his, but Balty sees it as a blessing in disguise because it frees him of the daily sight of the place where his crowning beauty died.

'Papa?' Betty's worried voice brings him back to the room.

'Yes,' he says to Joyne, 'I was here with Mr Pepys and my sister in October of '69. He introduced us to many people. He will remember me.'

Does FitzGerald know that the beautiful patient with the 'passing autumn fever' died? Would a sober doctor have made any difference? Balty tries to close off questions that still hurt, but a great fear keeps them open. Does his brother still blame him for suggesting the trip?

'If he confirms what you say, I will send a message. Where are your lodgings?'

Sam turns to him as they leave. 'Mr Joyne, sir? I was told about some cannons which exploded and a fat man with no hair who made the guns. Does he live here too?'

'Who told you that?'

'A boy called Lucien who came with his mother.'

'Oh them. He must have seen Sherwin on their way out.'

'Papa, will you give Mr Joyne a coin to thank him for his kindness.'

Balty sorts in his pocket, feeling for something smaller than a Louis d'or. A form of low-level trust has been established. 'My son wants to know how a cannon is made.'

'And he wants to ask Edward Sherwin?' The clockmaker laughs. 'He might have known once before his head was softened by bad wine. You're better off asking me.'

Sam jumps up and down. 'Lucien saw him fire a cannon that exploded beyond the Bastille.'

'He's right enough. Sherwin made two more that burst at Versailles and at least three that blew to pieces at Nevers.'

'Nevers?'

'Yes. That's where they make cannon.'

Sam stands in front of Joyne and looks up with eyes he has somehow made larger. 'I would like to talk to him,' he says. 'It is important to know how not to make cannon as well as how to make them.'

'Then he's definitely your man,' says Joyne. 'He's the top expert on knowing how not to make cannon.'

'Where can I see him?'

'It's not far. I'm going that way.'

It really isn't far. Joyne stares up at the first floor window and the smoke stains curling up the wall. 'So that explains all the fuss. That was his room up there. Looks like you missed your chance.'

Surprisingly, they haven't. Sherwin is still sound asleep on his sodden bed in what's left of his room. Local interest in his survival drained away with the departure of the Capuchins. Joyne shakes him until he rears upright and glares around at the wreckage, then at the visitors as if they must be to blame.

'What in the name of damnation and all the devils have you done?' he croaks.

Balty and Sam stare back at him. Betty is kicking stacks of burnt paper aside and tugging carbonized furniture out of the way.

'We are sorry to wake you, though glad to be able to,' says Balty. 'My son wants to learn about the guns you made. I will pay you to tell him.'

Sherwin glares. 'Do you know these arseholes, Joyne?' Old wine gusts on his breath. 'I don't know them and I fucking hate them already.'

'He does pay, Edward,' says Joyne. 'He's good for his word.' He turns to Balty. 'Come back when he's sober. Maybe tomorrow?'

'Not here,' says Balty.

Joyne considers the man marooned in his scorched bed. 'Edward. You can move in with me for a day or two. I can't abide you longer and you will not smoke your pipe because I like my rooms raw, not burnt. Mister St Michel, please bring your tribe to my rooms at noon tomorrow.'

On the way back to their lodgings, a man wrapped in a white sheet is accosting passers-by. He seizes Balty's arm, eyes rolling up in his head and points at Betty. 'I am surrounded by the saints,' he says. 'Sinners cannot see them. They show me a devil walks with you. This girl needs my intercession.'

Balty pries the fingers away. The man makes to bite him, snarls and turns his attention to the next group. Back in their rooms, he picks up the latest package of letters, slumps back in a chair and flips through them.

'Your godfather says your mother is well, enjoying Mr Hewer's hospitality and badgering them for news of you two. Ah, this next bit's good. Mr Pepys has found out why that marquis claims he told him all about our navy. It's true that De Seignelay was talking to the Secretary of the Navy but that was many years ago and it wasn't Pepys. Back then we were on the same side against the Dutch.'

Betty seems not to be listening. She is intent on a mass of scorched papers she has brought back with her.

Balty drops the letters. 'It doesn't help. Joyne doesn't trust us. I don't trust him. Sherwin is a drunk. Foster is drugged. Brother Pepys thinks I'm spending all his money and we're chasing a bunch of crazies who did such a bad job of making cannon that they're laughing-stocks.'

Sam picks up the letters, folds them and stacks them neatly. 'Papa, you need a glass of wine. You are perhaps over-tired. Let me list our progress. We have evidence that Colonel Scott sold King Louis maps of our coast. Also, we know that Scott was called back to England by a member of the nobility . . .'

'The Earl of Shaftesbury?'

'Let us not get ahead of ourselves. The earl is too clever to leave a clear trail. We know Scott wants revenge on my godfather. We know the cannon crew were traitors and we can link them to Scott.'

'By rumour only. We have nothing to prove that.'

'Except this?' Betty holds up the charred papers she has been studying. 'Did you not see what I was doing back there, papa?'

'Kicking burnt stuff around?'

'This adds up to more than nothing.' She holds up the first page. Large black capitals curve across it. 'EDWARD SHERWIN CANNON MASTER'S COMPLAINT AGAINST COL SCOTT AND HIS CRONIES.'

'It would be easier if he could spell and write in a straight line. It also upsets my nose. He soaked more than his bedding.'

The first sheet is dry now and dark flakes drift from the scorched circle in the middle of it. She shows them the other side. Sherwin has taken a pile of advertisement leaflets which all carry the same printed message 'By order of the King. An infallible remedy for the cure of secret diseases with no need to stay in your bed.'

'Secret diseases, papa?' says Sam, 'What are they?'

'They are not something we should talk about.'

'Oh, I see. They are promoting cures for the French disease as they call it in London, or the English disease as it is called in Paris.' He looks at the handbill thoughtfully. 'You should not believe what this message says. Such ailments are persistent and very unpleasant.'

'Ignore it. Betty, read out what Sherwin wrote on the other side.'

'He's very pompous.'

'Get on with it,' says Balty.

'It is headed "The accusation of Edward Sherwin, master of cannon founding, against Colonel John Scott. Myself, the afore-said Sherwin, left destitute by malicious treatment at the hands of Prince Rupert and dismissed in a peremptory manner from his foundry at Windsor, was solicited to travel to Paris at the end of May of the year sixteen hundred and seventy five by one Edward Manning to employ my skills in his project there ...'''

Betty sighs and runs a finger down the pages in silence, then she nods. 'May I summarize? You will fall asleep if I don't.'

Balty pours a glass of wine and waves her on.

'So ... Sherwin arrives here. Manning has been pushed out. Scott has taken over ... "vain and aggressive" ... Scott hides Sherwin in a house with a bunch of other Englishmen he's recruited ...'

'The cannon crew?'

'Exactly, but they knew nothing of Prince Rupert's cannon. Scott's after the money and ... yes, here we are. He signs up new backers. This is the scorched part. I think it lists them . . . "Marie de Cocq des . . ." I can't make out the next bit.'

Balty takes the sheet to the window and sees faint lines on the scorched centre of the page. 'It says "Marie de Cocq des Moulins . . . a woman of business in the city and her cousin . . ."' His voice trails off. 'Oh my dear Lord . . . We know these names, "Louis Heröuard, commander of Marines, known as le Sieur de la Piogerie." That's the second name. The third is the treasurer of the navy, Georges Pellissary. This is terrible. Why are you two smiling?'

'Because it is excellent news,' says Betty. 'It shows these people were not paying Mr Pepys to betray England. They were paying Scott. Do you not see? They were the investors he found. Sherwin may travel back to testify if you promise him enough gold.'

Sam takes the papers and reads on in silence, then he looks up. 'This des Moulins woman forces Scott to take communion with her to prove he is sincere . . . "but God was looking a different way on that day so she came away believing in Scott's fraud . . ." Then Manning challenges Scott to decide it "by a game of bowls at four in the morning outside the city walls . . ." What does that mean?'

'It's a secret challenge to a duel,' says Balty, 'which is banned by law. Who won?'

'Scott doesn't show up. Manning's gang beat him up. It's all mad. Fraud and fighting in the street. My head aches.'

'My turn,' says Betty. She studies the pages, sometimes turning back to check, then says, 'I think I've found the bit that matters. Mr Joyne mentioned the name Paul le Goux in the Rue Cléry? He matters and we're back to the house with the myrtles again. You see, Scott has used every bit of what happened there for his story, but he's twisted it all round to blame others for his own crimes.'

'Explain that simply if you can?'

'I can try. So . . . Scott muscles in to take over this traitorous crew of top English cannon experts – except most of them know nothing about cannon so they're not really traitors, more like saboteurs. Joyne, the hired hand, arranges things. But anyway, that day, the 17th of June, when Scott claims he overheard Sir Anthony Deane incriminating Mr Pepys, Scott really was in the house.'

'Oh no.'

'Oh *yes* and it is all good. Scott takes his cannon crew along to the myrtles and the orange trees to meet the investors. They are treated politely but as strangers, Sherwin says. Pellissary calls in his neighbour Paul le Goux, Louis's man in charge of cannon production, and le Goux sees they are rogues and rascals but the investors are besotted with Scott, so le Goux calls Scott's bluff. He sends the cannon crew south to make their magic guns. Nevers has all they need: furnaces, cauldrons and the Loire to power the machinery. If they can't make fine guns there, they can't make them anywhere.'

'And . . . it goes wrong?'

Betty waves the sheets in the air and smiles, 'So, so wrong. The Nevers gun-founders hate them. Scott plies them all with cognac. Sherwin assaults a visiting nobleman for doffing his hat to Scott and not to himself. He threatens to piss on the fire, says – oh yes listen to this bit, "Scott is seeking to destroy me, steal my secrets and keep the profits. He could no more make a turned and nealed gun than he could kiss his own manhood and

I will not suffer such infamy one moment longer."' She pauses there, looking thoughtful, 'He gets even ruder after that. Lots of words you would not like to hear me speak, papa.'

'Let's leave the rest for tomorrow. We may learn more from Sherwin when he is sober.'

CHAPTER 18

Sherwin is sober but he still stinks of smoke and urine. He is stumping up and down Joyne's room when they arrive and the watchmaker is looking annoyed, trying to align cogwheels as his workbench quivers.

Sherwin glares at them. 'Give me one good reason to talk to you.'

'Answer our questions for one hour and then we will take you to the wine shop to enjoy Bordeaux wine and fine tobacco.'

'Oh please do,' says Joyne. 'I have sent for clean clothes but you would earn my gratitude if you take the dirty ones out for a walk.'

Sherwin growls at Balty's suggestion. 'Fine tobacco? The shit they sell here burns your throat.'

'That will be the tobacco grown at Clairac,' says Sam, 'where the crop is often damaged by mould during the drying process.'

'Go fuck yourself smart-ass,' says Sherwin.

'We will buy you the best they have,' says Balty quickly, 'and I will have some very fine Virginia sent here from London.'

'A half hour,' says Sherwin. 'That's all you get.'

Sam takes out his notebook.

'Mr Sherwin,' says Balty, 'you were part of a contract to make cannon for the French.'

'Was I?'

'Our offer depends on you answering properly. We have a source for all this. We simply seek confirmation.'

Sherwin swings round to Joyne. 'Was that you, you bastard?'

'No,' says Joyne calmly.

Sam notes in his shorthand *Joyne knows everything.* Sherwin plucks the book from his fingers and stares at it, uncomprehending. 'The kid can't write,' he says and throws it back at Sam. 'You'll get me into trouble.'

'You are in trouble,' says Balty. 'You stand accused of betraying England, but you are just one of the victims of a great plot. Help us and we will destroy the plotters.'

Sherwin swings his gaze to Sam. 'So we can forget this shit about the kid and guns? Time you said what this is really about.' Sam seems to be drawing the view from the window, his eyes on the street while his ears are focused on the room. Betty is frowning, thinking hard.

'Mr Joyne already knows,' Balty says. 'It concerns a threat to a dear friend. Good information will earn a good reward. To show faith, I will put down money in advance.' He brings out another gold coin and the sunlight glints off it.

Sherwin takes the coin with a shaking hand, bounces its weight in that hand, then bites it. He puts it in his pocket. 'Depends,' he says. 'If you're after any of my lads, forget it. They didn't deserve what happened.'

'We're not after your lads. We're after Colonel John Scott.'

Sherwin's massive fist thunders down on the table. 'You're

after Scott?' He reaches into his pocket, takes out his hand and drops the coin on the table. 'Then here's your money back.'

Balty stares at the coin rolling towards him. 'You won't help us?'

'No, I won't help you for any money at all.'

Balty, Betty and Sam freeze. Sherwin cackles. 'I won't help you for money, I'll help you for free, matey. I want to see that bastard hang. Pick up your coin and put it away. Whistle up a bottle of the red gut-rot from down below and I'll talk until I run dry.'

Joyne rolls his eyes, but he extracts a promise that they will all go out afterwards and goes to fetch the wine, Sherwin sits brooding while they wait, then suddenly, after the first swig, he is ready to talk.

'I'm an iron master. King of the trade. I know how the metal likes to be heated and I know how it likes to be cooled. So what do *you* know?'

'We know about Manning and le Goux and what happened at Nevers.'

Sherwin recoils. Balty has said too much, too soon. 'I have enemies. You could have men outside waiting to grab me. Tell me who told you this or I won't say another word.'

Balty thinks he can't say they stole his document. He glances at the children and is shocked to see that Betty's eyes have rolled back in her head. She stands up with her arms thrust out before her.

'Hear me,' she intones in a shrill voice. 'A devil walks behind you. I can yet save you with the truths passed to me by the saints who walk with me. I am their voice on this earth.'

'God's wounds. You need to slap her,' says Sherwin derisively. 'She don't fool me.'

'Hear me,' says Betty again and gives a shriek which makes them all jump. 'The saints show me the place where you have planned a great swindle.'

Balty is as astonished as Sherwin.

'And what place might that be, little lassy?' demands Sherwin with a derisive laugh.

'A small land in the midst of the sea.'

Sherwin is smirking, inviting Joyne to share his sarcastic mirth.

Her voice drops to a whisper. 'It is an island named Man and that is where you have planned illegal alchemy.'

Sherwin stops smirking and stares, transfixed, at Betty, who brings her face close to the old drunk and hisses out her words. 'You planned a great crime. The punching out of false copper coins. The transmutation of that copper into the appearance of silver, masquerading as bullion and breaking all the laws.' She jerks back and stands upright, stock still with her eyes closed and continues in a lower monotone. 'Coins dispersed along the coasts to cheat the merchants of England, of Scotland and of Ireland, sent out in bags weighing exactly one hundred pounds and that is . . .' she ends with a shout, '. . . a capital crime.'

Sherwin is bolt upright as though a ghost has walked in. They all stare at Betty, aghast. She shakes all over and slumps slowly down to the floor. Sam and Balty rush to her and after several seconds she lifts her head, looks around the room blinking and says, in a weak voice, 'Is something wrong, papa? Why do you all stare so?'

'Because of what you said,' says Sherwin. 'Bloody horrible to listen to.'

'I spoke no words, sir.' Betty looks at Sam expectantly and

he speaks quietly, 'This comes upon her sometimes. She is always right.'

He glances at Balty who picks up the thread. 'Better perhaps that we hear it from you, Mr Sherwin, and not from her, because we never know where it will end. Have another glass. What is this scheme?'

There is a long silence, then Sherwin sighs. 'A mad plan of Scott's. Castles and cash piles. It came to nothing.'

'How could it?' says Balty. 'No one can turn copper into silver.'

Sherwin glares. 'I can. The blanching of copper is possible for those at the very top of the trade. Do not bloody doubt me, damn you.'

'Tell me about Prince Rupert,' says Balty hastily. 'I saw him twice, a grand and grizzled man.'

'Rupert had the idea for the cannon but he wasn't sure how to make them. It was all in the second heating, then the shock of the cold. Then . . .' He sweeps his hand across the table and knocks his empty mug into Joyne's lap. Joyne sets it back on the table and pours a small splash of wine into it. Sherwin pulls the bottle from his hand and tops it up. 'Then the final touch. You grind the iron to get rid of weak spots. You need water power for that but old Rupert was the constable at Windsor and that's got the whole Thames river flowing past it, hasn't it? All that water, just like the river down there at Nevers which you have to call "Nevair" or they don't know what you're talking about, though Nevers said the English way seemed a lot more to the point, cos it never got us anywhere.'

'How long did you work for Rupert?'

'Long enough to cast the finest cannon the world ever saw. A master gunner's dream, but there were a piece of shit at Windsor as wanted my job, said I was drunk. Said I blew up the powder store. Me? Drunk in the powder store? I would have died, wouldn't I? A few burns, that's all I had. That bastard took my candle, dropped it in the powder. After my job, don't you see? Well, don't you?'

'I do.'

'They threw me out. Me with nothing.'

'How did the French find you?'

'The Lord blind me,' Sherwin says. 'The top Frenchy, the London ambydassador man or whatever. Mister Barrel . . .'

'Monsieur Barrillon?'

'Him. He was with the king at Windsor. Heard all that fuss was going on. Sent a man to find me in a tavern. Made me an offer.'

'You didn't mind?'

'You calling me a traitor? We were on the same side then, us and the Frenchies and they knew what I was properly worth. Anyway it was an Englishman sent to find me. Man called Manning. A *man* called *Manning*.' He begins laughing as he reaches for the bottle again and a spreading dark patch on his britches foreshadows the smell of fresh urine.

'I think you need a bit of shut-eye, Edward,' says Joyne. 'You had a busy old day yesterday. What say you we carry on tomorrow?' Sherwin gropes his way to a bed in the other room.

'Mr Joyne,' says Balty, 'now it comes round to you. What exactly is your own connection to Scott? Tell us simply and directly. We already know a great deal.'

'Oh yes? How exactly? Don't try any spirit voices crap on

me. My earth goes around the sun like a cog wheel on a ring gear. It is not propelled around by angels.'

Betty joins in. 'We have information from others.'

'Who exactly?'

'We will not tell you, just as we will not tell others what you say unless you permit it.'

'Play your trick then, girlie. Tell me something you shouldn't rightly know to show that's true.'

'Scott pretended Sherwin's crew had been caught on their journey to France and needed to be freed.'

'So?'

'You cashed a money order from Scott's investors to set them free. I can give you the amount and the date if I think about it hard.'

Joyne takes his time replying, then shrugs. 'I don't know how you do that, but I prefer to be on the same side as you three. The colonel works for powerful men. I am not powerful. He is playing a dangerous game. I am not stupid. What more do you need to know?'

'Which powerful men?' says Balty.

'There's a nobleman among them.'

'Which one?' Balty knows the answer, but Joyne shakes his head.

'How long did Scott lodge with you?'

'Two years. He still owes me.'

'How much?'

'A great deal. Forty pistoles.'

'Money he did not have?'

'He had it all right. A chest full from one single deal.'

'What deal?' Balty asks.

'He made a grand map and he sold it for a grand price.'

'A large map on wooden rollers with a fringe of blue silk?'

Joyne nods slowly, frowning. 'I saw him off to the palace with it. He came back stuffed with silver and gold.'

'But he didn't pay you back?'

'One of the few constancies in the twisted life of John Scott is that he would rather spend the money on the person he loves most.'

'A woman?'

'Himself. He bought a suit with huge silver buttons, a shoulder belt with heavy silver buckles, the finest pair of pistols I ever saw – silver mounts, over-under barrels, waterproof pans. All paid from the coins in his chest.' He spits on the floor. 'When he vanished I went straight to the chest and it was empty.'

Sam opens his notebook. 'Two months after that meeting in Monsieur Pellissary's Paris house, can you confirm that Colonel Scott was still in Nevers, or at any rate not in Paris? That would be on August 5th of the year 1675.'

'Why?'

'Because that is the crucial date when Scott swears he heard treason enacted. If you can swear it is not possible, my godfather will be ever in your debt and will reward you well.'

Joyne considers, gets up and consults a box of papers and a worn ledger. He scratches his head and winds up a clock, then he checks the ledger again.

'Yes,' he says.

'Yes, you can say it is not possible?'

'The reverse. Yes, I can confirm Scott could very well have been in Paris on that day.'

Balty jumps in. 'So he may have visited the house in the Rue Cléry?'

'The Pellissary house? He may have done.'

'Damn,' says Balty. 'We have a powerful need to prove he is lying.'

'I can swear details of all Scott's duplicity and the money he took to sell the French all his other maps of England's defences. I could take Sherwin with me.'

'You would travel to England for that purpose?'

'I would be delighted to help your brother.'

Halfway back to their lodgings Betty breaks the silence. 'We can't trust him,' she says.

'Why?'

'I don't exactly know.'

'It's not the voices in your head?'

'Oh, papa. Really.'

'How did you know about the copper blanching in the Isle of Man?'

'It was all in Sherwin's document. He's clearly forgotten it entirely and you seem to have done the same.'

'Are you feeling tired Betty? Hungry perhaps?'

CHAPTER 19

And then the gloves come off.

The trio go on doggedly chasing leads. Letters go slowly back and forth so each end of the chain is always two or three weeks out of date with progress. Hubert grows from starving urchin into strong navy messenger, bringing packets to them twice a day through his back route into the house.

One afternoon, they are watching for him from the window and he comes into view as usual. Sam goes downstairs to meet him at the back. The other two see Hubert swerve round a slow-moving man and they realize it is the ancient embassy doorman. At that moment a figure in dun-coloured clothes bursts from a doorway behind Hubert and runs towards him with a cosh in his hand. Balty sprints down the stairs three at a time, shouting for Sam. Betty is right behind. Outside they stare at a bewildering sight. Hubert is racing away along the street. A body in dun-coloured clothing lies flat on the cobbles with the embassy doorman standing over it. The doorman spreads his arms. 'Back inside,' he says in an unrecognizable voice. He pushes them into the house. 'Upstairs, quick.'

It's not only his voice that has lost years. His movements are swift and athletic. Upstairs they go straight to the window as the attacker levers himself up, rubs his head and limps away.

'I should have hit him harder,' says the doorman.

'You did very well,' says Balty slowly and loudly.

'Pater, you have missed something,' says Sam.

Betty stares at the doorman, who smiles at her. 'Why?' she asks.

'Because I see what people are when their guard is down. Sometimes I can hit them before they hit me. That helps keep our embassy and Fat Harry better protected.'

'Good God above,' says Balty, 'I gave you a Louis d'or in recognition of your great age and infirmity.'

'Which I have kept to give back, having noted your expression. I am compensated very well in London for my extra services here.' He takes the coin from his pocket and places it on the table.

'Who are you really?'

'I serve my country and I report to the king's most trusted advisers.'

'Not to Mr Savile?'

'Fat Harry is not in that category. Now to business please. I have a pressing message from Secretary Coventry, which cannot be committed to paper.'

Balty remembers the brave agent Augier who serves Coventry in France and the way he was to introduce himself. 'What would you say if I was wearing a hat? Do you think you would like it?'

The doorman frowns. 'It is impossible to say as you're not wearing one.'

'Papa, this is someone else,' says Betty. 'Please carry on, sir.'

'Secretary Coventry wishes me to tell you that your information on the French naval build-up is useful. However, it is secondary material from their less important offices. He needs information on the battle squadrons in the northern ports and urges more effort in that direction. He says . . .' Here the man pauses for a moment as if the words come hard. 'He says his agreement on your personal future depends on the quality of that information from now forwards. I should add that the incident outside shows hostile operators are now aware of your use of that messenger.'

Sam is at the window. 'Hubert is back. He is looking up.'

The porter gets to his feet. 'I will go.'

'Tell your master we will do our best,' Balty says quietly, with no idea how to fulfil that.

The man gains twenty years before their eyes as he shuffles towards the door. 'Beg pardon, sir,' he says in the older voice, 'that sort of talk does you no credit. I'm a poor man and not here to be insulted.' He turns and winks at them as he goes out.

Hubert comes in soon afterwards. He is agitated. 'What happened? Who were those men?'

'A footpad and another man who chanced to be coming here.'

'A footpad? After me? I didn't even see him, then I heard the thump and he was on the ground so I legged it. I am found out.'

'The attacker was after your purse.'

'No.' Hubert shakes his head. 'Nobody knocks a messenger on the head for a few coins. Someone out there knows what we're doing and doesn't like it.'

'Perhaps. We're making a change. The Louvre fortress is

not very interesting. You should wait at the main office from now on.'

'A man attacks me for my not very interesting messages and you want me to take even bigger risks?'

'But you're a real messenger now.'

'Coming here is the risk. The packets from the main office go to Versailles Despatch. It's the opposite way.'

'We will rent a room somewhere on your route.'

'My skin is prickling. I listen to my skin.'

'We need better stuff, then there might be a bonus.'

Betty frowns when he has left. 'He is scared. I would be too. He deserves to be properly rewarded.'

'How do we get that past Trenchepain?'

'Tell him the reason is secret and Monsieur Houblon will approve.'

'Oh, I don't know . . .'

'Papa, the doorman says you will be sent to Tangier if we don't do better.'

'That's not quite what he said.'

'It is what he meant.'

Balty shakes his head in silence and she hugs him.

Sam restitches his sailor jacket into something closer to Hubert's correct one, ignoring Balty's questions. He cuts V endings into the ribbons, learning rapidly from his mistakes, and then adds the final touch, embroidering a one, a five and a six onto both sleeves in thick blue thread.

'That's Hubert's number,' says Betty.

'Safer than using someone else's number or one that might not exist.'

'You're not doing this yourself,' says Balty.

'Hubert might refuse.' Balty notes there is no 'papa' or even 'pater' and backs away.

Soon after Sam finishes, a message summons them to the house with the myrtle trees. An anxious Landry introduces them to a hard-faced man with an intelligent eye. This is Paul le Goux, head of the Nevers cannon foundries, his right cheek scarred by a splash of angry iron. He listens to Balty's polite and minimal explanation of their mission, and then nods slowly. They wait for polite words of equivocation, but instead he says, 'The man Scott is the most complete shit I ever met.' He stops. 'I am sorry to use such language. The words came unbidden.'

Sam smiles, 'I concur with your sentiments, sir, although my sister and I have not yet met him. We would like to hear what drove you to use such a scatological comparator.'

'Ah. Smart boy. I knew Scott was a crook from the start and the other man, the fat drunk . . .'

'Sherwin?' says Betty.

'Yes. Sherwin might once have known how to make Rupert's guns, but French iron is not English iron and French wine stopped him learning the difference. Scott didn't care. He was sure he could fool us. I chased him out of Nevers and I came back here to warn the people who had baptized him with their gold, then he had the nerve to turn up with his ragtag crew and six cannon.'

'Did his investors listen to you?' Balty asks.

'Most did even before they witnessed what happened next, except the des Moulins woman who was blinded by Scott fawning over her as if she were half her age. My dear friend Pellissary was horrified. He had dug deep in his pockets and that speeded his death in this very house.'

'All the guns failed?'

'One worked,' le Goux says. 'A pretty little thing, finely engraved and firing brass balls. Useful for parties, useless for warships. It is so much easier to make small ones. As for the rest ... They burst, one by one, spraying broken iron into broken men and the des Moulins woman on her knees in the wreckage, praying out loud. Scott had run for it. All that was left was wind and smoke.'

'Sir,' says Sam, 'will you help us save my godfather by testifying to all of this?'

'Let us sit under the trees and talk that through,' says le Goux.

CHAPTER 20

At exactly the same time, two hundred and ten miles to the north-west, two other men are already sitting under a tree that is entirely artificial. It has been dragged there on a heavy wheeled trolley to provide unnecessary shade on this sunless day. Gravel pathways divide this garden into a grid, sixteen squares of grass, flowers and somewhat modern sculptures. Henry Coventry, one foot swathed in a cushion of wool held in place by bandages, is carried to his chair by a careful team of footmen instructed by the man now sitting next to him. A towering iron device looms in front of them, the most compli- cated sundial Coventry has ever seen, conveying many more interpretations of the sun's position than a man could ever need, somewhat wasted now as the sun's position is behind a cloud. The man in the other chair owns the sundial and loves to explain all its functions, so Henry pre-empts him with utmost politeness.

'Such an extraordinary machine, sire. Your vivid description has stayed in my mind.'

The grand buildings which surround this garden have a chequered history. Some were part of Cardinal Wolsey's great house before the last Henry fell out with him and made it the centre of Whitehall Palace, surrounded by his hunting parks. A hundred and fifty years later, it is a sprawl of mismatched structures in the midst of the growing district of Westminster and Henry's old privy garden has somehow become a through route for passers-by.

Every now and then, King Charles the Second asserts his authority by stationing his guards at the access points to close it off. This time he has gone one stage further, ordering tall screens to be set up around these chairs and sending men from room to room in this part of the palace to empty them of any-one who can see the screens, let alone the men behind them. Whitehall Palace has one and a half thousand rooms, but for-tunately for those men, only eighty look this way.

Charles inspects his old ally. 'Comfortable, Henry?'

'Indeed, sire.'

'Nonsense. I see gout in every line of your face – and there are more of those than there used to be.' He reaches over and touches the back of Coventry's hand. Coventry looks down in surprise. They are as close as a king and his subject can be, but this is unfamiliar intimacy.

'We are going to be very plain with each other,' says Charles. 'Nothing of this will ever be passed on to any other living being. We share it only with our god. Yes?'

'Yes.'

'How long can you bear to continue in my service?'

'As long as you need me.'

'No. You have not rested for a decade. You deserve tranquil-lity and I know where your heart lies.'

'You do?'

'An hour's ride on from Oxford, you used to say ten years back. Half an hour at full gallop, you would say twenty years ago.'

'Now I say two hours in the slower comfort of my carriage . . . and not too often.'

Charles smiles. 'Minster Lovell. That kind old house by the well-named river.'

'The Windrush.'

'It winds among the rushes and the wind rushes over it and the house looking over it has warm memories soaked into twisted timber and aged stone. I yearn for such a house away from people and their plots. Minster Lovell is that perfect place.'

'My king, are you dismissing me?'

'I am rewarding you, dear friend, and protecting you from what may come next.'

Coventry stares at the sundial. 'The matter is finely balanced.'

'Henry, I know many things I would prefer not to know. You understand the danger of my proud brother succeeding me and the hatred that inspires, but I have to believe in royal succession ordered by God.' He meets Coventry's eyes as they turn back to him. 'The Duke of York will be my successor if he is spared. Your work to save us has focused the hatred of those who would destroy him and your old bones should not bear that load.'

'I may speak plainly?'

'You have rarely done anything else.'

'This is a dance of shadows. I have to add together a thousand hints and rumours and divide them by common sense. We both know the man who steers this plot does not live in Rome.'

'Take care before you name him. That would precipitate action and he . . .' Charles stops himself.

'It is surely plain enough? Let us take a name at random. The mob says a man called something quite like Shaftesbury leads their fight.'

'Ah,' says Charles and Coventry waits. The king seems to be thinking hard. 'The roll-call of his allies grows longer and they control my Privy Council . . . You're busy in France. More so than here in England?'

'My work in Paris has a wider purpose than just Mr Pepys's freedom. His brother-in-law works on our behalf. The deeds of Colonel Scott have infected your Privy Council. We need to cauterize that.'

'I have met St Michel. You could easily mistake him for a fool.'

'A fool might. A wise man could not. He and his children make a team that is much stronger than they look.'

'You have promised him a reward.'

'As long as he uncovers what we need. He wants to escape his posting to Tangier in order to stay alive.'

Charles frowns. 'You dare to be rude about my great wedding present from my wife?'

It is one of those moments when Coventry cannot be quite sure if his king is joking and he has seen Charles in too many sudden furies to take the risk. 'It would have been a still finer gift if they had wrapped it well and sent it here to London.'

Humour works. After a brief silence, Charles bursts out laughing. 'What exactly have you promised?'

'That we will not send him if he uncovers all those who have steered the damned plot. If he does, he can choose where he goes next.'

'That is the deal?' Charles frowns and Coventry wonders why he even has to think about it, but his expression clears. 'Thank you. Write that down so I follow it exactly and keep your side of the bargain. You will excuse me for a moment, Henry. Even kings have bladders.'

Coventry watches him head towards his apartments in the Stone Gallery, seeing a man who has walked a tightrope every day since his father's execution just one hundred yards from here. He knows more about that tightrope than the king realizes. This king has been one link in the triangular tug of European war since his childhood. Those Protestant Dutch would be natural allies except that they are rivals for control of rich far-off places. French King Louis has a strong link to Charles, whose sister is wife to the Duke of Orleans. Charles has to disguise his own Catholic leanings, but Coventry knows there is much more to this. Louis has curdled into open hostility more often in recent years and on top of it all Charles may be seen as a pleasure-seeking, smiling charmer, but his life is beset by the emptiness of his purse and the devilish bargains he must make to pay the bills. Tangier drains that purse like nowhere else on the globe.

Coventry sits there, worrying what will happen now. Who else can step into his experienced shoes to secure his king's safety? Royal footsteps crunch on the gravel and Charles stands over him. 'Henry, it is time to go home. I have my best ideas while taking a piss and it has come to me that we should allot two months at most, to pass on your tasks and free you.'

Coventry cannot stop himself. 'But who will you find to help you?'

'You have taught me much. Do you think I cannot do it all

myself?' Charles studies his friend's face and laughs. 'Do not answer that. You have fine people in your small team. I plan to use some of them. That young captain of yours, Clifton? I like him. As for the extraordinary St Michel, I have taken the weight of your promise off your shoulders. Then there is the matter of the capable Mr Pepys who has the bad luck to occupy the centre of the storm aimed at my brother. We have treasured him for many years and our navy needs him badly, but now he cannot be a blockage as we move boldly ahead. Sadly, there is more to the present difficulty than just Mr Pepys. Yes?'

Coventry studies him in silence, searching for the right words and feeling quite sick. Charles smiles. His reply sounds gentle but the words are not. 'You will not go against me, dear friend, because you know that would be treason.'

CHAPTER 21

In the years of hardship plodding towards him from below the horizon, Balty will exhaust himself trying to understand the events of the weeks to come. He will come to feel their rough shape, but he will never pin down the event that triggered all the others and he will never guess it was down to brother Pepys.

They get eighteen more letters from Pepys and send twelve back over the next two weeks. Instructions from London and responses to past queries only make sense if they refer to the right date and number of the letter in question. Adverse Channel winds confuse further by delays which build worries. The body of changing fact, fixed fact, instinct and guesswork builds ever higher and threatens to topple. There is no let-up from London. As the lists of people to persuade into a trip to England multiply, so does the vehemence of Pepys's insistence on economy. Even Sam begins to lose patience.

Esther's letters question their children's state of health with spelling that creates many puzzles. She is clearly enjoying the luxury of Will Hewer's house and Balty knows whatever comes next will be a rude shock.

A week on from his meeting with King Charles, Coventry

reads Balty's latest letter. The invisible part yields only a lemon juice apology for the shortage of fresh information and another request for money, so he has it copied and a trusted clerk takes the copy to Hewer's house. Pepys reads it through, reads it again and shouts for his friend. A surprised Hewer rushes into the room with Esther close behind him.

'He's done it,' says Pepys, waving the letter. 'I hardly dared hope. Balty has a fine English Protestant witness coming over to us. This watchmaker Joyne has full knowledge of Scott's treasonous acts. More. He has found two great men who will share their knowledge with the widow of the dead navy treasurer to cross the Channel on our behalf. They are Catholics but she is Protestant.'

Esther shrieks. 'So they can come home?'

'Soon. These people can show Scott is guilty of the crimes for which he has blamed me.'

Hewer sits down to read the letter and then, in their ignorance, they dig a deep hole. Their course of action seems so obvious to them because they both still believe in the rule of law. The prosecutor, Attorney-General Sir William Jones, has been against them but now he will realize he has been misled and do what the law dictates.

'We must seize the moment and speak to Jones at once,' says Pepys. 'He will have to arrest Scott.'

Hewer hesitates. He has not seen such joy on his old master's face for a deal of time, but it must be said. 'What if Scott gets wind of this? What if it spurs him on to find the second witness? That is all our enemies have ever needed – a second voice to swear to treason, conjured out of nowhere by a large bribe.' They contemplate that possibility in silence. With salvation in sight, the danger is doubled and trebled if the enemy knows the clock is ticking.

'The prosecutor must surely act,' says Pepys. 'The first Scott will know of it is when he steps ashore in England again.'

Hewer sends a footman to summon their diligent lawyer. Mr Hayes is a clever man with forty years' subtle experience of the law's many failings. He purses his lips. 'You ask me to demand a warrant for Scott's arrest?' he says in the end. 'We cannot be sure Jones will do that.'

'He must,' says Pepys. 'We will have all the witnesses we need.'

'You say "will." We *will* have all the witnesses. That is in the future. In the present we do not yet have them.' Hayes takes a silent pinch of snuff. Most men snort loudly as part of the ceremony. Hayes does nothing loudly.

'They continue to level their charges without producing evidence.'

'That, sir,' says Hayes, 'is because they have not enough witnesses, not because they have none at all. Always remember Scott has powerful allies.'

'He has Rolle and Peyton and the others. They will back away if they see they are losing.'

'Sir, he has the Earl of Shaftesbury behind him, for heaven's sake. The earl does not back away.'

Hewer disagrees. 'Even the earl will hesitate when he sees Scott's plan failing. Shaftesbury's mob see themselves as patriots. They will not like their earl's association with a traitor.'

'No, Mr Hewer. You are wrong. That mob is capable of mindless insurrection. Howling through the streets, hurling rocks through windows, heaping fuel on the fires they start.

There are not enough constables to overpower them. If the king had an army he could suppress them, but he has no army.'

Ever since Cromwell, the new politics bar any standing army without a clear foreign threat, because a standing army can be used against its own people. Warships are acceptable because they are an outward-facing protection against foreign powers, but radical voices point out that only dictators need large armies always on hand – absolute monarchs such as dangerous Louis across the Channel.

'The mob will change its view of Scott when it hears the accusations,' predicts Pepys.

Hayes tries again. 'Sir, not so. Consider how the mob gets its news. I go to the coffee houses where you cannot go as my face is not widely known. I watch and I listen to their political views and they don't read news sheets that don't please them. Truth does not find its way to the top of the heap, not in times like these. Truth that challenges their conception of their own righteousness cannot be truth. Do you know what drives them along?'

'Stupidity?'

'No, sir. Shame breeds blame and vengeance. They are privately ashamed of their lack of wealth and standing. Blame comes next because it makes that shame the fault of others, not themselves. Vengeance follows naturally from the vicious comfort of blame. *You* should not speak to Jones. I will go.'

'Mr Hayes, please do us that honour before any more time is wasted.'

Hayes is back again within the hour and shaking his head as he walks through the door. He is nearer anger than they have ever seen him. 'Jones has ducked the issue, sir,' he says to Pepys before the footman has even taken his coat. 'It is not his job, he says. What in God's name does he suppose his job to be? He suggests you speak to a higher authority. Who does he mean? King Charles? Jones could not wait to see the back of me.'

'Then I will go myself,' says Pepys, 'and force him to listen.'

Hewer's coach takes Pepys the short distance to Jones's chambers. He is announced then made to wait for a time that stretches far beyond the acceptable. Messengers come and go, sweaty from distance travelled at a rapid pace. They avoid Pepys's gaze. After far more than an hour, he is summoned by the insolent jerk of a footman's head and led to a room almost filled by a giant desk below shelves laden with books of the law. The window is very small. Jones sits in the gloom and does not even rise to greet him.

'Mr Pepys,' he says. 'I told your man Hayes there is nothing I can do. Why have you come to bother me?'

'Are you going to invite me to take a chair?'

'Are you going to stay long enough to need one?'

'I am staying until you make out an arrest warrant.'

'There is no chair yet made that will support you until then. Woodworm will have eaten them.'

'Sir,' says Pepys, speaking slowly and forcefully, 'we now have incontrovertible proof that Colonel John Scott is guilty of a great number of crimes, starting with fraud and theft in Long Island and then in the Low Countries. Most important of all, he stands accused by trustworthy witnesses of selling precisely those maps and informations to the court of King Louis that he has accused me of doing. My first witnesses are ready to swear to that and more will follow.'

'All papists I expect?' Jones has curled down behind his desk and bares yellow teeth as he speaks.

'No, sir, they are not.'

'I can do nothing for you,' says Jones. 'You may use all that in your defence when your own trial begins, for all the good it does you.'

'Your plain duty, sir, is to arrest Scott.'

'Do not tell me my duty, sir.'

'If your own brain does not, then I must.'

'I do not know where Colonel Scott is to be found,' says Jones. 'Perhaps you will get your chance to confront him yourself when he brings his second witness against you. I shall endeavour to speed that process, but I warn you that you are likely to very much regret the outcome.'

'I can now prove who is the real traitor, Sir William. It is the colonel himself.'

'He can also prove that it is you, sir.'

Pepys leaves in a rare fury, opening Jones's front door without waiting for the lounging footman and slamming it after him as hard as he can.

As soon as he leaves, a door to one side of Jones's study opens and a tall, burly man enters the room – a man with a military look and a slight cast in one eye.

'Did you hear all that?' Jones asks.

'I did,' says Colonel John Scott.

'Colonel, there is only so much more I can do for you and your patron. I am increasingly uncomfortable. You must soon find your second witness if you want me to continue. What progress have you made?'

'St Michel is rattling the cage bars in Paris. Those now prepared to support him make my task harder.'

'Do something now or lose me, Scott. I seek to retire soon. My successor may not be so inclined to help you.'

He recoils as Scott's fist thumps down on his desk. 'Hear me Jones. Do not go against me.'

'You threaten me?' Jones hears himself yelp and breathes hard to fight down panic. 'I am the highest officer of the law in the whole of England. You are not above that law, Colonel. It is in my sole power to decide whether Mr Pepys gets his arrest warrant.' Jones reaches for parchment and a pen. 'Twenty words written here will do it. Twenty words signed by me and *you* will be occupying a cell in the King's Bench prison.'

Scott picks up the inkwell and pours its contents all over the parchment. The ink runs over the edges and spreads across the Morocco leather of the desktop. Jones looks at it in astonishment and pushes his chair back to get away from the man standing over him.

The colonel speaks in a startlingly mild voice. 'Let me set you right, Sir William. Whether or not I am above the law, my patron, as you call him, is very far above it and you cannot reach high enough to touch his feet.'

'The earl is not the king.' He stops. 'Why do you laugh?'

Scott looms over him. 'I recommend you limit yourself to what you do best. Catching the pope's plotters. Otherwise . . .' He makes a cutthroat gesture with one finger and Jones watches him leave in utter silence.

Scott rides away. The next morning he sets out for Dover, intent on mischief – and he is not alone.

CHAPTER 22

Fourteen days pass. Two weeks of hard work for the team, treading the Paris streets to knock on often unresponsive doors. Trenchepain provides more bags of Houblon's silver and Balty rewards Hubert for every packet he brings. There is occasional material in them to give him hope. Instructions to question Cornish fishermen, new commands going out to the Americas ordering a squadron back to reinforce French Channel forces. That will raise Secretary Coventry's eyebrows.

The landlady knocks on their door, ignores Sam and Betty and melts into a pout as she looks past them to Balty. 'A note for you, sir,' she says.

'I am summoned to the embassy,' says Balty. 'Mr Savile wishes to speak to me. I hope I will not be long. You will look after Hubert?'

'We will.'

Sam goes back to his analysis of the conflicts in the information they have amassed. Hubert slides into the room, making just enough noise to avoid startling them. The landlady never spots him.

Sam pours him a small mug of red wine and pushes a plate

of dried meats across the table. Hubert has become his personal project and he enjoys the debriefing process. He carefully frees the seal on the latest packet with a hot blade. It takes him two lines of shorthand to cover the news contained inside but it will make little difference to anything.

Hubert puts down his mug. 'There is something new,' he says, 'but it needs us to work together. For the last few days, around eleven by the bell, the porter at the Rue Briboucher copy office hands out a fat packet to be run to the new Headquarters. It has three seals on it.'

'Triple seals?' Betty says, 'That does sound special.'

'There's more. The porter won't hand it over until there is a second messenger there to escort it. I want to try it before all the others get to hear about it and that means ...'

'... you need me to come with you,' says Sam.

'Exactly.'

Betty frowns. 'Won't they see you have the same number?'

'Not if you hang back a bit Sam. That way, I shout to you and you join me as I run past. They won't even see your number.'

'They won't like that.'

'No, but today we will see if it's worth the trouble and tomorrow we can work out what to do next if it is.'

Sam is already pulling on his sailor suit. 'Let's do it,' he says.

Balty arrives at the embassy and the porter opens the door in semi-senile mode. 'Do you have an appointment, sir?' he asks.

'Mr Savile has called me to a meeting.'

'Mr Savile, you say? And your name, sir?'

'You know my name. It is St Michel. Come on, there's only the two of us here. Stop it.'

'I'm sure I don't know what you mean, sir. Please wait here.'

He comes back frowning. 'Follow me, sir. Mr Savile will see you now.'

Savile rises from his desk as Balty is shown in. 'How good to see you, Mr Mitchell.'

'My name is St Michel.'

'Ah. To what do I owe the pleasure of this visit?'

'You told me to come.'

'I did? What was that about?' Savile stares at an open book on his desk, clearly puzzled. 'Remind me. Was it about the cognac?'

'You sent me a message not an hour ago.'

'Did I? It's not about Madame Després is it?'

'No, Mr Savile. I am Mr Pepys's brother-in-law and I hoped you had information for me.'

Savile's face clears. 'Yes. You upset Mr Brisbane. Great shame that he has gone. Far more work for me. A whole list of stuff to do for Pepys. I have to speak to that marquis and get in touch with someone, some relative of Mr Pepys. That would be you? A Frenchy? Well, well.'

'So *have* you spoken to the marquis?'

'Lord no and I don't actually think I asked you to come at all. Do please let Mr Pepys know I will do my very best. He may regain his influence one day and I would like to return to London.'

'I will be sure to mention that when I see him,' says Balty. 'If he survives, that is.'

It takes him fifteen minutes through the crowded streets to get back to their rooms and he is startled to find nobody there – not Sam, not Hubert and not Betty. The only trace is a sheet of paper on the table with notes he has not read before, seeming to give detailed movement orders for a dozen warships of the French Channel Fleet. Half an hour passes and now he is severely worried. That stretches to an hour and he is distraught. He has every reason to be.

It happens like this.

Sam tucks the pistol into his pocket when he puts on his sailor suit because it makes him feel just a tiny bit better. This exploit is a long stride into the unknown.

'We should not be seen together wearing the same number,' says Hubert. 'I will go first. Wait to a count of sixty. I will be halfway along the the Rue de la Harpe, where it is quieter. When I see you I will start running again. Follow me but keep your distance.'

'When you've finished, come straight back,' says Betty.

'I will,' says Sam. 'Don't go anywhere whatever happens, will you.'

Betty watches from the window as Hubert appears in the street and trots away to the left. She looks down again, waiting to see Sam, but instead she sees two men who have been standing outside the tavern turn and lope after Hubert. Sam appears a few seconds later when the men have already merged into the crowd and she wrestles with the iron latch trying to open the window to shout a warning. It is seized solid and she can only watch as he too disappears into the crowd.

She thinks for a fraction of a second about Sam's instruction to stay home and rejects it instantly. She goes to the cupboard, grabs the little pistol that Ezra gave her, checks the powder in the pan and tucks it away inside her waistband. Then she takes the stairs two at a time, reaching the street just in time to see a pair of heads, which may be the men, turning into the Rue de la Harpe. Betty can run like a hare, but she has to jink between all the people and she gets to the junction too late. The Rue de la Harpe is much quieter. A fiacre has been standing there some way down it and she is just in time to see the men bundle a cream-clad boy into it. The carriage moves off.

The prisoner must be Hubert, because Sam emerges from a deep doorway ahead of her, waits for the carriage to get further down the road, then runs off after it.

Betty thinks of the journey from Deal to Gravesend, feels the little pistol in her waistband and decides Sam is safer if he doesn't know she is there. She lets him get almost out of sight and follows, but when she gets to where the fiacre had been standing, she sees what he missed: Hubert's sailor's cap lying in the gutter. She picks it up, sees the red patch soaking into one side of it, then runs on.

Sam is using Hubert's method to follow the fiacre and stay out of sight, though it is moving at a testing pace and he starts to attract curious looks from passers-by who aren't used to seeing naval messengers take this route. His heart is pounding with fear on top of the exertion.

The fiacre slows for road menders and Sam thinks he may be in the upper part of the Rue de Tournon, but he has lost track. This road is lined by newly built mansions, small palaces, some bearing gilt coats of arms on the gates. Sam hangs back and sees the carriage turn in to stop at the steps of a very large house that looks dishevelled compared to its bright new neighbours. Its days are numbered and the vacant plot next door is already cleared for better things. Whatever previously stood there has been pulled apart and the stone is piled up for reuse. Bushes spring up along one side of the site and nettles cover the rest.

Sam tucks himself into a doorway behind a fence and looks through a gap between its planks at the house. Three men stand on its steps scanning the road, then go to the fiacre and flank the other two as they drag Hubert inside. Sam studies the windows and sees nobody, so he dashes across the road into the building site next door, heading for the screen of bushes along the fence boundary. He finds a narrow trodden pathway through the nettles, showing that something often comes this way. It takes him into the bushes just as a woman's head appears at a window high up on the side of the house. She calls out something and is cut off with a shriek of laughter as a man's arms enfold her and drag her back.

Sam dives into the foliage, expecting to have to struggle for cover, but it separates easily and he sprawls onto the beaten earth floor of a cleared dome, rolling on to his back. The remains of his breath is knocked out of him as a boy jumps to kneel on his chest, staring into his face and holding a long knife, which pricks his throat.

'Stay still,' says the boy. 'I can let out your blood before you can move and I will not think twice about it.'

'No need,' gasps Sam. 'I mean you no harm.'

'You lie. You have come from the house.'

'The house there? Beyond the fence? No I haven't. I was hiding from them.'

'Truly?'

'Yes.'

'Are you a navy messenger? Be very careful how you answer.'

Sam shakes his head. 'No. I am pretending for good reasons.'

The boy stares at Sam's outfit and stretches out a finger to touch the fabric. 'You tell the truth,' he says and clambers off him, laying the knife on the ground.

'This is ridiculous,' says Sam, remembering that first day with Hubert. 'You don't know anything about me. I might be lying.'

'You are not. I see it in your eyes. That is how I live. I do tricks and I juggle and I tell fortunes. I see what people want to hear in their eyes. I know when I am near the truth. What is your name?'

'Jacques.'

'No it is not.'

'My name is Sam.'

'That's right. Odd name.'

'English.'

'Sammm. Like a dog not sure whether to growl.'

Another extraordinary street boy. Sam sees Hubert, a bit cleaner, taller and just as thin, but where survival dominates Hubert's thoughts, this one has the light of another world about him. He has a healing cut down one cheek and a hand wrapped in a cloth showing a dark stain.

'What is your name?' Sam asks.

'Count Victor.'

'Really?'

'What is real? They hung a dull one on me in the orphanage. I found a better name inside my head and I like the sound it makes.'

'What happened to your hand?'

'They almost got me yesterday, the new bastards next door. I climbed in the kitchen. It was not theft because they had food for an army and I am just one. The man slashed me but he was too big for the window. I went back later so I didn't go hungry.'

'That was risky.'

'It was not. I have a hidden way.'

'You say they are new?'

'The house has been empty for months now. I lived in it until they showed up but I had this ready as my bolt hole. They won't stay long.'

'How do you know?'

'They act like soldiers. Here for a purpose. Only concerned with their mattresses, their food and their guns.'

Sam looks around. Count Victor has plaited long leaves into the branches of the bush above them. The earth floor occupies the surviving angle of two low brick walls, a last survival of the extinct house. Wooden planks are laid on the ground next to it, making a platform for a straw mattress and two neatly folded blankets. A decrepit wooden barrow holds an array of bowls and an earthenware jug. It is all surprisingly neat.

'Victor, they have seized a friend of mine . . .'

'*Count* Victor please.'

'Count Victor. He is a boy from the streets like you but he's a naval messenger now, dressed like me. Those men took him. I followed them here and they dragged him inside.'

'What can *you* do about it?'

'I don't know yet. Who are these people?'

'Foreigners. I can't tell what sort yet but I have ways to spy on them. There is one called quenelle.'

'Colonel? Colonel Scott?'

'That's it. You say it like they do. Kernel Scott.'

'They are English, like me.'

'You are not French?'

'Part of me. Who else is in there?'

'A few tough men. They get bossed around by this kernel. One more I think, but he is not visible. Yesterday two women joined them. Women with painted faces from expensive boudoirs.'

'I must save my friend. You say you have a way in?'

'My very best secret. If they find it, I will lose a dry bed when the house is empty and a full pantry when it is not.' He stares at Sam for a long moment. 'I have to live and go on living. You understand?'

'I will help you. If you take me over there, I will give you a gift when we get back.'

'What gift?'

Sam reaches inside his jacket and shows the little pistol. He sees Count Victor's eyes gleam.

'Oh,' he says. 'I would sleep better with that in my reach. May I hold it?'

Sam hesitates a moment, then hands it to him. The boy aims it, cradles it in both hands, nods and hands it back. Trust has been fully established. It is all Sam has to give, but a single shot from a small gun in this place teeming with threat is no use to him. The boy may use it better.

'How do we get in?' he says.

Count Victor moves his mattress to one side. They lift away the planks and there below are stone steps leading down into darkness.

'I like to think a prince lived here and his secret lover lived next door. Keep your hand on my shoulder. I don't need light but we must be silent or they will have us.'

At the bottom of the worn stairs there is a heavy wooden door. Count Victor takes a thick iron key from its concealment in the stonework and the lock grates open. He puts the key back and leaves it that way. 'In case we need to run,' he whispers. A

right-angle turn in the passage beyond cuts off much of the dim
light from the outside world. The short passage beyond opens
into a larger space, sensed more than seen. Sam feels a damp
draught on his cheeks. Rodents scamper from their intrusion. A
smell of ancient rot puts him sharply in mind of their house in
Deal and that floods him with sidelined childhood, a pang for
his mother, and a shock of surprise at how much has changed
in only weeks. The floor evens out and his feet tell him they
walk on tiles.

Across that space, the sounds change again as they enter
another passage. He sees faint light ahead of them and hears
hints of human voices. Thirty more steps and the passage
curves into another larger space. Flickering light comes from
the left through a small iron grille at head height. Count Victor
inches towards it, sliding his feet with slow movements to avoid
kicking any of the litter of empty bottles and splintered boxes
showing dimly around them. The grille is set in a door, secured
on their side by ancient iron bolts, swollen with rust. Sam sees
that Count Victor's dark clothing makes him almost invisible
in this gloom.

A man's voice raps out a question in the room beyond and
the words are English. 'Who has your father talked to in Paris?'

A boy's voice that Sam knows well replies in French. 'I don't
understand.' A fist smacks on flesh and Hubert screams.

Sam moves towards the grille and looks through for only a
moment before Count Victor pulls him back out of the light.

The momentary glimpse of that cellar room is seared into his
head. A boarded floor and whitewashed walls. Another door
with the same grille on the far side but standing half open. A
dozen candles around the room. Hubert, lashed to a chair in the

middle. A man sits to one side, wearing a silver-grey periwig and a dark blue coat with silver decoration. Two muscled brutes stand either side of Hubert. One is bald. The other has ginger hair tied in a pigtail. Sam only knows it is Hubert by the sailor suit because the boy's face is a mask of blood.

Sam takes the pistol from his pocket, but Count Victor grabs his hand and shakes his head violently. He is right. One uncertain shot cannot help.

The man in the chair says, 'Speak English, little man. Stop pretending.'

That is met by silence, not even a sob from Hubert.

The bald brute says, 'Mebbe time for the water, Colonel. That gets them talking.'

'Why not?' says Scott. 'Let's do it. Lash him to the floor.'

Hammering, grunts, wood splitting and a series of small shrieks. Sam creeps to the edge of the grille again, squints sideways and downward, and there is Hubert splayed out on the boards, his wrists and ankles tied to four iron spikes. The bald man spreads a thick cloth over the boy's head. A pump handle is working somewhere beyond his sight, water splashing into a bucket in gouts. The pigtailed man appears from the left, pours the bucketful onto the cloth and goes for another one. Hubert is gagging and choking under the heavy, drenched fabric that has moulded itself around his nose and mouth as a lethal mask, leaving him nothing to breathe but water. They tip another bucket and another, Scott shouting at the drowning boy, 'Say you'll talk. That's all you have to do and we will stop.'

They pause and lift the cloth and the water has washed away some of the blood but Hubert's broken face is barely recognizable. He spews water out of his mouth, coughs, retches it from his lungs and makes faint sounds. Scott leans towards him. 'Well?' he growls, and all Hubert can do is whisper wetly and in French.

The cloth goes back on and the buckets soak it again until the boy can say nothing more, but by that time Sam has crept away into the darkness, wishing he had never seen or heard any of it. That is when he steps on a piece of wood which snaps under his foot and a hush falls in the next room. The light coming from the room dims as a face is pressed to the far side of the grille. Sam freezes, seeing the remaining light shining faintly on the pale fabric of his uniform. The face disappears and Count Victor tugs him to one side. 'Lie down,' he hisses and he feels the boy lie in front of him. A lantern shines into the room through the grille, its outer edge just reaching them, but Count Victor's dark rags mask Sam's suit.

The lantern goes away and the men's voices return to normal. They hear no further sounds from Hubert.

CHAPTER 23

Balty is filled with fear and growing fury. It is three hours now and his children are still out there somewhere in the unknown. Pacing back and forth to the window does not help, so he immerses himself in cleaning his pair of heavy pistols and reloading with fresh powder. As he tamps in the wads that hold the balls in place, he is certain he will be using them soon – but where, when and against whom? When he's done he lays them carefully on the table within easy reach. They are elderly leftovers from Cromwell's war, with long barrels and dog locks, but they shoot straight.

Something niggles at him, something he should have seen in the cupboard but did not see. Wherever he has gone, Sam has taken his little pistol with him, but that's not much comfort. All that is left in the cupboard is Betty's little pistol in its leather case. He decides to reload that one too, just in case, but the case is empty. That makes him feel just a bit better. Betty has left at her own volition. She has taken the pistol and she has saved Sam once with it already. He vows he will buy them both much better weapons when this is over.

He crosses to the window again and scans the street in time

to see Madame Florentine leave the house with a group of friends. It is busy out there, the roast meat shops and taverns doing a fine trade. A man is standing opposite, out in the open, staring at their door. He keeps his head down under a wide-brimmed hat and he is wearing dun-coloured clothing. Fury fills Balty. Jamming both pistols in his belt, he runs down the stairs, hearing a fusillade of raps on the door as he crosses the hallway. He yanks the door open, grabs with his left hand and hauls the man inside, tripping him and pressing a pistol to his cheek as he slams the door shut. The man's hat falls off, revealing a bandage around his forehead.

'Don't move a muscle,' Balty growls.

'I don't think I can,' whispers the other man, 'but . . . I have to say I don't like your hat.'

'I'm not wearing a bloody . . . Ah . . .'

'Let go of me, St Michel. I'm only just walking in a straight line again after last time,' the other man says, rolling painfully on his side and waving away Balty's pistol. 'I will say it one more time slowly. I . . . don't . . . like . . . your . . . hat. Do you know who I am now?'

'You are . . .' Balty gropes for the name. 'You are . . . Angier?'

'Almost. I am Captain René Augier and I am at your service so long as you stop hitting me.'

'Captain Augier, yes. Are you all right?'

'Of course I'm not. I already had a concussion. Was that you too? I never saw it coming.'

'No. That was the man from the embassy.'

'What man?'

'The doorman, but he must know you're on the same side?'

'The embassy knows nothing about me. I have always

worked directly for Secretary Coventry and he, quite rightly, does not trust Fat Harry Savile with anything private.'

'But you were running to attack our little messenger friend.'

'I was running to save your little messenger friend from the tall man with the knife.'

'I didn't see any man with a knife.'

'No, the street was a little overcrowded with attackers and their victims. He got away.'

'But now my children are missing. I need help. Can you stand up?'

'If you give me a hand and then a strong drink.'

Up in the room, Balty pours him cognac. 'Today,' he asks, 'how long have you been out there for?'

'Hours.'

Hope springs up. 'Did you see my children leave?'

'First I saw your tame messenger leave. Then two men went after him into the crowd. Next I saw your son follow them up the road and just as I was about to go after them, your daughter did the same, keeping at a distance.'

'You did nothing?'

'Speed is not on my side today. Your children seemed to be the hunters not the hunted. I have heard about their skills from Secretary Coventry.'

'So . . . you just hid here and waited?'

'I watched for their return. I saw your face at the window over and over again and the look on it changing. I knew it was time to meet you. Please explain about the messenger clothes?'

Balty tells him about Hubert and the second sailor suit, then frowns at him. 'Why have you been watching this house without declaring yourself until now?'

'Secretary Coventry asked me to monitor your safety. He felt extra responsibility for your children and the hazard has increased. That is why I came back as soon as I could move again.'

'My children are smart and their French is perfect.' Balty says it to reassure himself. 'They will not be suspected.'

'They are in danger from the English, not the French. Colonel Scott came back to Paris yesterday.'

Balty crosses himself. 'Oh great heavens. He has come back here because of us?'

'Of course. He wants to ensure no witnesses go to England. He plans to kill you. They won't go if you are dead.'

'Kill me?'

'Unless I stop him and not just him. He has come in company.'

'Who?'

'I cannot yet say. They have gone to ground and I don't know where. Not to any of their usual places. I think they have found discreet lodgings somewhere and brought hired thugs with them.'

'Augier, I must find my children.'

'I have put my people on the job. You need to stay here. Don't let anyone in who you don't know.'

'I can help search the streets.'

'No. You must stay here and be on your guard. I will bring any news. Yes?'

'Yes,' says Balty, but he doesn't mean it.

Betty makes sure to stay out of sight when Sam ducks into shelter on the Rue de Tournon. She has an angled view of the old house further up the road on the other side, and she catches a glimpse of Hubert's uniform as the men haul him up its steps.

She watches Sam vanish into the wild undergrowth next door where the demolition crews have piled up old stone. She studies the front of the big house and when she is sure no one is watching from the windows, crosses the road to the vacant plot and follows Sam's faint track, crawling through the screen of vegetation to discover the neat little camp with planks piled up and steps descending into gloom. It feels like the entrance to a trap which may have already claimed Sam. Retracing her steps, she decides to walk boldly past the old house as if she has every right to be there. She gives it surreptitious glances, but a face appears at a window and as she walks on past, she hears the front door burst open. She turns her head and sees a woman in green silk, her face heavily painted, run down the steps. 'You,' the woman shouts, 'come back here right now.'

'Me?'

'Yes you, of course. Are you an imbecile? You are the maid sent by Chénier?'

Betty rapidly weighs up her choices. Going into the house has a high risk, but acting like an imbecile may offer some protection. She can explain later that she is not the maid. She giggles wildly and nods her head twice.

'So Chenier bestirred himself, did he?' says the woman and snorts. 'I wasn't going to have that. Tomorrow indeed. I told him we needed you yesterday. His nibs upstairs isn't familiar with dust.' She seems to be talking to herself, so Betty meekly climbs the wide front steps in the wake of her anger and follows her into the great entrance hall. It smells of decay.

The woman leads her to a passage behind the hallway and

points to a narrow spiral stair descending into darkness. 'You sleep down there. Find a room with a mattress. There is food in the kitchen. You get the leftovers. Have you no bag?'

'Yes,' she says, 'I have no bag at all!' and giggles again.

'Lord spare me. Do you know how to use a broom?'

'A broom? For sweeping? Backwards and forwards?'

'Oh great heavens. Find one. There is stuff like that downstairs. Sweep this floor. The hall here and the rooms each side. Do it well and I will find you more jobs. Work hard. I will be checking.'

The woman disappears up the left-hand staircase of the grand pair curving upwards each side of the hallway. Betty goes back to the servants' staircase, spiralling down, and hears faint voices from below. First she finds a broom and a pan and makes short work of the hallway to give herself cover in case the woman comes back quickly. The large reception rooms each side have dust sheets covering all the furniture, but she starts to sweep one of them and leaves the broom there as proof of work in progress, then she goes down the narrow stairs into the depths of the house. As her eyes get used to the gloom, she locates three small rooms to the left, with straw mattresses on the floor. To the right, a large kitchen is littered with recent food remains, then two big pantries have passages in all directions around them. One of those takes her past a wine cellar towards the room where she can now clearly hear men's voices and see flickering light through the half-open door.

Water splashes and someone shouts in English, 'Say you'll talk. That's all you have to do and we will stop.'

She realizes Hubert is in there and they must think he's Sam. She goes back up the stairs and starts to sweep the other room very slowly.

CHAPTER 24

When Augier leaves, Balty packs his pistols, powder horn, a bag of balls and another of wads in his leather shoulder bag and takes to the streets. He goes to all the places he knows that lie on the routes of the navy messengers and he talks to all of the messengers he can find. It gets him nowhere, but it is a very little bit better than doing nothing and there is brief hope every time he sees a flash of a small sailor's uniform ahead of him. Towards the end of that appalling day he realizes that for all he knows he may have walked straight past Colonel John Scott and wishes he knew what Scott looks like, remembering only phrases like 'a cast in one eye' and a 'tall, burly man'. Would Scott know him? Maybe, but he hopes not.

It is almost dark when he comes back to the house and Madame Florentine comes out into the hallway as he reaches the stairs. She shakes her head and hands him a beaker and a bottle of strong spirit. Upstairs, he swallows an ill-advised mouthful of something that could be marc, though the grape skins that generated this one might have been better left to rot. As he thinks about getting some sleep, he hears someone shouting in the street and looks down from the window to see Augier standing by a fiacre, waving his arms. He grabs his shoulder bag and hurries down.

Augier, white-faced and swaying, urges Balty into the carriage. 'There may be bad news,' he says and tells the coachman to take them to the King's Gardens. It is not far, but Balty can see Augier is in poor condition for walking. He does not suspect that Augier is thinking ahead to a moment when Balty himself may be in no state to come back on his own two feet.

'Have you found my children?' Balty asks.

'You must see for yourself, then we will know.'

Augier tells the coachman to wait at the entrance. They walk between beds of herbs to a long stone building which stirs Balty's memories into a growing feeling of dread. A man waits at the door and Balty recognizes Dr FitzGerald from a decade earlier. At once his dread redoubles. This is part of the medical school and he had stood with Pepys and Elizabeth in this very place. Here, FitzGerald had offered them the privilege of watching his students dissecting the bodies of the destitute, the criminals and the other unknown dead grappled from the Seine.

FitzGerald stares at Balty and grasps him by the shoulders. 'St Michel,' he says, 'I remember you. Monsieur de la Croisière here,' he indicates Augier, 'says you are searching for a naval messenger boy bearing the number 156 on his uniform. I regret to inform you that the body of a boy wearing that uniform was retrieved from the Seine this evening. I see from your face that this brings personal distress.'

'The boy . . .' Balty begins. 'The boy may be . . .' Completing the sentence feels lethal, words that once out there will make his worst fears come true.

Augier takes his arm gently. 'Shall we go to see? It is best to know.'

Balty nods dumbly, but the other possibility comes to him on the way up the stairs. Two boys, not one, wore that number 156: Sam and Hubert. The doom voice in his ear points out that it is Sam who has not come home, but hope has him nod and follow FitzGerald, climbing fast with Augier labouring behind them.

They arrive in a large chamber, lit by oil lamps. White-gowned students bend over things on tables that he chooses not to look at. He can smell spirits and something worse. FitzGerald leads them into a side room. A broom and a bucket occupy one corner. A shrouded body is stretched out on a table. He stares at this mystery, the sheet showing no hint of who lies under it. Balty knows the next second will tell. He seizes the sheet and pulls it gently back. What he sees is horrifying but makes him no wiser. The face he is looking at is massively swollen in shadows of maroon and grey, unrecognizable. He groans and switches his gaze to the hair, clotted with mud.

'Water,' he says. 'Quickly.' FitzGerald goes out and in fifteen very long seconds comes back with a jug. Balty pours it over the hair, washing away the Seine filth to show a darker brown. Sam's brown is lighter than Hubert's. This is the urchin, not his son, or does the wetting only make it seem darker? He turns to the clothing, soaking wet and stained with more of the mud and maroon patches. He fingers the stitching of the number 156 and knows then for certain that this is not Sam's careful work, but the rougher thread of the real uniform. He nerves himself to reach down. The swollen lips are stiff and shockingly cold to the touch. He separates them with difficulty and glimpses gap teeth. His heart roars back into life with the knowledge that this body is Hubert and not his son and feels immediately ashamed as he looks again at Hubert's ravaged face. He hears the boy's light voice in his head, expressing his ambitions and his brave view of the world. For the first time in many years, he says a short and silent prayer.

He turns to the other men. 'It is not my son, but I do know this boy. He is an orphan named Hubert who has been helping us.'

FitzGerald seems unsure what to say, but Balty knows the boy would not be dead but for him. 'We will pay for a proper funeral,' he says. We? He means the three of them and his panic immediately takes a new form. Sam and Betty are still missing. Hubert's death does not make them safe.

Augier is staring at the body. 'Can you tell how he died?' he asks.

'His lungs are full of water,' says FitzGerald. 'He drowned.'

'But the face?'

'The Seine is a busy river.'

'Thank you, sir,' says Augier and turns to Balty. 'Let us go back. There is nothing more to discover here.' He is soon shown to be wrong.

They walk back past the beds of herbs. Balty stops and looks down at them in the darkness. 'These are cures for all sorts of things,' he says, remembering FitzGerald's description all those years ago. 'One has curled leaves. It is good for taking away worry. I wish I could see it. Oh, poor Hubert. We put him in danger and those men did for him . . .' His voice rises. '*Where is my son?*'

The fiacre is waiting where the gardens reach the road, but

now a man astride a bay horse waits by it. 'Is that you, sir?' he calls and slips off it, holding out a roll of cloth to Augier. 'The patrol found this in a pond near the Luxembourg Palace. It's another one.'

'Another what?' Augier unrolls it, still cream in patches between the mud and the blood.

'Another uniform, just the same. Even the same number, 156.'

CHAPTER 25

After his clumsiness alerts Scott's thugs, Sam takes more care as they cross the cellar floor. Count Victor is leading him onward to the further corner of the cellars past the door with the grille. Another narrow passage takes them to a spiral brick staircase where Count Victor stops. 'You are an idiot,' he whispers.

'They soon gave up looking. They think it was a rat.'

'Rats don't break wood by standing on it. I have studied these men in their rooms up there. Even drunk, they have the smartness of the streets. They could be out there now, circling the house. I don't want to lose my shelter or my life. There is nothing you can do for your friend. Save your own neck. Get away from here.'

Sam looks back towards the cellar, feels the puny pistol in his pocket and knows that's right. Then he thinks of Hubert's bravery and cannot walk away. He needs to make them pay.

'You studied them? How did you do that?'

Count Victor points up the stairs to a faint glow. 'These were for the servants of the prince who lived here. An old woman still used to sleep here when I first came. She served here when she was my age. She told me the story of the prince who had magic servants who appeared out of nowhere when he wanted them. That way he never had to see the people who stoked his fires and cleaned his mess. She showed me the run of the hidden corridors. Then she died and I buried her.'

'Show me?'

Count Victor gives him a rapid tour of the secret ways with passages that ended at concealed doors, disguised as bookcases or the backs of tall cupboards. They move like ghosts, hearing men arguing in one room and a woman shriek with feigned pleasure in another. Back in the cellars, they pass a room with another smaller grille, thick with spider webs, and hear a man's booming voice. 'That's the son dealt with. The father comes next, right?' They stop, seeing shadows move on the back wall of their passageway, thrown there by the candlelight.

'You're very sure that's the boy?' It is the man in the blue coat with the silver buckles. It is Colonel Scott. 'He never spoke a single word of English when we were going at him. Kids can't take that much pain. I think you screwed up.'

'He came out of their house. Had to be him.'

'It's too late to ask him now, isn't it? Pour me some of that.'

A cork is pulled with a pop. Liquid splashes.

'What's the kid done to you anyway, Colonel?'

'His father's going round Paris making out I'm a traitor. I couldn't give Christ's right bollock for the kid. It's his god-damned uncle I want. Bastard had me chased out of England by half his bloody navy. Me! I was out to *save* England. Trusted by our noble friend with the mission to end all missions. A message to carry of national importance and a ship waiting at Gravesend. Whole place was in an uproar.'

'It was?'

'Course it was. They'd just found Godfrey blocking up a ditch, hadn't they?'

'And they said you did it?'

'That was what Mr bloody Pepys thought, but I had the better of him. I got safe out to sea, swapped ships off Dover, made it here and did my business.'

'What was your business?'

The crash of a bottle breaking makes Sam jump.

'*My* business is none of *your* business and you don't want to be poking your nose into *his* business.'

'No need for that, Colonel. Put it down before you cut yourself. I'll get another bottle. Just interested in you, that's all. You've done so much in your life. Anyway, you got back to England again, so it must have turned out all right in the end?'

'All right you say? I spent months kicking my heels over here. That tubby little bastard had warrants waiting for me at every port. I would have made my fortune. I should have been up there pulling the strings right now. Do you know what I would like to see? Pepys cut up in quarters and hung out for the birds to peck. Plus his family, what's left of them.'

A door creaks and a woman's voice says, 'Colonel, he wants you upstairs. You should come quickly.'

'Hello, darling,' says the other man's voice. 'What are you wearing, or should I say what aren't you wearing?' But they hear two pairs of feet hurrying away and the door is closed.

Sam and Count Victor creep away and put their heads together. 'Where do you think he's going?' says Sam. 'I want to hear them.'

'They made the blue room ready. Shipped in a huge bed and decked it all out with hangings. That's where he's going. There isn't a safe way in.' Count Victor fell silent, thinking. 'I do have an idea. It is dangerous. What is it worth to you if it works?'

'Powder and balls for your new pistol? My father will reward you well. Tell me.'

CHAPTER 26

Balty is in hell. Augier takes him back to the Rue de la Huchette. 'They won't stop at your son,' he says. 'They will be after you too. I will send men to be here with you.'

'Can you get me an army? We will find the people who did this and I will tear them to pieces.'

Augier inspects Balty's pistols. 'Put one on either side of your bed in case they come in the night. Shoot first. I will get the men here as soon as I can. Let nobody in until morning. Make sure the door stays barred.'

'Go.'

Augier nods and leaves in silence. Balty slumps down on the bed. He thinks of Esther and has no idea how he will be able to tell her any of this. He takes a swig from Madame Florentine's spirit bottle, recoils, then takes another and another, his hand reaching out to it without any more conscious thought to do so. The next thing he knows is he is abruptly awake, still fully dressed. The room is rotating slowly though he can see virtually nothing. The emptiness of the deep silence tells him it is that time of night when people die, the hours between three and four, but ... what has woken him? Hearing a scrape and the slightest of movements somewhere to his left, he creeps a hand out to the table beside the bed, feeling for the pistol that should be there – but there is no pistol. Sleep and the liquor had got to him first, so he touches only the mug and an unlit candle. A tiny noise again. The slightest creak of a board under a foot? Another one, closer. A killer is approaching from out there to his left. He rears up off the bed and lunges towards the sound, grabbing at shadows with both hands. As his eyes widen to the darkness, an outline forms that may be a face and a harsh voice says something he cannot understand. He lashes out and his wild fist strikes hard bone. His target shrieks and thuds down onto the floor. Silence.

Balty feels around in the dark, and his hands find a body, lying utterly still. He bends an ear to the face and hears shallow breathing. Panicking for light, he forces himself to breathe slowly, then feels all around the floor for his shoulder bag, pulls out the powder horn and dribbles some of its contents into the mug. The slow breathing of the man on the floor does not change. It is early summertime and the stove has not been lit for more than a day, so no embers will be found there. There is a tinderbox somewhere in the room, but where is another matter. It takes an age of groping in the dark before he finds it in the far corner, on the desk where Sam had left his notebook when he last rushed out of the room. Balty tears pages from the back of the book, hoping Sam will forgive him for the violation, then frowning as the futility of that hope hits him.

He shreds paper onto the gunpowder and it takes him three fumbling goes to strike a spark, but it catches and the powder flares. A tiny flame curls and grows as it spreads through the torn strips. He lights the candle, pushes it into a holder and then lights two more so that the darkness shrinks back to the walls of the room. Only then does he look down to see that this is no adult. This is another ragamuffin street urchin in dark clothes lying there on the floor, filthy, bloody and barely breathing, a burglar caught in the act. Balty cannot believe the damage his blow has done to the urchin's hugely swollen face. He bends down closer to look, but the boy stinks of decay and sewers and Balty's stomach revolts. One eye is closed, blood seeps and tufts of his hair are missing. What hair is left is dark and knotted with more blood, drying from a long scalp wound.

What to do with him? He may be a thief, but he is a child and grievously hurt. Balty lays a blanket on the floor and rolls him onto it, turning his head away and trying not to breathe in. He folds the rest of the blanket over the body and lays it on the sofa and lifts the unconscious form onto it and sharp tears come to his eyes. Three boys now, one dead, this one grievously hurt and one, the most precious one, missing. And then there is Betty. He confronts the hope still fluttering in him and tells himself not to be fooled by it. It is time to plan terrible revenge.

It is very hard to think. Taking the cords that tie back the curtains, he lashes the urchin's ankles together and secures them to the table leg. This time, he remembers Augier's instructions and places his pistols carefully, one each side of his bed, leaving one candle alight and a pile of others to take their turn. He settles down to watch, but his eyes quickly close. Sleep claims him and in that sleep, Balty dreams that Sam is crying out to him for rescue. It is not the self-assured Sam he has lost. This is the Sam of earlier childhood, crying 'papa, papa' over and over in a wavering voice that cuts straight to his bleeding heart. He opens his eyes and this dream lurches into a waking delusion,

because the weak voice goes on crying and the words remain
the same. 'Papa, papa.'

The voice is coming from the floor.

His candle has gone out and dawn is now creeping around
the edges of the curtains. He lurches up out of the bed, disori-
entated, reaches for the powder horn and does it all over again,
piling torn paper on the powder and groping in the dark for
the tinderbox. He cannot get the spark to strike and the voice
from the sofa rises in pitch and strength, getting in the way of
rational thought. He strikes it one more time, violently, and
this time a shower of sparks cascades onto a much larger pile of
powder than he intended to pour. In its light he sees that the
sparks are also cascading onto the primed lock of the pistol he
had forgotten all about – the pistol that is pointing towards him.
He lunges towards it, but as his hand gets to it there is a spurt of
flame, an almighty crash, and a slash of violent pain across his
left arm. Shocked, he manages to light a candle with a shaking
right hand and the room flickers into view, now filled with
powder smoke. Eyes smarting, he levers himself up and lights
two more and only then does he turn to look at the urchin on
the floor. One of the boy's eyes is open, though lurid swelling
keeps the other closed. The mouth moves and it is Sam's teeth
he sees. The voice struggles to speak and it is Sam's voice that
is struggling into his father's deafened ears.

'Papa,' Sam says, 'you have shot yourself.'

Rapid footsteps arrive outside and Madame Florentine rushes
into the room, horrified by what she sees and demanding expla-
nations, but when Balty tells her this is Sam and she sees their
injuries, she rises magnificently to the occasion.

'You first, sir. It will not take so long, then perhaps you

can help,' she says as she cleans the furrow in Balty's arm with stinging spirits and binds it up so that the blood is staunched. She lifts Sam onto the bed, unconcerned by what this does to her sheets, then drags a heavy armchair to the head of the bed. 'Talk to him,' she says. 'Hold his hand. I will get sponges and warm water.'

Sam starts to shiver and Balty wraps him up and holds him close, singing old rhymes from his boy's cradle days. Madame Florentine's servant girl brings a bottle of cognac and a mug of some fragrant infusion to warm him. He drips cognac into his son's mouth. They form a strangely intimate group, the four of them, three fully focused on bringing the fourth back to safety and the prospect of recovery. As full daylight arrives, a clean Sam is lying on the bed, his face withdrawn and deeply shocked.

Balty stares at him. 'Where is Betty?' he asks, but Sam shows no sign of responding.

He tries again. 'How did you get in?' realizing as he said it that Sam knew Hubert's secret way. Sam seems puzzled by the question and Balty looks at the damage to his head and his blood runs cold. He has seen sailors turned to silent hulks by such wounds as these.

Fists beat on the front door below.

'Go down,' says Madame Florentine to the serving girl. 'Do not unbar the door. Ask their name and come back.'

Her girl comes back up the stairs frowning. 'It is a man who will only say he was with you monsieur yesterday, in a herb garden.'

Sam beckons his father and raises his head to whisper in his ear. 'Who is ... who does ... ?'

His father whispers back. 'Don't worry. It is Captain Augier.'

Sam frowns. 'Who . . . ?' and Balty's heart sinks. He looks at the girl. 'Please let him in and then, if you wouldn't mind, we need to talk in private.'

'Of course,' says Madame Florentine and smiles down at Sam. 'But dear boy, where is your dear sister?'

'My sister? Where . . .' his voice tails off.

'That is why we need to talk,' says Balty.

Augier comes into the room staring at the boy on the bed in disbelief. Madame Florentine leaves them with a bell to call her. Augier closes the door and turns to Sam and Balty.

'This is a happy outcome,' he says. 'How can it possibly be?'

'Happy? No, no,' says Sam. 'Not happy . . .' He begins to cry. Balty holds him and feeds him a small spoonful of cognac, then turns to Augier. 'He is badly hurt. His head.'

'Has he told you where he has been?'

'No.'

'He must have been at the place where Scott and his crew have installed themselves. I have not yet found it. I am getting no responses from Mr Coventry. I fear he may be out of the game and I do not have the resources I need. We need men to protect you and spoil Scott's schemes closely. Would your brother Pepys send money?'

'By letter, but of course it takes two weeks. He already thinks I spend too much.'

'You are in huge danger and I cannot be everywhere at once.'

'I will send for the merchants who provide the funds. I will tell them a little of what has happened and . . . yes, I will force them to fund us. By the time it comes to an accounting, I will be forgiven – at least I hope so.'

'Do that now. I will recruit some stout fellows I trust. We will protect this house.'

'Is Coventry really out of the game? Do I still write my reports through him?'

'That is not clear. I hope at least that he still has the services of Captain Clifton and the *Moonstone* is still assigned to such secret duties.' Augier pauses, considering. Balty senses he is deciding whether to tell him something more. The man frowns. 'I do have a doomsday route for sending a rapid message. It eats up resources and money so I have only ever used it twice before. Perhaps the third moment has come.'

'How does it work?'

'A package delivered quickly to a trusted agent in this city marked by a single code word. Another packet inside that one in a code that is incomprehensible to those outside. It sends men racing to make sure fresh horses are staged along the route to the coast, to a place Captain Clifton knows.'

'I know it too. I have used it once before.'

'I will go to work on it immediately. As for you, get the money, look after the boy. Two men will be here within the hour. We will need to wake your boy soon. Above all, I need to know Scott's hiding place.'

If Sam remembers it, thought Balty, looking down at his boy, but he says nothing.

Two strong and silent men arrive who survey the house, fix bolts to certain windows and move a campaign bed into the room between Sam's bed and the hallway. One stays, the other goes. They will take shifts. Balty asks Madame Florentine to send her servant girl to Pelletier with his letter requesting two hundred more Louis d'or for life or for death. Better, he thinks, that Pelletier should be the one negotiating with Trenchepain.

Augier returns as Sam wakes up again, frowning around the room, unsure where he is. He has trouble speaking at all now and Balty watches him in fear as he struggles. Madame Florentine mixes up a tincture to ease his swollen mouth. She is deeply upset. 'Monsieur Balthasar,' she says, 'I despair of all this violence between Protestants and Catholics. Why must two religions which should be so close, instead hate each other so much that they will try to kill children?'

Balty is so upset that he speaks without thinking. 'It is terrible that our leaders are telling lies about papist . . .' Augier's frown stops him. Madame Florentine is looking at him expectantly, waiting for the end of the sentence, so he is forced to find one. '. . . about . . . beliefs. It is absurd that good people are divided.'

She goes on staring at him, so he ransacks his brain for something neutral to say that doesn't turn on the politics of English lies.

'Divided for such a silly reason . . . I mean, one religion thinks the wine *represents* blood and the other believes it is *changed into* blood and for that they may kill each other?'

He sees her frown, but Sam interrupts, suddenly in great distress, making choking noises as he tries to speak. Madame Florentine dribbles more of the tincture into his mouth and strokes his back as he coughs and coughs, then he lifts a finger and beckons them closer. Balty, terrified, takes his hand and bends down as the boy speaks in a whisper. 'Sad . . .' he says in English, 'I am so sad . . .'

'Oh Sam,' says Balty. 'You will feel better when . . .'

'No, no.' He waves for more of the tincture and his voice

strengthens just a little. 'Closer ...' he says, and they bend over him.

'It is sad,' he says, 'that so much suffering comes ...' He fights for breath and sips another spoonful. '... comes from arguing about ... about the doctrine of trans— transubstantiation.' Balty gapes at him as Sam points to the cognac and takes a whole spoonful of that. His voice immediately sounds stronger. 'When you compare communion wine with blood they have entirely different qualities. My ... my godfather's friend Mr ... Mr Newton helped me test a wide range of such liquids under different conditions.'

Madame Florentine stares, not understanding English.

Sam opens his eyes wide. 'A faulty translation from the Hebrew perhaps?'

'Welcome back, my dear son,' says Balty with tears trickling down his cheeks.

While Madame Florentine is preparing medicinal broth down below, Sam is able to describe what has been happening in the ancient house, though he is running short of strength. She brings up the broth and he stops. 'I will tell you more when I feel able. Colonel Scott and his gang have done all this and I know who commands them.'

'And you are quite sure you did not see Betty anywhere near?'

'I am sure.'

'Where are you, Betty?' Balty says to the ceiling above them.

He would be astonished to hear the answer to that question.

CHAPTER 27

The day before, Betty finds the hidden network within this house when she opens a cupboard door to see an unexpected dark corridor stretching away. She listens through cracks in walls to men boasting, men singing, men thumping fists on tables and women's false laughter. Back in the open, the servant's broom makes her invisible even to the rougher members of this crew. She tucks her head down to study a small patch of floor as they go by. She soon learns that one suite of rooms on the middle floor is quarantined from the harsher inhabitation of the rest of the house. It has its own lobby for access. The doors here stay closed and she sees the woman who first called her in from the street come and go. One other person, the man, in his blue coat with silver buttons, knocks and waits to be allowed entry. She works out where the servants' corridor backs on to it and stands in there listening, but the plasterwork is thick and all she hears is the drone of a commanding voice and an occasional deferential reply.

As the city outside shades into evening, she goes down to the basement where the great kitchen, mostly below ground level, still gets some light slanting down through dirty windows from the cutting outside. She inspects the small servants' rooms and chooses one with the least damp of the straw bag mattresses. She sits down on the one intact chair and searches for a plan. Where is Sam?

In her memory, she sees him disappear into the undergrowth of the plot next door. She has not yet followed the dark basement passages to their very end and she realizes there must be a way in from there. Taking out her little pistol, she wonders whether too much powder has dribbled out while it has been tucked away. She goes to search through cobwebbed kitchen drawers and finds a long-bladed knife for back-up. It tapers to a point which is still sharp.

That is when a boy starts to scream. A man laughs and she hears blows, one after another, until the screams stop. A door opens and she ducks down behind a table as heavy footsteps go by, then, knowing she must help, she creeps into the corridor. A flicker of light comes from an open door further along. It is a cell with the last stub of a candle showing her a small figure in dark clothing curled motionless in the middle of the floor. She takes one step towards him, knowing this is not Sam in his messenger suit, but as she does so, pandemonium breaks out beyond another grille in the back wall. A man is shouting and another boy shouts back. She races back to the kitchen, trying to get to the sounds, trying one deceitful passageway and then another until she sees figures struggling, silhouetted against faint light coming in from somewhere beyond.

Step by step she moves closer, her heart pounding, seeing the figure of a man, stabbing downwards. The boy in the pale messenger's clothes shrieks. She sees the man's arm jerk down again and then she is on the assailant with her own knife in her hand and no thought in her head but to stop him. She thrusts it at his body with all her strength, but it meets his leather jerkin and that's as far as it gets.

He backhands her, sending her slumping against the wall with the wind knocked out of her. It's the big, bald man she has seen upstairs. He kicks the boy's body. 'He's done. Your turn.' In the dim light he sees she is now holding something else in her hand and he laughs. 'The servant with the broom? What do you think yer doing, kid?' He lunges and the knife in his hand slices her left arm. He goes to stab again and Betty does the only thing she can, pulling the trigger to tell her if the little pistol is still primed and loaded. Until now she has only heard it pop gently in the open air on that road to Gravesend. In here it crashes and the man jerks backwards in the swirling smoke, clasping a hand to the centre of his forehead in surprise as his legs buckle under him.

She is horrified at the sight of him lying there with a darker pool spreading from his head in this dark place and she has no idea if the shot will have been heard higher up in the building. She goes to the heap on the floor in messenger clothing. 'Sam?' she says and there is no response, but she puts her ear to his mouth and hears faint breath. Putting her hands under his shoulders, she drags him along the corridor and through the rougher tunnel at its end to the base of the steps leading upwards into the night sky and the rising moon. Her left arm hurts sharply, but she hauls him up by sheer force of will, one step at a time, until they come out into that hollow under foliage with blankets neatly folded on a pile of planks.

Faint with pain but driven by desperation, she tips out bowls stacked in an old barrow, hauls it out of the shelter and drags out the unconscious boy. It takes most of her remaining strength to heave him into the barrow, worrying that she is hurting him. When it is done, she tucks a blanket over him, as if that will protect him from these enemies.

It takes another age to force the barrow through the hazards of the building plot, now lit by a bright moon rising. On the street she is staggering, bewildered, seeing danger everywhere and with no clear idea which way to go, except away from there. The few passers-by only glance curiously at the girl with the barrow, but even that troubles her and she wants to find somewhere safe where she and Sam can live or more likely die together. After an unknowable time, she comes to a double gate of wrought iron bars with an arched top and she sees trees and grass beyond. It looks locked, but when she pushes, the left half squeaks open wide enough to let them in. She trundles the barrow slowly on down a pathway to a shining pond and there she slumps to her knees on the grass, slips over on her side and closes her eyes. Discomfort soon wakes her up, but that short rest restores her to rationality and that is when she lifts the blanket off the boy's face and realizes within a shocked second that he is a complete stranger. Her heart plummets, but then she sees all the blood soaked into the cream cloth and is glad it is not Sam's blood. She peels the jacket carefully off to see if the wounds are still bleeding. There are four of them and the deep one under his ribs on his left side is producing gobs of blood.

The bloody jacket bunched in her hand repels her and she lobs it into the pond, then wraps him carefully in the blanket. He needs help and she won't find it here. Wheeling the barrow out through the gate again, she looks all around and sees the spire of the Notre-Dame cathedral in the moonlight. That is the way to her father and she forces the barrow into motion again. The task eats up her regained energy. It takes her an age to reach the next road junction, stopping every ten paces to get her breath but losing half of any regained strength just by lifting the weight of the handles. She comes abruptly to her breaking point by the high doors of a grand building, sagging to the ground. She leans back against the oak planks and closes her eyes. Time passes and other eyes peer at her through a slit window on one side of the doors. A small door creaks open and an old man shuffles towards her.

She wakes to find him stroking her cheek with his hand. 'Child,' he says, 'what has happened to you?'

'I . . . I am a little hurt, but the boy . . . the boy there under the blanket. He is sorely injured.' She begins to focus and sees that he is wearing a habit with a rope around his waist. 'You are a monk?'

'I am Brother Antoine.'

She thinks his habit is black but in the moonlight it is hard to be sure. 'Are you a Benedictine?'

'I am. This is our order's abbey of St Germain-des-Prés.'

'I have been here,' she says. 'You have an English sailor. He is called . . .' Her stressed memory fails her.

'You must mean Brother Ash,' says the man. 'He is coming out of the chapel as we speak.'

In no time at all, Betty and the injured boy are in the monastery infirmary, their wounds being cleaned and inspected by kind and knowledgeable men. Both the patients sleep, drugged by gentle herbs, and it is not until evening that Betty wakes to find someone is holding her hand. She opens her eyes to see Brother Ash.

'Betty,' he says quietly. 'You have a wound to your arm but it is all clean and it will mend. The lad. Who is he? That's not your brother.'

She tries to speak but her throat is too dry. He spoon-feeds warm cordial into her mouth and after a minute or two she can get words out again.

'I thought it was Sam but I think it must be a boy who was helping him. They changed clothes. Will he . . .'

'He's looking to make it through. It needs time and we will take good care. Did Scott do this to you?'

'His men did.'

'Scott is here in Paris?'

'Yes.'

The monk's face takes on a profoundly unholy expression. She remembers his account of his days at sea. Something about being good up the mast with a musket. She wouldn't want to be on the other end of that musket.

'First things first. Where's yer daddy?'

'We lodge with Madame Florentine in the Rue de la Huchette,' she says. 'It has a yellow door and it is opposite the roast meat seller.'

'I'm off there now.'

When Sam next wakes up, he is hungry, thirsty and anxious to talk. He has been washed and dressed in clean clothes and Balty holds up the crusted dark jerkin he had been wearing.

'How did you come to be dressed like this?' he asks gently.

In short bursts, Sam explains how he followed the fiacre, saw Hubert bundled into the house, stumbled over Count Victor and his hide-out and then witnessed Hubert's fate. He tells them how the boy showed him the servants' passageways and forgotten stairs and how he heard Scott explaining his lust for revenge against Pepys.

Balty thinks back what seems an age to Henry Coventry and the words of Henry Gals. 'So it really was all about Gravesend,' he says, 'when they thought he was escaping after murdering Sir Edmund Berry Godfrey.'

'But he did murder Godfrey,' says Sam. 'At least I heard him boast of it to his thugs, which is perhaps not quite the same thing. But that was not why he was trying to get to France . . .' Pain hits him and his bruised face contorts.

'Rest a while.'

'No. I must tell you how they found us. It waits for me when I close my eyes. I need to let it out into the room and the world outside. First Hubert and then Count Victor . . .'

Balty sees tears run down from the battered corners of Sam's eyes. Augier moves his chair further from the bed to give the father and son the space they need. Sam looks out towards the window and the light of day, then tiptoes towards the darkness at the end of the story.

'Before that,' he says quietly, 'there is a bigger question.'

'Which is?'

'Why was Colonel Scott really at Gravesend? Why did he have to go to France? It is not straight in my mind.' He closes his eyes and takes several slow breaths then he opens them again. 'He was carrying a message to King Louis. A very important message from the man who is in that house now behind the closed doors.'

'Sam, do you mean Shaftesbury is here in Paris with Scott? The earl himself?'

Augier is shaking his head in disbelief.

'I *must* tell it in order or it will slip away,' Sam says, frowning. 'We tried to listen from the servants' passage but the wall was too thick. He said we should listen from the dressing room.'

Sam reaches for Balty's arm. 'Father, he was a good, bold boy like Hubert. No, good is too poor a word. He was certain of himself and making the best of a bad, bad place. I promised him gold at the end of it. We went through a false cupboard into that room. But . . .'

Balty waits a long time before prompting him gently. 'But what?'

'He was too kind.' Sam stops to draw several deep breaths. 'We had almost been caught out by my clothes before. Any light showed up the white cloth. He said nobody would see me in his dark rags. I said they would see *him* in mine but he said he knew a hundred ways to get away. Papa, I agreed. Now I am here and he is not. So when . . . what . . . ?' Massive fists pounding on the door downstairs shake the glass in the windows.

CHAPTER 28

Someone forgot to pull the bar across the door below, because a man is shouting in an unfathomable language and a woman shrieks back at him in French, the quarrel moving rapidly up the stairs. Augier's on-duty guard runs down to challenge the intruder, but his own shouts end in a single thud. Augier leaps up, a dagger in one hand and a pistol in the other. Balty grabs both his pistols and they get between Sam and the door. A giant bursts through it with Madame Florentine hanging onto one of his arms and the serving girl on the other.

Balty knocks Augier's pistol out of his hand.

'He is a friend. Ezra. Great God above. How did you find your way?'

'Strong horses,' says Ezra. 'Yamma whee ow commensis curnyweck.'

'What?'

'I speak their language. It is my language too.'

Sam tries to say something and they all turn to look at him. Ezra stares at the bed. 'Who's this? It's not my Sam is it? It better not be. Who done this?'

'It is Sam,' says Balty. 'He looks bad but he's getting better.'

Sam holds up his hand. His voice still trembles.

'He said he speaks Cornish. It is very like the Breton language of north-western France.'

'Very impressive, sir,' says Augier. 'Did they understood you?'

'They got my drift,' says Ezra. 'I had to speak loudly and they hurried to set me on my way. I've come straight from the *Moonstone*.'

'Captain Clifton got my message then?' says Augier.

'You're the Frenchy? You were lucky. We were ready to up-anchor when your sweaty man arrived.' Ezra goes to the head of the bed, stares down in horror at Sam's face and says, 'Who did this to you, boy? They have me to answer to now.'

'That's what we're just finding out, Ezra,' says Balty.

Augier steps in. 'Have you brought me a message?'

Ezra hands him a folded sheet. Balty looks over Augier's shoulder and sees nothing but numbers.

Augier mutters as he works through it. 'I have it,' he says in the end. 'Orders for you, St Michel. Go to the coast with all speed, to wait in the appointed place until a boat comes.'

'Why?'

'To answer Clifton's questions I expect.'

'What of Sam?'

'He clearly cannot travel.'

'And Betty? I cannot leave until we find her . . . if . . . if she is to be found.'

'What's this about Betty?' says Ezra. 'I'm staying right here, sir. I am commanded to look after the children with my life and there's not much here to stop someone like me walking in whenever he wants.'

At that moment someone else does walk in. This time, the

knocking downstairs is polite and Madame Florentine looks puzzled as she puts her head round their door. 'Another person to see you, sir.'

'A man?'

'No, sir, a monk.'

She stands aside and Brother Ash walks in. His gaze goes straight to Sam. 'Thank the Lord,' he says and crosses to the bed, kneels down and carefully explores his injuries, but Ezra moves to stop him, only to throw up his hands. 'Ash Bolton. Can this be you?'

The monk turns and jumps to his feet. 'Ezra Penrose. Do I believe my eyes?'

'Oh, what?' says Balty. 'How . . . ?'

'We sailed together in the *Royal Oak* ten year or more back,' says Brother Ash, 'back when I were a sinner, but that can wait. I have news of your dear Betty.'

Silence falls and they stare.

'We have her safe,' he says. 'She has a wound to her arm but it will heal.'

Sam rears up from his bed. 'How did you find her?'

'She found us.'

'By herself?'

'She brought a badly injured boy.'

'Count Victor?'

'That's him. He was attacked with a knife and sorely wounded but I have great hopes for his recovery.'

Balty cannot speak. He hugs his son gently and blows three kisses in what he hopes is the right direction for his daughter.

'Before I came here,' Ash says, 'I asked my chum Brother Martin, who is a match for Ezra here, to come to that house in the Rue Tournon. I set out to find you, Sam. Betty told us about the back way so we went through those little corridors and then the main rooms. Not a soul in sight. They've legged it, Colonel sodding Scott and all his crew.'

'What do we do now?' says Balty.

Augier has finished decoding his message. 'You leave for the coast right now.'

'How?'

'There are horses waiting and a man to guide you.'

'What happens here?'

'I stay,' says Ezra. 'That's what happens.'

'Well, now I hear that,' says Brother Ash, 'I might stay with you.'

'No need. I can keep them safe from anything in this city.'

'I'm not bothered about *that*. I'm bothered about keeping Paris safe from you. I've had my fill of praying all night. The sea is a better place to pray. It's time I found a ship again, and maybe a new name that's good and Protestant.'

'My men will be here too,' says Augier. 'Your children will be safe, St Michel. Pack what you need and get going. I am ordered to see you to the city's edge.'

Balty looks down at Sam whose eyes have closed. 'Does Scott know my children are here?'

Sam's eyes open. 'Yes he does,' he says in a stronger voice. 'Scott was told about this house from watchers we never saw.'

Augier nods. 'We will move you to a safe place.'

'I don't know how long I'll be gone. How will I know where you all are?'

'Not hard,' said Brother Ash. 'I'll leave word with Brother Martin at the monastery.'

Sam looks around at all of them. 'Papa,' he says, 'I must now speak to you alone.'

Augier frowns but Ezra takes him by the arm and there can be no argument, so he nods. 'We will wait below with the brother here. No, I mean the *sailor* here, but be quick. When the captain demands speed, he has good reason.'

Left to themselves, Sam stares at Balty. 'Papa,' he says, 'I don't like to cry in front of you. I am too old for that.'

'I'm not,' says Balty, 'We can both cry.'

'It will slow down what I must tell you. It is said that clenching your buttocks together quells the emotions. I do not yet understand the anatomical logic but I will try.'

'You exchanged clothes. What happened next?'

'Count Victor jammed the cupboard catch. We sat on the floor. The man shooed a woman out and Colonel Scott came in. I knew his voice. We heard him report that the dead boy was not me. But there was a second boy in the same clothes.'

'Ah . . .'

'The other man was angry. Scott said they would set watch on this house. Then they started making new plans. I am trying to remember what they said but it is hard.'

'It will come back,' Balty says gently. 'Tell Augier when it does, but first tell me what happened to the two of you. I thought you were dead, my dear son.'

'Oh.' Sam frowns and Balty is pleased he can now tell it is a frown. The boy grunts. 'This clenching business hurts. We had been there through the day with nothing to drink, which was as well because we had nowhere to piss or anything else. We tried to get out twice. The first time I saw pistols on the table and some papers and I stopped to look, which was lucky, because we heard someone walk by along the corridor. The second time, a woman came with a message so while they were busy we crept out. Count Victor led me down the back corridors to the kitchen, but a door opened and one of Scott's thugs grabbed me. I saw his fist and I don't know what happened until I woke up in a dark room. It took an age to find my way out. I saw the bald man lying shot dead but I couldn't find Count Victor.'

He cries and Balty lets him take his time. 'I could see . . . oh dear . . . just . . . drips of blood. I got up the steps to his little camp but he wasn't there and I could hardly see at all.'

'My brave boy. How did you get here?'

'I knew I must walk and keep walking. Simple. But papa, the man beat me and he did his best to kill my friend.' He falls silent for a while, breathing hard, then speaks again in a small voice. 'This buttock squeezing business is not a complete answer. We have lost Hubert. We must take proper care of Count Victor.'

'We will, Sam, I promise we will. Now, I have to go to tell Captain Clifton what we know. Most of all, the name of the man in that room telling Scott what to do. Could that be a man called Peyton perhaps?'

Sam shakes his head, staring at him.

'Wentworth? No? Rolle maybe, that is Sir Frances Rolle?'

Sam pulls out a crumpled packet. 'I took this from the table with the pistols. I read part of it when we were back in the cupboard, then I pushed it into my pocket. The bald man never looked. It is the letter, papa, that the man in that room told Scott to deliver to King Louis. Take it with you.'

Balty thinks of the perils of the coming journey. 'No. Read it to me, then give it to Augier to keep safe.'

Two days later, Balty arrives at the cottage near Le Tréport, saddle-sore but elated by their unflagging speed. He has galloped north-west with the silent horse handler, four horses between the two of them, swapping mounts to keep up their speed and changing the whole team at two arranged stops. There are wet towels and food there, but the speed of their journey is refreshment itself. When they reach the five-way crossroads in Embreville, Balty swings his bag over his shoulder, hands the other man a gold coin and watches him out of sight before he sets out on the road to the rendezvous. He covers that last leg on foot because the horse handler must not guess his precise destination.

He has to skirt three hamlets to ensure he is not observed and he is pleased to find the familiar track coming down through bushes to the old oak by the fisherman's cottage, but he doesn't take it. He finds the smaller path up to the vantage point and spends time watching the cottage until he is sure nobody else is doing the same. A few coastal scows come by, broad-reaching westward, but he sees no other masts further out.

The cottage has a solid lock and he knows where to find the key. He checks all three rooms with his pistol ready, but all he finds is a small keg of wine on the table, salt beef under a cloth and two dozen apples. The pump in the back yard still draws sweet water. He bars the door and settles himself to think through all Sam has told him. Coventry will question him closely when he hears this, so he must get every part of it right. That thought chills him.

Before dusk, he climbs the hill once more to study the horizon and again at dawn – and the next day, and the next. It goes on until there is one apple left, not a shred of beef and nothing but air in the wine keg, then he sets a snare for rabbits on the heathland behind the cottage. In the middle of that night a knock comes on the door: three slow raps, a pause, then two more, repeated until he reaches the door. He remembers the words and calls, 'Stranger, who are you?' in French.

The correct answer comes in English, 'The men to slaughter the pig,' and he pushes back the bar. He sees one of Clifton's lieutenants, first encountered in the Deal ambush.

'St Michel,' the man says, 'we must make haste.'

The longboat is drawn up on the beach and half an hour's hard rowing takes them to the *Moonstone*, darkened and with sails aback in the lightest breeze, drifting gently. Balty climbs to the deck where Clifton is waiting in the light of a high half-moon. They shake hands.

'I have much to tell,' Balty says.

'Not to me,' Clifton replies quietly, 'come below.' At the door to the stern gallery, he stops. 'My master is within. He would speak directly with you.'

'Secretary Coventry is here? I heard he has been very sick.'

'Coventry is indeed sick. Gout is a terrible thing. No man of his condition should be forced to make a sea voyage.'

Clifton knocks on the door, opens it and says, 'Sire, St Michel is here.'

Balty steps into gloom, lit by the dim light of a small lantern. Its shine just reaches the further end of the gallery, making a portrait of King Charles the Second glisten – a painted face staring back at him. The portrait moves with the gentle motion of the ship, then its mouth opens and that mouth says, 'Let us not stand on ceremony, St Michel. You have travelled hard and I suspect you have endured much.'

Balty looks around the cabin for Coventry and finds nobody else there apart from this talking delusion.

'It is some time since you took a breath, St Michel,' says the king. 'I would recommend you to do so as I have travelled here solely to talk to you, which will be easier if you are still alive to reply.'

Balty draws in a shuddering gasp.

'Normally, I would remind you it is customary to bow to your monarch,' Charles remarks, 'but at this moment I am fast asleep in my cabin on my royal yacht close to the Isle of Wight so there is nobody here to bow to. You may sit down instead.'

Balty forces his throat to frame words. 'Your Highness,' he says, 'I . . . I was not . . . I expected to see Mr Coventry. Captain Clifton said that he wanted to speak directly with me so . . .'

'I could hear him clearly. If you interrogate your memory, you will find he did not say that at all. He said that his master wanted to speak directly with you. That is me. He also said no man of Mr Coventry's age and health should be expected to make a sea voyage. That is the precise truth. My old friend leads a quieter life now. My yacht met the *Moonstone* off Wight, close to the place where you once risked a great storm to bring me much-needed succour.'

'You remember that, sir?' Balty is astonished.

'June of '75. I was bound for Portsmouth to see those damned pond yachts for Louis which helped start all this trouble. I should have sunk them with my bare hands.'

Balty remembers it vividly, the signals telling them the king's yacht is ashore on the far side of the island, his own decision to set off with food and wine, the king's smile of gratitude.

'I was very hungry. You were very brave,' says Charles. 'That is why I backed your mission to Paris. I know you to be capable and daring.'

'Thank you, sir.'

'That first time,' says Charles, 'I failed to reward you properly. This time, I can make amends. As matters stand, you are still bound for Tangier and I hear that is not sitting well with you.'

'No, sir.'

'Clifton says your son and daughter also show remarkable daring. Are they well?'

'Both are being nursed in Paris, injured by Colonel Scott's men. They are in the care of men I trust, but I must get back there.'

'Hard news. Oh for goodness sake man, for the last time, sit down. How can we talk with you stooping over me and staring like that? Do you want to pinch me? I assure you I am real. May I pour you a glass of Bordeaux wine?'

Balty reaches out as the king hands it to him and isn't sure what to do. Does he wait for the king to drink first? The king does not appear to have a glass of his own. Is it worse not to drink the wine? Entirely out of his depth, he drinks.

'I have taken care to cover my tracks,' says Charles. 'I am trying out the paces of my new yacht. Clifton ran her up close and I boarded through this stern window so few would see. I am unaccountably unwell back there and the yacht will sail in slow circles until I am myself again. That will be soon after you and this illusion in front of you have done with each other. You have information I need and I hope to reward you with a better posting. In the royal record, this will be a blank page. If what we are about to discuss *ever* becomes the subject of wider discourse, I shall get to know of it and there will be no limit to my displeasure. Is that clear?'

The words are delivered without any change in his light-hearted tone and are all the more chilling for it.

'Quite clear, sir.'

'You look puzzled.'

'I am amazed your majesty has undertaken this voyage solely to speak to me.'

'What you say may decide the course of the monarchy from here on. I hear you have information on who commands Colonel Scott.'

'I have, sir. It has become clear through the efforts of my children.'

'Samuel and Elizabeth?'

Balty jumps. 'Betty and Sam, sir.'

'I will thank them. Now, I must have certain knowledge to direct my actions and prevent the fabric of England being further torn apart by these plots. Your duty is tell me only what you know to be absolute truth. Do you have indisputable knowledge of who accompanied Scott to France and dictates his actions?'

'I do, sir.'

'One man, or more?'

'One man, sir.'

'A papist?'

'No, sir.' Balty hesitates, acutely aware of the dangers of naming so high-ranking a person.

'Spit it out man. You cannot surprise me. You believe it to be Rolle? He is a key organizer of the Whig tendency.'

'Sir Francis Rolle?' Balty is startled. 'No, sir. It is . . . a more notable man, sir.'

A collapse in the candle's wick dims the flame in the lantern, then sends it soaring. In the flare, Balty sees the king's bright eyes fixed on him. 'How notable?'

'A nobleman. I . . . I hardly dare name him.'

'I know who he is.' He leans forward, narrowing his eyes. 'I have come to the end of my tolerance and I will stamp on him as hard as my feet will bear. Again, you are quite sure of the identity of this man with Scott, steering the plot?'

'Yes, sir.'

'Then. I order you, as your king, to name him.'

Here goes, thinks Balty, and once I have said this there is no going back. He thinks *what would my children do?* Something very clever that would steer him out of imminent danger.

'I am losing patience with you, St Michel. It is not a complicated question.'

A justifiable distraction comes to him to gain time to think. 'My son has discovered a signed message that Scott was to deliver to King Louis.'

The king frowns. 'Show it to me.'

'It is in Paris but the sense of it is fresh in my memory.'

'Go on.'

'It says there is a plot organized inside the Palace of Westminster to murder Louis using Irish assassins, and replace him on the throne of France. It asks for money to raise a strong London militia. It says there is already a secret treaty between the two kings that must now be used to thwart this plot.'

'What?' The king sounds shocked. 'Is it in secure hands?'

'Coventry's man Augier has it in his keeping, stained with my son's spilt blood.'

Charles is leaning forward, staring. 'Does it explain this secret treaty?'

'Sir, I don't think there was any detail.'

'And you are telling me the man *signed* this absurd message?' Charles is utterly incredulous. 'Shaftesbury dared to put his name to it?'

Balty is so shocked that the words which are about to change his life come flooding out. 'No, sir, no. Oh heavens no. The Earl of Shaftesbury does not come into this. The man with Colonel Scott in Paris is not *Shaftesbury.* The man who signed that letter is the duke.'

Charles stares at him, then half-stands, leaning towards him with his hands on the table, shaking his head. 'What do you say? The duke? My brother the Duke of York? You dare to lie to me? But . . . that makes no sense. He aims this letter at himself? Are you mad?'

'Oh no, no, sir. Oh my goodness. Sir, you misunderstand me. Not the Duke of *York.* Of course not. The man who signed the letter is the Duke of *Buckingham.*'

Five minutes later he is shackled to a cannon on the gun deck.

The half-moon is a handspan lower but there is no trace of dawn in the sky towards Abbeville. The *Moonstone*'s duty watch have jumped into action to wear the ship for a short tack back in towards the coast. They ignore Balty and he has curled into a miserable and baffled ball to try to ease the discomfort of the chains. Quiet footsteps come up behind him and a man bends to put a mug down on the deck next to him. Clifton's voice speaks gently.

'Drink,' he says. 'It is good coffee.'

'Just coffee? No belladonna? Nux vomica? Nothing intended to close my mouth for good?'

'A splash of cognac. That is all. I think our king has found his own way to close your mouth.'

'I have risked all to serve him. Why is this happening?'

Clifton sighs and looks around him. 'St Michel,' he says in a low voice, 'I should not answer that but . . . soon after you told me your own history on that first passage from Gravesend, I talked to a great friend who also served under Harman. He spoke of you in terms of the highest praise. You are, he said, far more than you care to seem.' He looks all around him again, then squats down on the deck next to Balty. 'I will choose my words carefully and you will not repeat them. Yes? Our king and Buckingham were raised as brothers. He knows the Duke can be wayward but he will never ever accept that Buckingham is a direct enemy.'

'But . . .'

'No. That is the way it is. We must alter course around that. Listen closely to me. You are to be sent to Tangier with your silence guaranteed until this peril passes.'

'Guaranteed?'

'I have suggested a way that will be to your family's advantage. I hope you accept it. Your brave boy Sam will be the first part.' Clifton stares straight into his eyes. 'He will join me onboard the *Moonstone* as a king's letter man.' He smiles and Balty tries to return the smile. They both know this is a change introduced by Pepys, transforming young men into good officers.

'How is that a *guarantee*?'

'In the unthinkable event that you suffer from a loose tongue, our king has decided that your Sam will be transferred to Captain Merrihew's command.'

Throughout the navy, Merrihew is known as a monstrous bully who takes savage delight in humiliating his men to the point of destruction. Balty groans.

'You may hear that as a threat,' Clifton goes on, 'but I urge you to see it as a promise. It means you have it in your power to ensure Sam remains under my command with Ezra as his watchful protector.'

Balty nods slowly, then frowns. 'You said there are *two* guarantees?'

'The second is more of a gift of thanks to you than a threat. Your quite remarkable Betty is to be offered a place in Queen Catherine's household at Somerset House. Our queen is the most gentle of women.'

'A Catholic. A hazardous place to be?'

'But in a most discreet way and less hazardous now. It was a condition of her marriage that she should enjoy her own free choice in that respect. Life in her household will be a safe and sweet place for Betty if all goes well. Much may change in the next year. The king feels that Betty's introduction to his queen should take place a year from now for the safety of all.'

'You mean so long as I behave?'

Clifton sighs. 'Do not blame me, St Michel. My master's burden is unimaginable, even to those closest to him. I take my example from our old friend Henry Coventry. I do my best to be a part of the king's protection while representing his natural humanity when he is under too much pressure to remember to do that himself.'

'Yes. I will resist blaming you if you unlock me, but . . . will you explain a mystery to me?'

'If I can and in exchange for a final stipulation.'

Balty looks all around and his whisper barely carries between them. 'Our king is a clever man. He knew this popish plot was nonsense but he let his Whig enemies take power and fire up a lethal mob with their storm of lies. Why?'

'I have come to my own conclusion on that very question. Will you be content with an answer that comes from me and not from any higher authority?'

'That is all I am going to get so, yes.'

'You are locked to this cannon because you gave our king the name he did not want to hear. I won't name him again but that man was always at a tangent to the main plot. He has lived by his own peculiar values and his objectives are seldom clear. Shaftesbury, on the other hand, has been at the very centre of the whole damned thing. He was delighted with Oates's lies and he used them to feed the flames until they were too hot to quell. Our king had no choice. He knew he must own the plot as entirely real while it ran its course and he knew he could make his move only when the flames began to flicker.'

'Will that be soon?'

Clifton shrugs. 'It may be a good time to be in Tangier.'

'There is no such time. I will accept the very weak hand dealt to me if you will now unlock me from this damned cannon.'

Clifton does so. Balty rubs his wrists as he gets to his feet and looks back towards Le Tréport. 'When do I go to Tangier and how long do I have to stay? That is, assuming I continue to breathe.'

Clifton glances up at the twitching sails. The *Moonstone* is hove-to again, going nowhere in particular within easy reach of the coast, but both men know the clock is ticking and it would be wise for the king to be far away from here before dawn. 'That,' he says in the end, 'is for Mr Pepys and my master to agree between them. You still have work to do here.' He sighs and slaps Balty on the shoulder. Three sailors trot past towards the stern and glance at Balty curiously.

'Come on,' says Clifton. 'It is time to get you ashore. You must walk back to the Embreville crossroads. You remember the way? Wait in the shack by the copse. It is empty and you will find a bottle of good water there. Be patient and your man will come with four strong horses. Two days should see you back with those you love and may they be safe, strong and mended.'

He reaches out his hands to grip Balty's shoulders. 'One more thing. My strong recommendation for your continued well-being is that you should never mention that matter of a supposed secret treaty with King Louis ever again and you should burn the absurd document that says so as soon as you get back to Paris.'

The young folk are safe. Ezra and Ash have seen to that. Back in Paris, Brother Martin sends him to the wine shop near Madame Florentine's house where Ash is waiting. He sees Balty and waves.

'Brother Ash, how are you?'

'Just plain Ash these days, sir. Maybe Bo'sun Ash some time soon if I play my cards right. Walk a respectful distance behind me keeping your eyes peeled and I will lead you to your new quarters across the river.'

They are well chosen. An iron gate in the archway of a

CHAPTER 29

Spring 1683

More than three years have passed since Balty returned to England, escorting Protestant witnesses from France to freeze the attempts to have Pepys hanged. Much has changed in the mood of the country, but not quite as much as King Charles would like and he has a lot on his mind. The danger is less clear now, but he has just been forced to recognize that it has not entirely vanished. The mobs are no longer on the street and Shaftesbury is no more. Charles has chased him out of England to exile in the Low Countries. The local physicians there do not understand the tricks needed to keep him alive, so Shaftesbury's tap stops working and his body follows suit. James, Duke of York is welcomed back from his own exile, but there is a posthumous hangover of the Great Plot. Only weeks after Shaftesbury's death, Charles and his brother go to Newmarket for the horse-racing, relaxing in Charles's modest palace of only a hundred and twenty rooms. It is late on the fourth Thursday in March when he is startled awake by a fist banging on his door. This is not a familiar way of waking for most kings.

blank wall blocks access from the street until they summon the concierge by pulling the bell rope. In the courtyard beyond, another bell-pull in another locked gate produces Ezra, who grins from ear to ear at the sight of him.

'Up you come', he says. 'You'll be hungry and thirsty and there's two young people upstairs anxious to see you.'

'Sire,' says an officer of the Life Guards, 'the town is afire.'

Charles goes to the sash window, pushes it up and his night-shirt is pressed against his chest by a hot wind from where an orange glow flickers beyond the next roof peak. He can hear people shouting in the distance and the crash of something falling. He smells smoke. 'Is my brother awake?'

A high-pitched voice says, 'Awake and here.' James joins him at the window. 'It's on the other side of town,' he says, 'and this wind will keep it there, pray God.'

That is not much comfort. Newmarket is a very small town. The main street runs north–south and separates the Suffolk half from the Cambridgeshire half where the palace and the richer houses stand. 'Send for all my men,' says Charles to the officer. 'Rouse everyone. Choose your fastest horse to take a man to Cambridge.'

By morning half the townsfolk are homeless and the king orders that they should be welcomed into empty barns and stables, except his own. The palace reeks of burnt timber and they move out into the Earl of Suffolk's mansion, but the wind shifts and clouds of ash whirl across the road from the devastation. Two days of this are enough and over the breakfast table when they are alone, James looks hard at him. 'No more racing then? Damned all point in staying. Can't abide this, can you?'

'It stinks of 1666,' Charles says. 'Shall we go back to town?'

'If that is what my king desires then so be it,' James replies.

'*If that is what my king desires?*' says Charles mockingly. He has to fight down irritation at the braying sound James often makes these days, the tone of a man who is not sure he still has power. 'Yes, he does so desire.'

The Stuart brothers can have no idea that the king's decision has saved both their lives. The last protagonists of the plot have set up a carefully planned assassination to interrupt their journey home, at the Rye House toll gate, halfway back to London. The fire has caught out the plotters and their murderers are not yet in place when the royal pair ride up three days too early. News of the conspiracy only leaks out a fortnight later and the arrests start. That shakes Charles out of his recovering sense of safety. He decides he wants a new base, his own Versailles Palace, in a safer part of England where his men can protect him and he can rule at a safe distance from the hotheads. He sets his sights on Winchester, sends Sir Christopher Wren on an urgent mission and groans when he sees the first estimates of cost. That is when he comes hard up against the drains on his royal purse and is forced to see it is time for drastic action. He gives orders to assemble a fleet of ships for a special mission and forgets to tell his somewhat distant friend, the queen, of its purpose until the very last moment.

Catherine of Braganza has lived quietly for most of her forty-five years on this earth. A childhood spent in a convent means the outside world comes as a surprise when she is sent to England at the age of twenty-four to marry its king. Nothing in her upbringing prepares her for the hedonistic chaos of Westminster but he has been kind to her, supporting her through sickness and miscarriages. She is mostly relieved that his stream of mistresses provides an outlet for his passions and the two of them stay surprisingly good friends. Catherine remains a Catholic, part of the wedding deal, and in the middle of the anti-papist uproar, Titus Oates claims she has been part of a plot to poison her husband. For her safety, Charles moves her a mile down the Thames to Somerset House. On this summer morning she is sitting in her favourite salon, attended only by her adviser and a servant, to be told that an unexpected delegation from her king is waiting outside.

She speaks in her native Portuguese as they always do when they are alone. 'Why do you suppose they are here?'

Her adviser recognizes her nervousness and takes care not to add to it. 'May it please your Majesty. They are two members of your king's Privy Council. I hear it may concern your port of Tangier, Portugal's great wedding gift. It would seem that your royal husband is sending an expedition to address the problems there. He may feel he should consult you as to its purpose.'

'Consult? A kinder word than inform. Do you think I will like what they come to say?'

'My queen will wish to listen to their words first and then I am at your service to reach your conclusion.'

'After *they* have gone. Who are *they*?'

'The Earl of Huntingdon.'

'You roll your eyes just a little bit. I know that roll. Do you trust him?'

'Not at all. He changes sides when it suits him but the other is Henry Mordaunt, Earl of Peterborough.'

'Peterborough? We do trust him I think?'

'Sometimes.'

'Oh, tush, tush, grumpy one. Shall we summon them in?'

The two men bow and glance from Catherine to the others present, the slightly stooping woman with steel-grey hair standing by the queen and the girl rubbing at the tarnish on a silver cup in the far corner of the room.

Catherine switches to English, in the deliberately more

halting version she uses to lower the guard of outsiders. 'Lords, I take pleasure in your appearance. What come you here to tell me? This is my personal chancellor and also my servant you see. My chancellor has my most full trust and my servant speaks only my own tongue. Please inform me at once of your message Lord Peterborough?'

'Your Majesty will know that I have great familiarity with Tangier.'

'You were, sir, the first Englishman commanding that great city after my country gifted it to my husband the king.'

'Indeed ma'am and you will know that it has often been under attack since then by those who do not accept our ownership.'

'Expensively for my king and most bloodily for many of his loyal soldiers.'

Peterborough winces and nods. 'Our king wishes me to inform you of steps he is taking to address those problems.'

'He is gathering vessels at Portsmouth. What purpose will they perform?'

Peterborough frowns, trying to frame a response and Huntingdon steps in. 'Majesty, the expedition will seek to strengthen the Tangier defences before passing it to another nation's ownership.'

'Another nation? Uncertain words. You surely intend Portugal, my dear birth country, who made the great gift?'

Huntingdon opens his mouth but Peterborough cuts him off. 'My queen, I am sure your gracious husband will wish to be the first to discuss such details of the matter with you.'

The meeting is over. Two minutes of necessary but vacuous leave-takings follow and then they are left alone. Queen

Catherine looks at the servant and says in Portuguese, 'You may go now. Wait outside.'

The woman with the steel-grey hair curtsies and leaves. The girl puts down the silver cup and crosses the room to the queen, who tousles her hair. 'Well my Bettina, what does your clever head make of all that?'

'My dear queenie, I think you will want your wedding gift to be returned in good order to your own country believing that to be natural and just?'

'You are right as always.'

'Then you will not be happy if I suggest a different plan?'

'Oh. Perhaps I may not be happy but I will be listening with care.'

'Your husband is reduced by Tangier. He is paying outrageous sums of money from his purse month by month to keep hold of it against surrounding armies who do not want England there for another day, let alone endless years ahead.'

'You are saying it was not after all such a great gift?'

'Bad Englishmen have spoiled the gift, corrupt men now in charge who steal his money, insult the Moors with their licentious behaviour and let the defences fall to ruin. If it is returned to your dear Portugal it will hang heavy around your country's neck.'

'*Filha escolhida*,' says the queen. 'Do you hear this from your poor dear father in Tangier?'

Betty's voice is a little choked as she starts to reply. Two years back when she joined the queen's household with some misgiving, Catherine had swiftly brought her from maids' duties to her side and had rapidly begun to call her '*menina sabia* – wise girl' and then '*meu dochino* – my sweetie' when they were alone and lately *'conselheira sabia* – wise counsellor' in company, but this is the first time she has been called chosen daughter.

'In all this time I have only once heard from my dear papa. I know he is alive but the bad men in charge of Tangier take care to see that his letters do not reach us. That single letter was delivered by a captain we trust.'

'I ask myself, could that be Captain Clifton?'

'Oh, queenie mama, how did you guess that?'

'Before you came to me, I visited a dear man in his retirement, a man who guarded my husband most zealously while he still could. That man said I was to have a new servant by order of the king. A very remarkable girl called Betty St Michel. He said I should take care to uncover her skills. He told me he met you and your father and your dear brother.'

'Mr Coventry?'

'Indeed. A fine man now nearing his eternal rest. He told me of his good opinion of your family. He said your uncle Pepys has been a true supporter of my dear husband and very ill used. Without him, my dear husband does not always know who to turn to. He and his brother relied on Coventry and Pepys. He does have Captain Clifton, which is much better than nothing, but still he has a wretched time.'

'I like the captain. He took us to France.'

'I know. He now serves my husband in his special ways and he would want me to tell you he had no choice as to what happened to your poor father.'

'If . . . if Tangier is given back, will . . . will . . . ?'

'Will your father be allowed home? We should set ourselves to thinking how. But before we come to that, you say it would hurt my beloved Portugal to throw despoiled Tangier back into its care?'

Betty takes a deep breath. 'Yes, and I hope clever people with clear heads are travelling with this convoy.'

'Who do you suggest?' says Catherine, with a hint in her face that she might already know the answer.

That is why, early the following morning, a hand raps at the knocker of Will Hewer's house and delivers two ornately sealed documents. Will Hewer's butler then knocks on the door of Samuel Pepys's apartment within and proffers a salver bearing one of them. 'Just brought here, sir, by a king's messenger in a great hurry.'

Pepys immediately knows who has sent it. In his lost days of importance only letters from Charles himself ever came with such intricate folds or so many wax seals. He counts eight of them on this one. To render this even more extraordinary, it is Sunday.

'Is he waiting for my reply?'

'No, sir.'

It must be an urgent command. He has not had direct communication with the king for all this time and now a message comes on the sabbath day? When the butler has closed the door he takes a knife to the wax and straightens out the interlocking folds. He reads the brief message with astonishment.

'*King Charles requires his subject Mr Samuel Pepys to undertake an expedition overseas on his behalf. Mr Pepys is required to attend the commander of the expedition, his most worthy and trusted Lord Dartmouth, on board His Majesty's ship* Grafton *at Portsmouth no later than the end of the first day of August, equipped for a voyage of some duration.*'

Switching from a wild flood of thoughts to the calm of organization, he counts the days backwards with his fingers. A day and half's travel to Portsmouth? He must leave London tomorrow afternoon at the latest. Half a day to buy what he needs and pack a bag? This afternoon with all merchants closed and tomorrow morning. There is one more line. It is short but delightful. '*His Majesty will be pleased to recompense his servant Pepys the sum of four pounds per diem for the duration of this engagement.*'

That lessens the sting. Twenty-eight pounds for a whole week, but this is an overseas voyage. Perhaps with travel it will take two weeks there and back or even more? That makes for a rich and royal sum after so many months of depending on his young friend Hewer's unflagging hospitality. He gets to his feet to tell Will, but as he opens the door Hewer is already standing there, hand raised to knock.

'Will!' Pepys says. 'You have heard about my letter no doubt. Come in and I will tell you all. It is most unexpected . . . but . . . you shake your head?'

'You need tell me nothing. There was also a letter for me. I suspect they are identical.' He holds it out and steps inside.

Pepys reads it and sees that Hewer's version lacks that final payment line. 'Indeed,' he says to spare his friend's feelings, 'identical. Come and sit yourself down. How can we plan for an expedition without knowing where we are going or how long for? A voyage of some duration? All voyages are of *some* duration.'

Hewer thinks. 'Portsmouth is a clue. Not Gravesend or the Downs, so that rules out the Baltic, the Low Countries and much of France. Unless it is the Americas, it might perhaps mean Spain or more likely Portugal? Something regarding his queen's affairs?'

'Think a little harder, Will. The two of us, together on this sudden mission. What is the one position I used to hold and which you hold now, concerning a distant port city which has eaten into our king's fortune. I was the treasurer of that awkward place. You are its treasurer now.'

'In heaven's name. Are we going to Tangier?'

'It makes sense.'

Hewer rubs his eyes with both hands and makes a face. 'Well at least let us start in comfort. My coach will take us to Portsmouth.'

The packing and the shopping is done in a terrible rush. As Monday's departure time looms, Pepys thinks that, fourteen years on, this might be the right time to start a new diary, so he buys a book bound in red Morocco leather with enough space for two or even three months of entries.

Running short of time, Hewer sends his coach off on the long loop to London Bridge and then back on the other side of the river, so the two of them and servants to carry their bags can cross on the horse ferry to Lambeth where the coach is waiting for them. Still feeling ill prepared, they set out from there at two in the afternoon. Hewer's carriage offers an uncommon degree of luxury, equipped with the best springs and the deepest cushions. They head south on the road known as the Sailor's Highway and Will says, 'I have met Lord Dartmouth only once and briefly. What sort of man is he?'

'He is two sorts of men. In simpler days he was George Legge. Promoted too young so quick to take insult until he trusts you, but grew mature in command of frigates. Last year you well know he and I shared a catastrophe and in the days that followed we came as close to friendship as he allowed. Since then he has been transformed into a lord and an admiral. I wonder what that has made him?'

Will is daunted by the 'catastrophe'. He hopes to get his old friend talking more about that, because silence has not been good for Samuel Pepys. He nods. Perhaps this unexpected voyage will open an opportunity. He has done all he can to provide his old friend with the comfort of his Buckingham Street house, looking through the Inigo Jones water gate at the great river. Pepys has his own apartment within as well as the use of the peaceful Hewer country manor out at Clapham Common, but Will is aware his old master has turned in on himself. He struggles to accept that he has no clear status, little contact with power and a smaller group of people brave enough to be open friends. The interrupted treason charges still hover somewhere over the horizon, threatening to return. He leans across the gap to pat Pepys's knee. 'This mission proves one thing. Charles knows he needs you and he never stopped trusting you.'

'Perhaps. It is almost certainly Tangier – but for what exactly?'

'To make it stronger?'

'I'm no stone mason.'

'You do logic and numbers. You spot weaknesses others miss.'

Pepys grunts. 'Well if we're right, at least I will see the place for the first time. It is most beautiful.'

Hewer opens his mouth, then closes it. Others have told him the pictures on the office wall are absurd depictions of a lethal city, but he has seen Pepys's angry denial of all that when Balty was resisting his posting. Argument will get nowhere.

'Have you heard from Brother Balty lately?'

'No.'

He has no need to ask about Esther. She has moved from house to house complaining of poverty, loneliness and inconvenience, mostly at his expense. 'The children?'

'A few letters. Their new lives keep them busy. I wish the queen allowed Betty more time of her own. She is some sort of maid, I think. I expect she sees the queen in the distance from time to time. Sam has been in far-off seas on Clifton's obscure business. He can give me few details of his voyages but they must be thousands of miles by now.'

That provides the opening for the question Will had hoped to ask. 'I forget. How many long voyages have you made? I mean proper passages across seas. Six is it?'

'More than that, Will. The first was before even you and I met. I was sworn to secrecy but it is old history now.'

'Can you lift the veil?'

'A different England, adrift, Cromwell dead. His son in charge, but that had the taint of a new dynasty. A real mess with only one locked exit door and two military men held the key. There was General Monck, with his army waiting up north.'

'The other?'

'My old master Edward Montagu, Earl of Sandwich. Admiral of the fleet patrolling the Baltic to keep our trade routes open. I was given a package to take to him.'

'How?'

'On board the *Hind* ketch. A pleasant voyage in warm weather plus a captain with a fine voice. Even his orders had a musical ring to make the hardest sailors smile. Four days from Greenwich to where Denmark and Sweden faced each other across the narrow sound with only our ships to keep them from each other's throats. If you could run on water, you would cross those narrows in half an hour. We found the fleet anchored off Helsingor.'

'And the package . . . ?'

'. . . spoke to me through its canvas wrapping and burned in Montagu's eyes as he read it. He wrote his reply and said it was more than my life was worth to open it, lose it, or let anyone have it except the person who wrote it.'

'Who was that?'

'Will, after all these years, I am still bound by my oath.'

'So you brought Montagu back with his fleet and another messenger set Monck to march south.' Will snaps his fingers. 'That's why your next voyage was with Montagu's fleet bringing Charles back home in triumph.'

'My father was a tailor, Will, and my mother a butcher's daughter. I owe everything to those journeys. King Charles and Duke James gave me their friendship and their trust.'

Will pushes further. 'Four fine voyages. The fifth was . . . ? Oh, perhaps we should pass that one by . . .' Too late, he sees the expression change on the face of the man opposite.

'You know all about that one.'

He does. Ten years on. Pepys and his lovely, furious French child bride Elizabeth are split apart by her husband's wanton behaviour with a new maid.

'Balty organized a fine holiday to break down the wall between us,' Pepys says quietly. 'That month in Paris started to open a door, but . . .' he stops, stares at the carriage floorboards, then looks up again with moist eyes. 'The pestilence invaded her and the voyage home was an agony.'

Will knows it ended in her death. He was there.

Pepys's eyes go to the window and his gaze locks on a far quarter of the sky while his friend waits patiently, then finally he asks again.

'The seventh voyage?'

'Will. The entire nation knows what happened then, or at least it thinks it does. I do not wish to talk of the wreck. Let the story sink as the *Gloucester* sank.'

Time for a change of subject. 'So, looking ahead . . . if it is to be Tangier, what are we expected to do?'

'Sew up the hole in the king's purse. It was meant to be a fountainhead of glorious trading profit. It has been a bloody disaster.'

'And how are we supposed to fix that?'

'By strengthening its defences and finding where the money leaks out. Some say it is a sink of corruption. If so, we will clean it out.'

'Then . . . I ask one favour. The Tangier treasurer's post was forced on me when you were locked away. You did it much better. When we return, I wish to hand it back to you.' They both know Pepys needs the large income that comes with the job and Will Hewer does not.

Falling silent, stuck in their own thoughts, they are both dozing off as they go through Corsham and on into the dusk. Pepys's waking thoughts merge into disturbing dreams so he stirs, slouched on the deep cushions, murmuring. Balty intrudes, waving a spear from a cave entrance, shouting furious words he cannot understand. A postilion wakes them at Portsmouth's first houses where a waiting messenger hands over directions. The shreds of his dream rush away but leave bruises.

A small measure of joy creeps back as they learn they will sleep on solid ground tonight at Dr Grundy's house where both have stayed before. Next morning, boarding the *Grafton* flagship in fine, calm weather, Captain William Booth welcomes them as old friends, then beckons forward a waiting figure. 'You know this young man, I believe,' he says.

'Sam Atkins,' says Hewer, 'and for once you're not in trouble. What a fine surprise and how do you do?'

Atkins smiles at him and bows to Pepys. 'It is a great pleasure to see you again, sirs.'

'Are you travelling with us?'

'I am, sir, as confidential secretary to Lord Dartmouth. He will join us tomorrow and he hopes you will enjoy your berths ashore until he returns.'

Pepys laughs. 'He knows me too well. Now Sam, speaking as your former master, do please tell me where we are bound?'

Atkins looks shocked for a moment then laughs with him. 'As your former servant, sir, I must politely remind you of the meaning of the word "confidential".'

CHAPTER 30

Balty stuffs a thin mattress into a wooden chest and emerges from his refuge into a wilderness. He goes round to the back of the shed to pull the rope that turns the hidden crank to jam the door in case of unwanted visitors. He knows that might stop a casual thief, but it won't stop determined men and they would have to be determined to get this far. He has to push his way through head-high vegetation, the plants clambering towards the sun beating down. He moves very slowly, listening for unexpected noises ahead, but all he hears are the normal sounds of the Tangier market, the Portuguese traders calling out their offerings and rude shouts from drunken soldiers. Abandoned fruit trees are knitted together by huge weeds, filling the once productive inner garden of this square. They are hemmed in by the four outer terraces of Portuguese houses, also going badly to seed under a complete lack of English care. A narrow arched passageway into the market place is the only way out, but he stops short of it. That passageway is even thicker with vegetation and at night he sometimes weaves the stems together to make the barrier still more forbidding. He goes to a blank wooden door close by it, looks back at the faint trail he has left and pulls the nearest stems together to minimize the signs of his passage, then he feels around the weeds at the base of the door and tugs the end of a length of cord.

He has lived like this since the beginning of spring. Before that, he could sit in any of Tangier's ramshackle taverns and join in the talking and the singing and sometimes, by no choice of his own, the fighting. He would keep out of the way, so far as he could, of the governor and his men. That all changed one evening in the bar behind the Portuguese church. There he was, minding his own business, thinking hard about another trip across to Spain to progress his private projects, when a hand was grabbing at his sleeve and the clerk, Appleby, half-slumps across his lap, as drunk as a lord. This had surprised him, as Appleby, usually the most sober of men, with a tonsure like the monk he seems to be, had showed no interest in anything except a column of figures. Appleby had immediately started to shout above the roar of swear words and ribald laughter.

'I have a tale for your ears, St Michel,' he yells. 'A tale of crime and crookedness. I hear you collect such things.'

'Is this the place to tell it?' Balty says. The bar is called The Good Shepherd and one man who frequents it is known as Monahan – just that and no more. The name makes good men shudder. Kirke brings Monahan with him to control Tangier with his private squad of murderers, the men the other soldiers call Kirke's Lambs. Monahan is now known as the Lambs' bad shepherd except when he's listening, and he is trying to listen right now through the hubbub. Balty sees him staring across the room at the two of them.

'Now or . . . never,' Appleby shouts and slaps him on the shoulder. 'It is about gold and crookedness and . . .'

'Stop there,' says Balty. 'Never is safer than now.'

'The gold was not lost,' Appleby yells into his ear. 'Those bags were filled with stones, not coins. Kirke has the gold in his private treasure chest. I have seen it.'

Other heads turn now and Monahan is pushing through the crowd.

Balty heads for outside and then for the small house he sometimes uses, two streets away. He bars the door when he gets there and is glad he did so when he hears it being rattled soon after midnight. He knows what Appleby meant. Ten bags of gold coins, overdue payment for the garrison, had been lost in deep water at the entrance to the bay as they were ferried from the *James* galley to the mole steps. The longboat capsized and no diver could go deep enough to find them. Does he believe Appleby? Yes, this is a truthful man known until now for shunning alcohol. Should he add this to his ledger of Kirke's crimes? He must verify it with the clerk in a quieter place.

Next morning he hears that Appleby is already in a quieter place. As dawn breaks, his broken body is found splayed across the rocks far below the ramparts, close by Lawson's Battery. That morning, Kirke's men stand in the road outside Balty's overnight lodgings to show they are watching him. From that day on, Balty widens his network of secret sleeping places. He has no wish to meet the rocks face first. Now he waits at the back door of Fernam Pereiro's shop. Inside, the Portuguese merchant sees the small wooden arrow hidden under his counter twitch up to the vertical as Balty pulls the cord. He completes the sale of a flagon of olive oil to the wife of the commander of the fusiliers, opens the door to let her out, then bolts it before he goes to the rear to let his good friend in, seeing the bag Balty is carrying.

'You are going away?' he asks. 'So soon?'

'I must keep moving now,' Balty says. 'It's getting harder all the time, Fernam. Kirke wants me dead.'

'He fears what you know. He thinks it will die with you.'

'It will not. It is all in my book,' says Balty. 'For now, it is in the usual place. Remember what you do if I don't return?'

Fernam hugs him. 'I cannot forget. A man will come. Perhaps from a ship called *Moonstone*. He will say your children's names. I will show him where to look but . . . Balthasar, you will come back. Where are you going?'

'If you don't know they cannot force you to say.'

'Not Barbate or Sancti Petri, nor Bonanza, I hope. There has been talk of your friends there.'

'Say Cadiz if you have to. I hope to see you in two weeks.' He wraps a white cloth around his face to hide it from the sun and from prying eyes, then dons his long robe. 'Have you ink and a scrap to write on?'

'Here.'

Balty writes one line. 'If the *Moonstone* comes, then give its commander this.'

'Tariq ibn-Ziyad? What man is he?'

'A man from long ago, now only bones. Goodbye Fernam.'

He slips out into the square. The Smyrna merchants are leaving the city for their camp out on the sands, so he merges in to pass through the gate. Within an hour he joins his friends, the fishermen, in his sailing skiff. The seven small boats sail out of the bay and he waves farewell as the others turn west. Steering north-east, propelled by the warm south wind, he heads for his great discovery, feeling much safer as he moves beyond Kirke's reach. The ebb tide sets in as he leaves the funnel of the narrow straits behind and it is early evening before he runs the boat up on the Spanish sand by the ancient Devil's Tower. Parts of this deserted place resemble Tangier, with a crumbling, deserted citadel sloping down to the sea, rocks rising behind it to ape the African mountains. Even this tower has its namesake at Tangier, but what this place does not have is other regular inhabitants bar the six men now walking down the sand towards him, waving.

That same day, the expedition fleet finally departs, carrying Samuel Pepys and Will Hewer with it on board the *Grafton*. After all that rush, ten days have passed since they arrived and Pepys's irritation has risen. He would mind less if he knew the delay is down to Betty. A young man from the Treasury visits Somerset House to hear the queen's quartet giving their weekly concert and afterwards Betty sweet-talks him into explaining the exact costs of maintaining Tangier. He enjoys her smile and tells her all. She conceals her shock at the total. 'My dear queenie mama,' she says when she and Catherine are alone, 'the place is a nightmare for any monarch who has the misfortune to own it. It should simply be abandoned.'

'Not so simple,' says Catherine. 'The devilish corsairs of that coast desire a stronghold to command the entrance to the entire middle sea. That monstrous structure that has cost my king-friend's fortune will make a perfect port for their raiding ships. I mean the . . . what do they call it? The *topeira?*'

This is a new word to Betty. 'What is that?'

'The little blind creature that digs tunnels?'

'A mole.'

'Just so. A most odd word for a vast stone thing above water not underground.'

Before Betty sleeps she has seen the only solution and she puts it to Catherine in such a way that the queen remembers it as her own idea. Catherine seeks an audience with the king, who is at Windsor. After hearing her, Charles sends a king's messenger galloping to Portsmouth to summon Lord Dartmouth.

Pepys and Hewer have a week to catch up on their shopping before they finally move from dry land to the *Grafton*. The flagship is the largest of the vessels now assembled at the Spithead mooring, a two-decker with a crew of four hundred, twice the size of the accompanying frigates. Pepys has a small cabin to himself and, anchored in sheltered waters, he thinks this ship will suit him for an ocean voyage, not so wild as the slender frigates. He changes his mind when they head out to the eastern shore of the Isle of Wight; the *Grafton* rolling as wind fights tide. An evil magic shrinks the ship to lurch like a wooden toy in a bath tub. It is a relief to anchor off St Helens to get their drinking water and when their tanks are full, they hoist a score of extra water butts on deck to fill those too. Captain Booth joins them watching. 'Tangier is ever thirsty,' he says. 'There is more wine drunk there than water and the garrison's folly spoilt their springs. They send daily water boats to Spain. We must supply ourselves.'

'Well, that confirms it,' says Will when Booth leaves them. 'Have you talked to Dartmouth yet?'

'He is keeping his distance. It's the only way to pretend this is a secret mission.'

Will looks back at the vessels queuing to take their turn for water. 'Nine warships? At least a dozen merchantmen so far?'

'It's a big job to strengthen the defences, Will. I think they also plan to extend the mole. The man who built it came on board at dawn.'

'Henry Shere?'

'Yes, everyone's favourite engineer.' Pepys's voice has a forced note. He means every woman's favourite engineer. Shere is a handsome hero who has grabbed a sword and leapt on a horse to save the day in several of Tangier's battles. Pepys came to resent the look on Elizabeth's face whenever Henry appeared at their London house, but in the years since, they pretend to be friends.

That afternoon, a violent westerly gale has the ship tossing at the anchors. The steward brings Pepys brandy in his cabin and sees his pallid face. 'On deck with you, sir. Grip the rail, fix your eyes on the horizon and keep them there.'

Up top he is clawing from handhold to handhold past the foot of the mainmast when someone screams from far above. Next moment, a violent shove sends him tumbling sideways as a dark mass thuds down on the deck where he had just been.

He sees a contorted body in a spreading pool of blood, then strong hands force him from the sight. Sam Atkins is holding him. 'No need to look. The man lost his hold. Are you hurt, sir?'

Pepys gasps in a breath. 'Sam, You saved me.'

'*You* saved *me* in Westminster Hall. Now come away. I am sent to bring you to his lordship.' He pulls Pepys away, then pauses at the door of the stern gallery, looking curiously at him. 'How are you now?' he asks quietly and Pepys is surprised to find himself entirely calm. It brings a sudden clarity that the prisons and the grey shadows of all those who want him dead have drained his capacity for fear. Atkins knocks and they hear a quiet summons.

'Give me one moment, sir,' says Atkins and slips inside. He is explaining what just happened, Pepys thinks, and when the door reopens he sees Dartmouth staring hard at him, so he takes care to show nothing but pleasant expectation on his face.

'Atkins, remain on guard out there. Make sure no one loiters near the door.' He clasps Pepys's hand between both of his and points to a chair. 'An excellent young man. He has told me many times what you did for him. Now . . .' he breaks off and turns to stare out of the stern windows.

'A new arrival. Oh great heavens, is that horrible scow joining us? Yes, I fear it is the damned *Comfort*. We'll be lucky to fly half our canvas. The pace of the slowest tub can drive a man mad.' He turns back. 'My dear friend, are you ready to talk?'

'You have my full attention, my lord.' Pepys looks to see what remains of young George Legge, the seaman. Not that young anymore, but there are fifteen years between these two. One day soon, he thinks, the two of them may drive out the ghosts of the *Gloucester* wreck, but perhaps not until England is safe enough for the truth to be properly examined.

Dartmouth drums his fingers on the table. 'Until I tell you otherwise, not one word of what I say may go beyond this cabin.'

'Indeed, my Lord.'

'Not even to Hewer.'

'I understand.' Pepys conceals a smile. Dartmouth clearly has no idea how much they have already guessed.

'You know where we are heading?'

'Tangier.'

Dartmouth's calm nod confirms he never thought this part would stay secret. 'And you, a famously clever man, will have considered what we are sent there to do?'

'I may speak plainly?'

'Mighty Lord Dartmouth might not accept that, Samuel, but at this moment in this cabin I see only your friend George. We have shared much and you command my high opinion. Speak freely within these private wooden walls.'

Pepys thinks carefully and Dartmouth waits patiently for his conclusion. 'We should have asked why the Portuguese were so ready to see the back of Tangier.'

'You were made Tangier treasurer. You saw what it might become.'

'It brought me undue wealth but ... I have received only three letters from my brother St Michel in all his time there. He wrote lately that those in charge are depraved thieves, stealing from our king.'

'You believe him?'

'Yes. He once had a habit of poetic exaggeration. Not anymore.'

'We agree Tangier is a problem. What would be your solution?'

'An impressive arrival is the first step. Sail into the bay with this grand display of force. Make it a stronger, better managed place to bring the foreign trade we expected.'

'How?'

'Examine the governor's staff. If they fall short, appoint trustworthy replacements. Complete the damned harbour. Send disciplined soldiers under a good commander. Reinforce the outer forts. Make it work better and reverse the flood of money so it streams back to King Charles instead of bankrupting him.'

George Legge stares at him with eyebrows raised and Pepys smiles inwardly. Did the man opposite think he hadn't worked this all out by now. 'My friend,' he says quietly, 'I may be able to face my poor brother Balty if I can tell him that all he hates about Tangier will be put right. That is so, is it not?'

'Samuel, you could not be more completely wrong.'

'What do you mean?' His voice betrays his shock.

'Be aware that Lord Dartmouth has now returned to convey to you the king's final decision and to lift the burden from George Legge's tender shoulders. Dartmouth finds it easier to be brutal and he needs both your help and your solemn vow of secrecy until he releases you from it.'

'Well ... I will, of course, swear to ...' The storm outside sluices rain across the glass of the stern gallery and the light level drops, but a moment later it becomes clear it is not an approaching cloud but an approaching ship. Spars, cordage and canvas suddenly fill their view as a vessel careens across their stern, men shouting as it scrapes past them in a series of thuds.

'It's the damned *Comfort*,' Dartmouth growls. 'God damn the idiots. Stupid name for a ship like that and nothing but trouble.'

They both stare out at the chaos of the wind and seas grinding the smaller vessel around their stern, seamen, so close they can see their tattoos, fighting to drop its remaining sail and fend it off from the flagship's gilded after-works. Pepys is surprised to see Dartmouth's degree of agitation. Such things happen in storms. Relative calm is restored and Dartmouth gives a huge sigh. His words course through Pepys's brain: *'you could not be more completely wrong ...'*

'You say I am wrong? You mean . . . ?'

'I mean I am commanded to destroy the city of Tangier utterly, not just the walls, the houses, the inner and outer castles, but also every stone of the harbour, the great mole and all its lesser works. I know this, young Atkins knows it, and now you know it too, but outside that not even Captain Booth, the commander of this my flagship, knows it.'

'Henry Shere?'

'He does not know it yet but I will soon have to tell him, because he made most of the harbour and hopefully will know how to unmake it.' He sighs. 'Two more ships laden like the *Comfort* will soon join this convoy. They will be ordered to sail some way astern because they are laden with powder to blast it all to rubble and they carry teams of miners, experienced in blowing up rock.'

'Laden like the *Comfort*?'

'In terms of their cargo, yes indeed. Four hundred barrels of powder in each one.'

'We were just rammed by a ship full of gunpowder? I thought you seemed concerned.'

'It needs a fuse and flame to become a problem. You know that. No, I was more concerned that we are short of paint to repair the damage. Now, as to the future of Tangier, I am wondering what you think as I cannot read your face.'

'My spinning head has not yet told my face what it thinks but, this being the king's order, it perhaps has nothing to add. I am not sure why I am here.'

'Oh Samuel, this is George back again. I need your wisdom. We will have to explain ourselves to those who have made Tangier their home. The king is sure you will find the right words. He may even hope that we will be blamed, not him. Also, you will determine the compensation to the owners of Tangier property which may take weeks to complete. Money in their hands will ease their sorrow and we carry that in plenty.'

And some of that will be mine, thinks Pepys. Weeks to complete? At twenty eight pounds for each week that will be a splendid reward. It could be two whole months before they get home. 'Where are they all to go?' he says.

'Anyone who calls England, Scotland, Wales and Ireland their home will be taken there. The rest? Back to their own lands.'

'Was there a change of plan? You were ordered to Windsor.'

Dartmouth drums his fingers. 'Queen Catherine expressed unhappiness as to the fate of her dowry. She had wanted it given back to Portugal.'

'So ... she changed her mind? Surely she didn't want it blown up?'

'She surprised the king. She somehow did the sums and found its return would impoverish Portugal just as it impoverished Charles. She urged it be destroyed for the greater good and my mission was utterly changed.'

'My Lord, could I not discuss this in the greatest secrecy with Hewer? He and I should start planning now.'

'No, Samuel. When I am sure of our arrival in Tangier perhaps, but not yet – and remember, if this goes wrong, you and I will be left with the blame.'

'George. If we let this go wrong, we will deserve it.'

'The deck will be clean by now. One last matter. You must bear with me when we arrive. I will have to greet the governor fondly as a great man and a strong ally.'

'I know little of him except that he has a beautiful wife. I admired her long before they met.'

'I have no choice but to work with him politely. I want you to know I don't mean it.' He looks at Pepys with his head cocked slightly sideways. 'You will be seeing your brother St Michel again. He is still in Tangier, is he not?'

'Indeed he is,' answers Pepys, entirely wrongly.

Five more days of high winds, the ships jerking at their anchors then being forced offshore for safety, see Pepys staying out of sight in his cabin, studying papers and avoiding questions. On Sunday, a fresh and friendly wind sends them beating towards Guernsey across a steady westerly, then back up to the Devon coast to anchor in Plymouth Sound. The next day, beyond Land's End, hostile winds force them towards the tip of Ireland before turning south to battle past the top corner of France. The waves rear higher still where the Atlantic swell hits the shallow bed of the wide Bay of Biscay. Their longitude slowly diminishes, not so Pepys's nausea until they reach better weather and tamer seas at Spain's northern cape and Sam Atkins comes to find him. 'His lordship requests the pleasure of your company on the quarterdeck.'

Dartmouth stands near the stern and leads him to the rail, looking back along their wake at the line of ships keeping station. 'I will share a secret with you, old friend. My thoughts often race when I should be sleeping and then I set myself a mathematical task. The curving distance from one point of latitude and longitude to another, the exact height of the head of a slanting mainmast, the course to be set across a confluence of ocean currents. Last night it was simpler.' He turns his head and stares at Pepys. 'I asked myself how many hours ago a particular

event occurred and I concluded it was eleven thousand, four
hundred and twenty. Can you name that event?'

Pepys is briefly puzzled as he tries to divide that by twenty-
four then he realizes that remote Lord Dartmouth is looking
more like uncertain George Legge and there is only one possible answer. 'Of course I can,' he says. 'Dawn on Saturday the
6th day of May last year when we encountered two sandbanks,
the Leman and the Ower.'

'To be more accurate,' says Legge, 'I encountered them and
you watched me and I think it is time for you to plainly tell me
why it was that way round.'

'Because . . . you were onboard the *Gloucester* frigate and I
was in the royal yacht *Katherine*?'

'But that was not the way it was meant to be, so I ask you
again, why was it so?' He is staring in a way Pepys has not seen
before and does not much like. 'I require your plain answer,
Samuel.'

'We were both summoned at the last moment,' says Pepys, to
buy a little thinking time. This is dangerous ground but perhaps
its moment has come.

The first part flashes through his head. With Shaftesbury
dead and his plot fading into memory, Charles brings his
brother James home from exile in careful stages, first to
Scotland then, leaving his wife there, for a test visit to London.
The king sees the capital's fickle crowds take to the streets to
cheer his brother and he acts. A fleet is gathered to sail north,
taking James and his entourage back to collect his wife and
return in glory.

Pepys's invitation shows the royal brothers can now reward
those who were punished for serving them. Legge watches him

closely. 'You were offered the chance to be at the duke's right hand. I was just another body to be stuffed into a lesser boat, well away from the people who mattered. Then . . . I am offered the exchange. I could not believe my luck.'

'I was not ready for crowds.'

'Tell me why it happened or I will transfer you to the *Comfort* for the rest of the voyage.'

Pepys sighs, 'There was something perhaps I did not fully explain.'

'What?'

'A man came to the door two days before we left. He gave me a letter and insisted I open it on the instant. It was not signed but . . . I knew the hand of my good friend Captain Gunman. It told me plainly not to sail in the *Gloucester*. Gunman said I would find it crowded and drunken. With my propensity for sea sickness, I would find greater dignity in the *Katherine* yacht, he said, the same *Katherine* which had already saved the life of Sam Atkins at his trial. I must pen a note to agree and hand it to this messenger. I did that.' He shakes his head. 'George, I had no notion that it was you who would take my place or what the outcome would be.'

Legge considers. 'The secret of the captains. Five words. Have you heard them before? Answer me with the greatest care.'

'No. What do they mean? You shake your head? Too secret for my ears? Listen to me George. There was no secret in this. Gunman named the thing I most feared. I did not want to vomit near the duke.'

Dartmouth takes a deep breath. 'That truly is how you hurled me into disaster?'

Pepys feels unwanted anger rising in him. 'George, if I had not chanced to do that, the Duke of York would be dead and me with him. I am too old, too weak and too poor a swimmer to have escaped from the sinking ship and you, George, would not have been on hand to pluck Duke James from death's clutch. You saved him.'

'While so very many drowned around us.'

'Oh yes, and I saw them die. The other boats hurling down their anchors, slewing to a stop. No captain certain of what might lie just beneath us, except for Gunman who had been right all along. Believe me, I will never forget one single moment of it.'

'Except for Gunman, you say?'

'Yes, and some even tried to blame him for it afterwards.'

'So . . . Samuel, tell me this, then. Did Gunman have second sight? But for him you would have been one more on the long list of the dead.'

Pepys frowns. 'Captains can be a law unto themselves and out for personal gain. He is not one of those. He had seen my seasickness at close range and was seeking to protect me.'

'Perhaps.' Legge waves his hand across the spread of ships following in their wake. 'There are officers with us now who were also in that fleet.' He turns and fixes his eyes on Pepys again. 'You have told me *what* happened but I asked *why*.'

'Some of the plotters saw their time was up and still designed to kill the duke.'

'You think the pilot, Ayres, agreed to be a martyr?'

'I do not. He was renowned as a strong swimmer. Other ships were close.'

'From my little boat, fending off the desperate men who

clawed at the gunwales and threatened to capsize the duke, he swam right past me without even trying to board. I believe I saw where he was heading. It was not the closest vessel and some of the frigates were far off. I steered for Gunman's *Mary*. He did not.'

'I remember he was taken on board the *Charlotte*, was he not?'

'Only because a swirl in the current took him there. He was heading for . . .'

'Yes?'

Legge opens his mouth to go on, then stops himself. 'No. My supposition may harden into fact if I release into other ears. We will leave that for another time, but Gunman was blamed by some . . .'

'Not by anyone who was there, surely? You witnessed every moment of it.'

James Ayres is brought in to set the fleet's course because, as a skilled pilot, he knows every inch of the lethal sandbank fingers just under the sea, stretching thirty miles from the Norfolk coast, and he knows the safe course between them. With him directing the helmsman, there need be no time-wasting tacks far offshore. Captain Gunman knows them too and he challenges the pilot's first chosen course, sailing the *Mary* under the *Gloucester*'s stern in the darkness to warn them off the Newarp Sands, tearing off his hat and stamping on it when Ayres resisted. He forces the five frigates and three other royal yachts to steer away, but hours later he is fast asleep when, out there amid the further hazards, Ayres alters course again. Alerted by his mate and rapidly diminishing soundings, Gunman reaches the *Mary*'s deck and tries desperately to warn the *Gloucester* coming up fast astern. His warnings go unseen in the early dawn and the ship buries its bows in the just-submerged Leman and Ower banks, eight hundred tons of solid wood travelling at seven knots. The ship's timbers split and it rapidly began to sink.

'My God, it made a noise,' says Legge. 'I had rarely heard strong oak torn apart with such brutality. The helmsman was killed by the flailing of the rudder as she struck.'

'George, the duke survived for two reasons – both of them were down to chance. Gunman forced that first change, so the wreck was hours later than intended and dawn had just come.'

'And second?'

'As you said, my seasickness.'

'What?'

'As I already said, it ensured a brave man was on hand to force the duke into that small boat despite his protests. You fought off those clutching men all the way to safety. I could not have done that.'

Legge stares out across the sea at the distant coast of Spain and shakes his head. 'We can both be glad we survived, Samuel. You are right. It was as well that we changed places. Let that be.' The topsails slat in a twist of wind and Legge cranes his gaze up the mainmast as the canvas cracks again. The helmsman sees him, bends their course a fraction more to larboard and smiles at Legge's approving nod. It breaks the conversation and the man who turns his head back to stare at Pepys is Lord Dartmouth again.

'Enough. This smooth sea and the kindly sun are a good omen for us.'

'I need more,' says Pepys. 'At the end of this voyage I must face my brother Balthasar who has been ill used in this tangle.'

With memories of the wreck exposed to the air, setting

things right with Balty is the next urgent task. A good omen seems unlikely, but as they stand side by side, staring at the *Grafton*'s wake, the sea answers them, boiling up with a display of wild, wet bodies arcing in their tens, then their hundreds through the wake of the ship and jinking to follow it, more and more and more until their numbers suggest thousands.

'Porpoises?' exclaims Pepys, astonished, and Lord Dartmouth is about to correct him, knowing dolphins when he sees them. George Legge steps back in for a moment and only says, 'There's your omen.'

CHAPTER 31

At the moment those distant dolphins veer away, Balty is sailing into Sanlucar de Barrameda, a small Spanish fishing town at the mouth of the Guadalquivir river. This is as far as he usually travels up the Atlantic coast beyond Cadiz. It is fifteen hours from Tangier on a good day and his small single-masted esquife, as the Spanish call it, is good at broad-reaching across a strong south-westerly. These days he never takes the straightest route, knowing unfriendly eyes may be observing his course from the high viewpoints above Tangier Bay. Instead he steers across the strait on the shortest route to Tarifa, the nearest town on the Spanish coast, and only then, knowing his skiff is out of sight, turns north-westward up the coast. He won the boat playing cards in Tarifa so it looks just like many others on both sides of the straits and Sanlucar is as safe a harbour as it gets in these dangerous months. Two or three of his closer friends here know that bad men may come looking. He drops the sail and moors the little boat to a jetty by a weary old warehouse. A friendly voice hails him from the darkness inside as if he had been expected.

'Balty. It is you.'

'Barto, it is.'

Bartolomé is tall, lean, sun-dried and darkened, with blazing blue eyes. His smile gleams in the sun and they hug each other. A friend from the moment they first met in the bar down the road, the near match of their names cemented it. He speaks in excellent French as always when Balty is there, learnt on his Mediterranean travels, though he also has some broken English. 'It is so good to see you,' he says. 'I have everything here that you wanted.'

'Did I leave you enough money?'

'Yes, easily and even enough perhaps to cover shipping it, depending on where it goes next.'

'Four days at most there and back including loading and unloading. I will have men at the other end to assist.'

'Four days? Then that is simple. I will take it there myself. Come and see.'

One entire side of the big warehouse is stacked with planking, spars, cordage and canvas. Balty inspects it because that is what Barto wants, even though he knows there is no need. It is all top quality, as good as anything he ever had tucked away back in Kent. That thought stops him. Deal. Another world. He misses the children, more perhaps than he misses Esther. In Deal he had to watch out for the odd vengeful skipper. In Tangier, he has to guard against Kirke's thugs every day of his life.

As if picking up that thought, Barto says, 'There have been six men here looking for you.'

'What sort of men?'

'Hard men. One in that silly uniform. Yellow, green and fluffy frills.'

'The Tangier Regiment?'

'Yes. For showing off, not fighting. He spoke bad Spanish. The others stayed silent.'

'What did they ask you?'

'They were looking for a man named St Michel to tell him he had great good fortune and would be returning to England if only he was located in time for the ship that was waiting at Tangier. I said I had never heard of such a man. Their eyes betrayed a different purpose.'

'They went away?'

'The man in his uniform came into the warehouse and saw your stores. He asked me what all that was for. I said it was a reserve for the Spanish navy in case Cadiz was besieged. He made a face. Balty, these were not friendly messengers, they were assassins. They gave up on me and went to the bar to ask more people, but I walked a little behind them and made the cut-throat sign so they met with silence.'

'They left quickly?'

'They stood talking to each other for a while and I was behind the fence listening. I think they said this was as far up the coast as they wanted to go and now they should try the other way.'

'Back past Cadiz and on north-eastward?'

'That was what I think they meant.'

'When was this?'

'The day before yesterday.'

'You saw them sail?'

'Yes, in a sloop with two guns. South-east towards the straits, as they said.'

And I just missed them going the other way, thought Balty. Would they have recognized me and my boat? Maybe not.

'Barto,' he says. 'Did the man in the regimental uniform give his name?'

'I think so. Something short.'

'Not Monahan?'

'No, not that. Shorter, Fipps or Fopps.'

'Can you find me some good men with weapons and a speedy vessel to go after them, straight away? I will pay well.'

'I can find five men right now. You need only pay for them. I will come for free and we will take my boat.'

'Here,' says Balty, dipping into his pouch and giving Barto a handful of heavy gold coins. 'Use these.'

'Oh, that is a lot. I hope this is not your money.'

'No. It belongs to King Charles. It was diverted into the pockets of our corrupt governor. I rescued it one night while he snored away his drunkenness. I am sure our king would approve.'

Two hours later, Barto's boat, a lateen rigged two-master, is beating into the brisk wind with the straits in sight. It tows Balty's skiff, leaping in its wake. The men on deck are cleaning muskets and polishing a variety of ancient swords, some straight, some curved, and all, says Barto, retrieved from battlefields. The wind drops with the evening and they make slow progress through the night. Barto takes the helm and calls Balty to join him.

'Tell me our destination,' he says. 'I know the tides and the currents well. I do not like sailing blind and close to a lee shore.'

'It may put you in a tricky place but you are about to see it anyway.'

'Tricky?'

'Barto, from the first moment I saw Tangier, I knew England

could not stay there much longer. Suppose, the Lord forbid, that we were once again at war with your delightful country and our fleet had nowhere near to go for repair and supplies? Cadiz would be barred to us. I looked for a remote place that might serve instead. A better place than Tangier. Defensible. I found one and I have done my duty for my king and country, I have built sheds there and I have sailors quartered there waiting for the supplies you will bring. Kirke and his men do not know.'

'A tricky place? That must mean it is not on the Moroccan shore but here in Spain.'

'Is that hard for you?'

Barto laughs. 'I guess we are steering towards a place in Andalusia. I am Andalusian. I am only loosely associated to what goes on in far-away Madrid. They are different people to us. Name this place, though I think I can guess.'

'In Tangier, I use the old words so any eavesdropper may be puzzled. There is a lot at stake. It is called after an ancient conqueror. Tarik ibn-Ziyad.'

Barto frowns then suddenly laughs. 'Yes. Jebel Tariq. Across the bay from the ruins of Al-Yazirat? You think that is where we will find these men?'

'I fear so.'

A waxing moon is rising in the sky and the rock of Jebel Tarik looms as they sail up the coast. They enter the bay two hours before dawn and silver moonlight is crisp on the shore. A stone watchtower stands gaunt sentinel where the sand-spit links the mainland to the crumbling fortifications below the steep rise of the rock. Balty stares across the water and sees no sloop, large or small. A longboat and a little boat much like his own are pulled up on the sand. He scans the shore and sees his store sheds are intact. As they drop the anchor a hundred yards offshore, he notices something between them and the sand that should not be there. Sticking up from the water, flashing with moonlight as it is splashed by waves, is a wooden pole.

Balty ferries them ashore in his skiff and they stand still staring ahead, muskets and sabres ready. Nothing stirs for a minute, then a door creaks ajar from the store sheds. A head peers round it and Balty shoves down the musket that the man next to him raises.

'It's me, Balthasar,' he shouts. 'Is that you, Jerome?'

'Aye, that it is,' the shout comes back. 'Come on. It is safe now.' Five men come out of the shed, muskets slung over their shoulders, and they meet halfway.

'You've missed a bit of howdedo,' says Jerome, the biggest of them. 'Unexpected guests. Dropped in out of nowhere in the early hours to wake us. Can't think for the life of me what they expected, but it didn't end well for the life of them.' He nods towards the bay. 'See that mast out there? That's got their boat underneath it and them tucked up cosy inside. Careless, I call it. No way for a proper seaman to do things. They acted like we'd be a pushover. Stores men. Didn't expect fighting sailors.'

'They attacked you?'

'When we heard them coming, I came out to see what they was about. Me and little Robbie Tyrell. They asked if Saint Michael was here, said they was friends bearing glad tidings. Well, no friend of yours would call you Saint Michael the English way so I says I never heard of such a man outside the scriptures. Bastards took a musket butt to Robbie's head, said that should open my mouth before I got the same treatment. Well, did they think we was stupid? I waved my arm and stepped left out of the way and my boys opened up from the sheds with their muskets. I had to stick my sword into the boss man and the one next to him, not having quite enough muskets to get them all in one volley, so anyway that was that.'

Jerome acts out the entire event as he speaks and Barto's crew smile their approval. Balty looks at the Englishmen and sees they are one short. 'Robbie's not here,' he says.

'He's sleeping off that kiss from the musket butt. He'll wake with a headache.' Jerome glances out towards the top of the mast. 'Whoops. That's a giveaway. Come low water, I'll nip out there and chop a bit off, then we'll all know it was nowt but a bad dream, right?'

Balty hands out more gold sovereigns from his dwindling stock, introduces Barto and his men properly, and they sit round a table drinking the roughest coffee he has ever tasted from three shared mugs. That done and arrangements made for the stores delivery trip, Balty looks in on the still-unconscious lad, then it's back on the boat. With the dawn, the wind has backed so they make good progress, but as they come closer to Tarifa, with Tangier's hills clear to the south, he is sprawled half-asleep across the stern when Barto shakes him.

All along the horizon, a few miles away, a low cloud of sails is stretched across the sea – not one ship, but ship after ship, a dozen, a score? They are coming from the ocean and slanting for Tangier.

'Barto,' he says, 'luff up. I will take my boat. I need a closer look.'

'We can bring you to them.'

'No. I must be the lone fisherman, so they glance at me and forget.'

'Then put on your headgear and all that Moorish stuff.'

He hoists his sail as they wave him farewell, then turns his boat to close with this startling fleet as it enters Tangier Bay. After half an hour he is sure of the distinctive outline of the *Grafton*, flying an Admiral's pennant. Following astern is a gaggle of frigates. He knows their little differences and who captains each one of them. Mixed in are a score of merchantmen. As they enter the bay he is close, resisting the temptation to wave, striving to look like any fisherman would, returning with his catch, intimidated by these alien visitors. He sees people staring all around them from the *Grafton*'s quarterdeck and cuts across below the stern for a closer view. A man who is nothing like a sailor peers down at him, blinking. Even at thirty feet, that face hits him in the gut because he knows it so well. Against all logic, he sees his brother Pepys, who turns away to look at other more remarkable sights.

It is a shocking moment for Samuel Pepys, but not because he has just seen Balty; indeed he has no inkling that he has. All his eyes have briefly registered is an African man in a small boat. He is shocked because for the very first time he is forced to confront the true nature of Tangier. The *Grafton* slowly turns and is manoeuvred alongside the great stone breakwater blocking the oceanic swell sent marching in by Atlantic winds. A third of a mile of wide stonework supports a line of warehouses, offices and gun batteries. Will Hewer, Lord Dartmouth and Captain William Booth appear one by one over the next two hours, but each looks at the back of the brooding figure standing at the rail and turns away. Pepys is facing up to horror. It is finally clear to him that during all those profitable years as Tangier's treasurer those rich images on his Westminster office walls had fed a fantasy. They had kept him reassured that the port controlled the mouth of the Mediterranean – the perfect, secure and profitable magnet for merchants from far around, protected by naval ships to tame the Barbary Coast and the harsh corsairs of Salee. On the quarterdeck Pepys grips the stern rail, staring at the city so close by and trying to reconcile it with those images he knows so well. The ship is more or less motionless at last, but his balance has been mauled by weeks of violent waves. The fluids inside his head still heave up and down to sicken him. From where he stands, Tangier is a great oblong of walls knocked aslant. The steep slope up from the water shows it to him like a twisted map and he knows the names of all he sees, but that is all – just words on parchment, not real life on African rock. To his left he sees where the waterfront's battlements meet the strong stonework of the Devil's Tower then climb inland. To the right, the landward end of the mole meets the massive walls of Yorke Castle, beyond which the edge of the sea curves gently west to the Atlantic. He looks further to his right and from this tip of Africa, he can see the coast of Spain across the narrowing straits, the white walls of a town bright in sunlight. That must be Tarifa, he thinks. Between here and there, the warm Mediterranean confronts the cold Atlantic, with this bottleneck of the narrow straits refereeing the fight. Turning back to the city, he see the ground rise steeply beyond Yorke Castle to a great walled bastion and high up there, beyond the governor's grand mansion, the summit of the city is the Peterborough Tower with the king's flag flying high.

He hadn't expected the sweet smell as they sailed in to Tangier Bay. The gentle wind comes at him straight off the shore, from ragged fields outside the walls and perhaps those wilder bands of green and yellow dimly visible in the foothills beyond. Orange blossom, he thinks, tangerines perhaps, what else? Something that might be vanilla and other unknown herbs. It makes a heady mixture, but he finds its strangeness as threatening as the land ahead. Tangier's buildings higher up the slope are crammed into narrow streets, parades of houses with white walls under flattened red tiles. The towers of two churches stand out and he slowly scans the gun batteries and the guard turrets along the top of all those great protective walls. Tangier matches the promise of the pictures he has so often stared at on his walls in almost every way.

Except for one.

He can now see that these grand defences add up to exactly zero. The city's parapets may be tall but they could never be tall enough, because the half-circle of surrounding terrain rises inland in steps, sand hills nearby, terraced faces of sheer rock further back, steepening where the vegetation ends, wilder and wilder as they climb. That savage landscape overlooks everything with an endless choice of vantage points to watch exactly what is happening inside the defences of the city below. What horrifies Pepys most is his first clear sight of the thousands of opposing soldiers plus their horses, tents and palisades which fill that landscape. A vast army is encamped outside the city's walls, a half-mile away in some parts, closer in others. These, he now knows, are the Moorish troops of Ali Benabdala, the Alcaïd of Alcazar, making it quite clear to the foreign upstarts that all this land is really theirs. The scales finally fall from his eyes and it is breath-sappingly painful. Oh my Lord, he thinks, how could anybody ever have thought this place could make a safe base? The Alcaïd's men can do as they will. King Charles has frittered a fortune into defending it and all for what?

He retreats to his cabin to be left alone and lies on his mattress in misery. The fear he has been squashing boils up to the surface. Somewhere in this town is brother Balty. Some time soon, they must encounter each other. Somehow he must accept that Balty was right all along. Tangier is a death trap. Later, as he dozes, the steward taps on his door. 'Captain Booth's compliments, sir, and the ship has been prepared for the dignitaries of the town. You would be most welcome to join them.'

He cannot refuse and leaves the gloomy cabin to go on deck where the sailors have spread awnings, yellow in the light of a hundred lanterns. Dusk is nearly on them and he looks again at the mountains masking the vast length of Africa curving down the globe beyond them. Those mountains are shading to a deep blue as the sun sinks, a colour he has seen in the paintings on his office wall and dismissed as fanciful. Now it gives him no pleasure.

Booth is checking the tables where stewards are laying out food and drink. He sees Pepys and comes over to him.

'Captain,' says Pepys. 'You have been to Tangier before?'

'Yes, indeed. When I commanded the *Newcastle* I was here before the great siege of three years back and twice more since then.'

'Were the Moors as close to the walls as they are now?'

'Not at first. We had forts out there to claim the ground. The siege put an end to most of them. Their armies have been close by since then, sir. We may think we own this place but they do not agree and that siege was a terrible affair.'

'Forgive me. I was fighting my own battles at the time,' says Pepys.

'Indeed you were. Omar ben Haddu led a well-trained army. This poor city had the idiot Earl of Inchiquin in command and he knew less of soldiering than I know of tapestry. He lost the outer forts in the time it takes to sneeze, then he insisted on leading an insane raid up there in the hills. He led his men into the woods and of course it was the perfect place for ambush. His poor men were slaughtered by the hundred. I regret to say they are still there, sir, deprived of burial. A brave man crept in a year after to bear witness. He found their white bones spread out in the undergrowth. He said they gleamed in the rays of sunlight through the leaves above.'

'Things turned?'

'Palmes Fairborne took over, a real soldier, shot in the chest at the very moment of breaking the siege.'

'My late wife's brother is here, you know? He was made agent, commissioner of the stores and muster-master.'

'Certainly, I know Balthasar St Michel. Indeed I brought him here in the year eighty.'

'Did you? A delayed journey. I am told he did all he could to stay in England.'

'Then you were told that by a malicious mouth. Any sensible man would have been in no hurry to get here, but in his case, sir, no blame is due to him at all. That siege delayed our voyage and he walked into a shocking degree of chaos. The catastrophe was kept as quiet as possible in England.'

'I am concerned for my brother. You have seen him since?'

'When I have passed this way he has not made himself known but I . . .'

'You hesitate?'

'Within the next hour you will meet the present governor. Sir Percy Kirke arrived some months ago. I must choose my words with care. Few honest people of any sensitivity have fared well. Have you met him?'

'I have met and admired his wife, before they married of course.'

Booth sighs. 'And she chose Percy Kirke.'

'He must have special qualities.'

'He has indeed, Mr Pepys. I will list them if I may. Sir Percy Kirke is the most disgusting, disgraceful, immoral, venial, violent and repulsive man I have ever had the extreme discomfort of knowing. I intend to make sure he takes passage back to England in a different ship, ideally one that leaks badly. I have heard he is no friend of your brother.'

The guests begin to come aboard and the stewards offer trays of unappealing food and more attractive drink. Pepys stands by himself at the stern, assessing the officers of the garrison. Some are clearly fighters with faraway eyes and bodies fried down to sinew under sand-blasted tunics. Others have bulges of fat strapped in tight with pudgy faces displaying greed as they peer at the markings on the silver dishes. They are portly, sweating administrators blinking and basted in elaborate brocade. Their wives are coated in powder to mask the sun's damage and desperate for diversion. They reach the deck, seize their first drink and add to the swelling babble, casting glances up towards Pepys where he stands beyond the limits of the crowd. They surround Will Hewer when he appears from below and Pepys sees them pointing towards him in the stern.

Hewer escapes to join him at the rail. 'They ask why we are here,' he says. 'I said to address the defences, but they scoff.'

'Then let us stare up at the top of the mast and appear to discuss the abstruse points of the rigging so no one disturbs us. That way, we can talk about whatever we choose.'

'Too late.'

A tall woman in green wobbles up to them on shoes not made for a ship nor for Africa. She spills her glass on Hewer's leg. 'The notorious traitor Pepys,' she says. 'Indeed the two of you together. Pepys and Hewer, the money men? You don't have the skills to strengthen our damaged walls, Mr Pepys, or did you learn the use of a chisel trying to escape the Tower when you faced certain death by ex——?'

She stops, diverted by shouts from the gangplank where the guests come aboard. A sun-roasted vagabond in tattered clothes is trying to push past the *Grafton*'s first lieutenant. A Tangier officer in ornate uniform rushes to intervene, trying to propel the intruder back the way he came, but the man resists. Pepys stares, then hurries down towards them, horrified, as he sees something in the way this stranger moves. The man's voice rises in urgent demand and he knows it for Balty's voice. The other men grasp the intruder's arms as they propel him away from the guests.

'Stop,' orders Pepys. 'Let him go at once.' The garrison officer stares at him in surprise.

'Do not concern yourself, sir. The man is a rogue.'

'The man is the king's appointed muster-master here.' Pepys stares at Balty. 'Brother, how do you come to be in this condition?'

A voice booms from behind as a hand clasps Pepys roughly by the shoulder. 'Mr Pepys, I believe!'

A heavy man with a hooked nose and red cheeks glistening with sweat towers over him, dressed in the richest of all the rich paraphernalia on the deck. Pepys is in no doubt who he is facing. This can only be Colonel Sir Percy Kirke, Governor of Tangier. His dark eyes swing towards Balty, then back to Pepys again.

'Pepys, ignore this son of a whore. We know him too well. My men will throw this fella over the side. A swim might wash out his mouth.'

Pepys turns and looks the man up and down. 'Damn you, sir,' he says. 'You insult me!'

Kirke is clearly startled. Does he really not know? 'Mr Pepys, you misunderstand me. I am speaking of him, not of you. I would not . . .'

Pepys, the anger rising sharply in him, cuts in. 'If he is the son of a whore, you, sir, are announcing to all the world that my much-loved and very much lamented wife was the daughter of a whore. I will seek satisfaction from you, damn you.'

The older timid part of him gibbers somewhere in the far reaches of his head. He knows he might last as much as ten seconds in a duel with this man, but the new Pepys no longer cares a jot and his vehemence astonishes him. He sees Kirke nonplussed, then struggling with the logic of what he has just said. 'You mean you are related to . . .'

'Indeed I am. Take care how you deal with this brave man because he is my good friend and the dear brother of my late wife. He has my protection and that of our king. What do you say to *that*, sir?'

He has the satisfaction of seeing Kirke step back a pace and then, astonishingly, turn and walk away without another word.

Balty switches his gaze from Pepys to Kirke's departing back. Captain Booth has been standing at a distance, listening. Now he hurries up. 'Good Mr Pepys, may I assist?'

'Yes, Sir William,' says Pepys. 'I request the liberty of your cabin to speak with my brother in private.'

'Indeed.' Booth's steward escorts them to it and produces a cork container. He tips in water and saltpetre crystals, carefully stands a flask of wine in the rapidly chilling liquid and leaves them to themselves.

They stare at each other. There is no flesh on Balty's bones. A white scar crosses his sunburnt cheek and another disappears up his sleeve. His eyes have lost the spark of his old, sideways humour.

'Brother, what has been done to you?' Pepys says.

'You know the answer to that. I have been sent to the Devil for a New Year's gift.'

'I did not send you.'

'I didn't say *you* did but you told me many, many times this would be paradise with added profits. Did you really not know?'

'I saw it clearly only today. This place is indefensible and so was my behaviour.'

'Yes. Your behaviour. I found you the French witnesses to set you free from Colonel John Scott and you let them send me here.'

'Let them? I lost all my power, brother, and it has not been returned to me. I was freed, for which I thank you with all my heart, but I was not returned to employment.'

'But you are now. You are sent here for a purpose and I think I know what it is. But first answer me this. Did my actions in Paris not save you from Scott?'

'Yes indeed.'

'Has he been seen in London since?'

'Not since the murder.'

'What murder? Brother, I stay out of sight here as much as I can. I hear little news. I repeat, what murder?'

'Scott had to run from England in a hurry last year. He killed a man.'

'What sort of a man?'

'A cab man. They argued over a fare at the Horseshoe Tavern on Tower Hill. Scott was drunk and angry. He stabbed the man with a five-shilling rapier.'

'Wait,' says Balty, 'when was this?'

'The spring of last year.'

'No. Exactly when?'

'The beginning of May. In fact, the first day of the month, I think.'

'*Before* you sailed towards Scotland with the duke?'

'You know about that, but not about Scott's flight?'

'I sailed to Cadiz on John Wyborne's *Happy Return* when he passed here last summer. He told me all about the *Gloucester* wreck. He said nothing at all of Scott. He talked only of Gunman and his part in the making of the wreck.'

'Wyborne is a fine and honest captain but that is nonsense. Gunman went out of his way to avert it.'

'That is not what Wyborne maintained but . . . brother, tell me the exact dates. This cab man died on the 1st of May?'

'No, he lingered almost a week.'

'But Scott did not wait around to see him perhaps recover?'

'No he did not. He left his lodgings that same night. It is thought he found a ship to Sweden.'

'He was drunk and angry, you said. Could that be because he heard the duke had survived the wreck?'

Pepys thinks hard, unsure where Balty is going with this, but dominated by his utter concentration and the look in his eyes. He trawls back through those days, a year ago. 'No,' he says, 'not possible. We sailed away two days after he stabbed the man. We had not even heard about it while poor Butler still lived. The wreck occurred on the morning of the next Saturday, which was the sixth day of the month. I am told news of it took three days or so to reach London and further news that the duke was alive another two days after that.'

Balty breaks into a fierce grin. 'As I thought,' he says. 'I know why Scott killed the cab man and I also know what that implies.'

'You are far ahead of me,' says Pepys, and realizes with some shame that this is something he has never let himself say before.

'Remember Gravesend,' says Balty. 'Scott kills Godfrey, races away to a ship and in so doing draws your attention to him as the possible murderer? You leave him trapped in France for months with your arrest warrants and magistrates waiting for his return. He hates you for it and he has learnt not to make that mistake twice.'

'What has that to do with stabbing a stranger?' Pepys asks in some confusion, but Balty just stares silently back at him until Pepys finally nods. 'You mean it was planned like that? He hears of the duke's preparations to sail north and organizes this pilot Ayres to do his business? But . . .'

'But by now justices across this country have come to know what sort of man he is and who he serves. He would be under immediate suspicion if he fled away with no other reason just before the duke's death.'

'But a murder is still a murder. There would be a hue and cry after him for Butler's killing?'

Balty frowns. 'Come now brother. Across the sea? We all know, do we not, that justice applies differently to the murder of a nobody than the murder of a king or his heir? Think of those who executed the first Charles. The regicides who signed his warrant have been pursued across the globe. Some still are. To search Sweden for the murder of a cab man? No, no, not the same at all. Doing what he did was his strategy to explain his flight by a much more forgettable killing.'

'So you think . . .'

'That this was Scott's final attempt to bring down the Stuart brothers and you are safe from him so long as they reign.'

'And . . . the plot of four months ago? The Rye House affair?'

Balty looks puzzled. 'I know nothing of that. What was it?'

Pepys tells him and finally Balty explains the furtive way he now has to live and the little he has in the way of open conversation with any of the occupiers of Tangier except ten fishermen and two Smyrna merchants. 'And John Wyborne,' he says. 'He knows ways to find me and he checks on my well-being when the *Happy Return* passes by. You cannot guess what this place is like now. It took you only one quick look and the Moorish army scared you? Well, you are right. The walls may not be tall enough to protect us, brother, but that is the least of it. Due to our governor, what now happens inside these walls is worse than all that may happen outside them.'

'Is Kirke a bad governor as well as a vile person?'

Balty seems lost for words, but then he shows there are too many, not too few jostling to get out. 'Kirke is not at the bottom of the ranked list of Tangier's governors but that is only because his name is inscribed in an entirely separate book entitled "Infamy", which should be torn into strips, burnt to ashes and buried in the deepest hole a man can dig. Kirke leads a criminal enterprise with no concern for anything except personal profit. He has promoted vicious villains to do his will to this tormented city and they obey his corrupt instructions like dogs. I was sent here, brother, to provide support for our fighting men and I did exactly that until he came.'

'And then?'

'You were out of office. Coventry was gone. I tried to alert you and those others who might warn the king, but my letters were stolen and torn up in my face by Kirke's bastards. I hid in a vile merchant tub with all the speed of a slug, which took me back to England to unmask him, but Kirke sent a sloop to beat me to Plymouth, where I was held, battered half to death and sent back here in chains.' He stares at Pepys, who has to look away. 'I have found bolt holes here to hide myself. My pay has been stolen by Kirke's men. I am threatened by the assassins they call Kirke's Lambs. Brother, I was sent here in the hope that I would quietly die, but I have fought to live. That is why you see the wreck of me before you, but I have gathered the means to expose Kirke for the villain he is and for that I demand your help.'

Pepys sees no trace left of Balty's old tendency to exaggeration. He goes back in his head to a minute earlier. I did not send you here to die, he had said, and what was Balty's reply? I didn't say *you* did.

'If it wasn't me,' he says, 'who *did* send you here to die?'

'You must know the answer to that?' Balty blinks as he sees genuine incomprehension in Pepys's face, so he seizes his brother by the shoulders and puts his face close. 'First, do you know how it goes with my boy and girl? Little news reaches me.'

'Brother, they have both been given fine chances for their future. Sam serves under Clifton in the *Moonstone*. Betty is in the queen's household, no less.'

'They are held hostage!'

'What do you mean?'

'I mean they are the means to seal my mouth. Listen to me.'

Balty tells him in searing sentences which impale Pepys. He tells him of Hubert and Count Victor, Brother Ash and Ezra, of his summons to the coast and the midnight row out to the *Moonstone*. Then he breaks the rules of his enforced silence because he cannot hold it in. 'I thought I was meeting Coventry,' he says. 'I was wrong. It was the king.'

'*Charles* crossed to France to meet you?'

'To trap me. He talked of the duke who pulls Scott's strings. I thought he meant his own brother. I was horrified. I told him the man Sam heard in that house was Buckingham, not York. He grew angry in an instant. He said Sam was entirely wrong and . . .' His voice tails off.

'What?'

'I saw Sam's beaten face and I had to set him right. I told him Sam was *not* wrong. He flew into a rage and had me shackled to a cannon.'

'Oh Balty, they were raised together. Buckingham was like his twin, his dearest friend. Charles forgives Buckingham everything he ever does.'

'Even to conspiring with plans to overthrow him?'

'Yes, perhaps even that, preferring to believe someone else had misled him.'

'How could I guess that?'

'Tell me what happened then?'

'Clifton set me loose. He said Sam would serve under him on the *Moonstone* and his fine future would be guaranteed by my silence. If I was found to have named Buckingham again, he would be moved to Merrihew's command.'

That brings a deep silence.

Balty breaks it with indignation in his voice. 'He said the king would consult you about what to do with me.'

'The king has not spoken to me since this whole affair began.'

'I have kept my lips glued shut,' says Balty simply. 'Can you find out where Sam is now? I heard the *Moonstone* went to the Indies.'

'I will try.'

'Ingratitude,' says Balty, 'just as the man wrote in his Caesar play. Ingratitude more strong than traitors' arms. I am owed more than a try.'

'I told you, I have no power these days.'

'We do get some news here, you know. Shaftesbury is dead. The mobs have burned his effigy. The king has regained control. I know why you are here and it is your ladder back to power.'

'You know?'

'Brother of mine, husband to my lost sister, as soon as we sail away from Tangier, the bloody pirates of these coasts will grab it to command the straits exactly as they choose. The Moors' armies are deadly on land but powerless to stop them at sea. Portugal will not want this place back. Spain? France? You shake your head. Quite so.' He hammers his fist down on the table. 'That leaves gunpowder. You will blow it to pieces and send the people home.'

Pepys cannot prevent the smallest of nods and Balty's mouth twists. 'Yes, that is why you are here. So, for my safety, will you take me home with you when this is done and the *Grafton* sails?'

'I will get you back to England, brother. His lordship will allow me that.'

'I so much want to see my wife and my children again and I must stay alive until then, but what awaits me back there?' He looks around the cabin. 'This is the most comfortable place I have been for many months. I move from place to place in empty houses to spend my nights. Sometimes I live in a shed hidden in a wild garden, other times in a fisherman's hut by the old city.' He points a finger off to the south-east where the bay curves around into the Mediterranean. 'Ruins now. A few men live there to fish and I have made them my friends. If Kirke knows I will reach England to tell all I know, he will try harder to find me and he *will* kill me. You put a low value on my judgement, brother, but you do know I hate corruption.'

Pepys frowns, aware of the vastly different rewards the two of them have received over their navy years and the steady stream of messages from Deal, registering Balty's increasing anger at the behaviour of certain captains. 'I do not doubt it. What sort of corruption in this case?'

'Kirke steals. He threatens. He takes bribes. He terrorises any trader who does not pay him for protection. I saw him stave in all the barrels of an honest wine dealer who refused his demands. He ruins anyone who stands against him and even has them murdered.'

'Murdered?'

'His squad of assassins is proud to be called Kirke's Lambs and Monahan, the bad shepherd of those lambs, is the worst

man I have yet met. He has a slanting smile fixed on his face by
the slash of a sword and he is soft-spoken through the botched
job a dagger did on his throat. If he whispers to you, don't be
fooled into bending closer. That is the last thing many men have
done. So far I have counted eighteen people he has killed, five
of them women.'

'You can swear to it all?'

'Swear? Better than that. I have detailed it in a ledger with
the times and places and the nature of crimes that should be the
death of him. I have the names of those witnesses who are still
alive and will testify if they stay that way. My book is securely
hidden. He has ransacked some places where I used to sleep but
I think he will not risk killing me until he has it.'

'You can live here on board, protected while we do our
work.'

'Kirke has arranged that you will be housed ashore. They
would get to me here. I bless you for confronting Kirke but I
had best stay hidden. I will tiptoe further away until you have
done your work.'

'Away? To where?'

The *Grafton* has slowly swung in the evening breeze and
Balty points out across at Spain. 'I have people to shelter me.'

'Tarifa?'

'Too close. A crossing for men with minds set on murder.
When I first came here, the graves from the Great Siege were
raw, turned earth. The weeds had not yet risen. The soldiers
stared with sleepless eyes. You schooled me to think ahead,
brother. I knew Tangier would soon be lost to us so I found a
safer base for our ships.' He stops at a knock, but it is only the
steward asking if they need more wine. When they are alone

again, Balty says, 'Another time. I must depart. Tonight no one must see where I go.'

'Balty, I can ask Lord Dartmouth to protect you until we leave and I promise you safe passage home.'

Balty clasps his hand. 'Brother you have no notion of the evil we face. I have pressing business to finish and I am safer elsewhere.'

'How do I find you if I need you?'

'I may be gone some time. Weeks, probably. You will be here longer. I have my small boat close by to take me across the water.'

'When you come back, you will find me?'

'Yes. They have prepared a house next to the Court of the Guard for Lord Dartmouth and his people, including you. Will Hewer will be two streets away in St John's yellow house with two brass crosses on the door. If . . . if for any reason I do not come within five weeks, go to Fernam's shop by the market place. He is Portuguese and a trusted friend. Alongside his shop is a narrow alley that looks impossibly overgrown, but you can force through. It is the only way into the square within. The Portuguese grew vines and fruit but now it is smothered under towering weeds and wild bushes above your head. Push south-ward through them. A hidden shed is my hiding place when I have nowhere else. And . . .'

'Yes?'

'Behind it is a dry well. Under stones at the bottom you may find a leather-wrapped package. That will be my ledger of Kirke's crimes. I move it in the dark from place to place but it is often there. If you find it and I am dead, keep it safe and use it well.'

Balty slips away. Pepys retires to his own cabin but he cannot rest. In his head until now he has carried memories of unjust privations from his incarceration in the Tower of London and then those weeks in the Southwark prison but ... really? His friend Houblon's money bought him cushioned comfort in the Tower even though death loomed. He had the best of the prison cells and since then Will Hewer has made sure he lives in even greater luxury than ever before in his life – but Balty? He finds himself marvelling for the first time at the sheer courage of this man. He feels startling shame because he knows he has enjoyed lording it over this remarkable brother, choosing not to see his skills. He opens his document case and takes out that first, savage letter Balty sent him on arrival in Tangier. It tells of his attempts to obey delayed departure orders to join the *Newcastle*, far out in the Thames estuary. Hours of rowing through a violent storm strand him on the Essex shore, but the ship has up-anchored and gone. Four more days of passages begged from passing vessels take him through fresh gales round the corner of Kent, where he finds the *Newcastle* at anchor in the Downs, the very place he had left a week before. The letter ends in a desperate plea to be forgiven this cruel and unjust posting.

In Pepys's head, the image of the man he thought he had known for so many years is shoved aside by the scarred, determined survivor he has just met. Pushing that letter under other documents so he doesn't have to look at it, he opens the red leather journal he brought from London, his diary of this expedition. It is a decision moment. Does he bare his soul on the coming pages as he did of old? He finds he cannot bear the thought. This diary will be no more than a terse list of what happens. He takes a quill, opens the ink and slowly writes: 'Then upon the quarterdeck, full of officers walking, and among others, my brother St Michel came, who is mightily altered in his looks — with hard usage as he tells me.' He closes the book, forgetting to blot it first, and reopens it to see the accidental mirror-writing on the facing page. Of old, this would have distressed him, but now he knows it is entirely apt, because this business has been arse about face from the start. He picks up the pen again, feeling a duty to add Balty's startling declaration, his words soaked in sadness marinaded in Tangier heat: 'I have been sent to the Devil for a New Year's gift.' Then he thinks there is no point. He knows those words are etched on his brain for the rest of his life.

CHAPTER 32

Five weeks have passed since the fleet reached Tangier. The ships fill the protected anchorage inside the mole and spill out into the bay. Their physical presence dominates everything. The Alcaïd sends polite emissaries, hoping to discover the purpose of all this. His army mostly keeps its distance except when called upon to show off its skills in almost-friendly tournaments. Hundreds of Dartmouth's sailors dress in army garb to add numbers to the answering displays of fire power. Added to the garrison, the message is clear. They outnumber the Alcaïd, who cannot quickly call reinforcements from the other end of his country. Their meetings take place on the sands outside the city to deny knowledge of the work of destruction starting inside, and that work is planned to stay invisible within the walls for as long as possible. Most of the remaining Portuguese residents are spirited unobtrusively into ships to be taken back home, only a few essential merchants remaining. Sir Percy Kirke decides it is in his interest to moderate his behaviour and does his best to be Dartmouth's keen supporter. Pepys and Hewer get on with the tedious work of arranging compensation for the city's property owners.

Only one thing is missing. There is no sign of Balty.

Will Hewer knows something is bothering his old master and has a good idea what it might be, but Pepys needs to keep his fears to himself to stop them ballooning out. He explores the city as best he can, even risking the areas outside the walls where he feels himself inspected by the Alcaïd's sentries.

On Friday October 19th, Pepys can stand it no longer. He goes to ask Henry Sheres, busy drilling into the stonework of the mole, for a rope and a capable man to climb down it. He decides to visit Fernam, the Portuguese merchant still in his shop, and ask to see Balty's overgrown hut. Sheres sees his face. 'We're trying out the first mine down by the mole this very afternoon,' he says. 'You will want to watch it, I'm sure. I will find a rope and do whatever you need straight afterwards.'

'Thank you,' says Pepys. 'The first mine? That is good news.'

'Not really. It's all taking an age. The rocks blunt the miners' drills and I mixed the mortar to last a century, fool that I was. It is harder than the rock itself. Anyway, I have no great hopes because this particular mine is Captain Leake's creation. It's not done the way I would do it. You saw a better one yesterday, I hear?'

'Captain Silver told you? Yes, I was walking outside the Peterborough Tower and he showed me the tunnel they have made. I crawled down on my knees to the charges and the fuses, laid out and ready.'

'My friend Pepys, I hear you are being very bold in your perambulations outside the walls. The Moors have good sharpshooters. One might choose to test out the sighting of his musket.'

'It is safe enough.'

Sheres considers him and shakes his head. 'Only until it is suddenly not.'

At five they gather near the landward end of the mole to watch the first mine explode under an arched section. Boats have been moved a cable's length away but the plan has been kept quiet to avoid a crowd. No more than twenty people are in the know. They see a man in the distance bend to light a fuse and then run hard towards them. He needn't have bothered, because there is only the mildest of thuds and a small upward rush of dust. Then, by some freak of acoustics, a far more violent echo crashes back at them from the farther stone walls of the city rising behind them. Only when they look that way do they see a ragged fountain of smoky dirt has erupted into the air from somewhere up the hill.

'What in hell . . .' says Sheres. 'Come on!'

It is not until they reach the market place that a breathless Pepys sees the remains of that smoke still rising from behind the terrace of houses facing them on its far side and sees the name 'Fernam' on the shop with the arched alleyway next to it. Debris lies around and two soldiers of Kirke's Tangier Regiment are blocking the narrow alley, stopping people going in to see what has happened.

'Not allowed, sirs,' says one of them. 'Something blew up. Could be more to come.'

'Stand aside,' says Pepys, but they ignore him. Sheres picks one of them up by the waist and throws him into the gutter. The other shuffles sideways. 'Let no one else in,' Sheres shouts and they push through the coiling weeds to get into the enclosed garden within. It is just as Balty described, with wild vegetation towering over their heads. They force a way through and come out into a flattened circle of chaos in the evening light. The only sign of a hut is a swathe of splintered wood and a ragged crater beyond it where the well had been.

Pepys groans and Sheres stares at him. 'Do you have any idea what happened here?' he says.

'A mine.'

'An accident? No, of course not. There should be no mines here.'

'No accident. This was deliberate.'

Sheres stares. 'They sought to confuse us by firing it under cover of Leake's mine. But this one made a hundred times the noise of Leake's squib. Stay here.'

He pushes back the way they came in while Pepys gazes at what he fears may be Balty's grave.

Sheres is only gone for a minute and he comes back with a fierce look on his face. 'That was no accident,' he says. 'I have found the burnt powder marks of a fuse on the earth running back to the alley. What do you know?'

'This is why I needed you and a rope. My brother Balthasar often used a hut here as a hidden place to sleep. There is a well in the middle of this mess.'

'Hidden from who? Oh yes, don't tell me. The bastard Kirke and his men.'

'Henry, I think my brother had something of great value concealed in the well. I fear ... I fear he may be down there with it.'

'Right. I have met your brother on occasion since the siege. I have a great respect for him, whereas Kirke ... You stay here. Block any interference. I will find trustworthy men to guard the alley and I will bring miners with ladders. I knew these wells when they still tapped into water running down from the hills. This one will not be deep. We will soon know.' He pats Pepys on the back and leaves him alone with his thoughts.

Pepys stares at the crater in misery and his understanding of the real Balty takes another lurch forwards. He has avoided recognizing Balty's true qualities because they somehow lessened his own. Balty has bravery that his supposed superior is only now trying to match. He has failed to prevent Balty being sent here to die and he fights down the unbidden response that says he could not have stopped it. Before he reaches the end of these dizzying revelations, Henry Sheres is back with three miners carrying shovels, buckets and a ladder. It takes them only minutes to delve down eight or nine feet to the stony bottom of the dry well. Hauling up the buckets takes more time than the digging as the gunpowder has pulverized the soil and the loose stone.

'Nothing here, sirs,' the man in the hole calls up. 'I'm down to bedrock.'

Pepys feels a wave of relief and then thinks of Balty's ledger of evidence. 'No sign of anything burnt? Leather perhaps, or parchment?'

'Clean rock. That's all. Nowt else, I swear.'

'No trace of anything else . . . anything dead?'

'No, sir. Nowt dead, excepting the rock. Nowt living, excepting myself. That's the whole story.'

The absence of the ledger is more than balanced by the absence of a body and he has no doubt this has been done at Kirke's command. The confirmation of how far the governor is prepared to go chills Pepys and he parries further questions until Sheres gives up asking.

'Thank you,' he says to Sheres and the men. 'Let me not take you from your many tasks.'

After they have gone, he sorts through the wooden wreckage of the hut, but finds nothing, then he fights his way back through the vegetation. Just before he reaches the alley, a door in the back wall of the terrace creaks open and he stops abruptly.

A face looks out at him, a stranger with a livid cut across his cheek. It oozes blood. 'My name is Fernam Pereiro,' says the man. 'You, I do not know.'

'My name is Samuel Pepys.'

'Who do you look for?'

'My brother. I call him Balty.'

'Ah.' The man touches his cheek and looks at the blood. 'This man. Has he young ones?'

'Children? Yes, two.'

'Name them to me please.'

'Elisabeth and Samuel.'

The man frowns, 'No,' he says, 'wrong answer.' He starts to pull the door closed.

'Betty and Sam,' Pepys says quickly. 'Their short names. Please, Fernam. We must talk.' He reaches in his pocket for the pass Dartmouth has given him. 'You see? My name is written.'

The merchant sighs and seems to relax. 'Come inside,' he says. 'Stay away from my window. Soldiers pass near.'

'You are my brother Balty's friend,' says Pepys. 'When I saw what they had done, I thought he was dead.'

'Alive by God's grace and my warning.'

'You saw the men who did this?'

'Men from the lambs of evil Kirke.' Fernam spits on the

floor. 'Looking, plotting no good. They left and Balty came after. Went away fast when I said. Now I go home to Lisbon at sunrise where my uncle has his shop and we have no drunken English customers.'

'Please, where is my brother?'

'With the fishermen perhaps? He did not say.'

'Fernam, I will send men to protect you until you leave. They will bring you gold for what you have done.'

'No gold. I have this for you,' Fernam says, opening a drawer.

'His book?'

Fernam's eyes swivel sharply to lock on his. 'I will speak of no book. Look.'

Pepys squints at the small piece of torn parchment. 'Tariq ibn-Ziyad,' he said slowly. 'Who is this?'

'All I know is that is the name of a dead man and it may take you to a safe place. The commander of the *Moonstone* boat knows more.'

'Clifton?'

'I do not know that name.'

'But he is not here.'

Fernam shrugs. 'I have done what I can.'

That night Pepys talks with Will Hewer and asks if they should tell Dartmouth what they know.

Hewer shakes his head. 'I have a great regard for his lordship,' he says, 'but he has to spend much of his days with the odious Kirke. We should keep this to ourselves and ask quiet questions of people we trust.'

'There are not many of those. Is there nothing I can do to help Balty now?'

'Only remind yourself that he has lived a dangerous life, that he has the skills to continue living it and that he is safely out of reach in Spain.'

'Will, all the Portuguese will soon have left. The English families will be next. Our own work is nearly done and we can't help the men blow the place to pieces. It will take weeks. Why don't we look for Balty? I will ask Dartmouth to let us cross the straits and see the sights. Seville is said to be a most beautiful city and that is not so far from Cadiz. We could ask for Balty as we go. He named some places where he has friends. I made a note.'

'Up the Atlantic coast?'

'Yes . . . ah, no. There is one more to the east that remains a mystery.'

Two more weeks pass with slow progress on the demolition. Only soldiers and sailors are left in Tangier now. They have started pulling down some of the empty houses. The Alcaïd's forces, puzzled by the noise and dust from behind the city walls, parade their strength around the hills and gullies facing the Peterborough Tower and all along the inland wall to the Irish Battery at the far corner. Pepys suspends his walks outside the walls. As they head into November, the great day approaches when Sheres will blow up a massive mine at the head of the mole. He has buried iron tubes and heavy timbers in the 'iole, bound tight, engineered to channel all the force of the powder sideways, and the detonation is planned for sunset.

In the early afternoon, Pepys sits poring over the papers submitted by the clergy of the garrison church of St Charles the Martyr, due to be pulled down at the very end of the destruction. He stares at the pages, carried back to that moment nearly thirty-five years ago when he stood in the Whitehall crowd to watch King Charles the first, no obvious saint, become that martyr. He remembers a glimpse through the wall of guards of the king's head being held high and knew that Cromwell ordered it sewn back on so the family could mourn. Who got *that* job, he is wondering, when he is interrupted by a polite cough and he sees a young officer standing in the doorway.

'Your pardon, sir.'

'Yes?'

'I am commanded to invite you to join a pleasant expedition if you wish.'

'Where to, young man?'

'The Roman buildings towards the Tangier river. It is close by and we will escort you.'

'Roman buildings? Yes, certainly.'

A saddled horse waits for him and they join a dozen horsemen outside the sally-port gate. Pepys has walked this way, through the broken remains of the old Seamen's Battery. He has looked at the goods that the Smyrna traders display in the stockade there and he has seen the rest of the bay from rowing boats. He follows in the hoof marks of the mounted squad towards the scatter of fishermen's huts and remembers that Balty uses one such hut.

The leader of the squad holds up his arm to halt them, turns his horse and trots back to Pepys. It is only then that Pepys sees his grotesque smile. The man swings his horse round and it steps sideways so that Pepys's left leg is forced hard against the other man's right. 'Mr Pepys,' he says in a voice like the sigh of a final breath. 'My name is Monahan. Let me show you what utter ruin looks like.' He stands in his stirrups and all heads pivot towards him. They know it is hard to hear him and often lethal not to. 'You men,' he hisses, 'stay here. Eyes open.'

Monahan beckons him to follow and leads him from one giant lump of broken masonry to another, pointing a finger as if he might not otherwise see them and whispering 'A temple, they say' or 'the base for a statue, perhaps'. Pepys is silent and alert, wondering if he himself is at risk of joining the ruins, then the other man turns his horse to crowd against him again. There are no clouds today and they are both sweating. Monahan smells of decay. He whispers, 'You are looking at disaster, Mr Pepys. What do you think of our city now it is to emulate this wreckage? Yet I am told you chose to send your brother here?'

'You were told a lie. This would be the last place on earth I would send any man. I would sooner send him to hell. Sir, since I arrived I have witnessed drunken excess, vile cruelty and roguery everywhere I look. I think it high time it is blasted entirely into dust.'

'You disapprove?'

'You have somehow come to that conclusion?'

'How goes it with your dear brother St Michel? I have not seen him for some time. Is he well?'

'My brother?' Pepys thinks a little distance would be a safer thing. 'Oh, he likes to call me that. In truth he was brother to my late wife. We are not close.'

Monahan leans sideways even closer to him and Pepys feels pure aggression carried on the breath that hisses from his damaged mouth. 'You defended him from my master when you first arrived.'

Pepys feels the threat level rising. 'Sir, let me tell you I defended myself against an insult to me. St Michel has been a burden to me for many years, my family obligation. He is excessively French.'

Monahan nods. 'I understand. He has tried your patience as he has also tried ours, but we must consult him on urgent business and he cannot be found.'

'What business?'

'I have money due to him and I know he has papers that demand attention.'

'You can give me the money. I will see it reaches him. I know of no papers.'

'Perhaps they are with Mr Hewer?' Pepys feels Monahan is watching him very closely. He shrugs.

'He has made no such mention.'

'Will you watch the great explosion tonight?'

'My dinner companions will not be able to resist the spectacle.'

'Where will you be dining?'

Pepys resents the questions, but Monahan's low voice has dropped to an even quieter whisper and it lures him into minimal answers which can surely do no harm. 'With Mr Hewer at his lodgings. My Lord Dartmouth is joining us.'

'Will you have a clear view?'

'I don't know.'

'I do hope so. If not, I will advise you of a nearby vantage point. Which is the house?'

'He lodges with Captain St John.'

'Ah, a fine house for the occasion.'

'Good.'

'I have heard there was a previous explosion last week that you did inspect?'

'I'm not sure what you . . . ah, you mean that business near the market? Mr Sheres went to investigate. He took me with him.'

'And sent for men to dig into the hole?'

'I believe Mr Sheres is interested in the rock structures under the city. It helps inform his careful mining.'

'Yes, Mr Pepys. Please mark my words.' Monahan locks eyes on him. 'With so much gunpowder on hand all around our city, it pays to take great care. Do make sure you have a good view this evening and that nothing gets in the way of a safe outcome to your journey. I hope you understand. We will return now.'

Pepys has had quite enough of his company. 'You go back, sir. I shall stretch my horse's legs a little further,' he says and persuades the unwilling horse to trot off down the firm sand into Old Tangier, leaving Monahan watching him. He looks sideways at the scattered huts with driftwood piled up in front of them, trying not to show it in the movement of his head, but sees no sign of Balty, so he turns the horse slowly back to the walls of the city.

That evening, he walks in procession with Lord Dartmouth and his guards to Captain St John's capacious house. After dining well, they stand at the windows looking down the slope of the city into the bay where bright moonlight is shining on the water. They see a knot of men who had been gathered at the mole's far end, half a mile out, now heading back towards the land.

'There are still two lanterns there,' says Hewer, looking through a long glass. 'One must be Sheres. It's certainly a big man. Ah! Now they're both moving. I think they're running, do you see? The fuse must be alight.'

Dartmouth is peering through his own glass. 'If this works well we could be done by . . .' He seems to think better of declaring yet another date. 'We could be done quite soon. I have had my fill of damp squibs.'

It is a very long fuse and the two running men are off the mole, out of sight below the city walls. Still nothing happens and then, just as the watchers start to doubt, a jet of orange light streaks high up into the air. 'Oh my Lord,' Dartmouth says, 'It has worked . . .' but the mighty noise of the blast and the scream of tearing rock swamps all else. They stare as the flame shrinks, but now another sound is taking over, a hailstorm starting down there by the water and moving up the slope towards them louder and louder, shattering windows nearby then rattling hard on the tiles above their heads for a count of five, until the sky has spat back the vast mushroom of fragmented stone forced up into it.

Dartmouth and Pepys are escorted back to their own house and Pepys is glad of the sailors around them. Only now does he let himself recognize that Monahan's interest in this evening's location has been disturbing him. Dartmouth is clearly pleased. 'That is how it should be done,' he says.

Pepys is hard at work in his own office next morning when handbells start ringing and voices shouting. 'House afire, house afire. Bring your buckets. Hurry now.'

He opens the front door as one of the bell ringers goes past. 'Where is the fire?' he demands and the man points up the slope. 'Thomas Sinjon's house. Hard ablaze.'

The man has gone before the name sinks in. Sinjon is how some say 'St John'. Pepys steps into the narrow road and sees smoke billowing up. What to do? Is Will Hewer inside that house? He does something that he rarely does these days. He runs. It is uphill on deceitful cobbles, but he arrives in the short street where the flames roar upward with some breath still left in him and is vastly relieved to see Will Hewer, face and hands blackened, stacking books and papers into a cart. Empty buckets lie all around and a dozen soldiers have given up on trying to save the house. Instead they are using iron hooks to pull planks off the next building before that catches fire as well.

Will comes to him. 'We rescued the money and the documents and much of the library. Captain St John and his wife are safe.'

'You've been lucky, Will.'

'We were due to move in three days to the Stewart House. This whole street is coming down. To look on the bright side, it saves a bit of time. We have two carts full of my stuff and the chests. Can we take it to yours? It requires a proper guard.'

They follow the carts down to the big house. Pepys takes Hewer up to his own room, opens the door and stops in astonished indignation. His papers are strewn across the floor.

No one in the house has seen anything. It seems likely the intruder climbed onto the balcony. The only explanation bursts in to fill his head. 'Will,' he says, 'Kirke's vile man Monahan questioned me yesterday. He wanted to know where you lived. The fire was a distraction to get me out of here.'

'Why?'

'Balty has kept a book of Kirke's evils. Monahan seeks it.'

'But you don't have it, do you?'

'No. I hope Balty has it with him and we must find him to make sure he is protected.'

'Then, my friend, it is time. You must get us leave to travel.'

That same night the weather breaks. A violent storm sends

lightning to ignite a mine buried near the city wall. The *Montagu* breaks her chains and collides with two others and just misses the *Happy Return* as that frigate charges into the relative shelter of the bay from a patrol in the straits.

In the middle of the morning, as Pepys works to understand a document regarding the compensation due to the Portuguese church, there is a tap on his door and he opens it to find a man he knows well and who looks as if he has had a sleepless night. John Wyborne, captain of the *Happy Return*, has many qualities that Pepys admired in past years. He has never enriched himself by the 'good voyages' which have so often undermined the navy's efficiency as less honest captains take huge rewards from bankers and other men of business to carry high-value cargoes of gold, silver and other precious things to ports far away from their designated duties. It is rife and it is how captains build the fortunes to let them retire in great comfort.

'Samuel,' says Wyborne, 'I come from Cadiz. Aylmer and Shovell are there, damn them, quarrelling over a cargo of fine plate to go to Genoa. Advise his lordship he should order them home to England.'

'John, he hates that trade as you and I both do, but he has more on his plate than . . . well, plate. Anyway, it is good to see you back here.'

'I will leave you to your work,' says Wyborne with a smile and clasps Pepys's hand. 'I wish to speak with your brother.'

'He is nowhere to be found.'

'Well, if he comes back, please do let me know. I have much to discuss with him.'

'Where are you bound next? Hewer and I have a mind to cross to Spain to see some sights.'

'Speak with Killigrew. His precious *Montagu* was sadly damaged last night. He must take her to Cadiz for repair.'

Will Hewer needs repair too. His new lodgings have no glass in the windows and the rain sheeting sideways through the gaps between the shutters is only diverted by more rain tumbling vertically from gaps between the tiles. Dartmouth takes pity on him when hail follows and allows the pair of them to join the *Montagu* for Cadiz as soon as the weather permits. A blunt message from his lordship just before the ship sets sail insists they must be back by the end of the Christmas week.

The storms relent only long enough to trap them. They tour Cadiz, finding no trace of Balty and nothing worth hearing from the English there, then, in a lull after three more days of downpour, a hired carriage takes them up the coast to Sanlucar, that fishing town at the mouth of the Guadalquivir river which winds inland to Seville. They ask for a boatman, but the first to respond looks up at the lowering clouds and says he has many better things to do. They also ask if anyone knows a man called Balty St Michel and that produces a tanned and muscled man with vivid blue eyes who speaks some English and says his name is Barto. He takes them to his boat, hoists a sail and stands silent at the tiller for the first hour, following the hidden curves of the river that has now spread wide into the fields either side.

He breaks that silence when they are moving slowly through the widest part of the flood so far. 'This person, St Michel,' he says. 'Who is he to you?'

'He is the dear brother of my sadly departed wife,' says Pepys. 'I must find him.'

'Then you will know the answer to two questions.'

'Will I?'

'You had better, because otherwise it is a long swim to wherever the riverbank may now be. Stay still, sir,' he says to Hewer,
who has risen from his wooden seat. 'You are no match for me.'

'What questions are these?' says Pepys, realizing that this
man must know Balty if the answers are to mean anything.

'I have been thinking about that. First, how does he ride a
horse?'

'With long stirrups,' Pepys says with no hesitation. 'He likes
his legs almost straight.'

Barto nods slowly.

Pepys waits, then grows impatient. 'That might have been
a lucky guess. There aren't many choices. Short, normal, long,
side-saddle maybe. Standing on his head. I hope your second
question is better.'

'What wine does he prefer?'

'Almost anything,' says Pepys, annoyed.

'No,' says Hewer. 'Not so. He has always preferred a black
wine, a wine like those he favours in France. The difficult wine
they make in Cahors from the Malbec grape.'

The man by the tiller relaxes into a smile. 'I have worked in
that region,' he says. 'Yes. Your Balty likes our old Monastrell
and that is close to a Malbec. Both wines taste of earth and
smoke.' He smiles. 'I am persuaded. You come in good faith,
unlike the last men.'

'Last men?'

'Yes, sir. I have been cautious because you are not the first
to seek him. Some English came asking for him a month ago
and they were sour and vicious men.'

'But you have not seen him?'

'Not for many weeks now.'

'Barto, he is in some danger.' Pepys delves into his satchel. 'Do you know this name? Tariq ibn-Ziyad?'

'Yes.'

'Who is he?'

'A forgotten man from long ago. "Where is it" makes a better question. Jebel Tariq ibn-Ziyad is back through the straits and up the coast of Spain. Balty calls it simply Jebel Tariq. There is not much there, except his stores and his men. Oh, and a sunken boat containing the assassins who went to kill him. We dealt with them.'

He tells them the story as he sets sail again. They pass a cold night with the boat tied to a tree, wading to an isolated church through the floodwater that is lapping almost to the top of its steps.

He leaves them at Seville, recommends an inn and arranges to collect them in two weeks. They explore the sights of Seville for only half a day before the storms return. The inn has comfortable beds, good food and fires to dry their clothes, but this time the storms set new records. Flood water funnels into the streets. The inn runs short of food and fuel. River travel is impossible. Days of scurrying around the city under a series of short-lived umbrellas turn into weeks spent in their rooms. Pepys's only comfort is to tally what his daily four pounds is adding up to. He likes the total, but his sums have been far too cautious. It is halfway through February before they see Tangier again.

CHAPTER 33

News of the Iberian floods arrives slowly in London because an excess of water in a place far from home is way down the list of interesting tales, unless you are a homesick queen wanting to see that home again and perhaps even see some winter sunshine. The summons to the king's palace comes at eleven in the morning and John Clifton is there ninety minutes later, a fast ride in the ship's longboat upstream on the tide from the *Moonstone*'s mooring at St Katherine's.

Charles is reading poetry to three women when Clifton is shown into his presence. He recognizes two of them immediately, both the subject of much notorious gossip in the streets. Hortense Mancini, Duchess of Mazarin and Louise de Kérouaille, Duchess of Portsmouth are somehow tolerating being in the same room at the same time, though the former is smiling because the poem is in Italian and the latter is staring out of the window, frowning, for exactly the same reason. The third woman, in the half-way noble garb of a lady-in-waiting, sits in a corner with a studiously blank face. Charles reaches the end of the verses and glances at his mistresses. 'Ladies,' he says, 'please indulge me for some minutes while I speak to the captain.' Confusion then reigns as the two duchesses remain in their seats, clearly expecting the king to take himself elsewhere. Only the lady-in-waiting stands. 'You, sit,' says Charles, firmly and she does. 'And you two, pray stand. The green saloon awaits you and I will join you shortly.' There is a further pregnant silence while the mistresses try to outlast each other in staying seated, but Charles waves them away with a frown and their bulky skirts collide in the doorway.

'Clifton,' says Charles, 'I need your services. This dear girl comes with a disturbing message from my queen. I believe you know her of old.'

'I fear not, sire. It is my pleasure to . . .' but then Betty smiles at him and he knows the smile, even if the young woman in front of him has now entirely eclipsed the girl. 'But it is Betty,' he exclaims. 'You have . . . you are grown up and you . . .' He stops himself babbling. 'It is only three years, or perhaps four? How can that be?'

'The beneficial influence of my dear queen,' gasps Charles, trying to suppress laughter at the expression on Clifton's face. 'Catherine's patronage has even changed her name. 'May I introduce you to Bettina Saint Michael. She brings an urgent request from Somerset House that requires your expertise.'

That is why, later in the afternoon, Clifton is crouched uncomfortably in the bilges of a vessel he greatly mistrusts, poking a spike into the places where its ribs meet the keel and feeling profoundly grateful that it is propped up in dry-dock and therefore at no immediate danger of sinking. He inspects the results by flickering lantern light. Bosun Ezra is doing the same a few feet away. The dry-dock is ten miles east by twisting loops of river at the Woolwich dockyard, where fifty acres of warehouses stand ready to put any damaged naval vessel back in order and the Royal Arsenal stands next door to provide all the lethal powder and shot they will need to fight again. This strange boat carries small guns but has never had any call for more powder or shot and hardly belongs in a proud navy. It is one of the fleet of royal yachts, but it carries more eccentricities than most.

This is HMS *Saudadoes*, the most frequently misspelt name in the entire navy.

'Ezra?' Clifton calls. 'How's your bit looking?'

'Passable on a calm sea half a mile from land, but more like cheese than chalk in my opinion, sir.'

'Not fit to cross Biscay this month as the queen desires?'

'Oh lawdie, lawdie, sir. Not fit to reach Gravesend from here, not in a winter like this one.'

Footsteps sound on the boards above. 'Sir,' says another man. 'I believe you should inspect the bow timbers. The forestem is an unsettling sight.'

They go on deck and climb down the ladder to the puddled surface of the dock. Clifton reaches up to push his spike in where the curving bow timber joins the keel and feels it penetrate by an inch or more with little resistance. 'That's no damned good. This thing needs to come apart now. The king demands magic but he won't fool the queen twice.'

'Twice, sir?'

'Twice, Mister Mitchell. King Charles gave it to his queen a dozen years ago but that was a mistake. A fifty-foot yacht was all very well for wandering up and down the Thames, but she determined to show it off to her people in Lisbon and by all accounts that went badly ... Barely space for a dozen of her household and a terrible time wallowing down through Biscay. They say she threw a fit when she got back. It quite shocked the king, so he took to wizardry.'

Clifton stops and considers whether he is treading on the wrong side of the loyalty ditch, but he trusts both his companions with his life, so he smiles and carries on. 'Coventry told me what happened. Charles told Catherine that kings could sometimes perform miracles for their loved ones and he babbled some nonsense, waving his arms in the air. "There," he said, "it is done. Your yacht is growing larger at my command. It will be hidden in a dark place where no one can watch as it swells." She believed his every word. She asked how long it would take because she was having a party on board in a month and he was perhaps a little carried away, because he said it would have done its growing by that time.'

Ezra is turning his head back and forth inspecting the length of the vessel. 'How did he do it, sir? That's not enough time for sure.'

'My guess is he went and bought another one, Ezra,' said the young man, laughing. 'But, sir, how did he make her think it was the same boat?'

'By commandeering the best ship's carpenters in this yard and loading them with coin to buy their silence. He had them strip all the recognizable bits from the old tub and fit them in this one. The queen walked on board up the same gangplank, held the same railings, went down into a cabin panelled just like the old one, though twice as big. All the fancy bits were put back up in all the right places, then they burned what was left of the old hulk.'

'But . . . now this one's rotting away, sir.'

'Yes and that's because they bought it in a hurry and this was the only one that came near to fitting the bill. Now we have another job on our hands and I'm unsure what advice I should give in Westminster and I fear my view is unlikely to make me popular.' He turns to the giant bo'sun. 'Ezra, go down to the stern and take a very good look at the state of the frames and the keel back there. Mr Mitchell and I will finish off at this end.'

When Ezra disappears, Clifton looks at young Mitchell. 'I doubt you will guess who gave me my instructions this morning.'

'The king, sir? No, that would be anyone's first guess. The queen then? Did she come to Westminster to see you?'

'No. She sent her new adviser in her place.'

'New adviser, sir?'

'Your sister.'

Sam starts to laugh, then stops abruptly when he sees this is no tease. 'Adviser sir? Ah, so that is what she meant. Her last letter said she was very busy these days.'

'What a pair you make. It's like this boat. You grow at twice the usual speed.' He looks Sam up and down. The boy can't be more than sixteen now, he thinks. He must be all of six feet tall now, slim but certainly strong. This is not the eccentric prodigy he first met, but a confident, resourceful man in the making, coached by Ezra, brave in action and respected by the crew. Is he too young to make lieutenant when there is a gap? No of course he isn't, probably never has been.

'If I could gently persuade our king that it would be much safer to let us take his queen to Lisbon, as she wishes, you would look after your sister on board, would you not?'

'Oh yes, sir, yes, yes.'

This idea of a voyage to Lisbon is first broached by the queen a week earlier. A February day when the sun surprises them by peeping over the Somerset House roof to light up the court-yard deceives her. Looking down, she sees men digging up the wrong flower beds for this spring's replanting and calls Betty to go with her to set things right. The sky fools them and a squall of freezing rain hits them as they do so. Running back inside, they are standing in front of a fire, being dried and dressed again, when Catherine breaks a thoughtful silence.

'*Filha amada*, do you like this winter?'

'I am accustomed to the cold; our houses were always freez-ing except the last one.' Betty thinks back to Deal and feels a pang. 'My papa had piles of old planks and he would chop them up.'

Queen Catherine has to think about that. In her whole life, fires have burned in grates without any need to pay attention to how the perfect logs arrive to feed the flames.

'My dear country is a kinder winter place than this England,' she says. 'It is some time since I last went home. *Saudadoes* can mean a heartfelt greeting for dear friends who have been missed. Did I ever tell you that the king performed magic to make her much, much larger?'

Betty looks at her, eyebrows raised, and the queen chuckles. '*Querida filha*, you are wise beyond your years, but here is one new wise thought for your future happiness. When a man who is important to you invents a tale to please you, never show you doubt him. Anyway, would you like me to show you Lisbon and other beauties of my country?'

The word comes that the *Saudadoes* is entirely unsafe for a long winter voyage and they are both delighted when the king offers them Clifton's frigate instead. '*Moonstone* is a good name too,' the queen tells Betty. 'It is the gem that stands for love, hope and healing. Shall we prepare to go?'

So it comes about that Betty revels in Sam's company as the *Moonstone* races down-channel then knifes across the Biscay swell to the warmer realm. It is only eight days in this fine ship from the Thames to the Portuguese capital and Betty spends as much time with Sam as his duties allow, both of them talking non-stop. They enter the Tagus river, drift slowly through the narrows past the grand guard Tower of Bethlehem to moor by the busy, bleached city. Lavish festivities begin and Catherine is swept up in them with Betty at her side, but after a week Betty is missing Sam, out there where she can see the *Moonstone* at anchor. It is only then that the queen lifts the lid on the plan she has been brewing since the start.

'*Filha escolhida*,' she says when they are alone. 'I have a mission for you. You must leave here tomorrow and I am gifting to you the use of our fine ship.'

'Where am I to go?'

'Our dear captain knows all. I need someone I trust deeply to do this and you are that one. Will you go?'

'Well yes, of course, queenie mama, but you are being most mysterious.'

'You accept?' She opens her hand and holds out a small badge that catches the winter sun. 'Pin it to your dress where all can see it and do not lose it whatever happens.'

Betty looks at the golden symbol and recognizes it with a shock. 'You are making me a queen's messenger?'

'Yes,' the queen says. 'For this occasion only. Do not worry. You will not have to run around delivering my other messages.

This will protect you from any attempt to stop you while you take a message to a place not far south from here. Here it is.' She hands her a folded document, tied with red ribbon and closed with six large seals. It is marked on the outside only with a large '2' in red ink.

'What does that mean? Who is it for?'

'The captain knows and he will come for you in one hour from now. Your maids are packing your bags.'

Three men collect her, Clifton, Ezra and Sam, wearing freshly laundered clothes. They progress in silent dignity down to the quay flanked by twin columns of Portuguese guards in perfect step, the crowds separating to stare at them. When they are in the longboat and heading for the frigate, Sam and Ezra are soon laughing with her while Clifton watches them. As the crew prepares to sail, Clifton takes her to his cabin.

'Can you tell me where we are going?' Betty demands.

'In one moment,' says Clifton, 'but first I have to endow you with proper authority for the task ahead of you.' He opens a drawer, picks something out of it, then turns back and says, 'Please remove your coat and pin this on.'

'I will,' she says, 'but I already have one. See?'

His eyebrows rise as he sees the gold emblem pinned to her dress. 'Ah,' he says, 'now there is a surprise. My badge is only of silver. I'm not sure how this will work. A king's messenger is only supposed to serve one person, but I suppose the king must make an exception when he is married to the other one.'

'Captain, the queen gave me a sealed letter with no name on it, just a number 2.'

'That must mean that this is number 1.' He hands her another document with even more elaborate seals.

'My queen,' says Betty, 'said you would tell me where we are bound as soon as the anchor was up.'

'Do you hear that rumble out there? That is the capstan turning and the chain beginning to leave the wet sea for the dry air. That means, yes, I can tell you. We are bound for Tangier, or whatever now remains of it.'

'To see my father? Oh, my prayers are answered . . .'

'Betty, our first task is to find your father.'

Pepys and Hewer have that same thought in mind and are also finally converging on Tangier. Barto has kept his promise as soon as the floods allow and finds them in Seville for their much-delayed return to Sanlucar, more than eight weeks after they left. A carriage takes them on to Cadiz and their first clear view of the harbour is startling because they see half the English warships of Dartmouth's fleet moored there.

It is easy to find the officers in the taverns around the port area, busy about their private business, making lucrative arrangements for those 'good voyages' that Pepys has always abhorred. He cannot see Wyborne or any of the few more honest captains he respects. They are still in Tangier and it is the rogue captains who have slipped away to get here early who are feathering their nests. In his cups, Aylmer boasts to them that he stands to make five thousand pounds from this one very 'good voyage' home. They laugh when Pepys shows them Dartmouth's order commanding any navy ship he encounters to transport him straight back to Tangier. They say they are done with Dartmouth's orders and tell Pepys to shut his mouth and enjoy himself. The *Grafton* and the others will be here soon enough and anyway, what's the point of going back to see a horrible sight?

Pepys and Hewer fume helplessly until, eleven weeks after they left Tangier, news spreads that the *Grafton* and the rest of the fleet have dropped their anchors in the Bay of Bulls, close by. It is Pepys's fifty-first birthday but this is not destined to be a day of any celebration.

Captain Booth meets them when they step on to the *Grafton*'s deck and makes a face when Pepys asks if Kirke is on board.

'Oh no, sir. We put him and his men into the *Sapphire*. She has a lively ride though sadly she is unlikely to sink. Did you want to speak with him?'

'No, I want to strangle him.'

'You are far from alone, but try not to strangle Lord Dartmouth. He is most keen to see you.'

Dartmouth is beyond exasperation and there is no softer George Legge to be seen. His lordship is on the very edge of anger, furious with those corrupted captains who have made every unlikely excuse to avoid his orders, worn down by the strain of igniting mines in incessant downpours and desperate to water the fleet, replenish supplies and get back to England as fast as possible. He has praise only for the very few people he still trusts.

'Henry Sheres has done a splendid job. I am sorry you will not see it. Wyborne has also done much. He would rather stay poor than make his fortune with these venal captains and he has brought me some remarkably good news. Now first, did you find your brother?'

'No. Kirke's thugs have been chasing him. I hoped he might have found you.'

'Kirke's thugs? Kirke is thankfully gone from here. We shipped him and his household home early on the *Sapphire*. I